"Romances that offer intensity, humor, and well-developed characters whose memorable stories are heartfelt." —*USA Today*

"Scintillating sexual chemistry, wonderfully drawn characters—a total winner." —Lauren Dane, *New York Times* bestselling author

"Beautifully written and emotionally charged, Anne Calhoun's romances define the erotic." —Alison Kent

"Anne Calhoun is one of the best writers of contemporary erotic fiction." —*Kirkus Reviews* blog

"Features the deep, simmering desires and fiery chemistry that has earned [Calhoun] legions of adoring readers." —*RT Book Reviews*

"Calhoun has a winner, and romance readers will be enchanted by this couple and their love story." —Fiction Vixen

"Romance readers who enjoy a solid love story with some heat will appreciate this steamy, emotionally complex novel." —*Publishers Weekly*

"Entirely refreshing." —HeroesandHeartbreakers.com

"One of the best erotic romances I've read in a long time . . . An emotional read with two characters that I can fall in love with." —Dear Author

"A must-read." —Smexy Books

"Filled to the brim with pleasure and passion." —Under the Covers Book Blog

TITLES BY ANNE CALHOUN

Uncommon Passion
Unforgiven
Uncommon Pleasure
Jaded
The List
The Muse

SPECIALS

Afternoon Delight
Transcendent

– THE –

Muse

ANNE CALHOUN

HEAT | NEW YORK

HEAT

An imprint of Penguin Random House LLC
375 Hudson Street, New York, New York 10014

This book is an original publication of Penguin Random House LLC.

Library of Congress Cataloging-in-Publication Data

Calhoun, Anne.
The Muse / by Anne Calhoun.—Heat trade paperback edition.
p. cm.
ISBN 978-0-425-27690-7
1. Erotic fiction.   2. Love stories.   I. Title.
PS3603.A43867M87 2015
813'.6—dc23
2015003537

PUBLISHING HISTORY
Heat trade paperback edition / December 2015

PRINTED IN THE UNITED STATES OF AMERICA

10 9 8 7 6 5 4 3 2 1

Cover photograph: "Woman with Feather Over Her Mouth" © Mohamad Itani / Trevillion Images.
Cover design by Diana Kolsky.
Text design by Kelly Lipovich.

Penguin
Random
House

− ONE −

The cab's horn went off like a shot, twice, then settled into a long, indignant blare, shattering what passed for quiet on Fifth Avenue on a Sunday afternoon. Arden MacCarren's heart rate spiked abruptly as adrenaline flooded her nervous system. Startled in the act of removing her bags from the backseat of the SUV, she banged her head on the doorframe. With one hand clapped to the back of her head, she hunched over to extricate herself from the car when the horn blared three times. Her heart rate spiked again, nearing the terrifying sharp thrum that was the precursor to passing out. She reached out blindly for any solid surface, and gripped the door handle until her fingers went numb, then forced herself to relax her grip slightly. Balanced on the razor wire between frightened and a panic attack, her body would interpret even the slightest stimuli as a reason to tip over the edge.

You're overreacting. Calm yourself. Brain over body. Mind over matter.

Her brain snapped into hyperalert mode, cataloging her surroundings. Fifth Avenue. Sunlight glinting off chrome and mirrors, coating the trees with gold. The cabdriver righteously taking to task the driver of a Mercedes double-parked while a woman unloaded her take from an afternoon of shopping. Hermès, Tory Burch, Barneys, Irresistible. Arden scanned the woman's sharp features without the click of recognition, but her brain, already on a hair trigger thanks to the horn, slid into the worst-case scenario like tires on black ice. No one she knew, but in her New York world it was only one degree of separation. She knew someone who knew this woman.

This woman knew.

The woman stalked up the red carpet leading to her building's front door, and the Mercedes turned the corner onto the side street, allowing the cab to roar off down Fifth Avenue with one final blaring honk. Arden's heart stutter-stepped up a notch, the resulting spike in blood pressure throbbing in the sore spot on the back of her head. Not good. She forced in a deep breath, inhaling long past the point her lungs thought possible, then exhaled as she focused on what was right in front of her: the black leather backseat of her SUV, the tote holding her sketchbook, pencils, charcoal. *Reach out, ignore the tremor in your hand, and close your fingers around the handles. Good. Don't forget your purse.*

Derek, her driver, waited patiently until she closed the door. Arden turned to find Tony, the doorman, sweltering in his gray wool uniform and white gloves as he hovered under the canopy stretching from the building's heavy brass doors to the sidewalk, his normally friendly face a smooth mask. "Allow me, Ms. MacCarren," he said, reaching for her bag.

"I'm fine, Tony, thank you," she said, and ordered her knees to quit shaking. But Tony's unusual formality sent a new wave of anxious thoughts surging to the forefront. *The woman in the street knew. Tony knows. The only people who didn't know your father and brother were arrested for orchestrating a decade-long Ponzi scheme that swindled thousands out of hundreds of millions of dollars were living under rocks or in yurts somewhere without electricity or satellite television, and how many of those people were left? Six, maybe eight? Everyone knows. You're exposed; you're all exposed for everyone to see, stare at, a shining example of how the mighty have fallen . . .*

The cool air in the building's marble-tiled lobby swirled against her skin, drying the sweat at her nape and sending goose bumps down her spine. Without meeting her gaze, Tony pushed the button to call the elevator. "Ms. Cottlin said to send you straight up," he said.

"Thank you," she said.

The doors opened and she stepped inside. Tony pushed the button for fourteen, then stepped back.

When the doors closed, she held it together through sheer will, inhaling slowly, filling her lungs, forcing her diaphragm to expand into her belly, safe in the cocoon of the elevator. That's all it took to make her feel safe: several layers of thick walls between her and the outside world.

No. I've given up on finding peace, inside or out. I will not give up on feeling safe.

At the ding the elevator doors opened, revealing the marble floor of the fourteenth floor. She strode off and nearly collided with a woman obscured by a marble-topped table holding a profuse arrangement of flowers. Her heart jackrabbited again. "Excuse me," Arden said as her face flushed.

The woman looked up from her phone, and did a double take before her jaw dropped in shock. That's the way it would be from now on, stares and double takes, whispers behind her back and tirades on social media, their honor dragged through the mud again and again, for ratings. The woman's gaze flicked over Arden's clothes, the sizable oval ruby ring on the middle finger of her right hand.

"I hope your father burns in hell," she said, teeth bared in hatred.

Arden froze. The woman sidestepped into the elevator, the doors closing, leaving Arden with the spray of flowers and her reflection in the mirror. Unbrushed blonde hair spilling around her shoulders. Pale skin. Near-colorless lips. A lavender tunic her personal shopper chose to draw attention to her eyes, which only served to highlight the smudges under her eyes and the scar tissue on her shoulder and chest. White jeans. Gold sandals.

Put on some lipstick, Arden. It brightens your face.

Her mother's voice echoed in her ears until a door at the end of the hallway flung open, and Betsy Cottlin peered nearsightedly into the hallway. "I thought I heard the elevator," she said. "Why are you standing in the hallway? Come in and help me find my glasses."

"You live next door to a former investor," Arden said as she hurried down the hall, glad for the distraction. Her voice was almost normal, but Betsy knew all of Arden's tells. "She hopes Dad burns in hell."

"Her dog craps in the elevator at least twice a week. I hope she sees him there," Betsy said. She closed the door and resumed patting tabletops and rifling through the pockets of coats hanging in the closet by the door. "Carlotta, have you seen—?"

Betsy's housekeeper appeared in the door to the kitchen, a pair of red-rimmed glasses in one hand and a scraper smeared with what looked like spinach dip in the other.

"Thank you," Betsy said, and took the glasses.

"Hello, Arden," Carlotta said, then disappeared as Betsy slid the glasses on her nose to study Arden. Her gaze, sharpened by both corrective lenses and two decades of BFF status, missed nothing. "Oh, honey."

Arden surrendered to the enveloping hug Betsy gave her. "It's fine," Arden said automatically into her friend's loose dark hair.

"I call bullshit," Betsy said.

"Okay, I'm at the end of my rope," Arden said.

"That's better," Betsy said. "How's your mother? Still in denial?"

When the FBI raided their Hamptons house a week earlier, Arden and her mother had no idea what was happening, or why. Shunted off to the side and under the watchful gaze of an armed agent, Arden immediately called her cousin Neil, who served as the family's attorney, and got him off the sidelines of his son's soccer game. When the FBI left, taking her father and brother away in handcuffs, she turned on the television and watched a CNBC reporter narrate the devastation of their family's reputation.

MacCarren, the investment bank carrying their family name and headed by her father and oldest brother, Charles, was a front for one of the largest Ponzi schemes in history. The screen cut from a report to video of men and women in cargo pants and polos with FBI emblazoned on the back and guns strapped to their thighs, carrying boxes and computers out of the firm's offices in Midtown, the principals' homes in New York, Aspen, and Palm Springs. She had been so stunned, it took her a moment to realize the reporter was broadcasting from the front lawn of the house in which she'd been standing. In the next ninety seconds, Arden watched her mother age a decade, right in front of her eyes. She wouldn't have been surprised if her hair had gone white.

In the moment, Arden kept it together, called lawyers, took the house phone off the hook. When the scope of the accusations became clear, Charles's wife, Serena, laid her crying, shivering girls down in the back of her Land Rover and covered them with blankets before driving through the reporters and back to her family home in Connecticut. Her mother refused to leave, then spiraled into an attack of hysterics. It was Arden who shut off the television, Arden who found her mother's pharmacopeia, Arden who helped her mother into bed, as if the shock had numbed her system to whiteout overload that staved off a panic attack. But she knew one was coming, perhaps the mother of all panic attacks, and if history repeated itself, the monster inside her head would arrive at the worst possible time.

"She's still refusing to leave Breakers Point," Arden said. Her pulse had slowed, her breathing deepened, but the scent of flop sweat hovered in the air around her, and her legs were still unsteady. She held out her hand, tremors running through her fingers, out into the air. "A cab honked while I was getting my bags out of the car."

Betsy's eyes sharpened even more. She reached for Arden's hand and held it palm-down in hers. "I've seen worse," she said, her voice oddly gentle. "If you want, I'll reschedule this for another time. This probably isn't the best week for us to brush up our rusty drawing skills. Libby and Sally won't mind."

It was tempting, except it felt like quitting, and quitting felt like failure. "Who's here?"

"Everyone except the model."

Which meant Micah Russo, on faculty at NYU and an accomplished artist, was also here. "No," Arden said. "This is a good idea. I need a distraction. It might even help."

"Fine, but say the word and we shut this down in favor of a really good pinot," Betsy said decisively. "Come have a glass of wine."

"Where's Nick?" Arden asked as they walked down the hall into a classic eight overlooking Central Park.

"Dubai," Betsy said. "He said to tell you whatever you need."

As Betsy's husband, Nick was still Arden's friend, although he had dated Arden all through college before they parted ways just after graduation. All three of them pretended there was nothing awkward about this. "Thanks," Arden said automatically.

"All right. Forget about it. For the next two hours, you're in a Parisian atelier. Nothing exists but this moment," she said grandly, leading Arden down the hallway.

Betsy did nothing by half, including turning her spacious, high-ceilinged living room into an atelier overlooking Central Park. The furniture now resided against one wall. Four easels were arranged on the antique Turkish rugs in a semicircle around a simple wooden box draped with a soft blanket. Libby Harmand and Sally Kettering-Stevens were arranging their pencils in the easel trays, but they stopped to kiss Arden's cheek and hug her.

"I'm so sorry," Sally said.

"How are you?" Libby said, squeezing her hand.

"Fine," Arden said automatically. "Which one's mine?"

"That one, unless the sun is too bright," Sally said, pointing to the easel at the top of the circle, facing the windows. "I can switch with you."

Sally erred on the side of oversolicitous, unlike Betsy, who would crack dirty jokes until Arden howled with laughter. They'd clearly circled the wagons before Arden arrived, maybe even had a conference, and while Arden knew they meant well, this group of friends who'd seen her through crises before, this time it rankled.

"It's fine," she said to Sally, and forced a smile. "We'll switch it up each class."

Libby brought her a glass of wine, placing it on the barstool beside her easel. Arden set up her large sketchpad and arranged her pencils, then sipped the wine. Sometimes alcohol helped and sometimes it acted as a trigger. She just didn't know which would happen, but she refused to stop drinking wine because something bad might happen. The instructor, Micah, stopped by to say hello. They'd met before, moved in the same art circles, which enabled them to keep the greeting casual. His blond hair brushed his fine-cut jaw, and his brown eyes reflected a calm, if abstracted, wisdom.

"We're just missing our model," he said.

The buzzer from the doorman went off, startling Arden nearly out of her skin. She covered by adjusting her sketchpad on the easel. A few moments later the door opened, and Arden heard Carlotta's low welcome.

"That way?" came from behind her.

A male voice, smooth and dense, like the caramels her grandmother used to keep in her pocket for Arden. A thud of a heavy bag hitting the floor, then the hair on Arden's arms lifted as he strode between her easel and Libby's. Her gaze focused down at her pencil tray, Arden saw bike shoes, knee-length cargo shorts, and a tight-fitting jersey, unzipped to the end of his breastbone. Tattoos swirled up his forearms to disappear into the jersey's short sleeves, and reappeared in the gap between the unzipped edges. A day or two's worth of stubble accentuated his square chin and full lips. His hair was buzzed close to his head, indentations flattened into the hair and his forehead from a bike helmet that had left a distinct line on his forehead and around his ears from the straps. The heavy sunlight streaming through the west-facing windows slid through his irises, turning them the pale green of sea glass.

He shook Micah's hand. "Sorry I'm late. I took one last job in Midtown."

"You're fine," Micah said amiably. "We've just set up, so you're in good time."

The model scanned the room, his gaze searching corners high and low. Arden got the impression he wasn't interested in the crown molding. "Now?" the model asked.

Micah nodded. In two seconds the model tugged the zipper of his bike jersey free and shrugged out of it. Arden's first impression was of skin stretched over muscles, revealing veins, tendons, ligaments, flat planes of muscle. The cargo shorts hung low on his hipbones, held up by God-only-knew-what force of nature because the man didn't have an ounce of fat on his body, but was absolutely covered in tattoos. Ink curled up both arms to the shoulder, but the first thing Arden could distinguish in the swirl of color was a sword, the hilt spreading over his collarbone, the blade arrowing down his pectoral, ribs, and hip to end just above his thigh. The second thing was a dragon, prowling restlessly over his other shoulder. The third thing was an oddly bare spot just over his left pectoral, a patch of skin remarkable for its lack of ink.

Micah turned to the circled easels. "This is Seth. Seth, this is Libby, Betsy, Arden, and Sally," he said, pointing to each woman in turn.

Seth paused in the act of unzipping his cargo shorts to give them a short nod, then, with absolutely no ceremony or coyness, hooked his thumbs in his shorts and boxers, and pushed them to his ankles. In one movement he stepped out of them, kicked them behind the platform, and then he was up onto the blanket-draped box. Hands on his hips, weight on one hip, he looked at Micah. "Say when."

"Now's good," Micah said, and moved from the center of the circle to the outer edge. "We'll open with fifteen-second poses. Big movements, not details. Warm up your arm, and your brain," he said. "Whenever you're ready, ladies," he said gently.

Arden blinked. Stared. Came back to her senses. Ducked her head behind her easel, and slid Betsy a look, only to find her best friend gaping. Flat-out gaping, which was worth savoring. Very little took Betsy by surprise, and the sheer shock on her face almost made the past week worthwhile. Clearly Micah hadn't vetted his choice of model with Betsy.

This wasn't happening. This kind of person didn't show up to model for a private drawing class hosted in a Fifth Avenue apartment overlooking Central Park. Classes like this hired dancers of either sex, slender, supple, waxed, capable of holding languid, elegant poses while beginning artists struggled to capture the way fingertips dented the air, the slope of a thigh into negative space. Seth was almost too much to look at.

She'd done this before, taken drawing classes at boarding school and in college before her business-and-math course load edged out electives. The fact that she hadn't drawn anything in nearly a decade didn't make her a novice, just rusty, so there was no reason for her heart to pound. She picked up her pencil and glanced back at Seth. Still tattooed. Still naked. His sparse body hair thickened at his navel and groin, and his genitals hung heavy between thighs bulging with muscle. His skin darkened abruptly just above his knees, then lightened just as abruptly at his ankle. A tan from riding a bike in the city's sunny summer, delineated by the shorts and socks.

Color heated her cheeks, a stupid, schoolgirl reaction. She'd seen naked men before, slept with them, gone to strip clubs and hired dancers for bachelorette parties, so this shouldn't have caused a blush. Libby wasn't blushing. Betsy wasn't blushing. Arden couldn't see Sally, but Sally was a pathologist; it was unlikely anything about the human body made her blush. But Arden's body was on high alert after the incident in the cab, calling blood to the surface more quickly, triggering that rush of goose bumps when he passed her.

The hushed scrape of pencil against paper pricked at Arden's awareness. To her right and left, Betsy and Libby were drawing, pencils held between first and middle fingers, arms moving in sweeping arcs, capturing broad shoulders, jutting elbows, long, thickly muscled legs.

Seth's gaze caught hers, his green eyes even more shocking without the light rendering them translucent. One eyebrow lifted ever so slightly. *Breaking the fourth wall,* she thought hysterically. Things like this worked because everyone pretended one of the people in the room wasn't stark naked. On display.

"Change."

Without batting an eyelash, Seth dropped into a pose Arden recognized from yoga class. Warrior one. Knee bent, leg extended behind him, arms extended to either side.

Micah stopped at her easel and smiled at her. "Big gestures," he repeated. "Just loosen up your arm and hand. That's all."

She went for the obvious, the stretch of his hands from fingertips to fingertips, a long, slender oval, then the line of his spine from the crown of his head to the sharp swell of buttocks, angling down to his foot.

"Change."

Flip her paper and leave the bent leg behind. Warrior two. He'd either taken yoga, maybe to combat hours hunched over a bike, the constant jarring of flying over the city streets, potholes, cracks, debris, curbs, or knew someone who had. A girlfriend, perhaps.

"Change."

She stopped thinking as Seth shifted smoothly through a series of poses, all long lines and unfocused eyes. He turned as he changed postures, giving each student a different angle. It took two minutes to run through ten postures. By the last one, Arden was over her blush, more comfortable in the room.

"Time," Micah said. "We'll do two forties, with a break in between. Sound good to everyone?"

Seth stepped off the pedestal and waited for Micah to use blocks and blankets to support him in the pose he would hold for forty minutes. Arden sharpened her pencil and watched covertly as Micah had him sit on the pedestal—one leg stretched onto the polished parquet—then twist to his right so his right arm bore most of his weight.

"Music?" Micah asked belatedly. The standard rule of thumb for a class was that the model chose the music. If the artists didn't like it, they wore headphones.

"Anything from my phone is fine," Seth said without moving. "Left cargo pocket."

Micah opened it and connected the phone to Betsy's wireless speakers. To her surprise, the opening lines of New Orleans jazz colored the air. Definitely not what she expected.

She leaned over to Betsy's easel. "This is ridiculous," she murmured under her breath. "Mom's so medicated she doesn't know what century it is, Garry's not returning my calls, and Neil says we should prepare for the worst."

"Life is ridiculous," Betsy shot back. "Is this taking your mind off your life?"

"Yes," Arden said.

"Then shut up and draw."

"Ladies," Micah said gently as he passed behind them. "The pose."

That was the point. When Betsy suggested the class, she had been thinking of Arden's panic attacks, but now any break at all from the swirling hell of her life was not only welcome but vital.

Seth was different. Rather than lulling Arden into a sense of beauty and order, stylized into a smooth imperturbability, she hardly knew where to start—the taut swell of buttock braced on the pedestal, the sword or dragon, the way his toes spread and flexed against the floor—yes. Start there. Toes. She lightly sketched the shape of his foot, oval, the arch a pale shadowy arc underneath, before defining the slope of his toes, rectangular, then making each a distinct, flattened circle topped with toenails, a tuft of hair gilded by the sunlight. Narrow to the bones of the ankle, that defenseless bump of bone, the Achilles tendon, then the curve of his calf, an odd slope of muscle, not rounded like hers, but a plane that dropped off into space then reappeared as the back of his knee, bent at a slight angle, the back of his thigh, the muscles taut oblongs narrowing at the connections with hip and knee. Kneecap, a circle, the bulge of muscle alongside the knee.

His penis hung soft between his spread legs. She sketched in a suggestion before continuing the line from his pubic bone to his other leg, bent and dangling in the space between the table legs and top. The proportions stymied her until Micah stopped at her side.

"Don't think too much," he said. "Find the essence of the pose, the line of energy," he said quietly, one arm folded across his abdomen, his chin braced on his thumb, his fingers obscuring his lips.

Arden blinked, then looked again at Seth. If she had to use one phrase to describe the essence of the pose, his energy in the room, it would be *hidden in plain sight*. He was physically there, irresistible, but somehow not in his body.

Don't make this more difficult than it is, Arden. Just draw his body.

She re-created the twisted line from his hipbone to his opposite shoulder, then added his arm, braced to hold his weight, and the table under the palm. Micah nodded, gave her an abstracted smile, and moved away to stand beside Libby.

When it came, Micah's soft "Time" took her by surprise. Seth waited until all four artists had set down their pencils and stepped back before he abandoned the pose. He snagged his boxers and shorts from the floor, stepped into them, zipped and buttoned the fly, then stretched side to side while his spine cracked all the way down. Carlotta brought out chilled white wine and water, trays of grapes, cheese, crackers, hummus, vegetables for dipping, olives, little pastries and cakes, setting them on the dining room table next to plates, napkins, glasses.

"Well?" Micah began, looking first at Libby.

"I can tell it's been years since I've done that," Libby said, cradling her wineglass between her palms.

Arden took two of Carlotta's truffles and nodded a *yes, please* to Betsy, who filled her wineglass. Seth poured water into a wine goblet, filled his plate, and sat down across from her. Close up his bare chest was even more daunting.

"Betsy?"

She looked up from her phone. Everyone besides Micah and Arden had their phones out, tapping and scrolling. Arden's would contain ninety percent bad news, if not more, so she focused on the strawberries and not sneaking glances at Seth.

"I can't remember the last time I went forty minutes without looking at this," Betsy said, waggling it at the group.

"Sally?"

"Focus isn't my problem," she said. "Drawing live bodies without turning them into an anatomical exercise, however, that's different."

A little laughter. Libby leaned over and said, "She's a pathologist," to Seth.

"Arden?"

A weird silence, because everyone in the room knew about MacCarren's downfall, and most of them knew about the panic attacks. "There's just so much to look at."

More laughter. At that, Seth looked up from his phone. His face broke into a smile that wrinkled the skin around his eyes and carved lines on either side of his lips, adding entirely new layers and nuances to his already unfathomable self.

"That's a Marine Corps symbol," Sally said. Arden followed her gaze to a globe and anchor on his upper right shoulder.

"Yes, ma'am," he said easily, but while the smile remained on his mouth, it disappeared from his eyes.

"I see a lot of tattoos in my line of work."

"No shoptalk," Betsy said gently.

Sally looked quickly at Arden. Yes, she was the reason for the no-shoptalk rule. Usually Sally's tendency to describe the trickier parts of autopsies was the most socially awkward thing to happen, but now they were making a space for Arden to not have to think about, much less talk about, work.

"It's not a problem," Seth said. "If it was, I wouldn't take off my clothes for art students."

Slightly nervous laughter, but Arden sensed tension underneath the accurate statement. Just because you showed your soft underbelly to people didn't mean you wanted people to poke it.

"Let's talk about the introductory exercise," Micah said. "What's the connection between the warm-up and the longer session?"

"Switching on the right brain?" Betsy offered.

"In part," Micah said. "Getting down a quick sketch is the foundation for a drawing. When we come at drawing from the left brain, we want to make each line perfect the first time. It makes us hesitant. Building from a quick sketch captures the pose's energy and relies on intuition. If you learn to follow your instincts, the rest will fall into place."

"I knew this was easy," Libby quipped.

"It's that easy, and that hard," Micah said, and finished off his wine.

They pushed their chairs back from the table. Seth leaned over. "How are the truffles?" he asked, his voice carrying under the conversation at the head of the table. Sally was already back at her place, frowning as she erased a line and redrew it.

"Really good," Arden said. "Carlotta makes them with red chili powder."

"Don't give away all her secrets," Betsy chided.

Seth snagged a truffle on his way to the circle of easels, consuming it in two bites before stripping as casually as he did before. Micah arranged him in a reclining pose that allowed him to relax entirely. Betsy got Seth's front while Arden the long line of his back, from the crown of his head to his heels. Libby and Sally got a serious challenge in foreshortening.

She flipped to a new page in her sketchbook and set to her task. The sword was repeated on his back, as if someone had driven it through his shoulder and now the thing pulsed inside him, the edges, carved hilt, and ornate text on the blade radiating through his skin. Arden ignored the ink and focused on the muscled cleft of his spine.

"Time."

She'd done it again, lost track of time as she drew. Micah stopped at her easel, his slender finger tracing over the line of Seth's torso from shoulder to knee. "Good," he said quietly.

"It's out of proportion."

"He's out of proportion," Micah said, then nodded at Seth. "Look again. It's good."

Seth had risen from the pedestal and was in the act of stretching, his fingers reaching for Betsy's nine-foot ceilings, toes pushing against the floor. Arden looked again, and discovered Micah's eye had seen what her brain denied. Seth's torso was shorter than his legs would suggest, something the energy of his presence hid. Her brain tried to make it "right," but her instinct captured the truth.

Seth stepped into his shorts, zipped up, then paused at Sally's shoulder as he pulled on his bike jersey. As Arden watched, Sally all but melted. He continued around the circle, looking at each drawing, before turning to Arden.

"Don't," she said, blocking his body with hers. His forward momentum carried him into a split second of thrilling full-body contact. The heat from his bare chest seared through her linen tank to her skin, and the shift of his hips against hers sent a deep quake through her lower belly. She drew in her breath in response and the scent of him, the inevitable sweat of a humid New York City summer, warm skin, something deeper and darker she recognized from her study abroad year in Oxford as the grease used to lubricate a bike chain. The scent of the oil lingered long after she'd scrubbed her fingers.

With an innate grace, he shifted back from the balls of his feet to his heels, putting an inch of space between his body and hers. "Okay," he said, very gently, his gaze searching hers.

It wasn't defensive, accusatory, but a caress. Arden knew she'd been abrupt, if not rude, but there was a limit to how exposed she could stand to be, and after the events of the last week, she was at her limit, all the time. It wasn't rational, but a self-protective instinct. She looked up at him, into those green eyes and saw them flick to the thick scar that started just below her collarbone, disappeared into the V-neck of her sleeveless top, then emerged at the ball of her shoulder.

Seth took two steps back, purposely not looking at her easel. "Okay," he said again, soft, reassuring.

"Same time next week," Micah said. Arden gathered her pencils into the box.

"Leave your sketchpads here," Betsy said over her shoulder as she escorted Seth and Micah to the door. "I'll store them with the easels. No point in hauling them all over Manhattan."

The door closed behind Micah and Seth. Between them, Betsy and Arden shoved one of the sofas back into place, then collapsed on it. They all looked at one another, then lost it laughing. For a moment the lightness of sheer relief swept through Arden.

"My God," Libby said. "Where on earth did you find that *man*?"

"I didn't!" Betsy gasped. "Micah said he'd arrange for the model."

"He'll bring him back, right? Can we request a specific model?"

"He'll probably alternate," Sally said. "Men and women, different body sizes and shapes. Crap. Did I really ask him about his tattoos?"

"You did," Betsy said, lifting her glass to toast Sally.

"I'd love to know the story behind them," Sally continued, thinking out loud.

"You could just ask him," Betsy said, eyes twinkling.

Sally opened her mouth, closed it again, then looked at Arden. "It's nice to see you laugh," she said.

The mood in the room instantly dampened. "I feel like I've forgotten how," she said, and finally pulled out her phone. She had voice mails and missed calls, but none of them from Garry. Now. To download or not to download? Normally her emails downloaded automatically, but after the news broke, she set the retrieve option to manual so she could handle them when she felt up to it.

Might as well get it over with. She should be inured to the near-constant stream of anger, hatred, and vitriol. She swiped her thumb over the list of her accounts and watched the wheel spin as the phone connected to the servers.

"What's the latest?" Libby asked.

"I don't even know how to describe it." Where the hell was Garry? New Zealand, where it was apparently possible to just disappear off the grid into the mountains.

"Why are people angry with you? You ran the foundation, not the investment side of the house."

"My name is on the firm. I'm on the board. It's all about the name. We are MacCarren." She waited for the emails to finish downloading. Three hundred and eight in the three hours she'd been in Betsy's apartment. She'd given her assistant paid leave and taken over managing her own email. The sheer numbers were overwhelming, as was the hatred and pain many of them now contained.

"Have you seen your dad since . . . ?"

"Since the FBI raided the house and took him away in hand-cuffs?" she asked, refusing to mince words. "No. I looked through the evidence, and it's clear the accusations are true. He and Charles were running a Ponzi scheme. I'm too angry to go see him, or Charles."

Silence. Arden tried to get used to the fact that no one wanted to talk about MacCarren anymore. Before, it was the only thing people wanted to talk to her about. How did her father do it? Could they buy in or was he closed to new investors? On the surface, she, too, was MacCarren. They got close to her to get close to him, not knowing that she, like the rest of the family, like the rest of the world, was being told a great big lie.

Sally picked up her purse and tote. "I have to work in the morning. Brunch soon?"

"I'll walk out with you," Libby said.

Betsy walked them to the door, then came back to top off Arden's wine and set the plate of truffles in front of her. "Want me to help you put the furniture back?"

"Carlotta and I will take care of it in the morning," Betsy said. She looked around the room. "It's rather bohemian. I might keep it this way." Arden contemplated a second truffle, settled for top-ping off her glass of wine, then dragged Betsy's cashmere throw from the back of the sofa. Betsy pulled the trailing end over her feet and snuggled them companionably against Arden's calf.

"He was hot."

No need to name the subject of that sentence. Except *hot* didn't quite cover Seth Last-name-unknown. He was compelling, and Arden was suddenly of the opinion that *hot* was what you settled for when *compelling* wasn't available.

"He was," Arden said, assuming Betsy would stop there. They had a deal: they were ruthlessly honest with each other about everything except the fact that Arden never got over Nick leaving her for Betsy. In exchange for Arden being the smiling, attentive, picture-perfect maid of honor at the wedding of her best friend to her former lover, Betsy stayed out of Arden's love life.

"He was interested in you."

Arden flicked Betsy a look. "Everyone's interested in me at the moment."

"He didn't do the double take," Betsy said. "Either he doesn't know, or he doesn't care."

"The last thing I need right now is a date."

"So don't date him."

"Let me rephrase that. The last thing I need right now is a man."

Betsy shrugged. "Your family name is being dragged through the mud by every news outlet on the planet. People are sending you hate mail, picketing outside your offices, and you're vibrating like a hummingbird on crack. Maybe you don't need a date, but you could sure as hell put that man to good use."

"The drawing class was supposed to help with the humming-bird thing."

"So try two things at once."

"How will I know which one worked?" Arden said lightly. Betsy knew all about randomized double-blind controlled studies because she was trained as an epidemiologist. After she married Nick she put that training to use on boards and charities focused on public health. Arden used to donate significant sums of both her personal money and the MacCarren Foundation's annual budget to programs Betsy vetted.

"If you get drawing *and* him, who cares which one works?"

Arden threw Betsy a glance her oldest friend had no trouble interpreting. *Enough. Move on.*

"What comes next?"

"Neil's cleared his schedule to handle this full-time. I have an appointment with the FBI in a couple of days."

"Again? I thought they interviewed you."

"They have done. Twice. I suspect I'll be at their beck and call for a very long time," Arden said. "This time they want to go over the family assets."

"That sounds ominous," Betsy said.

"It is. Neil's been rather vague on the subject, which is even more ominous."

Betsy reached out and clasped Arden's hand. "Want to stay the night? Carlotta will make you crepes."

Derek was waiting downstairs, but he could just as easily drive the SUV back to the garage and head home whether she was in the back or not. A week ago she had work, a schedule filled with both professional and personal obligations, but right now she had only one goal: to salvage what she could from the wreckage of her family. She found herself remembering the ease with which Seth undressed, his confidence in his own skin. He'd forged that confidence in the Marine Corps, while she couldn't even handle Manhattan traffic.

Daydreaming about a tattooed former Marine wasn't in her plan at the moment, let alone actually dating or sleeping with him. "Why not?" she said, and put Seth out of her mind.

— TWO —

The gap between the alley wall and the delivery truck narrowed as the truck slowed to make its left turn. Seth knew to the micron how wide he was on the bike; the question wasn't fitting his body through the gap, or the bike's handlebars, but rather the messenger backpack slung across his back. He had two boxes crammed in there, the straps straining to close. If he misjudged the space, the box would catch between the truck box and the wall, snagging him off his bike as neatly as a bomb blast blew souls into the afterlife.

He'd proved fucking hard to kill, so he probably wouldn't die. The digital monitor strapped to his handlebars ticked relentlessly; three minutes to deliver the contents of his messenger bag. All senses focused on the narrowing gap, his thrumming heart rate, his lungs straining for air to fuel his muscles, he leaned forward and found another gear deep inside. He shot through the gap and out of the alley into the intersection, and felt only the faintest brush of metal against Cordura nylon as he did. The truck driver honked indignantly and extensively, right next to his head, but Seth heard only a faint bleat. He swerved around a taxi, popped up over the median and back down into what would be oncoming traffic when the lights turned, dropped his head and ignored his screaming lungs, and dipped into what he mentally dubbed the *I don't give a fuck if you're dead, you hold your goddamn position, marine* reserve tank and made it across the avenue before the traffic arrived.

One minute. Six blocks. Not enough time, or air in his lungs, in the city, in the entire fucking ecosystem. He blew past a line of cars waiting for the light at the end of the street, hit the light just as it changed, swerved to avoid a left-turning black SUV, lather, rinse, repeat at the next intersection. He was going too fast to time the lights right, so there'd be a red in the next block.

He blew through it.

Brakes, a horn barely denting the thick, pervasive silence enveloping him, twenty seconds. Three blocks. Too close but he could see the building now, and surely he hadn't survived Iraq and Afghanistan to die of a heart attack on a Manhattan city street. Slight uphill he knew only because his quads quivered on the verge of giving out on him, but he was through the last intersection and braking at the building's entrance. His bike would disappear if he left it unlocked on the street for more than a split second, so he rode right through the open door beside the revolving doors, startling the man holding the door for the women behind him, swerved to avoid them, ignored the indignant *Hey*, braked in front of the reception desk, and glanced down at the digital readout on his handlebars.

Six seconds to spare. Fuck, yeah. "Mirinda Castille," he said with the last air in his lungs, then heaved in a breath. Sweat dripped from his jaw. He used his shoulder to smear the droplets, but his jersey was as soaked as his skin. The fabric snagged on his stubble and the still-unfamiliar arrangement of straps. The bike helmet's straps didn't quite match the configuration of his combat helmet. It was the little things that hooked him out of the adrenaline rush, back into reality.

A woman stepped up beside him. "I'm Mirinda," she said, her voice faint under the thrumming heartbeat in his ears.

"Sign there," he said, handing her his phone, then shrugged off the messenger bag, opened the clips, and pulled out the packages. "What is it?" he asked. His heart rate was separating into distinct jackrabbit beats, not the chest-exploding thrum of high-intensity exercise.

"Running shoes."

"What?"

"Running shoes, and wing tips," she said, and opened the box for him to see. "My boss is on his way to the Hamptons for the weekend and he forgot his shoes at his club."

Seth peered into the bag. They were Nikes, blue with red accents, showing some road wear, and *what the ever-loving fuck*? He damned near killed himself getting some hedge fund manager his running shoes for a weekend in the Hamptons? The irony tasted like blood, or maybe he'd bitten his lip when he hit a bump. He touched his hand to his mouth. Yup. Bitten his lip. Didn't feel the sting until the adrenaline started to ebb.

"He could buy new shoes for what that delivery cost."

"But not for what the wing tips cost," she said in the mild tone of a woman who'd long since given up making sense of unreasonable demands.

Seth peered into the box. There was no identifying mark on the insole or leather, so . . . handmade? He had no idea. "Shoes."

"I would have waited," she said with a smile he'd seen fairly regularly since leaving the Corps. He questioned her sanity, given that he was dripping sweat onto pink granite floors and his legs were literally shaking.

"It's the principle," he said. "I said I'd be here by two fifteen, and I was."

"Let's hear it for principles," Mirinda said.

"Sir, on principle, we'd like you to remove your bike from the lobby," said the receptionist.

"Understood," he said, and popped the bike up on its back wheel to walk it out the door.

"Thanks," Mirinda said. Running shoes firmly tucked under her arm, she climbed into a Lexus SUV not that much smaller than a tank, leaving Seth on the sidewalk.

He walked his bike over to a low wall separating the building's plaza from the sidewalk, sat down, and fumbled his cell phone from his cargo shorts pocket. The phone was like his rifle now. He always knew where it was, constantly checking for it like he'd check for his rifle. He was registered with three different online delivery services, picking up jobs based on where he ended up, taking multiple jobs at once if he could do a quick delivery in one zone while on a longer one between zones.

Sweat dripped from his chin and elbows to plunk on the side- walk, dripped onto his phone's screen. Absently, he wiped the screen, then activated it. The screen saver was a picture of him and his three best friends, a candid shot taken by their lieutenant of them laugh- ing just after they'd shrugged out of body armor and flak jackets. Seth looked at it, looked at the tremor in his hand and the quiver in his legs, and felt nothing. He'd just chased down a legendary run, set every neuron and nerve ending in his body on fire. He should feel something. At a minimum he should *hear* something.

He didn't. He had, of course, held conversations, but they all echoed across a canyon, like someone was standing on the other cliff face, shouting at him through cupped hands. He'd had his hearing checked during his discharge physical. It was perfectly normal. Except it wasn't.

The app refreshed while he scratched at the stubble on his jaw, where the sweat itched under his bike-helmet straps, then dried his fingers on his cargo shorts. A new job was available, a pickup in Midtown with the delivery on Wall Street, to the building that used to house MacCarren. When the news broke about MacCarren, Seth hadn't paid much attention to the story until Ryan Hamilton, who'd retained him to make deliveries to Irresistible, a high-end lingerie shop in the Fashion District, was identified as the whistleblower who brought the entire scheme crashing down.

That explained a lot about Ryan's demeanor over the course of the summer. Seth joined the Corps at eighteen, so while he didn't know much about a lot of things relevant to civilian life, he recognized all the signs of someone under incredible pressure: sleeplessness, weight loss, but the big tip-off to Seth was the extravagant, inexplicable way he threw money around. To secure Seth's services to make deliveries to Simone at Irresistible, he had handed Seth a manila envelope full of more money than Seth made in a year with the Marines, including the bonus for combat pay. Seth had been worried that the guy was going to eat a gun, but then again, he saw potential suicides everywhere these days.

He swiped over to his texts, tapped on Ryan's name, and sent a quick one. You okay? Back in the app, he tapped on the Wall Street run to claim it, then set his bike upright, swung his leg over the seat, adjusted the messenger bag to his back, and set off into traffic again.

He waited for a light near a flower shop in Midtown. The blooms of vibrant purple orchids caught his eye. The color reminded him of Arden's violet gaze, flicking from him to her drawing paper during the class on Fifth Avenue. He really had to stop thinking about her, or just think about her less, which was low-hanging fruit because he thought about her basically all the time. Not actively, but sunlight reminded him of her hair, and a certain pensive expression glimpsed as he waited in a lobby or foyer reminded him of the way she looked as she drew, thoughtful, brow furrowed, attacking the drawing with a fierce concentration that made him want to run his thumb over the lines between her golden eyebrows, tell her to ease up, just let it flow. But Micah didn't do that, so Seth sure as hell wouldn't. He was the model, not the instructor. She and Betsy were friends, and Betsy lived on Fifth Avenue; maybe there was some sort of "wrong side of the track" friendship there, but he didn't think so. She was beautiful, expensive, and while he could make the effort to get to know her, in the end she was something he couldn't have.

Where did she get those scars?

The train of thought was wearing a groove in his brain. Back on the bike, he rode slowly downtown, stopping at the intersection of Broadway and Morris, across the street from the fabled bull. There was still a fair amount of foot traffic in the area, heading for the Staten Island Ferry terminal or the Lex Avenue line, but he found a delivery doorway where he could lean the bike against the building and hunker down out of the way. With a sigh of relief, he lifted the messenger bag over his head and set it down beside him. Unfastening the seat-belt clasp, he rummaged around in the front pockets and pulled out his Moleskine journal and a Micron pen.

Ease up. Let it flow.

He'd never had official drawing classes like the ones he modeled for, just books checked out from the school or public library and thousands of hours of practice on long, solitary walks back home in Wyoming, his muse a constant, subtly demanding presence in his life. He had every sketchbook he'd ever used, one continuous record of what he saw, where he was, from fourth grade on, but the one in his bag was brand-new, the cover a pristine black, the pages cream and crisp, ready for his pen.

Open the cover and flip to the first page. Uncap the pen.

He couldn't do it. It felt wrong, a jump in time, like gaps in the fossil record, because the last one he'd been using during his last tour in Afghanistan was jammed in a bag in the tiny closet in his motor home.

Just start. Draw the bull. It's a New York City landmark, and a fine piece of sculpture. Just draw the curve of the nostrils and the horns, the bellied side of the bull leaning mid-breath, the lifted forefoot.

Hunkered down on his heels, he watched suits stride past him, talking on Bluetooth headsets or on phones, rarely to each other. He felt invisible here, enveloped in silence and the smell of cement and asphalt, which was just fine with him. In this city of art students and designers, no one paid any attention to a man with a notebook. It should have been the easiest thing in the world to whip off a quick sketch of the bull.

Not today. He shut the sketchbook, snapped the elastic strap over the cover to keep it closed, and jammed it back in his messenger backpack. Then he got back on the bike and merged with traffic heading outbound on the Brooklyn Bridge. He easily outpaced the vehicle traffic by splitting the lanes. The practice of riding between cars was technically illegal but almost impossible to enforce, as long as he didn't ride past a police cruiser. When traffic picked up, he reached out and snagged a strap holding down a truckload of lumber, and let the truck power him the rest of the way into Prospect Heights.

Home. Home until he was eighteen was Laramie, Wyoming. Then, for the next ten years, it was an assortment of bases, barracks, camps, and forward operating bases, both stateside and in Iraq and Afghanistan. Now he was living in a twenty-three-foot motor home he bought from a former city employee, parked a couple of blocks from the west edge of Prospect Park. After detaching the front wheel from his bike, he unlocked the heavy metal chain from around his waist, and secured the bike's frame to a rack attached to the motor home's grill. It wasn't the most secure thing in the world; anyone determined enough to steal the bike could work the bolts free and make off with both the rack and the bike in very little time. Taking the front wheel inside was a more effective deterrent. Even more effective was the fact that the bike was an old ten-speed, and not really worth the trouble it would take to steal it.

By the time he unlocked the door, took the three steps up into the motor home, and flicked on the lights and the air-conditioning, all he could smell was himself, the garlic from three slices of pizza working its way out through his pores. The first order of business was to take a shower. Every few days he filled up the motor home's hundred-gallon tank at an open fire hydrant or the local VFW, but he was stingy with water, as stingy as he had been on deployment. He rinsed out his compression shorts and his bike jersey, then hung them up to dry on a clothesline strung the width of the bathroom. He had a couple of sets of each—one to wash, one to wear, each set drying in the heat accumulated in the motor home over the course of the day.

A life executed within normal tolerances was a life, no matter if the silence threatened to crush him. He'd shared the same amount of square footage with three other Marines. Of course it was quieter.

He opened the tiny closet and pulled out jeans and a river driver's shirt, resolutely ignoring the blood-stained pair of cammies neatly folded on the top shelf, the Moleskine in the left-side pocket. Wallet and keys in hand, he scuffed his feet into flip-flops and set off for dinner with Phil.

But when Seth arrived at the bar, a trendy combination of micro-brews and Middle Eastern food, Phil wasn't there yet, probably caught in some delay on the subway in from Manhattan. Seth snagged the last table and ordered a beer to nurse while he waited, his gaze divided between the television screens tuned to the Yankees game over the bar, and the door. Twenty minutes late, Phil walked in the door. He lifted his chin in greeting and stopped at the bar for a beer before making his way through the crowd to Seth. The resemblance to his brother was unmistakable. Same dark hair, pale blue eyes, but at twenty-three and four years younger than Doug, Phil hadn't developed into the wall of muscle Doug was. *Used to be,* Seth corrected himself. *Doug used to be, and that's why you're here.*

"Hey," he said.

Seth nodded a greeting.

"You look wiped," Phil said.

"Rode forty-two miles today, pretty average," Seth said with a shrug, "except for one delivery to Midtown. I damn near exploded my heart. Guess what the package was."

"Fuck," Phil said. "Don't make me guess. I fucking hate guessing games."

"Tennis shoes."

"No shit."

"No shit," Seth agreed. "Some guy wanted his running shoes for his weekend in the Hamptons. I got them from his club, and took them to his assistant at his office. She and the shoes took off in an eighty-thousand-dollar Lexus."

Phil was a lifelong city resident and too jaded to find this truly insane, but it was worth a laugh, and that was enough for Seth. It wasn't the same as the camaraderie he had in the Corps, but it was close, close enough to trigger a little of the endorphin rush he used to get sitting around after patrol with Doug, Brian, and Manny. Normal tolerances.

"It's a fucking crazy way to make a living," Phil said. "Playing in Manhattan traffic? Crazy."

Seth remembered the sweet rush of adrenaline, the conviction of his invincibility as he blew through light after light. A shiver skittered up his spine. "You're a Marine," Seth scoffed. "You're calling bike messengers crazy?"

"There's crazy and then there's really crazy," Phil said. "That's what you're doing with your life?"

He was doing exactly what he wanted to do with his life. "I make better money than I did in the Corps," Seth said, like it mattered.

Phil grunted. "You want falafel?" He waved off Seth's automatic reach for his wallet. "I've got it."

He walked up to the bar, waiting to order. Someone switched one of the TVs to the news. He caught the tail end of the Mac-Carren scandal update, then a story Seth was already too familiar with: reports of more deaths in Afghanistan. Two dead, four injured. His gaze switched from the TV to Phil, knocking back his draft beer.

"—The whole thing was a total fucking waste of time."

The speaker at the table behind Phil, with his beard and nerd glasses and his flannel shirt unbuttoned over a Bright Eyes concert T-shirt and carefully cuffed sleeves, was three microbrews to the wind and holding court for the people gathered around him. His commentary registered when Seth walked into the bar, but biking forty miles a day left him too tired to take offense at civilian attitudes, another advantage to making his living with his body. The guy offered a steady stream of opinions about US foreign policy, the complete debacle that was the war in Iraq and Afghanistan, complete with totally uninformed opinions on the war, the fallout, the geopolitical situation in the Middle East. Adrenaline dumped into Seth's nervous system, and he went into hypervigilant mode, gaze flicking from the TV to the hipster to Phil and back again.

Phil's shoulders were hunched, his face growing more and more stony with every use of *geopolitical situation.* The next thing Seth heard over the cut to commercial and a cheer from the Yankee fans was a fragment of a sentence that sounded like "dumb enough to join . . . deserve to die." That was all it took. Phil's face went from stony to blank.

What happened next took less time than it took Seth to set his glass on the table and rise. One second, bearded guy was standing in Phil's vicinity. The next second, he took two giant, stumbling steps backward into a crowd of people, his arms flailing like a pinwheel in a stiff breeze. Beer arced into the space he once occupied, and glass shattered. Stifled screams and gasps filled the air, the half of the bar that wasn't protecting glasses or plates had their phones out and pointed at the scene.

Seth shoved his way to Phil, standing over the bearded guy, who was now sprawled on the floor. He had one hand cupped to his nose, blood trickling down his cheek and jaw. He stared at the red liquid, then looked up at Phil, who stood over him, shoulders hunched, fists clenched, brows lowered, breathing through flared nostrils like the bull on Wall Street.

"What the fuck is your problem?" the guy on the floor all but shrieked.

"My brother was *dumb enough* to join up and defend your right to say what you said," Phil said. "He died doing it. Show some fucking respect." His voice was a whisper, but Seth heard it loud and clear. So did the guy on the floor. His eyes widened, and he had the look of someone who'd gone from pleasantly drunk to stone-cold sober in the space of a heartbeat.

Seth took hold of Phil's upper arm and got half his body between him and the dude on the floor, purposefully turning his back on the guy to show he wasn't a threat. "Let's go."

Phil turned to look at Seth. Seth stared back, not flinching, into eyes a startling shade of blue, the color of the winter sky over the mountains, and as impenetrable as a layer of ice. The lights were on, but nobody was home. As Seth watched, some form of humanity returned to Phil's face. He looked at the guy bleeding on the floor, then at Seth. His brows slightly furrowed, he blinked, and Seth knew he had no memory of what he had just done.

The bartender leaned over the end of the bar. "You have ten seconds to get him out of here or I'm calling the cops."

"We're gone," Seth said.

"I didn't mean . . ." Phil started.

Seth took a firmer grip on Phil's arm and turned him toward the door. "Go."

The crowd parted for them, eyes flickering from Seth's tattoos to Phil's bloody knuckles to their haircuts. He shoved through the door with a little more force than necessary to open it, and found himself in the lingering heat of the day. The parking meters seemed to sway in the heat rising off the sidewalk. He let go of Phil's arm, but kept a close eye on him as he paced up and down the sidewalk. He felt dizzy, a little sick to his stomach from the adrenaline flooding his system and no easy way to burn it off. He did what he always did and channeled it into Phil. "You okay?"

Phil shook out his hand and looked at his bleeding knuckles. "What did I just do?"

Seth braced up on the sidewalk and watched Phil pace, his hands linked behind his head. "You don't remember?"

Phil shook his head slowly, then said, "Some hipster jerk-off said something about anyone stupid enough to sign up deserved to die." He stopped pacing, linked his hands together and slid them over his buzz cut. Hands still behind his back, he looked at Seth. "That would do it," he said. "That would set me off. Shit." A rough exhale, then, "I was hungry, too, and they make damn good falafel."

"I'll get a couple of orders to go," Seth said, and went back inside. The bartender's eyes widened. "I just want the falafel," Seth said placatingly.

"Couple of minutes," the bartender said, eyeing him warily.

While he was waiting he checked on the hipster, now sitting on a barstool with a napkin clasped to his nose. "I think it's broken," the kid said.

Seth took one cursory look at the slow trickle of blood saturating the napkin. Phil had pulled his punch. "It's not broken," he said in tandem with a woman standing beside the guy.

"I'm a nurse," she said in explanation.

"I've had mine broken twice," Seth said.

"He'll be fine," the woman said. "He's sorry for running his mouth off and being a dick."

"My friend's sorry for talking with his fist," Seth said.

The bartender called out Seth's order. The kid stopped him before he claimed it. "I am sorry for his loss," he said grudgingly.

They all were. Everyone was sorry for a dead soldier or Marine, but that's where it ended. They didn't understand Phil's loss, or what he was going through now, three months out of the Corps, missing his brother, no idea what to do with his life next. Seth was as clueless as the kid. There was no road map, no story, no movies made about What Happened Next, when the mission ended not in victorious homecomings and a fadeaway shot of a big family meal, but rather in body bags, explosions, and dust that never seemed to settle. "He was my friend, too. My brother," Seth said, and snagged the warm brown paper bag.

He had this. Doug was gone, and Phil was his responsibility now.

Outside the bar he collected Phil with a tilt of his head and started walking back to the motor home. Fat droplets of rain smacked the sidewalk as they walked, but they made it back before Mother Nature got serious. Seth unlocked the door and led the way inside. Phil stepped up and closed the door behind him. "You weren't kidding when you said you lived in a motor home."

"Who'd joke about that?" Seth said as he set the food on the small table.

Phil eyed the spokes Seth had trued, dangling from the frame over the window. "Looks like the shed in *Twister*, the one full of scythes, just before the big one hit. Is it legal?"

"There's no law that says it's illegal," Seth said, tipping his hand back and forth. Rain spattered against the windshield and the aluminum roof. Within moments the intermittent drops became a steady deluge. Seth flipped on the lights, automatically noting the full charge and the battery from the day's earlier sunshine. He switched on the TV he hardly ever used when he was alone, and they ate while watching the game. It was normal. Two guys eating dinner, drinking beer, watching a game. Exactly the kind of thing that would help Phil keep it together.

"It's five months today," Phil said during a commercial for razors.

Five months. Five months since the day an IED went off and killed Phil's brother, Doug, and two other Marines, Manny Lopez and Brian Gibson, riding in the same Humvee. Five months since Seth watched a giant fist of fire burst inside the vehicle carrying his three best friends in the world.

That's why he lived in a land of asphalt and cement and concrete canyons, a place so noisy all he heard was silence, far away from wadis and dusty roads and explosions. Hell yes, he knew exactly what he was doing with his life, and why. It didn't matter how much he thought about Arden's fierce, fragile face or the pale gold of her hair. He had responsibilities to his friends, to the loved ones they left behind. Phil, Doug's younger brother. Brittany, Brian's wife, a widow at twenty-three and a single mother to a seven-month-old son. Manny, who let Seth observe, draw, record their daily life as Marines, but eventually teased him into putting away his sketchbook and joining the group for a meal, a movie, a game of basketball. Semper Fi never ended. Faithfulness never ended.

"I know," Seth said.

"It's supposed to get easier," Phil said. His voice cracked. He cleared his throat, swallowed hard, and the tears gleaming in his eyes didn't spill down his cheeks.

Seth eyed him in his peripheral vision. Phil had started drinking long before he met Seth at the bar, and if he was anything like Seth, he slept better with another human being breathing next to him.

"Why don't you stay here tonight?"

Another throat clearing. "Sure," Phil said.

Together they transformed the dining area into a single bed. Phil rolled out Seth's surplus sleeping bag. They were both too accustomed to camp life to find the arrangement awkward. Seth stripped to his boxers, brushed his teeth, then lay down on the bed at the back of the space, arranged his pillows behind him, and turned on the TV over the motor home's queen-size bed. He was accustomed to sleeping on a narrow cot, which meant he could use the other side of the bed as a dumping ground for his laptop, cell phone, books, magazines. The drawing supplies he hadn't touched in months, pencils, colored pencils, a barely touched watercolor kit, charcoal and pastels and the bundle of Moleskines from his last tour, were stuffed in the bottom drawer of the bedside table, always at the periphery of his mind. He focused on the TV and let his mind wander through his to-do list. Pick up a few groceries on the way home from work tomorrow; the messenger backpack made transporting a week's worth of groceries easy. Convert the stash of cash in the coffee can into a money order and send it to Brittany. Call his parents, distracted academics caught up in the frenzy of a new school year, and not thinking much beyond the relief that Seth was home in one piece.

His phone vibrated in the pocket of his cargo shorts. When he pulled it out, fading from the notification screen was a text from Micah. Can you sub for René on Sunday?

He had met Micah when he made a delivery to his studio and walked in on the tail end of a life drawing class. He ended up walking out with the model. They struck up a conversation while he was waiting for his next delivery, and it turned out that modeling in the nude actually paid like whoa and goddamn. He turned around and walked right back into the studio, and told Micah that if he ever needed a sub, to keep Seth in mind. He tried not to think about what his fellow Marines would say about his sideline. Taking an art class in order to see naked women would make perfect sense to them, but being the one posing on the pedestal would've made him the butt of jokes, including jokes about butts, for the rest of his life. The money was part of the reason why he was doing it. The other part was that Manny the trickster would've found it hilarious, and a great way to get laid.

That was a bad idea, for two reasons. First, he didn't want to get taken off Micah's roster by causing a shitton of drama that nobody needed. Second, when he modeled for classes at NYU or City College, most of the students felt far too young to him. Everyone involved was above the age of consent, so the difference in age wasn't all that significant, eight to ten years, but the difference in experience was so vast it felt impossible to cross, and ultimately felt like cradle robbing.

Arden's class was different. The interesting thing about the drawing class last Sunday was the sense he got that he was not the most wounded person in the room. By the end of a front-line tour of duty, everyone was wounded in some way, from the sheer stress to death—killing, seeing friends wounded or killed. Arden seemed shell-shocked, dazed, the expression on her face reminiscent of Marines who had a big fucking explosion go off next to them. He remembered what that felt like: the total absence of sound, the flare of light burned into your retinas, the settling dust giving everything a hazy, unreal patina. Arden looked like she'd been through a firefight, no doubt about it, and the lines that remained made her face as interesting as any he'd ever drawn.

He skimmed his thumb over his phone's screen, thinking it through. She was pretty. Really pretty. In the light streaming in through the west-facing windows overlooking Central Park, her hair was a multilayered blond, with strands of gold and silver and wheat hanging tousled around her shoulders. Rich and gleaming and vibrant, all at the same time. It looked like it hadn't been brushed since she got out of bed, which made him think of her in bed. He would've sworn her eyes were brown from the way the light slid through the irises, but when he sat across the table from her during the break, they were clearly Elizabeth Taylor violet. Again, rich and vibrant, surrounded by the pale skin of someone who spent every second indoors, and shadows under her eyes that told him she was getting about as much sleep as he was.

He could hear Manny. *Why you gotta be looking for a project? Millions of single girls in the city happy to welcome a Marine home, and you focus on the one who looks like she dropped her ice-cream cone.*

He wasn't looking for a project, especially not a woman with friends who lived on Fifth Avenue, and wore a ruby ring the size and shape of an oyster shell. He owed too much to people who laid down their lives for his. He wasn't going to waste the time or energy giving something to someone who didn't need him. He'd model for her class, and keep his mind on the people who needed him.

No problem. See you then.

He sent the text to Micah and added the appointment to his calendar. Ignoring the pang of disappointment inside him, he set down his phone and turned onto his side. Phil had started snoring on his cramped bed in the dining area. This was his life now. He was a former Marine with obligations to the dead, working as a bike messenger and an artist's model, and he had no regrets. As much as he wanted her, it wasn't going to happen. The last thing Arden needed was a man like him.

When he woke up the next morning, Phil was gone. Seth pulled on his bike gear and started searching the apps for a Brooklyn-to-Manhattan run.

— THREE —

"Don't say a word unless I give you the okay. Not one word."
Arden stared at her cousin Neil as the elevator doors
slid closed on the crowd in the lobby. That wasn't going to be a
problem. Her stomach had crawled up to the top of her throat and
lodged itself at the back of her mouth around the time Derek
opened the SUV's back door and used his big body to clear a path
through the gauntlet of photographers, reporters, news cameras,
people with their cell phones held up and recording her every
move, and people she assumed were victims of the Ponzi scheme,
based on the way they were screaming obscenities at her. Once
she was inside the Midtown building that was home to Levinsky,
Strewthan, MacCarren, and Martin, the furor died down, but the
aftereffects left Arden with a heart thumping like a twitchy rab-
bit's hind leg and with a very familiar tightness in her chest.

Neil finished thumbing away at his iPhone, then slid it into his
jacket pocket and shifted his briefcase from his left hand to his right.

He reached out and gripped Arden's hand, then gave it a tight squeeze. "How's Aunt Lyd?"

Arden's heart fluttered in her chest like a trapped bird. She'd spent most of the week in East Hampton, holed up in Breakers Point, the house her family had occupied in one form or another for over a century, alternately arguing with and consoling her mother. "Devastated," she said. "One minute she's furious with Dad and vowing never to speak to him again. The next she's chastising me for not calling him since that day. Then she's pleading with me to fly to New Zealand and find Garry, who seems to have disappeared into another dimension."

"You can't go to New Zealand," Neil said. "You're not allowed to leave the country."

"I know, Neil," she said. "But Mom can't seem to remember that. She's been able to fly anywhere in the world she wants to go, on about two hours' notice. The idea that we're not allowed to leave the state, let alone the country, just won't take hold in her mind. Not that she's going anywhere. I talked to her again about leaving Breakers, but she won't do it. I don't think she believes they can evict her, much less that they will."

"I'll talk to her again. Then what?"

"Then she gets furious because the FBI confiscated every electronic device she and Dad owned, and she can't remember her passwords to get into the email account she uses to bid on eBay. Then she needs to take a Valium and lie down."

Neil's gaze was fixed on the numbers flashing on the elevator's LED screen. "Speaking of electronic devices . . . until you're officially cleared, which may be months from now, assume the government thinks you're guilty and could confiscate your phone, tablet, or computer at any point in time. They're going to dig through every piece of electronic communication between you, your father, and your brother going as far back as they can convince the judge to subpoena. Even the slightest hint that you were involved, or even knew that something like this was going on, and they'll indict you so fast it'll make your head spin."

This was the thing she liked about Neil. Of all her family members, he never pulled his punches with her, and never treated her like she was a second-class citizen in a family full of financial superstars.

The elevator dinged, signaling their arrival at the twenty-second floor. "What are you going to do at this meeting?" Neil said.

"Say absolutely nothing unless you tell me to," Arden repeated.

Neil pushed the button that held the doors closed, giving them a few more seconds of privacy. His gaze searched hers. "I know you hate it, Arden. I know you had nothing to do with this, and that you want to go on the offensive to defend your family, but until we have a better idea of their case against you, it's in your best interests to give them nothing at all."

She did hate it. In the past, she would have been relegated to the background, the panic attacks unpredictable and embarrassing enough for people to solicitously ensure she could avoid the press gauntlets and the combative, frankly dangerous meetings with government entities and law enforcement agencies. That was no longer an option. All MacCarren had was her.

"Who's going to be at this meeting?"

"The SEC, FBI, NYPD, the Justice Department, the attorney general for the state of New York, The U.S. Postal Service—"

"The post office?" Arden said, incredulous.

"Mail fraud," Neil said succinctly. "At this point, anyone who can sue or get a court case that looks like a good conviction on their records is going to want a piece of this action. Think of them as sharks in the water—"

"—and we're the chum," Arden finished.

As she walked through the doorway, a wave of energy hit her, not unlike the moment she used to experience when she was a child playing on the beach. Every so often she would have her back turned, and her brothers, thinking this was hilarious, wouldn't warn her when a larger-than-expected wave was approaching. She would be knocked down, then swept out as the wave receded, to surface spitting out saltwater and crying from the burn in her eyes and sinus passages. This was a feeding frenzy, the sharks circling in to rip out chunks of flesh and thrash around in the blood in the water, her family's blood—

"How are you doing?" Neil asked in a low voice as they took their seats.

"Fine," she said. Pretending to search her handbag, she bent her head and closed her eyes, the better to shut out the visual stimuli, and focused on inhaling slowly through her nose to avoid gasping, and exhaling equally slowly through her mouth for a double count. Initially it was inhale for two, exhale for four, but after a couple of breath cycles, she was able to stretch it to three and six, then to four and eight. She could do nothing about the cold sweats that broke out, except hope no one else at the table would notice.

His gaze scanned the table, not her. "You sure?" Neil said quietly.

The situation was ripe for a panic attack of truly spectacular proportions, but she couldn't allow that to happen. Not now, not in front of all these people who would rejoice at watching another MacCarren tumble and fall.

Failure was not an option. "I'm sure."

She lifted her head and looked around the room. Lawyers, lawyers, and more lawyers. The firm who handled the family's business, the firm who handled the foundation's business, the firm who handled their personal business, and of course, the FBI's and the SEC's lawyers, and FBI agents, two of whom she recognized from the raid. The room wasn't really big enough to hold them all, so there was a fair bit of jostling for space at the table, then the seats arrayed along the walls and windows behind the table. For a moment, Arden was reminded of seconds at duels. If someone collapsed, would their second rush forward to take his seat?

Undoubtedly. The only person who didn't want to be at this table was Arden.

"Let's get started." Recording devices were turned on, then the man at the head of the table continued. "Let's do a quick round of introductions for the record."

Everyone around the table stated their name and agency affiliation for the record. The room got very quiet when her turn arose. "Arden Catherine MacCarren," she said clearly. "I'm the chief executive officer of the MacCarren Foundation."

"Ms. MacCarren," Agent Jenkins began, "would you please describe for the record how you were affiliated with MacCarren Investments."

"I have no affiliation with MacCarren Investments," she said, remembering Neil's injunction to answer the question and offer nothing more.

"You've never worked for MacCarren Investments?"

"I worked for the firm briefly after I graduated from business school three years ago," Arden said.

"And that was . . . ?"

Arden gave the dates. They were clear in her head because she'd fought for a job that had been offered without question to Charles and Garry, and won. She began work as every other new associate would, the Monday after Labor Day. The end was equally clear, as it dated to exactly one week after her epic panic attack on the trading floor.

"Why did you leave the investment bank your family had run in one form or another for over a century?"

"It was decided that the family's interests would be better served if I went to work for the foundation."

"And why was that?"

"My father and brother already comprised a significant portion of the leadership team at MacCarren Investments. My brother Garry was not interested in taking a leadership position in any of the family's other interests. My mother was getting older and wanted to step back. It was time for new blood at the foundation," she added hastily, remembering the party line in the press releases.

"And since that time you had no dealings, no discussions, no involvement whatsoever with the day-to-day operation of Mac-Carren Investments?"

"That's correct."

"It's unbelievable," Jenkins said. "You expect me to believe that your family never talked about the investment side of the house over dinner, at meetings, with other members of the family?"

She bristled at his incredulous tone. Under the table, for her eyes only, Neil's hand lifted in a placating gesture. "My mother's rule was that we did not discuss business at family events."

Jenkins's gaze flicked over her suit, the pearls in her ears, the ring on her finger. "What did you discuss?"

She felt her eyebrows lift a little, knew she was straying dangerously close to imperious arrogance. "The same sorts of things that any family would discuss over dinner," she said. "Art, music, concerts, books, newspaper or magazine or blog articles of interest, friends, family, vacations—"

"So anything but business?"

Arden felt her face flush at the agent's disparaging tone of voice. As if he'd just tarred Arden and her mother with the same brush her father and brother always had. Her mother loved conversation about beautiful things, the arts, fashion, decorating, and approached them as seriously as her father approached making money. She didn't feel like explaining golden handcuffs shaped by class and generational expectations, or giving this man any more ammunition. "Yes," she said.

"And will your mother corroborate that?" Jenkins asked.

At that, all the blood drained from Arden's face. Her heart seemed to stop beating for moments, even though years of conversations with doctors told her that was a physical impossibility. But stop it did. In that one smooth sentence, the agent made perfectly clear that whatever privacy and independence Arden had was now gone. This man had the right to demand Arden's presence, her mother's presence, and to drag every single element of her family's personal, professional, and financial lives into the public view.

The possibility terrified her.

Beside her, Neil had done that thing men so frequently seem to be able to do, somehow making himself a little larger, and a little more intimidating, all without moving. "Watch your tone of voice, agent," he began.

It was Arden's turn to put her hand on Neil's arm. "Agent Jenkins," she said, quietly, because she'd learned that was the best way to keep her voice steady, "if you've done even a cursory examination of my family and our business, you know my mother never worked a day in her life, much less at MacCarren. She raised three children, and nearly half a billion dollars for various charitable organizations in New York and around the country. Confine your questions to the investment banking side of the house and leave my mother out of it."

There was a moment of silence while everyone in the room digested her statement. Then Agent Jenkins smiled gently, as if he were allowing an obstinate child to think she was getting her own way. "Of course, Ms. MacCarren," he said. "When do you expect your brother back in town?"

It was a calculated slap. Garry, older than her by nearly five years, had turned his back on the family business shortly after entering MacCarren Investments. He first moved to Colorado to work as a ski instructor, spending his summers on various dude ranches, moving cattle from one pasture to the other. Over time he worked in Canada and then made his way to New Zealand, where he was currently raising sheep. What would have stood out in an examination of phone records for her father and brother is that neither of them had talked to Garry since he left six years earlier. Maybe they thought Charles or her father fed her scheme details and she passed them on to Garry, who did what with them?

All the family's chickens were coming home to roost, in a very public way.

Remembering Neil's injunction, she merely said, "He's out of cell phone range in New Zealand. As I'm sure you know. He's had no contact with Dad or Charles since he quit MacCarren. As I'm sure you know. I'm doing my best to get in touch with him. As soon as I do, I'll let you know."

Jenkins smiled genially. "We have some questions about your family's financial records," he said.

The next few hours detailed exactly how the Ponzi scheme worked, every horrible detail of money coming in, then being spent on some expensive new toy or trip or home or piece of art for Charles or her father, and were the longest, most painful of Arden's life. That included the night Nick sat down and told her he was in love with her best friend, and he had to call off their engagement. It also included Nick and Betsy's wedding day, and funerals for three of her grandparents, a beloved aunt, and two friends who had died of overdoses. But sitting at that oval table in the conference room while lawyers and accountants from the SEC and the FBI crawled through every financial record ever generated by the Mac-Carrens was almost as humiliating and painful as the day she had a panic attack on MacCarren's trading floor.

Neil guided her out of the conference room and down the hall to his corner office, where he closed the door behind her. Arden all but folded into the white leather sofa that made up part of the seating area in Neil's large office.

"You did well," Neil said. He set his laptop on the large credenza aligned on the wall by the door. "Really well."

"How else could I do?" she asked, twisting the ring on her right hand. "There's no one else to do this."

"What the hell is up with Garry?"

"He owns a ranch outside Wellington, and all his manager can tell us is that he's out with the herds. It's like he's gone back in time to the 1860s."

"You don't have to go that far back," Neil said with a smile. "He's basically back in the mid-1980s."

She massaged her scalp with her fingertips, seeking out all the tight muscles behind her ears and at the nape of her neck. "I can hardly remember a time when people weren't instantly reachable 24/7/365."

"Arden, what happened with Garry?"

She thought about her artistic, sensitive, gay-as-the-day-is-long brother, trying as hard as she had to measure up to Charles in their father's eyes. "Dad happened to Garry," she said, knowing Neil would understand the shorthand.

"Is that all?"

She looked at Neil, remembering the fights over the dinner table, the cutting remarks, wondering how he could classify the total dismissal of a human being as *all*, when the other shoe dropped. "You think he left because he figured out what they were doing?"

"I'm asking if it's possible."

The fist tightened in her chest at the implication. Had her brother known about a long-running scam to defraud investors of tens of millions of dollars, and done nothing about it? "Oh, God," she said faintly. "The timing is right."

"The timing is your problem, too," Neil said. "You both quit right after starting at MacCarren. It looks suspicious as hell—like you knew, but didn't tell."

"I didn't know," she said. "Dad and Charles kept us at a football field's length. Garry didn't know. He would have said something. I would have said something! What is the point of playing the game if you cheat? Everyone finds loopholes in regulations and exploits them, but stealing from investors? It's all meaningless! How could they not understand that?"

"Let's hope that's the case," Neil said. "From now on, you have to treat your cell phone, laptop, your work computer, as if they can be seized and searched by any law enforcement agency at any point in time. Do not, under any circumstances, put anything in writing that you would not want repeated in court. Don't comment on the case to anyone, not even in circumstances you would normally consider to be trustworthy." He pulled a cell phone out of his jacket pocket and held it up and demonstrated. "Remember Mitt Romney and a video that was made by a waiter at what was considered to be a private, supportive event. Everything you say and do in public from here on out will be considered not just tabloid fodder but media fodder, and relevant to the case. We cleaned out your cloud account. I suggest for the time being you stop saving things there, and change your passwords. And try not . . ."

"Try not to what?" she said.

"I mean." He stopped, obviously considering how to phrase what he needed to say. Arden took pity on him.

"You mean, if I can help it at all, don't have an epic, flailing panic attack in some public place where people will see it."

"That's not what I meant."

"Yes, it is." She stood up and straightened the jacket of her tailored black pantsuit. "I'm the face of MacCarren. I know that as well as you do. I'm the last person in the family anyone would choose to be the one who holds us together through a crisis. I know that, too. But I'm the person we've got right now."

"You'll be fine," Neil said.

She wasn't sure who he was trying to convince—himself or her—but either way the statements were not reassuring. Simply repeating something over and over again like an incantation did not make it true. "Anything else?"

Neil nodded, then gave her a wry grin. "This isn't the end of this. Don't go anywhere without letting me know, not even to the Hamptons. I'll call your car for you and have your driver meet you in the parking garage underground."

Two weeks ago she could walk out the front door of the building without being photographed. "I appreciate it," she said, and let herself out of his office.

Derek was waiting for her in the secured-access parking garage underground. He opened the door to the SUV and held her back as she got into the backseat. "Where to?" he asked when he buckled himself then.

"Home," she said. "Thank you."

Only a few photographers had staked out the exit from the parking garage. Through the tinted window glass she could see the flashbulbs going off, and hear the clamor of people shouting questions and insults at the window before Derek pulled out into traffic and headed uptown. The street outside her Ninety-second Street town house was clear; with cops routinely on duty outside the Jewish Museum, it was easy enough for her neighbors to complain to the police to run off the press. Derek pulled up outside. Arden opened the low black wrought-iron gate at the sidewalk level, then hurried up the offset flight of stairs to the front door, half a story up from the sidewalk. Derek waited, passenger window open, while she jammed her key into the front door and disabled the security system, then he drove away, headed for the garage in East Harlem where she paid to park the car.

When the door opened, she felt a sense of relief so profound it nearly made her weep. Mail was scattered on the doormat at her feet, so she picked it up, carried it up the stairs to her home office on the same floor as the small kitchen and dining room. The dining room overlooked the back garden while the office faced the street. Up another flight was the main living room and her bedroom, where she stripped out of the suit and the silk tank top she'd worn underneath it, and changed into jeans and a tailored button-down shirt.

After that first panic attack, she had developed a number of different tactics for dealing with stress, but tonight nothing appealed to her. Having converted one of the unused bedrooms into an exercise room, she had installed an elliptical machine, a rowing machine, and a treadmill, as well as a full complement of weights. She had an enormous bathtub with massaging jets she could soak in. She had cable, streaming video, seasons of television shows she hadn't seen, books available on her e-reader. If there was any time in American history to suffer from a self-enforced house arrest, this was it.

Except, she wanted to do none of those things.

What she wanted to do was draw. Specifically, she wanted to

draw Seth. Right now she wasn't questioning impulses, desires, needs. She had to do something to stave off the panic attacks.

She texted Betsy and asked for the instructor's phone number. Betsy sent it to her thirty seconds later, no questions asked. Still moving on autopilot as she paced the apartment, she texted Micah, and asked if he thought Seth would be willing to model for a private session. Micah's response came equally quickly; I don't know, ask him, followed by a phone number.

She then texted Seth. Hi, Seth. It's Arden from the drawing class. Would you be interested in modeling for me?

She reread the text. She purposely did not include her last name; she hadn't used it at their first class and there was no point in asking for trouble. Her brain raced ahead, composing explanations or justifications for why she was asking him, but in the end she decided not to include any. It was a simple question, easily answered with a yes or no, and she didn't need to explain herself.

She tapped send, then set her phone down and went to the kitchen to make herself something to eat. She wasn't hungry, hadn't felt hungry since the FBI showed up at Breakers Point a lifetime ago, but she knew she had to eat. Already her clothes were loose enough to tell her that the five pounds she always wanted to lose were long gone. She made herself a spinach salad with a piece of broiled salmon on top, and only after she finished it did she let herself look at her phone again.

Sure. When?

Alrighty then. Tonight?

She sent the text, and as she watched, the dots appeared on the screen indicating that he was composing a reply.

Address?

She texted him her address then added Just off Fifth.

Give me 30 minutes.

She added his name to her contacts, then looked around her

living room. Betsy had gone to the efforts of setting up what felt like an art class, but Arden settled for sliding the rug in the center of her living space off to the side, taking the glass-topped coffee table with it, and moving one of her dining room chairs into the cleared space. She found her easel in a top-floor bedroom closet and carried it down to the living room to set it up off to one side from the chair so the light from the setting sun would fall on Seth. She arranged her sketchpad and her pencils on the easel, then quickly tidied up the kitchen.

Her heart was racing, and not in a good way. It fluttered like a trapped bird, with the occasional bumps as the bird knocked itself against walls and ceilings in an effort to get free. Her mind began to spiral *What if drawing didn't work nothing else had worked not cognitive behavioral therapy not biofeedback not talk therapy not exercise or diet nothing worked she had no control over this if drawing didn't work either she had no idea what she would do*

The buzzer rang, startling her nearly out of her skin. Her heart gave one last gigantic *whump*, forcing the sweat from her skin, then did something very odd. It settled into a regular rhythm, fast, but one where she could count the beats. She took a deep breath, then walked forward to open the door.

He stood between the potted miniature evergreens, and the sheer, visceral presence of him was like tripping and stumbling into a wall. Before, she had been overwhelmed by his energy, the way he moved as he walked into the room and took off his clothes, but now she could pay attention to the details. His hair was dark brown and showed the indentations of the bike helmet. She'd retained an impression of caramel; on closer inspection, his eyes were an odd, unique shade of light brown and fringed with dark thick lashes. He had a strong nose with a couple of bumps in the bridge that came from breaks. She knew this because both her brothers had had their noses broken—Garry's in lacrosse, and Charles's in baseball. And her mother despaired of the unsightly bumps that came as the broken bone and cartilage healed. Charles eventually had plastic surgery to repair the damage, but Garry flatly refused.

It looked like Seth had also refused, or perhaps that simply wasn't an option.

"Hi," he said. His eyebrows lifted as the end of the word did, and she came back into herself with a start.

"Hi! Hi," she said in a more normal tone of voice.

"Where should I leave my bike?"

"In here," she said, and stepped back to let him wheel it into the foyer.

He did, lifting the single strap of the bike messenger bag over his head and setting it down on the floor by the door as he looked around.

"Nice place," he said.

"Thank you," she said. "It's very quiet." The town house was still in her grandfather's trust's name, along with the farm in upstate New York, and had been renovated a few years earlier. Despite leading to the Reservoir, the street was infrequently traveled, and had lots of private town houses that had been in families for generations. Charles and Serena thought it was too small for their brood, which included a nanny, a housekeeper, and Serena's personal assistant, who accompanied her everywhere; they had opted for a larger space on Park Avenue. Arden loved the location, just down the block from Sarabeth's and around the corner from The Corner Bookstore, and had happily moved in.

She led him to her main living space, a front room furnished with cozy castoffs from their property upstate, Hollow Hill Farm, and Breakers Point. Her bedroom, on the same floor, overlooked the town house's garden and had an en suite bathroom. She turned on the floor lamps, casting pools of light over the ottoman that held her laptop and tablet, and a couple of coffee-table books. "Did you have any trouble finding me?" she asked over her shoulder.

"None," he said. Something in his wary expression eased when he saw the living room furniture and the easel, a single straight-backed chair between them.

Best to get the financials out of the way first. "How much do you charge?"

He shoved his hands in his cargo pants pockets and looked at her. "Micah pays me seventy-five for classes and a hundred even for the session at your friend's apartment."

She did the mental math, and factored in how stressful the next few months were likely to be. "I'll pay you two hundred per session. It will run just like any other class, warm-up exercises, a ten-minute sit, two forty-minute sits, with breaks in between. Plus, of course, your travel time. Does that seem fair?"

He was shaking his head before she finished. "It's too much. It's no big deal for me to bike from Brooklyn to Manhattan."

"When I'm learning a new skill, I can be rather tenacious about it, and I'm at loose ends at the moment. I want to make this worth your while."

"You want to make it worth my while," he repeated. His eyes were amused, and one corner of his mouth lifted. "In Manhattan, models are a dime a dozen. I've been doing this for a couple of months and nobody else has asked for private sessions."

There was something dark and delicious about negotiating for his time like this, especially because he seemed to take it all in stride. "Going once," she said lightly.

"It's your money," he said, the shrug both verbal and physical. He reached back and pulled his T-shirt over his head.

Flustered, she made her way along the wall of windows, lowering the white silk blinds but angling them to filter the sunlight rather than block it entirely. The effect muted the light, and for moments, the dust, raised by the movements of lowering the blinds, hung suspended in the warm, pearly air.

When she turned back to face him, he was naked.

She could no sooner stop herself from looking at him than she could stop herself from breathing, her eyes flickering from jaw to throat to the sword arrowing down his left side, the ridges of his abdominal muscles, the line of dark hair beginning below his navel and narrowing over his groin. From this distance, the scar tissue nestled in the hair on his legs was invisible other than small spots where the hair thinned. The light did nothing to soften the hard muscles and planes of his body but managed to heighten the colors in the tattoos adorning his forearms, biceps, and chest.

"You ready?"

"Yes," she said.

She skirted the open area, and therefore him, and took up her position at her easel. When she nodded at him, Seth pushed a button on the watch he wore. It beeped and he took a position, standing with his feet together, his arms outstretched, and his head tilted back. It was an excellent starting pose, and Arden raced to draw a quick line at the center of her paper trying to capture the indentation of his narrow waist, the swell of his chest, and the curve of his throat. The watch beeped, and Seth folded his hands under his chin, and crouched down. This time the line was about the curve of his spine nestled in the deeply muscled valley running down his back. Another beep, another shift in pose, this time down into a runner stretch. She flipped the page and drew a single line from the top of his head around his cranium down his nape to his spine, caching the swell of buttock, thigh, calf. One line. One single line. For the ten seconds of the pose, it was the only thing on her mind.

"That's ten," he said, resetting his watch.

"Do you want something to drink before we continue? I have water, wine, sparkling water, cranberry juice . . ."

"Water would be great, thanks. Staying hydrated in these temperatures is hard to do."

She trotted down the stairs into the kitchen and poured him a glass of water, and brought it back up the stairs. He drank most of it, completely unself-conscious about his nudity or the fact that she was dressed. She couldn't remember another time when nudity wasn't something embarrassing or mysterious, something to be revealed slowly, then hidden again. Seth was an open book.

When he finished he set the glass down on the floor by the chair. "Do you have a pose in mind?"

She turned the chair so that it was facing the windows. "How about if you sit down," she demonstrated, slouching down so that her bottom was on the edge of the seat, her legs extended in front of her, and crossed at the ankles.

She got up. He sat down and mirrored her pose, working his shoulders against the back of the chair until he was comfortable. "That's fine. Where do you want my arms?"

Back behind the easel, she perched on the barstool she'd snagged from under the breakfast counter, considered the pose, and then said, "Can you put one hand on your belly and let the other hang?"

He tried it, resting first his right hand and then his left on his abdomen.

"Good. Thank you."

He set his watch, settled into the pose. For a long minute she watched him breathe. The inhales and exhales animated his torso, lifting his shoulders, the sword moving like a held blade, threatening and protective all at once. She sketched in the big blocks of torso, head, thigh, calf, foot, the chair underneath him, then went to work at his shoulder. The line was wrong, too flat, lifeless, muddy. Frustrated, she set the pencil down and erased, then started over.

"Do you mind talking?" she said.

"Not if you don't."

"How can you sit still for so long?" The question formed in her mouth before her brain knew it was coming. She was restless, her brain jumpy and anxious, constantly analyzing her internal state, always on the lookout for a threat or a way to defuse the threat of a panic attack. He seemed the opposite, resting in suspended animation until he brought his body to bear on the situation.

A smile bloomed in his eyes without moving his mouth. "I learned when I was a kid, hunting with my friend's dad. He threatened to leave us at home if we spooked the deer. I wanted to go hunting with them more than I wanted to move. When I was in the Corps, moving meant drawing attention to our position and possibly getting Marines killed."

"Oh."

Frowning, she sketched his arm, curved ridges of muscles and veins running under his skin, erased, tried again, added the general shape of his hand, then retraced her path back up the inside of his forearm, marking the faint tan lines.

"Explain the different tan lines," she said, distantly noting that her hand was moving of its own accord now. *Shut up, left brain.*

"The one at my elbow is from rolled sleeves on my cammies, my uniform blouse. The one at my biceps is from the bike jersey. The one at my shoulder is from the shirt with the cut-out sleeves I wear when I'm running."

"Uniform blouse?"

"It's the Marine Corps. We have different terms for everything. A man's shirt is a blouse."

"Um, why?"

"Doesn't matter," he said, his voice slow and amused before he answered the question anyway. "Tradition. History. It just is."

"I didn't know that," she said. This was working, as if one thing wasn't enough to shut down the racing, chattering part of her brain. Two things, however—idle conversation and a tight focus on the shape of his chest, the way his ribs curved up to his sternum—and her frantic brain spun down. The tattoos were too much to replicate, so she focused on his body, making her way up to the notches of his collarbone, the hollow in between. Here the edges were smoother, more rounded, general. Shoulder. Chest. Until she really saw them, the way the collarbone emerged from the shoulder joint to sit atop the pectoral, lifting the skin at the base of his throat before disappearing into the strong line.

Somehow the component pieces of him fit together, the line of his jaw, his full mouth, the twice-broken nose. Distantly noticing a confidence in her hand, she followed the shape of his skull, the way the muscles in his neck held his head up, then sweeping down to his abdomen.

"Is that scar tissue?"

"Yes."

"How did it happen?" she heard herself ask, adding shading to the hollow of his throat.

"IED," he said.

Funny how that came out so easily. An explosion, then, ripping through . . . what? A vehicle? It must have hurt, searing into his skin as it had. She'd lost the line, was back in her head, so the persistent electronic beep coming from his watch was actually a relief. "Okay if I move?"

"Yes, thank you," she said, and risked a glance at the page. The sketch was absurd, like something drawn by someone high on pot and red wine. It was going to take some time to regain her hand skills.

"More water? Something stronger?"

His whiskey eyes were smiling at her. She forced herself to stop fluttering and hovering, and met his gaze. "I'm fine. I don't need a twenty-minute break," he said. "Can I offer some constructive criticism?"

Arden considered herself reasonably sophisticated, but never before had she been offered constructive criticism by a man standing naked in her music room. "Sure," she said, not sure what he meant.

"You're working too hard at it," he said.

And there was another first. She'd never been told she was working too hard at something. The bar was always out there, always just beyond her reach. "I beg your pardon?"

"You're attacking drawing like it's an obstacle course. You're not getting graded at the end of the semester."

"If I put anything in the show at the end of the class, it's worse than getting graded. At least grades are private."

He gave her an utterly disarming little smile that was mostly about the corners of his mouth. "I bet you got really good grades, and I bet you never bragged about them."

She bit her lower lip because he was right, on both counts.

"Do you know what a blind contour drawing is?"

"Yes," she said, her brain scrolling up an exercise she'd learned a long time ago, drawing with her pencil poked through a sheet of stiff cardboard so she couldn't look at the picture and judge it. "You draw without looking at the page, following the edge with your eyes, slowly, attentively. It's an exercise in seeing, in being in the moment, not accurately rendering the subject material."

Again with the smile at her automatic recital. "Next time try that."

It felt like admitting defeat, to attempt anything less than a perfect drawing each and every time. But while she tried to come up with a polite way to decline, he gave her that half grin again, then settled himself on the chair, elbows braced on knees, fingers woven together. "Grab a chair and come out from behind the easel," he said as he set his watch. "Twenty-five minutes. Go."

Fine. Fine. It was one session. She pulled the sketchpad from the easel and spun a wingback chair to face him, braced the pad on her lap, and looked at him.

Dear God. He couldn't possibly be real.

Edges. Start with the edges.

She chose one at random, the point of contact between the sole of his foot and the wide-plank floor, then followed the curve of his heel to his calf and up, not looking at the page, moving her pencil very slowly, seeing each dip, hollow, and swell. She tried not to look at the page, but her gaze kept flickering back and forth, checking in, judging.

"You're looking. Don't look."

He was so close. She could smell his skin, almost taste it. Exasperated with herself, she started again, this time with his ear. In her peripheral vision, she could see his eyes, fixed on her face, his mouth solemn, easy to hold.

"Don't look," he said, a split second before her eyes flicked down.

"Dammit." She lifted her chin, and this time looked straight into his eyes. The connection was visceral, immediate, and as her hand moved, she really saw his face. Dark stubble emerged on his jaw, highlighting his full lips, the sensual curve of the lower lip, the bracket of the upper lip, the twin ridges leading to his nostrils, and from there to his left eye.

He really had gorgeous eyes, the striations and variation in color ranging from dark brown at the edges to a fawn color near the center. His eyelashes were thick, short, almost spiky straight, and very dense along both lids. The creases at the outer edge were easier to see up close, a dense web of lines that came from squinting into the sun. His blade shades had left a distinct tan line along his temple and across the bridge of his nose.

Her heart rate shifted as she drew, blood heating her face, then fading as the connection between them tightened like a knot in silk. She startled when his watch beeped again, and quickly set her pencil down. The finished product reminded her of a tangle of thread found in her grandmother's embroidery basket.

"Don't often do this with people looking at my face," he said, and stepped into his shorts.

She chuckled. Naked tattooed man with the sculpted body of an athlete, and she drew his face. "Your face is very interesting. Lots of contours."

She felt better, though, her muscles loosened, her mind ever so slightly calmer, less like a hamster on crack and more aware of little details around her. The rough brick of the fireplace, the pale yellow paint on the walls. Seth's body, and the promise it held.

No. The last thing she needed was a man.

Her purse lay on her bed, through the landing and bathroom in the master suite. Arden brought it back into the living room and opened it, and riffled through her cash. Her hands engaged, her mind sent up another memory from a long-ago art class, the instructor giving them all lemons to handle, explaining the connection between touching an object and drawing it. They were, he said, to draw like they were touching what they saw. It all sounded vaguely ridiculous to Arden then.

Right now it made all kinds of sense.

Seth thrust his arms into the sleeves of his T-shirt, the fabric stretching over his elbows and partially obscuring his tattoos. "Wait," she said.

He paused, looking at her expectantly.

"May I touch you?" she asked, peering at him.

– FOUR –

Her hair slid free from behind her ear and slid to her cheek-bone, obstructing her view but not enough to miss the fact that he stopped breathing. She hastened to add, "I remembered something from the contour drawing lesson. Supposedly there's a connection between touch and drawing."

It sounded really awkward when she explained the request. He hesitated, probably searching for a polite way to tell her no, that she remembered wrong. "Sure."

She walked back to stand in front of him. For the first time she felt the difference in their heights in a way that made her heart skip and her stomach flutter. He stood right in front of her, back-lit by the soft light from the floor lamps. His head was bent, look-ing down at her, his soft exhales warming the hair at her temple, an intimate touch she registered deep in her belly. He didn't discard his shirt, but left it where it was, his arms thrust into the sleeves to the elbow, the fabric drawn taut, like a shield.

She secured her hair behind her ear and hesitated for a moment then reached out tentatively to place the tips of her first two fingers on the sword's hilt. Despite nearly two hours of constant exposure, his skin was warm to the touch. He'd resumed breathing shallowly, but once again stopped entirely when her skin made contact with his. She glanced up, and saw that his eyes were closed, his lips parted ever so slightly. His shoulders were rigid, steeled against an assault, she realized.

"Are you sure this is all right?"

"It's fine." Brusque, but deeper. Resonant with something she didn't quite recognize.

Permission given not once, but twice, she continued her exploration, following the line of the sword to the dense muscle of his shoulder, then back again to his collarbone, startlingly vulnerable under his skin. The bare patch under the hilt drew her eye, incongruous next to the sword and the elaborate dragon that coiled over his right shoulder, ready to launch itself from his skin. He was literally skin and bone and muscle, his abdominals visible in a way she knew came not just from being physically fit but carrying no body fat. She wanted to follow the sword blade down his side to his hip, where his cargo shorts rested, but that felt too much like an invitation.

"May I see your back?" she asked softly.

He turned, allowing her to explore the sword, a different set of runes running down the blade that disappeared into his waistband. Touching him did help, she realized. She had a better sense of the density of his body, the thinness of the skin over muscle that was, even at rest, a threat and a promise all rolled into one. Heat seemed to pulse from his body through her fingertips and into her veins, where each feed of her heart carried it to the edges of her skin. Her lips. Her nipples. Her sex.

"Thank you," she said, and heard something else entirely in her voice.

He turned again, full circle, and faced her. He made no move to pull the T-shirt over his head, but rather, looked at her with an expression that was part challenge, part invitation. "Get what you needed?" he asked, low and steady.

"No," she said.

She wondered if she should say something else, something more flirtatious like *I didn't get what I needed* or *I could use a little more of you*. But she wasn't wired that way, and not even the total collapse of her family's business and reputation could change that. So she left it at *no*, hooked her fingers in the hem of his T-shirt, snagged between his elbows, and went on tiptoe to kiss him. His mouth was firm, soft, and resilient under hers, and the heat of his mouth, the promise of his tongue sent sensation flickering along her nerves. The rough scratch of a couple days of stubble around his mouth sent another wave of input surging into her nerve endings.

He let his hands drop a little, giving some slack to the fabric. Arden pulled it free from his hands and wrists and dropped it on the floor beside her. Then she curled her fingers in the waistband of his tough cargo pants, and pulled him to her. This time there was nothing tentative about the kiss, just pure need driving her to tilt her head and slide her mouth across his. He took advantage of her open lips and touched his tongue to hers. Then exactly what she'd been hoping and praying for the past horrible days happened. Desire flooded her brain, and she stopped thinking, worrying, processing, and shut down, simply recording sensation, movement.

Her body took over, but with none of the breathless terror that came with a panic attack. Instead her dominant rational mind disappeared, leaving her a purely physical creature. Her finger tightened around his waistband, and his abdomen jumped, flexing against the backs of her fingers. One of his hands slid through her hair to cup the back of her head; the other flattened at the base of her spine, sealing them together from thighs to chests. The kiss deepened, his tongue dancing against hers, then withdrawing.

"Oh," she said indistinctly, and took advantage, sliding her tongue into his mouth to glide along the edges of his teeth, then touch, tip to tip, then retreat ever so slightly.

He groaned, and his grip tightened as the sound rumbled from his throat into her mouth. She stroked at his throat, intrigued by the noises he made, wondering whether the texture was as rough as the sound. They would shape the way she drew him, she thought. The heel of her palm rested against silky skin, while the tips of her fingers rasped against bristly stubble under his jaw.

A second groan worked its way up from his chest, rough and desperate under her hand. He tugged his hand free from her hair, taking a few strands with him. The pain, stinging sweet, made her shift her pelvis against his. Now she could feel his erection against her belly, then brushing the fingers gripping his waistband as he shifted in response, freeing the thick shaft to strain upward. The soft tip left a smear of fluid on her knuckles.

She was distracted from her focus on his cock when he grasped the hand at his throat and dragged it across his jaw to nip at the tips of her fingers, then suck them into his mouth. The combination of heat and slick pressure was so viscerally shocking she gasped at the intimacy, but before she could pull them away, he bit down with just enough strength to hold her fingertips while he licked them. Still holding her wrist, he released her fingers, then, without breaking eye contact, drew her hand down his chest to his nipple.

She circled the hard nub, watched it stiffen under her fingertips as the cool air washed over the moisture. His cock pulsed against her hand. It was the most honest chain reaction she'd ever experienced. She bent her head and licked his other nipple while pinching the first between her thumb and forefinger, and caught the groan with her mouth.

"Bed," he muttered indistinctly.

"This way," she whispered, tugging him through the bathroom to her bedroom. Once inside the door she set to work at his button fly, ripping it open and shoving his boxers and pants to the floor with hurried moves, then dropped to her knees, desperate to taste and touch at the same time.

"Whoa, whoa, slow down, oh, fuck," he said, the word drawing out on a sound as thick and salty as the fluid on her tongue. But this would do, stroking the ridged muscles in his abdomen with her fingertips while licking the tip of his cock, then taking him deep until her lips met her fingers, wrapped around the base of his shaft.

Yes. It was taste, and the smell of soap and sweat nestled in the crease of his thigh, and the hair on his leg rough under her palm, punctuated by the raised, smooth shrapnel scars. She smoothed her hand back up his thigh until she could brush his balls with her thumb as she slowly took him in, drowning in wave after wave of sensation, the sound of his rough breathing in her ears. She risked a glance up at him. His head lolled on his neck, and his hand hovered near her head, fingers flexing, as if he wanted to grip her head but was holding back.

No holding back. She patted blindly at the air until her hand made contact with his, then drew it down to rest on her hair. His eyes snapped open, peering directly into hers, part rough need, part question. In response she let her lashes drift closed, pulled off so the tip of his cock rested on her tongue, then closed her lips around it and sank down again, saliva slicking her way.

"Oh, fuck, that's good," he said, and slid his fingers into her hair.

More sensation upon more, well past enough and into whiteout overload. His hand tightened in her hair; his hips, quivering with the effort to stay still and not fuck her mouth, gave up the battle.

She left her circling fingers snug against her lips and let him thrust through her grip, into her mouth. A fresh burst of semen flared on her tongue, and she stopped.

This time his groan held a pissed-off edge. Although she hadn't known when she started, that's what she wanted. That was exactly what she wanted, oh, yes, please. She swiped the back of her hand across her mouth, then scrambled backward, off her knees and up over the foot of her bed. Once in the middle, she yanked her top over her head, wriggled out of her bra, and went to work on the zipper of her jeans.

"What the everloving fuck?"

She looked up. He stood at the foot of her bed, gloriously naked, hands on his hips, brows lowered, sweat gleaming on his chest and shoulders, his cock bobbing with his pulse, red and slick with her saliva. Her scars were clearly on display on her left shoulder and knee, some thin, fine white lines, others thick and heavy from becoming keloid scars. His gaze flicked from them to her face.

"Fuck me like that," she said, and shimmied her jeans down her hips. The denim was halfway down her thighs when she remembered protection, and rolled onto her stomach to scrabble in her nightstand. She wouldn't need lubricant. Her sex felt full and heavy, the slickness apparent as she moved.

From this awkward angle, the drawer stuck, so she yanked it open. It dropped to the floor with a clatter, spilling a box of tissues, lotion, two alarm clocks, a timer, and thank you God, condoms on the floor. Still wearing her jeans at half-mast but beyond caring what she looked like, she snagged a strip of condoms and tore one off.

"Like this?" he asked, deceptively calm.

"Yes," she demanded.

"You got it," he said, and dropped on top of her.

He caught some of his weight with his hands beside her

shoulders, and knees to either side of hers, but the shock of his skin against hers sent air rushing from her throat as much as the weight of his torso on her back. His erect cock snugged against her backside. He shifted his hips until it settled between the cleft of her buttocks, then rolled his pelvis into her ass with too much purpose and intent to be anything as playful as suggestive.

It was her turn to moan. The mattress stifled the sound until he rested his weight on one forearm and fisted the other hand in her hair and not-quite-gently turned her face to the side. The rest of the sound vibrated into the twilight settling in her bedroom, and ended on a gasp when he tightened his grip on her hair.

"Okay?" he asked roughly.

He could have been asking about any number of things, permission, affirmation that she liked the direction he was taking things, confirmation that he wasn't hurting her. It didn't matter. Her answer was the same. "Yes," she said.

His mouth landed hot and heavy on her ear, the unpredictable combination of kisses, licks, and nips jolting her from shudder to pliancy and back again. There was no getting lost in what he did, mind wandering to the grocery list, much less spiraling into the barbed wire of anxiety. He commanded her attention as he gathered more of her hair in his hand, baring her nape to his mouth. She braced her arms underneath her and pushed up. He didn't take more of his weight but rather made her bear it, giving her something to writhe against. This was real, physical, definitely not in her head. She tipped her head forward, giving him full access to her neck, and felt the position resonate deep in her back brain. Pinned under a bigger, stronger male, oh *yes*.

He rewarded this surrender by closing his teeth on the sensitive skin and biting down. She cried out again, the sound somewhere between a yelp and a groan. He treated this with all the attention she wanted him to pay it, which was none. Instead he rolled his hips into her buttocks until she could feel his balls rasping against the backs of her thighs and the slick fluid coating her skin, the rhythm elemental and compelling, crushing her between his heavy body and the bed.

She struggled, torn between trying to spread her legs and getting out from underneath him so she could get her jeans off in the first place. Desire trashed her normally analytical brain, made her try to do everything at once, because if she didn't get him inside her and moving with that same weight and power, she might go out of her mind.

"Fuck, that's good," he growled in her ear, bringing her attention to how her struggles must feel to him.

"Let me get my jeans off," she snapped back.

With a chuckle he eased back onto his knees, his hand moving heavily from her hair to her shoulder, gentling over the scars, then down her back to her bottom, cupping and squeezing.

"Get to it," he said, then plucked the condom from her fingers. She rolled on her side enough to get at the bunched denim, working the stubborn fabric over her feet and off. For a split second she watched him smooth the condom over his shaft. He knelt above her, the sword arrowing down his lean body, the dragon perched on his shoulder, fierce and ready to pounce, hands unselfconsciously dealing with the practicalities of safe sex, his muscular body and taut expression as unsafe as anything she'd ever seen.

Then he coaxed her over until she was flat on her stomach again. The bed dipped as he braced himself on his elbow, gripped her hip and lifted her. Her heart rate tripled in a matter of moments. She'd done this before, of course, and there were two ways it could go. His legs outside of hers gave her control. His legs between hers gave him control. For a thrumming moment she wasn't sure which option she wanted.

He spread her legs with his knees, and all thinking shut off again. She wedged her forearms under her shoulders and let her head drop forward. The curtain of her hair shut off her view in the mirrors on her closet doors, forcing her to focus on what she felt, but not before the starkly erotic lines of her spine and spread legs seared into her brain. She tried to ascertain where his cock was, but all she could feel was the rough strength of his thighs against hers, holding her open for the penetration she craved.

It came not hard and fast as she expected, the slamming thrust that would pitch her forward, into the bed, but as a single, teasing nudge that opened her soft folds before withdrawing. The movement triggered a cascade of sensation along her nerves, tightening her muscles and drawing her head back. He did it again, no deeper, and she could hear the slick gliding sound as he dipped into her a third time.

"Not fun, is it?" he asked. He was braced over her, legs and arms confining her but giving her little actual contact with his skin. "Getting all worked up, then changing pace?"

She stared blankly at the headboard, white silk against the pale yellow walls, too focused on the promise of his cock to bother formulating words. His next thrust took him deep enough for the head to glide teasingly over her sweet spot. She gasped, tightened, arched even more.

"Hmm, found that," he said, meditatively, then shifted his weight back to kiss her tailbone. "I like this line, from here," he said, then licked his way up to the sensitive spot between her shoulder blades, "to here. Very provocative."

The soles of her feet and palms of her hands tingled, then ignited into a burn the next time he thrust in, just a bit deeper, just a bit harder, the angle just a bit more precise. "Seth, please, I know you know what you're doing to me," she gasped.

"Sure do," he said, amused.

She tried to push back and finish the process of getting him inside her, but he shifted his hand and prevented her from just getting it over with. As a result, she felt every half inch of his gliding strokes into her, setting off a cacophony of conflicting demands from her body. Her inner walls parted for him in soft, slow stages, but each stroke over her sweet spot curled her fingers and toes. By the time he seated himself fully inside her, she trembled on the verge of an orgasm, past pleading, past words, her entire body tight and shaking.

The first full thrust ended the quivering.

The second flung her into white heat and bright light. He thrust through it, changing nothing about his tempo or depth, but she could hear tight little grunts that made her think of air forced through clenched teeth. Her legs trembled until she relaxed enough to let her weight rest on his thighs. A second wave of pleasure hovered promisingly behind the first, something that had happened before, but never came to much of anything before her partner finished, so she let her head droop to the mattress.

Except, he wasn't rushing to finish. His hand scudded across her sweat-dampened skin to cup her sex. She flinched, anticipating contact on hypersensitive nerves, but he hushed her and curled around her, and did nothing more than press the pads of his fingers to the top of her sex. The pressure against the bundle of nerves added momentum and power to the climax building deep inside her.

"Oh, God," she said indistinctly.

Seth didn't respond, just curled around her, his cheek stubble scratching her erratically through the curtain of her hair. It was in her mouth, and likely in his, and all she could think about was the second wave looming like God's own fist. Someone was making sharp cries, almost in time to the sharp smack of skin against skin, the box spring had developed an audible squeak, and her arms and legs were shaking with the strain, and she was going to come again. Hard. Now.

The pressure of his fingers against her clit and his cock, stretching her each time it buried deep inside her, drowned out everything—sound, sense, sight, everything—for a long moment. She came to when he finally, finally slammed into her, the rhythmic pulses of his release riding the ebbing crest of hers.

"My leg hurts," she said. That knee had never quite been the same after three surgeries.

"Sorry," he mumbled and shifted to one side. She lay down flat on the mattress. At some level she knew she would be sore tomorrow. She knew there were things in her mind that would trap her, but for the moment, she savored the absence of anything threatening, anything at all. Laughter welled up in her chest. That worked. That really, really worked, although in hindsight, she had no idea how touching him would add depth or unity to her drawings. Amazing what the brain could come up with to rationalize desire.

"What's so funny?" he asked.

"I can't believe I told you that would help me learn to draw."

He laughed, a short, rough, satisfied sound that rasped over her nerves like a cat's tongue. "I haven't heard that one before," he said. "Okay if I get dressed now?"

"Of course," she said, answering the smile she heard in his voice with a real one of her own.

He snagged his clothes from the bedroom floor on the way to the bathroom. She pulled on a robe and headed for the hallway, returning to her original goal of paying him. "I'm surprised no one else asked for private sessions," she said, and held out his fee when he approached her and scuffed into his shoes.

He thumbed through the bills. "There's too much—"

His head came up, eyes sharp with something so potent her body recognized anger before her brain did. She felt herself go quite still in response.

"Is that the going rate for a rent boy?"

She blinked, astonished, then it all came together. The text, for private sessions. The simmering charge in the air between them. The conversation about getting aroused while modeling. The request for him to leave his shirt off. Sex. Money exchanged.

"No. No! Oh, God. It's a tip. See?" She took back the money, thumbed the bills into two groups. "Two hundred for the session, plus a twenty percent tip. Forty dollars. I'm not . . . I didn't mean . . . I'm not paying you for sex. I swear. I didn't plan this, or think it would happen. It's just a tip."

He stared at her.

"Oh, God," she repeated, then shoved her hair back from her face. The strands snagged on the ruby ring. "Look, the going rate for a rent boy in Manhattan starts around four hundred dollars an hour and goes into the thousands if you want a good companion. A friend of mine has a standing arrangement with one of the best. If I wanted a rent boy, I would have called her and asked for a referral, not texted you on the vague hope you'd sleep with me."

His lips, still full from kissing, curved ever so slightly.

"I probably seemed desperate," she said. "It's been a while. I swear to you I didn't plan that. I just wanted to draw you."

She'd meant to stop at *draw* because *draw you* sounded so needy. But she'd told him the truth.

"You didn't seem desperate," he said. "You were amazing."

His voice swirled around the words, heating them, making her heart pound. Face flaming, she neatly stacked the bills, aligning the edges lengthwise, then slid both piles onto the table between them. "Whether you take the tip is up to you. I apologize for insulting you."

Without a word he picked up both stacks, combined them, and zipped them into one of the pockets in his messenger bag. As she watched him, so careful with the money, so careful as he checked for wallet, keys, phone, testing all the straps and clips and buckles, a wave of remorse flowed through her. She should have told him beforehand, before he took off his clothes and posed for her, much less let her touch him, even less took him to bed. Wanting him to help her work off some stress was no excuse for using him without his full consent.

She opened her mouth to tell him, but he spoke first. "Why are you taking the drawing class?"

I have panic attacks. I'm trying to find a way to cope with them. She'd admitted this to any number of professional therapists, counselors, advisers, life coaches, but she couldn't bring herself to say the words, to bring them into this. Adding *My family has just been accused of running a Ponzi scheme,* standing under the blinding glare of the klieg lights shining into every nook and cranny of her family and personal life, made it that much harder to admit this long-standing weakness.

"I used to draw. My life is a little complicated right now," she said finally. "I needed something . . . uncomplicated."

She almost winced when she heard the words, implying nothing would come of this. Seth, however, didn't seem to notice, or if he noticed, didn't care. He nodded at the phone. "Uncomplicated works. You know how to find me."

After she let him out, she tossed her sketchpad and pencil box on the sofa, then folded the easel against the wall by the fireplace. Reclaiming the sketchpad, she curled up on the sofa and studied her first sketch, fumbled one of the pencils out of the box, and strengthened the line created where his legs were crossed, retracing the shared edge from his thighs over his knees to his ankles.

It did help, touching what you drew. The tactile experience informed what she saw in a way she hadn't expected. Except touching Seth wasn't like handling a pear, an apple, and an empty wine bottle from a still life. Sharing skin and breath with Seth was more than creating a shared edge.

The inspiration ran out when she tried to clean up the lines of his hand and bent arm, but it was enough, a good stopping point. Maybe Betsy was right. Maybe the drawing class and Seth were exactly what she needed, distraction and stress relief in one hard-muscled package. She set the sketchbook on the large leather ottoman and hefted her laptop instead. With the noise inside silenced, she could deal with her email.

A window popped up from her calendar, reminding her of Melissa Schumann's baby shower over the weekend. Arden checked her email and found one from Mel, staunchly assuring her that of course she was welcome at the shower, that she was one of Arden's oldest friends, and it wouldn't be the same without her.

Another perfect distraction, thinking about new life and soft, pretty things. In all the chaos of the last weeks, she'd forgotten to buy a present for Mel and baby girl Schumann, due just as fall was beginning. Arden knew exactly where to go for the perfect present.

– FIVE –

"Thanks," the lawyer said. "They're about twenty minutes out, so if you could step on it, or pedal fast, or whatever."

"No problem. My pleasure," Seth said. He zipped the ring of keys into the front pocket of his messenger bag, pushed through the door to the law firm's reception area, and hit the button for the ground floor. He didn't ask questions about deliveries, but assumed the lawyer now hurrying back to her office was renting her apartment to out-of-town visitors for the weekend. The guests were on their way in from LaGuardia and would meet Seth farther up in Midtown.

Outside the office building he unlocked his bike, looped the Kryptonite chain around his waist and secured it with the disc lock, then set off uptown. As he rode, his mind wandered to all the different kinds of sex he had had since the IED went off. He'd had what he called "I didn't die in Afghanistan" sex, a frantic encounter with a woman he met at a bar near Lejune hours after he touched down on American soil. He'd been drunk as hell and barely remembered the encounter.

He delivered the keys, then spent the next three runs—a bag of cold medicine from a Duane Reade in Tribeca, lunch from Whole Foods in Union Square to a town house in the West Village, and a dress coming straight from a designer's workshop to someone he assumed was a celebrity, based on the enormous sunglasses and skeletal frame—working his way through the memories of a series of one-night stands interspersed with memories of buying the motor home, his bike, and registering with delivery services. He hung out with Phil, sent money to Brittany and Baby B. He picked up women, had sex, went home alone. For a while now, his life fell into the "I didn't die at all" category.

Until the moment Arden kissed him.

The next customer was waiting outside a gallery in the West Village, arms folded as she watched a mother push an empty stroller while her toddler studiously navigated her doll's stroller along the sidewalk. "Thanks," she said, and took the thick envelope Seth had picked up at a printer's office.

He paused on the corner of Bleecker and Hudson, and swiped the app to refresh available jobs. Nothing below 110th Street at the moment, so he took a break to drink some water and categorize what happened last night. He remembered the look on her face as she drew him the first time, all fierce focus, gripping the pencil so tightly her knuckles were white. He liked that, a woman who squared up for an assault on whatever was in her path, but not for art. Drawing came from a different place, and while she obviously thought the contour drawing suggestion was bullshit, when she settled in and started to draw, it was like she saw every single cell in his body. There was a longing, a want in her eyes, all the more powerful for the fierceness in every line of her body. But the real kicker was the way he responded to it. She wanted like he wanted, from so deep in the body it felt raw and red and hot, like an open wound.

The memory made his cock lift as blood pulsed into it with his heartbeat, something that hadn't happened during the session, thank fuck, but he'd had to purposefully block her out during the first sitting. Physical exhaustion was pretty effective at shutting down his libido during the workweek, but on the weekends, it was like all the stored-up testosterone needed an outlet. So far, the series of no-last-name hookups had somewhat successfully pushed down the questions he didn't want to answer. So far he'd not associated the urge to have sex with a particular woman.

Then Arden's touch, her tousled, witchy hair, the ragged edge of her breathing, hooked on something deep inside him.

He wasn't quite sure what to call what they had done. He had gone to her apartment expecting to model, and left with his worldview completely reordered. Not just because they had sex, either. There had been little, startling jolts the whole way through, the way the lamplight picked out the gold highlights in her hair and her jeans hung from her hipbones. The way she took charge of the sitting, then reluctantly gave it back to him. She was accustomed to being in charge, in some ways held herself like an officer, but there were these flashes of vulnerability. Like the way she asked to touch him, but once he said yes she had gotten really bold, really quickly. The scars on her shoulder and knee, a couple on her chest that were probably from ports and indicated a longer hospital stay. She was a paradox, strong and fragile. Ferocious, fighting something he couldn't see but knew had to be there.

There was something else. Something different. It niggled at the back of his brain, just out of his reach. He tucked his water bottle back into the mesh pocket on his bag, switched to the browser on his phone and typed Arden Upper East Side Manhattan into a search engine. The first couple of hits, the promoted ones, were links to some cosmetics company, but underneath that were hours-old news reports about Arden MacCarren, daughter of Donald MacCarren, sister to Charles, both of whom had been indicted in a massive Ponzi scheme a couple of weeks prior.

"Damn," he said, then let out a long, low whistle as he clicked through to a couple of pictures showing a smiling Arden in posed family portraits, her smile not quite reaching her eyes. MacCarren, an investment bank so powerful it didn't need a description like *Bank* or *Investments* or *Fund* or *Brokerage* behind the name. Simply MacCarren. According to the articles, Arden headed the MacCarren Foundation. He read her bio on the foundation's website, then a couple of lengthy articles detailing the rise and fall of the MacCarrens, Arden's brief tenure with the investment side of the family business. He knew the Ponzi-scheme details, but the newspaper article repeated speculation from various unnamed sources that the reason Arden and her brother Garry had left was because they discovered their father's illegal activities and refused to be a part of it.

Seth shut the browser window. That explained the hunted, haunted look on her face. The fact that she was upright and coherent made him respect her even more.

The delivery app beeped with new jobs added. He closed the browser, scanned the new jobs, and jumped on one that required him to pick up a book at Three Lives and Company and deliver it to an address less than two blocks away. When he'd handed over the book, he locked the bike to a no-parking sign and swung into the post office branch on Hudson. At the counter he bought a money order with Arden's twenties and the tips he'd accumulated over the past few days, then sent it registered mail to Brittany. Back outside, he tucked the confirmation slip in his jersey and called her.

"Hey, Seth," she said when she answered.

She sounded tired. No surprise. "Hey, Britt," he said. Two shops down from the post office was a stationery store that always had really interesting window displays. Today was no exception, a dragon made of sticky notes breathing flame at a brave knight defending a castle below. "How's it going?"

"The usual," she said. "Baby B's teething again, so he's not sleeping well and he's fussy during the day. My mom's coming over to get him before I go to work."

He studied the window display. It was the kind of thing he used to draw, back when he drew. One of the shop's employees, a tall woman with tousled black curls, smiled at him from the other side of the window display, then lifted a leather-bound notebook from the stack comprising the castle's walls.

"That's six teeth?" he asked.

"Yeah," she said. "Two on the top, four on the bottom. I just . . ." Baby B's whimpers cut off, replaced by a satisfied smacking sound. Seth heard Brittany's sharp intake. "The only thing he wants to teethe on is my finger, but those tiny teeth are so sharp," she said.

Her voice trembled, increasing in pitch toward the end of the sentence. "I know," he said, although the only thing he knew about babies and teething he'd learned from Brian—who compulsively read ahead in the baby books—and other Marines with kids.

"I just . . . it's another thing he won't see."

Brian had been home for the birth of his son. Cut the cord. Held him, sung to him, brought back a hastily made photo book of pictures he showed to anyone who would sit still. Seth did a lot of sitting still. He'd seen Britt with her exhausted-new-mother smile often enough to memorize it and draw his own version for Brian. And now he would see Baby B's baby teeth come in, and later fall out, his first steps.

"Tell me about it," he said gently, watching the dragon sway as the stationery shop's door closed. The knight's sword was so small and flimsy against the dragon's fiery paper flames.

"It's just poked through the gum," Britt said. He heard the sound of the fridge opening, then closing. "I freeze damp washcloths for him," she said, her voice going soothing. "There you go. Ouch. I wrapped it around my finger, but it sure does make my finger stiff."

Brittany cut hair at a discount salon and was going to school nights to become an elementary school teacher. "I just sent you something," he said.

"Seth," she said. "I'm going to pay you back. I promise."

"No, you're not," he said. "We take care of our own, Britt. That's all I'm doing."

"You must need the money, too."

"I'm fine," he said. "Did you get the car plated?"

"Yes, a couple of days ago. It's such a relief to have a car I know will start every time I turn the key. I can't thank you enough."

"Not a problem."

"Where did you get that kind of money, anyway?"

"A tip," he said, remembering the moment Ryan Hamilton handed him an envelope with twenty-five thousand dollars in cash inside it. He'd wired it to Britt so she could replace her clunker Escort with a used Nissan Altima still under warranty. "You wouldn't believe New York money," he said, remembering Arden's town house. He'd expected an apartment, not the whole building, fireplaces in every room he saw, original brick and crown molding and hardwood floors, new windows that shut out the city sounds, her own private garden in the back.

"I probably wouldn't," she said. "I have to go. My mom's here."

"Send me a picture of the new tooth," he said. "Be safe."

"You, too, in that crazy Manhattan traffic," she said.

The call disconnected. Without taking his eyes off the fantasy landscape, Seth slid his phone into his pocket. The knight was a woman, like the lionesses he'd served with—female Marines tasked with searching female Iraqis at roadblocks. The shape was subtle, just a hint of curves in the breastplate, blonde paper hair under the helmet obscuring her face. The resolute set of her shoulders and grip on the sword reminded him of Arden.

Upright, coherent, and fighting. He lived and fought with female Marines, had blunt conversations with them about the physiological response to fear and shock, to a massive adrenaline dump, to being in a fight for your life. All that adrenaline had to go somewhere. Being on the receiving end of passion that honest and desperate was the hottest thing to happen to him in years. Even the role reversal, the nuances of power and money in play, sent an electric charge skittering over his nerves.

Then it hit him, the thing that was really different. When he was with her, he heard things. Her breathing. Her heartbeat, the soft, shocked noises she made when he pushed into her, tightened his hand on her hip, lowered his chest to her back. The hours he'd spent with Arden, he heard the world again.

Why not ask her out? You have her number.

He looked over his shoulder at his bike, the only mode of transportation he owned at the moment, then mentally compared his motor home to Arden's apartment. He got points for creative living, a small environmental footprint, but he could probably fit his entire living space—cab, kitchen, dining table, bathroom, bed—into her living room/bathroom/bedroom floor. The motor home wasn't one of the new, six-figure models made by Mercedes, currently in favor with retirees on the move. It was about thirty years old, and if the pumps and hoses didn't blow on the way back to Wyoming, he'd count himself lucky.

He looked past the clutter of apps on his phone to the background, the same favorite picture of the four of them. The four of them, wearing full combat gear, cradling rifles like babies, and deliriously happy in the middle of a war zone. Together. Alive. In their faces he saw Phil, Brittany, Baby B.

That's why he wouldn't call her. He didn't die in Afghanistan, but three other Marines did. Their deaths, his survival, dictated the terms of his life: to serve the people left behind. Taking care of people made him who he was, what made him check in with Ryan Hamilton, but there were limits to how much he could give outside of his family from the Corps. He wasn't going to ask her on a date, because she hadn't even told him who she was. Maybe she assumed he knew and didn't want to talk about it. It wasn't his place to bring it up. She knew what she wanted, and that suited him just fine. If sleeping with him helped her deal, it was just another way to have "get on with life" sex.

He took one last look at the hopeless situation in the stationery shop window, the dragon laying waste to the landscape, the lone knight defending the civilians. Then he got back on the bike and searched the delivery app for another run.

— SIX —

"We're here, Ms. MacCarren."
Arden snapped out of her reverie and looked through the tinted windows at West Village Stationery's eye-catching window display of a single knight bravely holding an enormous paper fire-breathing dragon at bay with a sword while the villagers scrambled for the safety of the castle walls. As accustomed as she was to the creativity normally on display in Manhattan's shop windows, this one caught Arden entirely by surprise.

She knew how that knight felt. Wearing a version of armor, facing insurmountable odds, refusing to back down.

When she didn't move, Derek hitched around in the driver's seat. "West Village Stationery, right?" he said over the sound of the flashing hazard lights. They were double-parked in the right-hand lane, and even on a Saturday morning, someone would honk.

"Right. Thank you, Derek," she said.

In the space of a year, Tilda Davies's shop had gone from yet another stationery shop to an international sensation, helped along by her role as agent for Sheba Clark's latest works. Buying the present here would please Mel, who liked both the traditional elegance of paper and cutting-edge art. Hence the trip downtown for the gift before going back uptown to the shower at an apartment on Central Park West.

Arden settled her sunglasses firmly on her nose, opened the passenger door, and swung her legs out, feeling for the street, then tucked her handbag into the crook of her elbow. Only after she stepped between the cars and onto the sidewalk did she realize she was holding her breath.

Breathing seemed so simple until your body resisted doing it.

She forced herself to exhale, which would automatically generate an inhale, then opened the door and walked into the elegant interior, created with polished maple flooring, white walls and cabinets, and glass cases displaying pens, pencils, leather journals, and address books. The walls held pictures and several Sheba pieces with sold labels discreetly placed over the prices, and the window display of the knight and dragon cast a gorgeous shadow on the maple floor.

If the woman straightening a shelf holding cloth-covered journals recognized Arden, she didn't show it. Her gaze flicked appreciatively over Arden's couture suit, perhaps a bit fancy for a baby shower, but wearing it lifted her spirits. "May I help you?"

"I'm looking for a baby shower gift," Arden said.

"We have several lovely options." She led Arden to a display in the corner by the window. Leather baby books in shades ranging from classic white to baby blue and pink to vibrant shades of red, purple, and green. "It's a husband-and-wife team based in Maine. He tans and dyes the leather and sews it together. She makes the paper and does the calligraphy. Each one is unique," she said, opening two on a table to their right so Arden could see the pages, hand-drawn and lettered like an illuminated Bible, whimsical fairies in one, teddy bears in another, dragons in a third.

The dragons, charming infants emerging from shells, breathing fire with surprised expressions, curled up to nap by a mama dragon's side, reminded her of Seth. "They're exquisite," Arden said, setting aside the dragons in their butter-soft green leather cover to pick up one in midnight blue. Constellations decorated the pages inside.

"They make a limited number. We don't expect another shipment until the first of the year," the shop assistant said.

"Choosing one will be the difficult part," Arden said. Melissa was having a girl, but had also gone through a rather enthusiastic comic book–cosplay phase in college. She might appreciate the superheroine book with the dark violet cover. "This one," Arden said, then wandered over to the shelf of journals. One caught her eye, red leather with a snap closure and slots so the blank pages could be removed and new folios inserted. It appealed to her, for drawing and journaling. "And this, please."

"May I wrap these for you?"

"Just the baby book. I'll take the journal," she said, and tucked the red leather book in her bag. "I'd also like to get something for the mother-to-be. Do you have any of Sheba Clark's pieces left?"

"Only small ones, in the display case," the assistant said regretfully.

Arden followed her to the counter in the center of the store. While the assistant wrapped the book, she chose a Central Park West scene in which the seasons overlaid each other, winter blending to spring, then summer into fall. It was almost the exact view from Melissa's apartment. "Wrap this as well, please," she said.

She handed over her credit card and was texting Derek when a door opened in the back wall. Tilda Davies, tall and slender with riotous black curls, walked out of the space, followed by a whipcord-lean blond man. Their eyes met. Arden's heart kicked hard against her breastbone before rabbiting off into the red zone, her gut lurched, and a cold sweat broke out at her temples before her brain made sense of what she was seeing.

Special Agent Daniel Logan. His name was unforgettable. He'd handed her a search warrant while the FBI streamed through the front doors at Breakers Point. Of course Arden knew of Tilda, had even met her once or twice. But how was Tilda connected to Daniel Logan, one of the agents working on the MacCarren case? Was it a setup of some kind? Had she been lured out of her apartment into a trap to arrest her in some horrible, public way?

The thought spun wildly in her brain, drilling deep into her fight-or-flight response. Her heart rate soared and her breathing halted, leaving her light-headed and dry-mouthed, until the sunlight streaming through the windows glinted off gold, and sanity returned.

Agent Logan was holding Tilda Davies's hand. Arden looked at Tilda's left hand, then Agent Logan's. Gold ring. A slender platinum band on Tilda's fingers, and no other jewelry but a Cartier Love bracelet on her left wrist. The casual intimacy and the age-old symbols clicked. Married. They were married. Tilda Davies was *married* to the FBI agent instrumental in bringing down MacCarren.

For a moment, no one spoke, then Agent Logan murmured something into Tilda's ear. She nodded, turned her head for a quick kiss, and let him go.

"Ma'am," he said quietly. There was something of the courtier's bow in the way he inclined his head as he passed her.

Tilda stepped behind the counter, and the assistant, bless her hardworking little heart, said, "She's taking a Fiorentina journal, one of the Kinney baby books, and a Sheba for the mom-to-be."

"Those baby books are truly one of a kind, and so beautifully done. She'll love it," Tilda said.

"Yes," Arden said, latching onto the normal, if superficial, conversation. "I'm sure she will."

The assistant handed over the bag and went back to the shelf of journals. Arden and Tilda stared at each other, and for a moment, Arden was wildly jealous of the woman's composure.

"I didn't know you were married."

"We eloped last December. It was all very whirlwind, never formally announced, and I kept my maiden name," Tilda said in an exceedingly British way that somehow made the uncomfortable situation entirely her fault, not Arden's. "I'm very sorry for your trouble."

What had Agent Logan told his wife over dinner? The story was all over the news media, and Arden's skin crawled at this immediate, potent reminder of exactly how public her life was at the moment. But Tilda's eyes were kind, sincere. Like she knew trouble all too well.

"Thank you," Arden said.

Her phone buzzed. Derek was outside in the SUV, blocking traffic. "Excuse me," she said, and took the bag and hurried out the shop's door. Derek met her at the back passenger door, opened it, handed her in. Arden fumbled with her seat belt as Derek climbed in and merged into traffic.

So much for normal.

Her hands trembled as she reached into her handbag and found the leather book she'd just purchased, and the pencil case she'd bought when she picked up her drawing supplies for the class. Pencils splayed over the backseat before she got one tucked between her index and middle finger. She remembered Seth's words. *Don't look. Just draw.*

Something simple. A contour drawing of the bag. A rectangle, sitting on the smooth leather seat, the arcs of the handles. No fussy tissue emerging from the top of the bag, which was a relief. Clean lines. Find the line and follow it in the light filtered by the tinted windows. Don't look at the page. In this moment, all you have to do is see the thing in front of you, its emptiness, straight lines, its clarity.

Her heart rate declined in hitches and starts as the SUV crawled uptown. Resolute, she blocked out everything except the feel of the pencil between her fingers, the page under her hand, the gray bag with its discreet West Village Stationery logo in a dark gray the color of Tilda's eyes. Something in her brain disconnected, and when Derek said, "We're here," she came back to reality with a start.

She'd added a dragon to the bag. A poorly drawn dragon with one weirdly bulging eye and a snout that looked more like a horse's head than a fierce, predatory beast, but it was clawing its way out of the bag with as much determination as Seth's prowled down his chest.

She looked out the window. They should have come uptown on Eighth Avenue and pulled to the side by Central Park, but instead they faced downtown again. Derek had made the block to ensure she could exit the car right under the awning. Until recently he'd done this so she didn't have to cross a street. Now, she realized, he did it so she could hurry into the building.

"Thank you, Derek," she said.

"My pleasure, miss," he replied.

"I'll be a couple of hours," she said. "Park somewhere and take a walk. It's too nice a day to be inside."

The doorman opened her door. She stuffed the new journal back in her bag, grabbed both the handbag and the gift bag, and hurried across the wide sidewalk to the door, held open by another doorman.

"Arden MacCarren to see Melissa Schumann," she said.

The doorman buzzed the apartment and repeated her name. His face changed ever so slightly at the response. "Ms. Schumann says she'll be down in a moment."

Arden froze in shock.

"You can wait over there," he added, not unkindly, and pointed at a pair of wingback chairs grouped around a low mahogany table. An aspidistra and a fern sheltered the occupants from street view. Moving on autopilot, Arden walked over to the chair and sank into it. She set the gifts on the table, smoothed the perfectly tied ribbon as an all-too-familiar emotion crawled up her spine. Shame.

Two women walked past, chattering away. Arden recognized both of them, both school friends who'd known Mel as long as she had. They looked at her, then kept walking right up to the elevator. Exclamations of greetings, a third voice, then Melissa emerged.

"You don't have to say one word to her," said one of the new arrivals.

Something indistinct but firm from Melissa. Arden smoothed the ribbon again, and following the lines with her gaze as she trailed her finger along the grosgrain edge.

"Arden. Hi. Thanks for coming."

"Hello, Melissa. You look wonderful." She did, tall and slender, blonde hair pulled back in a ponytail, her skin glowing, the baby a pretty basketball under her silk maternity dress. From the back she wouldn't look pregnant at all.

Melissa didn't lean in for a kiss. "Arden, I'm sorry. I thought it would be all right if you came, but then Geneva called me last night, in tears. Apparently Randall had invested more than he'd let on in MacCarren, and . . ." Melissa's voice trailed off.

"And she can't stand to be in the same room with me right now."

"I'm sorry. She's one of my oldest friends—"

"I'm one of your oldest friends, too. We all met at Tripp Lake, remember?"

"I know. I just don't want to make anyone uncomfortable. She's a wreck, not sure if they'll be able to buy the place in Vail after all."

Arden forced a smile onto her face. "I understand, Mel. Really. I do."

"You're stronger than she is, Arden," Melissa said stoutly. "She fell apart when it rained through the cabin's screens. You led us three miles through the wilderness, remember? You'll get through this. You get through everything."

She barely remembered that girl, the one who led them to the meeting point when they were lost in the Adirondacks, back when kids could get lost at summer camp. "It wasn't three miles, Mel," she said, and reached for the wrapped presents. "But thanks for the vote of confidence. For you and baby girl Schumann."

Mel sat down in the other wingback and unwrapped the presents. "Oh, Arden," she breathed, when she unwrapped the baby book and opened the pages to the hand-inked superheroine drawings. "You remembered. This is gorgeous. And something else? A Sheba?" She looked up. "Arden. You shouldn't have."

"Congratulations, Mel," she said as sincerely as she could muster. Keeping her voice even, pleasant, unaffected took most of her effort.

"Thank you so very much. I'm sorry about this."

"So am I," Arden said.

Mel gave her an awkward hug, one-armed, shoulders only, and mostly behind the aspidistra. She turned and went back to the elevators. Arden settled her sunglasses on her nose, straightened her spine, and walked out the door. She could text Derek and have him get her car out of the parking garage, but she'd given him the impression he could have a couple of hours to himself.

Traffic flowed past on Central Park West, the bus's air brakes whooshing when it made the corner, heading for Broadway. Across the street, Central Park's giant trees and shaded paths beckoned. It was surprising how quiet the interior of the park could be, given that over a million people lived on the island of Manhattan, and on any given day another million visited for one reason or another. All she had to do was cross the street. Most days she barely had to talk herself into it. But today, with her nerves shot and her stomach in knots, it took every ounce of concentration she could muster.

She turned right and walked to the corner, where a traffic signal would halt the rush of cabs, buses, cars, bikes, scooters, motorcycles. The light turned green and the little white walk man appeared, but Arden couldn't move. The man started to flash red, then went solid. She waited, watching the light. The moment the little white man appeared, his sturdy legs striding confidently forward, she inched into the street. *Look left, look right, double yellow line, look right, look left, the cars are stopped, they're all stopped, no one is turning, two more steps, there's the curb.*

No one stared at her. This was Manhattan. When she'd been hit by the cab, people stopped until it was clear the situation was in hand. Then no one gawked. They just kept walking. That's what she did, following the wide, curving path into the park's interior. Chattering children scrambled up and down a mound of rock surfacing from the park's grass like a breaching whale left in place as part of the park's rustic ambience; she sank onto a bench across from them and tried to catch her breath.

She was an idiot to think she'd be welcome at the baby shower. An *idiot.* Her throat tightened, but whether from humiliation, tears, or the early stages of a panic attack, she couldn't be sure.

Her phone chirped in her bag. She withdrew the drawing journal, pencil bag, and her sunglasses case before finding the phone. A text from Betsy.

That fucking bitch.

Arden gave a choked little giggle. Betsy's next text appeared while she was thumbing She's trying to keep the peace for—

Where are you?

She looked around. Umpire Rock.

On my way.

Arden scrabbled a pencil from the bag and opened the journal, then stared fixedly at the rock. A blind contour drawing was exactly what she needed right now. She'd followed the jagged, irregular line of the immense rock through several peaks and shadowy faces when "That bitch!" fractured her concentration.

Betsy. Phone in one hand, her Miu Miu bag in the other, teetering on four-inch Louboutin heels and a geometric print Diane von Furstenberg wrap dress, holding the skirt closed as she trotted down the sidewalk. "That *bitch*!"

"Betsy," she said.

"*Fuck* Geneva. Fuck *her*! Who does she fucking think she is, keeping you away from Mel's shower?"

Her friend stood in the middle of the path, making big, sweeping gestures with her arms. "Betsy, I love you with all my heart and soul, but the last thing I need right now is you making a scene."

Betsy looked around, then sat down on the bench and looked at Arden more closely. "Sorry, sweetie. I'm very protective of you, that's all," she said quietly. "Look, why don't you take Mom up on her offer and head down to Palm Beach for a few weeks, until this blows over? Because it will blow over. All you need is another big scandal, and everyone will forget about this."

"No one's going to forget about this," Arden said distantly, her eye still following the peaks and cuts in the rock face. "No one we know. The media will, but everyone in our world has the memory of elephants. There is no escaping, so there's no point in leaving, and I'm not going to back down."

"Fine, be that way." Betsy sighed. She settled back onto the bench, and peeked over Arden's shoulder. "What are you doing?"

"Blind contour drawing," Arden said without looking down. She kept her hand moving, her eyes fixed on the exposed bedrock. Solid, immovable, the core on which Manhattan was built. Far more stable than the flibbertigibbet landfill at the tip of the island, or the long drop under Arden.

For a moment longer, Betsy looked at the drawing, but made no comment. "Why are you doing it in the middle of Central Park?"

"I expected to be at the shower until midafternoon, so I told Derek to park the car and do whatever it is he does when I'm shopping or having lunch or working. Just because I was summarily kicked to the curb doesn't mean I should ruin his afternoon."

"It's such a farce," Betsy said, but her voice had lost its rancor. "Dressing up for each other. It's her third, for Christ's sake. What did you get her?"

"A handmade baby book and a Sheba Clark from West Village Stationery. You look really nice, by the way," Arden said. The dress was vintage, passed down to Betsy by her mother. Betsy couldn't be bothered to dress up for anyone.

"So do you. Sarah Burton?"

Arden just nodded. The suit felt ridiculous now, with its silk fabric, feathery hem, and slender gold belt, especially because she wasn't in a Central Park West penthouse but sitting on a chipped-paint, pigeon-stained bench in the park.

"It's gorgeous," Betsy added.

"Thank you," she said. "She said it would be fine."

"I know."

"I asked. I never looked at people and saw a MacCarren investor. I never looked at them and saw whales or minnows. I just saw friends, classmates, acquaintances. Now I look at them and see amounts above their heads, in red, for losses. Of course, I didn't just *assume* I would be welcome after . . ."

"You should be welcome," Betsy said, and crossed her leg. "You were welcome until Geneva discovered how much Randall invested with your father. That's not your fault. Randall was always looking for the get-richer-faster inside track. *You* didn't know."

"I should have known. That's what everyone's thinking. I should have known. How could I have not known?"

"Because it's your dad and Charles. Literally thick as thieves, those two. Because they didn't want you to know." Betsy eyed the hot dog vendor at the intersection of two paths.

"You know that, Betsy. Not many other people do."

Betsy shrugged. "Did you eat?" When Arden shook her head, she added, "Want a hot dog?"

"Sure."

Betsy returned with two hot dogs, a pretzel, and two bottles of water. She cracked the seal on one and held it out to Arden. "Drink one of those. You look pale. You can't blame yourself for not knowing what your father and brother obviously went to great lengths to hide."

Reluctant to give up the tiny measure of comfort she felt from guiding the pencil across the page, Arden focused on the waves in the outcropping of Manhattan schist in front of her, waves formed over eons, the bedrock on which Manhattan skyscrapers towered. "What are the grief stages? I don't think I'm at the blame stage yet. I think I'm still in shock."

Betsy set down the water and started in on her hot dog as she watched Arden draw. "You asked me for Micah's phone number. I assume you were tracking down Seth."

"I was," Arden said. "After the meeting with the government agencies fighting over the MacCarren carcass, I wanted something to take my mind off . . . everything."

"And?"

"He came over and modeled for me. Then we had sex."

It was amazing what came out of her mouth when she'd partially disengaged the filtering, processing, fear-based side of her brain. A tiny girl in a white sundress and matching hat scrambled up the side. Without thinking about it, Arden added the girl's hat brim to the drawing and kept her hand moving.

"Good," Betsy said. "Or, I assume good."

"Very good," she said, remembering the shape of his cock in her mouth, the heat of his body over hers when he'd flipped her to her stomach. Her right brain sent up vivid, flashing images, and her hand quivered for a moment, then resumed the measured pace. One millimeter at a time. She'd spent literally thousands of hours in Central Park since she was the age of the little girl in a sundress and hat, and never before really looked at a rock.

"It's helping," Arden said. "Drawing. It's helping. I breathe in naturally, but I forget to breathe out. When I'm drawing, I remember to exhale, like I'm taking all of the data coming at me and channeling it. I nearly had a panic attack just crossing Central Park West, and that hasn't happened in a long time. I'm holding my breath, waiting for the next hit, but when I do this, I'm okay."

"Good," Betsy said again, this time quieter.

Arden let everything except the rock fade into the background, the tourists strolling by, Betsy, the children playing while their parents hovered. A thought struggled through the sediment settling in her brain, something about the way Special Agent Logan had looked at her, a flash of something under the impassive facade, leaking out in the unusual, awkward circumstances. The FBI and the SEC and everyone else would go through the motions, searching for more people to indict, try, blame, but Logan believed she'd known nothing about it.

He thought she was a victim, too. And here she was, sitting on a park bench, unable to cross a street without breaking into a cold sweat. The panic attacks weren't getting better. They hadn't been before the night when the FBI raided their home in East Hampton.

She should have been grateful for his compassion; he might even help manage the agents who wanted to interrogate her mother, but all she felt was frustration. Other than Betsy, people saw her as either a thief or a victim, too much a MacCarren or not quite enough of one, prone to inconvenient panic attacks. If the drawing helped, then she would master it.

Galvanized, she closed the journal and snapped it shut and jammed it back in her bag. Betsy lifted one eyebrow. "Better?"

"Yes," Arden said decisively. "Is your mother sincere in her offer to host my mother in Palm Beach?"

"Of course," Betsy said. "Frankly, I'm surprised Lyd's still here."

"She wants to be close to Dad. I think a change of setting would do her good."

"I'll tell Mom to try again. See you in class on Sunday?"

"Yes."

But she was hanging by a thread, clinging to anything that helped her deal with the ruins of her life. As she walked slowly toward the East Side, the memory of Seth's gaze flooded her mind. She wanted him, a man who'd fought real battles, who saw her as strong. Maybe she could learn to be the woman he saw.

Just before she reached Fifth Avenue, she pulled out her cell phone and texted him. Are you busy?

Now?

Yes.

No.

Meet me at my place.

– SEVEN –

W hen Arden's blue front door opened, Seth wasn't sure who was more surprised: him, or her. He didn't have words to describe what she was wearing; he'd need metallic pastels and hours of focused drawing time to re-create her outfit. A jacket and skirt, he supposed, in a shade slightly darker than cream. The cuffs and hem of the jacket were ruffles of gold matching the skirt's frilly hem. The jacket's high collar made up for the deep V-neckline, softened with elegant ruffled folds. A slim gold belt encircled her waist, and something about the structure gave him the impression of a corset. On her feet were strappy gold sandals with a killer heel. The whole outfit had a sheen to it he could only describe as expensive, like a car, leather and walnut, perfect fit and finish, or a gun, well-oiled, precisely engineered. Her hair curtained her face with the same sheen as her outfit. Expensive. Luxurious. No tousled, tangled strands here. Everything from her pores out gleamed like it had been buffed.

Without a word she stepped back and let him in. He leaned his bike against the wall next to the table, the one now holding a purse, keys tossed on the polished wood, a red leather journal, the same wallet she'd pulled a sheaf of twenties from last time, tossed negligently on top. So far so good.

What tipped him off was the wineglass. Red wine, held negligently in her hand as she stared at him at four o'clock on a Saturday afternoon. She didn't look like a woman about to dirty herself with charcoals, pastels, or even pencils, so the modeling/art student thing was bullshit, at least for now. What really tipped him off was the way her eyes flicked over him, hitting the highlights. She started with his face—he'd give her points for that—but in a split second she checked him out, shoulders, chest, thighs, then back to his face. He was glad he'd gotten decently dressed, in dark jeans, a white shirt. But when she looked at him like a bored, rich, thrill-seeking woman checking out the rent boy she'd hired, everything else dropped away.

Her life was in ruins; she was coping in a way he recognized. Alcohol and sex were two legitimate methods for combating anxiety. That was his job now. Be helpful.

The decision to play this out didn't happen in his left brain, rational mind. Some element of creativity in the right brain took the primitive signals pulsing up from his brain stem, added a healthy dollop of simmering lust, and formed a single word in his mouth.

"Arden?"

Her name came out of his mouth in a rough, businesslike tone with enough of a question to give her the hint. See if she'd catch the ball on the fly, throw it back to him, or at him, or duck.

"And you are?"

A one-handed catch, sent right back at him, fast ball down the center of the plate. Don't let the jeans and loose cotton top and fresh face from last time fool you. She's sophisticated in ways you cannot begin to imagine. "Seth."

Another glance, just haughty enough to send blood pulsing to his cock and a fresh rush of lust darkening the edges of his vision, then she nodded. He crossed to stand in front of her. After a few seconds it became clear she wasn't going to break the ice by offering something to drink. Without breaking eye contact he took the glass of wine from her hand, inhaled, then sipped it. It was good, deep and full-bodied, filling his mouth and nose the way one look at her blocked out everything else in his vision.

He set the glass on the table. "What do you have in mind?" he asked, playing along. He of all people had no reason to contact a woman like this. Maybe at some level he was asking for permission to put his hands, his tanned, scarred, killing hands with a faint ring of bike grease in the cuticles, on her suit.

One shoulder lifted in a shrug. The fabric whispered against the strands of her hair, a susurrus of sound. Like she didn't care. Like it didn't matter as long as he fucked her.

"Come on," he said, his voice still foreign in his ears, "a woman like you has to know what she wants." He leaned close enough to see the fine hairs on the skin covering her cheekbones, watched them lift as he whispered. "I bet you always get it."

Her eyelids, covered in a shadow barely one shade darker than her skin, flickered, but remained open. She turned to look at him, as if she couldn't believe the disrespectful words coming from his mouth. Like a dancer at a barre, she straightened, then stepped to the side and circled him. His heart beat four times to every slow click of her heels on the polished floor. She stopped behind him, waited. His heart was pounding hard enough now to strike sparks in his blood, making his skin tingle from the inside out. He could hear her breathing, shallow, giving away some of her arousal.

She set one fingertip to the base of his spine, just above his waistband. This time she wasn't asking permission to touch him. He automatically straightened and squared up. His cock pulsed, too, just from one single touch. In his peripheral vision he saw her arms curve around his waist. His mind, rushing ahead, envisioned her leaning her forehead into the triangle between his shoulder blades and his neck.

Wrong. He'd expected her to need something from him, to lean on him, use his strength. Instead, her fingers, the nails perfectly manicured, tugged his shirt from his waistband, then unfastened each button from pelvis to throat. His pulse beat crazily in his head, in his cock, lust a physical weight surging in his veins. Why did he feel her touch like a hot, sweet weight? He had seventy pounds on her, easy, all of it muscle and bone. She should make no impression on him at all.

Surprised by his own words, he thought about it for a second. Spending most of his days on the bike kept him near fighting shape, but as her fingers moved deftly up his shirt, he realized he'd lost something that couldn't be measured in pounds or kilograms. He spent most of his days anchored by constant contact with his friends, keeping one another alive on patrol, laughing, shooting the shit, cleaning gear, watching movies. He never noticed that both their noise and presence weighed him down in all the best ways, until Arden put her hands on him like she owned him.

Again, his vision darkened at the edges. She didn't help matters any when her hands stroked up his abdominal wall to fan out over his chest, pausing at his nipples just long enough to halt his breathing when she teased them into peaks. One hand slid up his throat, like she fucking owned him, then back down to shift his shirt fronts to the edges of his shoulders. Without pausing, her fingertips skimmed both dragon and the sword.

Crazy turned on, he stopped breathing. She finished her circuit of his body, the tip of her finger tracing the edge of his waistband to his belt buckle. She paused, her gaze lingering on his body. It wasn't the body he'd fought with. Those muscles were gone, lengthened and strengthened into the bike messenger's body, constantly burning more calories than he could easily consume. She hooked her finger in his waistband, barely brushing his erect cock, straining against the denim. He heard the soft, satisfied noise she made, completely in character, like he met with her approval. Her gaze traveled up again, this time all the way to his face.

Her gaze still locked on his mouth, she trailed her finger back up his torso, along his throat to his jaw, then over the day's worth of stubble there to his lips. She traced first the lower lip, then the upper before sliding along the corner to touch his lower teeth. The tone in her eyes changed, and fuck, he recognized that look, too. It was entirely possible he wouldn't get to fuck her in this role. That added to the edge, too.

She negligently snagged the handles of her enormous handbag, then turned away and walked up the gently curved staircase leading to her main living space, crooking her finger over her shoulder as she went. She didn't look over her shoulder as she did, though. That would make the command an enticement. Instead, she beckoned without looking, utterly, transparently confident he'd come to heel.

Heels against floor, heart against ribcage, cock against fly. His own shoes, soundless on the parquet, as if he weren't really there. When she reached the living room she tossed her bag on the sofa, then turned the chair away from the windows and sat in it, easing down with her back straight and her head bent. The sunlight permeated her suit, turned it to gold, her hair to gleaming chestnut. It was a Saturday afternoon, time in abeyance by gold sunlight, gold suit, molten eyes. Where the hell had she been, dressed like that? Head cocked, she looked up at him, tucked her hair behind her ear, and crossed her legs at the knee. "On your knees, please."

The please was a formality offered because she didn't have to give commands to a rent boy. Or a companion. She could mask them in requests, knowing he was bought and paid for. What the hell had he been thinking when he started this?

He hadn't been thinking. Just acting. His body knew what it wanted. He heard Manny's voice in his head. *Just go with it.*

He went to his knees, thinking about all the times he'd done this with kneepads on to protect him from rocks and shrapnel and debris from bomb blasts. All the ways you tried to protect your body from injury, how ineffective they were in the end. Something bigger, stronger, meaner was always waiting.

But right now a woman drenched in gold was waiting for him to play his role. Up close her suit was even more incomprehensible, the skirt's frilly hem lying soft and easy against her knees. He tried to get a handle on the lust flooding his system by taking her uppermost foot in his hand and putting his fingers to the buckle.

"Leave them on," she said.

He couldn't look at her. That should have been his line. He wasn't sure what would come out of his mouth if he tried to flip something back to her, disbelieving laughter, or begging. Instead he bent his head and kissed her instep. Eased his palm along the swell of her calf, to the pressed flesh of her crossed legs, and lifted the top one off. The tight skirt didn't allow for much movement, so he left her knees pressed primly together and hitched the skirt up. She didn't do anything so gauche, or helpful, as wiggle. Instead, when he got the confection of what had to be silk in some form or another to midthigh, she lifted her bottom so he could push the skirt to her hipbones.

Baring panties in the same shade of gold. Lace. The fabric laid waste to the demure construction. Without thinking, he bent forward and touched the tip of his tongue to the tiny triangle at the juncture of her thighs. He traced the edge of the leg openings from hip to thighs, heard her breath catch as he did, then release on a slow, breathy exhale as he licked and kissed his way down to her knees. Her thighs were soft; she was thin but lacked the muscle tone of an athlete. Her skin was smooth, freshly shaved, more likely waxed. The lace contained darker curls, neatly trimmed; he breathed heat and humidity into them, then pushed his tongue against the top of her cleft.

She made that soft, pleased noise again. His cock leaped in his pants, then again when she said, "Yes, please."

There was role playing and there was ridiculous; he drew the line at removing her panties with his teeth. Instead he reached under her backside, curled his fingers into the top elastic edge, and pulled them off, letting his fists brush her bottom as he did. Humor lightened the heat simmering in her eyes but disappeared when he put his mouth to her bared mound.

She shifted, intending to kick her panties free from her ankles, but he pressed down on her knees, keeping her in place. She looked at him, one eyebrow lifted, despite their positions, imperious in her shining suit and hair. He smoothed his hands up her outer thighs, curled his fingers around to the soft inner flesh, and drew them down and open, spreading her.

Her eyelids drooped. "It would be less awkward," she said, one ankle tugging at the entrapping panties.

"You like me like this," he said, meaning his bared chest and jeans. "I like you like this."

"The shoes work for you," she said with satisfaction.

"Even more with lace panties against them," he said, and spread her knees wide.

It was awkward, until he bent forward and set his mouth to the top of her pussy. He was looking up at her as he did, so he saw her eyes close, her teeth dent her lower lip, the faint quiver of her lashes. Less awkward already; he spread his own knees to make room for her feet between his legs. He wanted to grind his cock against something, but there was nothing in reach. Shifting his hips made it better and worse at the same time, so he sat back on his heels and focused all of his attention on her.

Ignore how that makes your heart race, because this is really fucking hot.

He curved both arms under her thighs and gripped her hips, the better to feel her squirm. Then he nuzzled at the soft hair and softer flesh, darkening pink. The scent of slick heat filled his nostrils. One of her hands gripped the edge of the seat. The other came to rest on his head, heel by his temple, her long fingers curving through his hair to press against his skull.

They all but left dents in bone when he brushed closed-mouth kisses to the soft folds, lacking urgency, teasing them open before letting them close again. Her clit was swollen, slick, he noted before he shifted to the tender skin by her thigh. She tried to squirm down and open farther. He clamped his hands around her hips and held her where she was.

"Seth," she snapped, or tried to, except it was hard to snap when the only air you got was from panting gasps.

"I can leave any time," he said, neatly shifting the balance of power back to something resembling level.

"Seth, please," she tried again.

"Hush," he said, and brushed the very top of her sex with his fingertips. "You're distracting me."

He went back to work with her low groan of surrender echoing in his ears, making the golden light vibrate. He rode out the furious struggle as she wriggled her feet free from her panties then slid down and lifted her leg to his shoulder. He squared up to take her weight and teased open her folds with his tongue. Her fingers curled in his hair, seeking a grip on strands he hadn't had cut since he was discharged.

The first time he circled her clit, she sighed with relief. The second time she breathed *yes god yes*, barely audible over the air-conditioner. The third time she lifted her hips, pleading for more, harder, with body and mouth. In response, he slid his tongue down to her opening, circled there, felt her salty slick juices coat his tongue, his chin, his lips. She arched, lifting, trying to get his mouth where she wanted it, but he flattened his forearm across her belly and used the fingers of the other to hold open the top of her folds, exposing her clit to the cool air he could feel against the hot skin of his chest and belly. Even with him holding her up and open, her thighs were quivering with tension. He wedged his shoulders more firmly between her legs and resisted the powerful urge to grind the air.

Her ferocious cry when he returned to her clit made him look up at her. He almost came in his jeans. Her head was thrown back in a position of utter abandon, but she was clothed from the top of her mound to her collarbones, and something about the tightly fitted jacket and skirt, the incongruous frills, the long sleeves, made his heart thump against his chest.

She was close, tense, quivering, the pink sex flush blooming in the deep V of her jacket and spreading up her throat. Oh yes, she was close, helpless, pleading wordlessly. He closed his eyes and licked his circles a little harder, a little tighter until she went rigid in his arms and a soft, hoarse cry tore from her throat. He held her through it, pressing gently with tongue and hands until she subsided.

When her eyes opened, they were spaced out, satisfied, clearly adrift on endorphins. He palmed her juices off his face then went to work on his belt and fly. All this did was remind him of how the speed and thrill of playing in traffic wasn't enough, that there was a personal element, the element of touch necessary to keep the mental wolves at bay. They were both stuck in nightmares of lives, but together they'd forget everything.

"Stop," she murmured.

"What?" Incredulous, his hand halted mid-zip. Was this some kind of role-play ending in which she sent him home unsatisfied? His brain short-circuited in the overload of no meant no, but fuck if he was coming back for another round of any-goddamn-hundred-bucks-an-hour-thing if he wasn't getting off. Playtime was fun, but he was no masochist.

She reached out and swiped her thumb across his lower lip, and Christ, the look in her eyes. "I want to draw you like that."

EIGHT

Her brain was offline. The observer whose voice ranged from snarky to shrill to shrieking was all but silenced. The spaciousness in her head was brilliant, a negative space that seemed to go on forever. Afraid of disturbing the fragile balance giving her the first sense of peace she'd had in weeks, she didn't move, didn't say anything else, just watched him with the feral, female part of her brain.

His face. Traces of her juices gleamed on his cheek, and his lips were an invitation to sin, swollen under her thumb. She pressed, very gently, watched his eyelids droop and his cheeks heat. Drawing him was no longer the idle pastime of a rich woman with a panic disorder. It was an imperative. She could breathe, and it was glorious.

"You want to draw me like this," he said. It wasn't a question. A fine tremor ran through his hands, halted on his buckle and zipper. At some level she knew the intricacies of fingers, hand, buckle, belt, zipper, fly, and hips were beyond her, but Lord have mercy, she wanted to try. And that mouth. Five lines. She could do that, capture the swoop of his lower lip, the bracket of the upper, the tantalizing space in between. It was their density that would evade her, but again, imperative that she try.

"Yes," she said, her voice distant, like that of the observer.

"Naked?"

Tacit permission granted, she scrambled to her feet, knocking him back on his heels, then stumbled over the shoes and panties strewn on the floor. She shoved her skirt down as she hurried to the easel. "I don't care," she said abstractly. Breathing was *glorious*. "Just . . . stay there."

Her hands were unsteady, so the first attempts to capture him sitting on his heels with his back to her were shaky. Then he changed position, smoothly rising and turning to take her place on the edge of the chair. His elbows came to rest on his knees. He scrubbed the heels of his hands over his face once, twice, all fantastic action poses to capture, both the motion and the impulse that made them. Frustrated desire, sublimating something, just as he had when he saw her. He slid his cupped hands over his hair and linked his fingers at the nape of his neck. A pause, trying to come to terms with something. A single low breath shuddered to the floor, disturbing the eddies of air in the room, control found. The scent of sex reached her nostrils, calling a faint response from her nipples and clit. She ignored it. Later. She grabbed for this as avidly as she'd grabbed for the game he'd offered.

She'd seen him in bike messenger gear, cargo shorts, and a tight jersey. He'd come to her apartment last time in something similar, cargo pants and a T-shirt. This time he wore a tailored white oxford and dark jeans fitted to his lean hips and thighs. In his current position the shirt gapped open, giving tantalizing glimpses of his chest, the tattoos, the scar—the lines and angles irresistible. Without thinking about it, she drew quickly, bold, confident lines, working from the silent space in her head, glancing from him to the page, not judging or erasing or thinking, just capturing. The essence of the pose was in his shoulders and the intricate play of angles at elbows, knees, the negative space between them. The impulse and motivation were more difficult to grasp. Why was he here, not just in the chair but in her town house, in Manhattan? Her own frustration grew. She saw the surfaces of him, but not the essence of Seth Malone.

A horn went off down below. Arden made an inarticulate noise of protest as her concentration shattered. He looked up from his steady contemplation of his hands, his sharp gaze a delicious contrast to the sex flush fading on his cheeks and chest. She shook her head as an avalanche buried the quiet. He sprawled in the chair, the shirt dropping away to expose ribs and muscles, the unabashed jut of his erection against his jeans. He still wore his shoes, highly polished brown with good tread. The contrast caught her attention for a moment, the workingman's shoes polished bright. He was dressed to go out, she realized. As was she. But not together.

"Lost the moment?"

"Yes," she said. "They don't seem to last very long."

He glanced at his watch, a thick functional digital thing, battered, on a worn canvas strap. "That was about twenty minutes. Not bad for picking it up after a decade."

"How do you know all this? Did you pick it up from modeling sessions?"

"I draw, too."

She blinked. "You draw."

"Yeah. It takes a while to learn to switch off the right brain on command. You'll get there. It just takes practice."

Right now it felt as if she'd never do it again. The numbing effect of the shock that got her through the last couple of weeks was wearing off. Her stomach was a swirl of emotions, the heat that had ebbed to a simmer, the residual humiliation of the party. Oddly enough, that party wasn't the worst thing she had to do this weekend. Tomorrow morning bright and early, Derek was driving her out to East Hampton to see her mother. Neil had promised to stop by the house on his way back into the city. More lawyer talk, probably bad news she'd have to brace her mother for.

But despite the observer voice in her brain shrieking that it was temporary and therefore pointless, on a deep and profound level, she felt better than she had in ages. Since she'd been hit by the cab, to be precise.

She forced her brain back to the lines on her sketchpad. It . . . wasn't bad. It wasn't good, either, but at least it wasn't bad. She knew what she was doing, attacking drawing for something to do, because the risk she'd have a panic attack was too dangerous right now.

"I'm trying to get the feel of you on paper. The weight," she said, feeling rather inarticulate.

He gave a soft huff that wasn't quite a laugh. "Good thing I weigh less than I did in the Corps," he said.

She peered around the easel, head tilted, her hair sliding free from its mooring behind her ear. Something about that changed the way he looked at her. It had been a long time since she'd felt this dance between herself and a man, where all it took was a look to convey desire. "I can't imagine you heavier," she said.

"I'm down about ten pounds. Between biking thirty to forty miles a day and not lifting weights like I used to, some of it got redistributed."

The initial burst of enthusiasm was long gone, but looking at him, at the sheer energy and ability in his body, was too enticing to let go. That was definitely part of who he was, but she was still missing something. "Forty miles a day?" she said, incredulous.

"Easy."

Looking at him was no hardship. "Do you mind if we continue before we . . . continue?"

The corners of his mouth quirked. "What do you want?"

"Take off your shirt," she said.

After a moment, he stood and shrugged the white shirt from his shoulders. His erection strained at his fly, and there was something predatory in his gaze, reminding her wordlessly that they weren't finished. All she could think was that sex with Nick, now married to her best friend, had never been like this. Never.

"Requests?" he asked.

"I've always wanted to try that Spiderman upside-down kissing thing," she said offhandedly.

She startled a bark of laughter from him. "We'll have to put hooks in the ceiling," he said, studying the plaster.

"Too much work. Suit yourself."

The filmy ruffles of her skirt tickled her knees and the lining brushed her bare bottom as she arranged her pencils and he sprawled on the chair again, his hands linked behind his head, presenting the flat plane of his chest and abdomen, the length of his legs, the triangles between his bent arms and his head. "Okay?"

"Perfect," she said, and picked up her pencil.

"Why the . . . I guess you'd call that a suit?"

"I had a party this afternoon," she said. "A baby shower for a friend."

"And you wore that?"

She remembered Betsy's acerbic comment about the women dressing up for each other. "I wore this," she said. "What about your clothes?"

"I thought I'd have time to go to the movies after you'd finished with me."

"Are you meeting someone?"

She tried to make it casual, distantly answering his questions while she focused on drawing him. Light, curved strokes for his ribs and abdominal wall to give his torso dimensionality on the page. It was harder than it looked, creating three dimensions on a flat page. Knowing she was missing something gave the effort to draw him new purpose.

"No," he said. "I was going to meet a friend, but he bailed on me just before you texted."

"A bike messenger friend?" she asked.

"No. Phil. A friend from the Corps."

"Someone you served with," she said.

"No. I served with Doug, his brother."

"Why aren't you going to the movies with Doug?"

"He died. An IED killed him and two other guys."

She peered around the easel, the shortening responses and clipped phrases coalescing into an increasing pattern of discomfort.

"Also your friends?"

"My best friends," he said.

"I'm sorry," she said.

The anguish on his face, covered only by a thin layer of bravado, mirrored the way she felt so much of the time, even before the raid, always putting on a show of being fine, just fine, so she gave him the space she longed for, the space he'd given her, and went back to the drawing.

She worked in silence for a while, until the tension in the room thickened into irresistible desire. "I'm done," she said, and stepped out from behind the easel.

He got to his feet, stretching overhead on the tips of his toes, then each arm across his chest, with the opposite forearm holding his elbow. Then he beckoned to her, one finger, one step down from imperious. Suddenly acutely aware of her bare feet and bare bottom under the suit, she crossed the floor to stand in front of him. He looked down at her, a hint of concern flashing under the long-simmering desire in his eyes, thick and potent.

Please don't say I don't owe you this. Please don't.

As if he read her mind, he reached out and rubbed one of the filmy ruffles lining the V-neck of her jacket between his fingers. The rasping sound was loud in the room, ending when he trailed his finger down to the intersection of the ruffles and the corset-inspired waist made of a darker gold silk. She wore nothing under the jacket but a bra, and the heated look in his eyes told her he'd figured that out, and he knew exactly what to do with that piece of information.

Both hands went to work on the narrow belt at her waist, unfastening the toggles to toss it on the sofa next to his shirt.

"Do you want me to put the shoes back on?" she asked.

"No," he said.

It was his turn to sound distant and distracted. He was exploring the jacket by touch, fingertips ghosting over each seam and shift in fabric, coming together at the hook-and-eye closure, then parting to slide down the V created by the jacket's ruffled, open hem. Back up, this time unfastening each hook as he went, baring her as she'd bared him several hours earlier.

She wore a bra of gold lace, her breasts peeking out from the jacket's edges. His expression, possessive and as pleased as any sultan in a harem, made her nipples peak. He touched each one, then cupped her breasts and rolled the tight peaks. The rasp of microfiber against her nipples sent a bolt of pleasure straight to her already swollen sex.

He wasn't looking at her face, so she glanced down. It wasn't hard to figure out what he liked about this. His hands were tanned, dry, and had remnants of bike grease embedded in the nail beds, but they touched her skin gently, almost reverently.

"How old are you?" she blurted.

"Just turned thirty," he said absently, obviously not bothering to waste any mental energy on wondering why she was asking such an irrelevant question.

Two years older than she was. Her brain ground, trying to

make sense of what they were doing together, her life, her shattered world.

"Stop thinking," he said.

"Make me," she demanded. Like her life wasn't complicated enough? Why wouldn't she just stop thinking, if it were that easy? Like what else was he here for, as her model, as her lover, if not to make her stop thinking?

The look in his eyes. Oh, goodness, the look in his eyes, total disbelief and total commitment to doing exactly that. Like it was Christmas and his birthday all at once. "Come here." He wrapped his fingers around her wrist and drew her to the sofa. He thumped down, knees spread, and unceremoniously pulled her down on top of him. Except the tight skirt, for all its ruffly, frilly movement at her knees, wouldn't let her spread her legs to straddle him.

An awkward moment ensued when she almost kneed him in the balls because she couldn't get her legs spread. The muscles in his arms flexed as he braced his palms against her hipbones to balance her weight, then straightened her. "Is your knee okay with this?"

"Yes," she said, beyond thinking about her knee, prepared to do battle with him if he coddled her.

"Then get your skirt up."

That helped. Short commands, rough tone. All men had that enough point, not a breaking point, but a point where they'd taken all they were going to take from a woman. She'd reached Seth's enough point. She curled her fingers in the fabric, working it up inch by inch while he watched. When the frilly ruff cleared midthigh, he reached out, ran his hands up the backs of her legs to cup her bottom and pull her down onto his lap. She braced with one hand on his shoulder and the flounces dropped down to cover her sex. She straddled his lap, but he stopped her from slotting their hips together.

"Kiss me. No, from there," he added when she tried once again to scoot forward and get big swaths of skin-to-skin contact. It wouldn't be complete, as she was still wearing her bra and jacket, but it would be something.

His hands left her bottom to skim her silk-covered hips, then the transition point from her waistband to her ribs, then up to her breasts. "Come on. Kiss me."

She leaned forward and set her mouth to his, open and avaricious, and licked her way inside. His tongue flickered back, responsive, teasing, but his attention was focused on his hands, skimming every part of her he could reach, flexing into certain spots. Her breasts, still in the bra, her hips, her bottom, but uncommon places, too. He curled his fingers around her instep and squeezed, a touch that made her groan helplessly. She reached blindly for his hand and wrapped her fingers around the edge of his palm. Her brain went haywire, stopped recording and started connecting touch and being touched, the rough skin, all of it coalescing deep in her mind to flesh out her impression of Seth.

He let go of her hand and wove his fingers through hers, squeezed again, then let go to run his circling fingers up and down the sleeve's frilly cuff once, twice, then up the sleeve itself to her shoulder. Another firm clasp at the joint, then he bent forward, tugged the fabric back to reveal her shoulder, and set his mouth to the skin.

She gasped. Started to wriggle. "Take it off," she said.

"Leave it on," he replied against her collarbone.

"Why?"

"It's making me really hot," he said, without any sense of shame.

She wasted no time with words, which were rapidly disappearing anyway, instead flattening her palm over his fly. Even with denim, underwear, and zipper separating their skin, she felt his cock jump. He looked at her, eyes intense, heavy lidded, pupils dilated, as he pushed his hands through her hair then slid them down again, cupping her ears, then stroking his thumbs down her throat, pausing at the notch of her collarbones, then down over her breasts to her belly, then to the hem of the skirt.

She turned her wrist and cupped his testicles.

"Get me out," he said, and worked his hands under her skirt. With his thumbs he brushed the crease where her legs met her hips, near enough to the top of her mound to keep her distracted, make her fingers twitch as she jerked open his belt, unzipped his fly. He leaned into the sofa's back just enough to lift his hips so she could yank his jeans down. They stopped just below his balls.

"I've got a condom in my wallet," he said, his hands not moving. The implication was clear; if she wanted to fuck him, she'd have to get the condom out herself.

"So do I," she said, and reached for her purse.

An amused smile lifted one corner of his mouth. She ignored it as she unzipped the lining pocket and found the condom, tucked into an assortment of rewards cards. She tore open the packet, situated the latex over the head of his cock when his hand curled around her nape. Again with the squeeze as he pulled her mouth to a bare breath from his.

"Go on," he said. When she did, unrolling the condom by feel, he added, "It's really fucking hot that you've got your own protection. Suits your personality. Tough. Sexy. Taking what you want."

"I'm not tough," she said, thinking of all the things she hadn't told him, who she was, the panic attacks.

"The hell you aren't," he said. His lips brushed hers as he spoke, kiss and conversation and seduction all in one. Heat glittered along her nerves with each soft contact, intensified by the teasing contact of her fingers, his erection, her aching, sensitized sex, the brush of silk and ruffle against her thighs, her hands. She'd have to get this suit dry-cleaned. She was sweating into the jacket and about to come for the second time while wearing the skirt.

Taking what she wanted, she held up her skirt with one hand and took hold of his cock at the base with the other. His grip on her nape tightened as he slid the other hand to her hip, holding the jacket open with his forearm. They were both looking down as she lifted herself just enough to center over his erection. He jerked when the tip nestled just inside, a choked sound forcing itself from his throat. Once she had him securely inside her, she kept hold of her lifted skirt and scudded the other hand up his sweat-sheened torso to his throat. Going on instinct she tightened her fingers and thumb before she lowered herself onto his cock.

He groaned, the sound rumbling out of his chest, through his throat, into the sun-soaked air as his eyes closed and his head dropped back. Muscles, tendons, arteries all vibrated or tightened under her fingers, and she got it, the varied touches, the full-body approach. He was turning her on, yes, but he was learning her, too.

She paused when he was fully embedded inside her, savoring the tiny pulses as her body stretched to accommodate him, nerves firing in response to a hard throb from his erection. The complex flex of his throat came alive in her mind; she didn't need to be able to name the anatomy of his neck in order to feel its strength and power in a new way. Dressed in the rumpled remains of her Sarah Burton suit, she had his cock inside her and her hand on his throat. She bent forward and bit his chin, feeling the emerging stubble scrape against her teeth.

His head lifted, and she captured his mouth with hers. All-out war, teeth in his lip, copper with saliva, her fingernails tightening on his neck, the other dropping her skirt to sting his waist. Grunting in response, he moved fast, using a fist in her hair to pull her mouth off his, capturing both wrists behind her back in one of his, lifting her skirt with a hand on her hip. His hands were so big he could guide her hip and press his thumb to the top of her clit.

"Ride me."

She lasted no time at all, smoothly rising and falling on his cock, at the back of her brain grateful for childhood summers spent on horseback, because the motions were shockingly similar. Her breasts bounced in her bra, the sheer fabric rough enough to stimulate her nipples. Her hair clung to her cheeks and lips. With each downstroke he filled her, the delicious stretch magnifying the pleasure building under his thumb. Her head dropped back, as pleasure swelled against her skin, then burst, pulsing out in waves, forcing short, sharp cries from her throat. He thrust up into her, somehow timing his strokes to the contractions wringing her out, then held her down by her hip and wrists as he came inside her.

She slumped forward, her forehead bumping his before she collapsed to the side. His hands tightened reflexively on her wrists, hip, then let go. She brought her arms around, resting one hand under her forehead on the back of the sofa, the other by his ear. Each gasping inhale brought the musky scent of sex and the tang of fresh sweat to her nostrils.

His hand slid between their joined bodies. Securing the condom, her brain told her, but distantly, faintly, like her left brain lost the lightning round and was down for the count. Aware it would help if she got off him, she tipped right and sprawled rather inelegantly on her side, her head pillowed on one of the throw cushions. He scooted down a few inches to make room for her, but her feet still lay on his thighs.

"I know why you were doing that," she said.

"Doing what?" he said, eyes still closed, head tipped back.

"Touching me the way you were. You were learning me, to draw me."

His head swiveled on his neck, and he opened his eyes to look at her. "It's not all about drawing. That's fairly typical male behavior during sex," he said with an amused smile. "I was touching you because I get grabby when I'm turned on. Just like you use nails and teeth."

She lifted her head a little and looked at his torso. Faint red lines marred the path from groin to throat, and yes, she remembered the taste of blood, too.

He got to his feet. "Mind if I take a quick shower?"

"No," she said.

He hitched his jeans up around his hips and walked into the bedroom. She heard the water turn on, then the clank of his belt buckle against the marble floor. She sat up and closed the hooks and eyes to fasten her jacket, but didn't bother with the belt. When he was gone she'd take a long, hot shower. Until then she'd sit here and let the scent of them wash in and out of her lungs.

He emerged just a few minutes later, smelling faintly of her almond body wash, which made her smile.

"I'm just glad it's not fruit," he said, unerringly picking up on what made her smile as he snagged his shirt from the back of the sofa. "Strawberries, pomegranate, peaches. Smelling like peaches is the worst."

"I think your masculinity is secure whether you smell like peaches or bike grease," she said, watching the tattoos disappear behind white cotton.

He smiled at her, then tucked in his shirt. "I don't like the smell of peaches," he said.

She reached for her wallet and withdrew the twenties, counting them out as she spoke. "If I don't tip you, are you going to come back as a loan shark or a hit man?"

Hands on his hips, he tipped his head back and laughed, the sound real and utterly delightful. "No," he said. "Probably not, anyway."

Heat quivered inside her. She bit her lower lip and handed him two hundred and forty dollars, watched him respond to the zing that went through her when their fingers brushed. As they went down the stairs to the foyer, she made a mental note to call Garry yet again and order him an answering machine and have it sent to New Zealand.

The way Seth unself-consciously picked up his bike and turned it so it faced the front door broke her open. He'd given her a tiny part of himself, something she could see he didn't easily share. The least she could do was be honest with him in return. "Seth, I need to tell you something."

He looked back over his shoulder, eyebrow raised.

"I'm Arden MacCarren. My family has been in the news the last couple of weeks. My father and brother were indicted for running a Ponzi scheme."

His eyes were calm, unsurprised. "I know," he said. "I searched you online after the first drawing session."

She blinked. "Why didn't you say something?"

"Because you didn't say something. We all have secrets we want to hide."

"It was hardly a secret." Embarrassed, she ran her hand through her hair. "I feel like an idiot."

"I have something to tell you, too," he said. "I delivered packages for Ryan Hamilton for most of the summer. They were all private deliveries, mostly to a woman he was . . . well, I don't know what they were doing, and I didn't ask."

Ryan had made an absolute spectacle of himself over the summer, something that raised Arden's eyebrows, until the news broke. Then it made perfect sense. They'd all been talking about his shenanigans rather than what he might know. Seth could have been delivering gifts to any number of women. "Oh. Oh," she said again, when the implications spun up in her head. Should she hire him to model for her? Should she *sleep with him*? "Have you been subpoenaed?"

"No," he said. "I don't think it had anything to do with the case. You know Irresistible?"

"I love Simone's designs," she said ruefully. "I wear a fair number of them."

"I delivered an orchid, a couple of other things in envelopes. He paid me in cash. That was it. Does it matter?" he said.

"I don't know if it matters. I'm more worried about you getting caught up in this . . . this . . ."

"Shitstorm?" he supplied helpfully.

"Precisely."

He shrugged. "No big deal."

"If the FBI wanted you, you'd know by now. That's probably why he paid cash," she mused. Especially if he wanted to keep Simone Demarchelier out of it as well. "Nothing to trace. I'd wager no one other than you and Simone knows you had any contact with . . . him."

It was still difficult to say his name. He'd done the right thing. Intellectually, she knew that, but as she was the one standing in the ruins while a wake of vultures stripped meat from bones, it was hard to remain objective.

Seth's brows drew together. "I haven't heard from Ryan for a couple of weeks. He seems to have disappeared."

For a moment she was fiercely envious of Ryan's ability to walk away from the mess, but ultimately, it wasn't his mess. He'd just exposed it. "I heard he was in Vermont, or Maine, or somewhere like that. Far, far away."

"But okay?"

"We'd know if he wasn't," Arden pointed out. "There is no way on God's green earth to keep the press from something that big."

Seth's face eased, and Arden realized he'd been genuinely worried about Ryan. "Is the Ponzi scheme coming to light the reason why you're taking the drawing class?"

Yes and no. "Betsy arranged it because it might help me . . . deal with things," she said belatedly remembering that he didn't know about the panic attacks.

"Does it?"

"Does what what?"

"Does the drawing help?"

"Yes," she said, then continued with painful honesty. "What happened after . . . the sex . . . that helps."

"Good enough for me," he said with a shrug. "Stop worrying about me. I'm fine. Why aren't you worried about me selling this story to Gawker or TMZ or whoever?"

She scoffed. "You wouldn't do that. I barely know you, but integrity and honor are written all over you. Literally," she said, and nodded at his chest. "Which is why we should end this. I really don't think you understand what being associated with me could do—"

"I need this, too," he said. For a split second he looked like he wished he could take back the words, but instead he straightened his shoulders and went on. "This is an arrangement that works for both of us. I model. You draw. Anything else that happens is our business. No one else's." He unlocked the front door and hoisted the bike by its frame. "Text me. I can't say I'll be free. I work evenings, too. But if you don't mind late hours . . ."

"I'll text you," she said quietly, and closed the door behind him. But she couldn't erase her memory of the look on his face when he said he needed this, too.

- NINE -

S eth hoisted his messenger bag over his head so the strap rested across his body, then lifted his bike by the crossbar and carried it down the stairs to the sidewalk in front of Arden's town house. He looked at his watch. Just before eight. Scanning the movie listings in his phone told him he had a couple of hours to kill before the next round of movies started.

He set off along Ninety-second Street toward Fifth Avenue, pleasantly relaxed. He should be wiped out. The sex had lasted for a couple of hours, from the moment she opened the door to the moment he walked out. It felt like one long session, with big surges and equally powerful ebbs while she drew him. His heart felt too big for his chest, beating in a rhythm that sent flickers of heat to his nipples, trickled down to pool in his groin, his fingertips. He wanted to fuck her again.

More important, he wanted to draw her, and he knew why. She was taking up residence in the space inside him where Brian,

Manny, and Doug used to live, the space hollowed into a charred husk by a searing explosion and fire.

Which was unexpected, and ridiculous. He'd given her the barest of bare-bones details about Phil and Doug, and gotten her last name in return. MacCarren. Arden MacCarren, a woman everyone thought they knew, and no one knew. But he did. He knew her at the instinctive, physical level. He'd let her touch him, thought it wouldn't affect him. He'd been wrong. He'd touched her, thought *that* wouldn't affect him, either.

Again, he'd been wrong. He'd touched her, and now he wanted to draw her. The urge was both unfamiliar and bone certain, making his fingers grope down his thigh in search of the sketchbook he used to carry in his cammie pocket. Not there. But it was in the messenger bag. Carrying one was like the pain from a phantom limb. He didn't draw like he used to, but he carried the sketchbook. After the IED went off, he put away the journal he'd carried, but found himself compulsively reaching for it, patting pockets, driving other Marines nuts with his unfamiliar restlessness. The LT took him aside and all but begged him to carry one. *Not that one, Malone, you don't have to carry that one. Another one. Please. We're all skittish, all freaked, all grieving, and you're making it worse. Just carry it.*

I can't draw, LT.

You don't have to draw. Just put the goddamn thing in your pocket.

He'd done it, shoved the old one he had carried to the bottom of his locker, put another one in his pocket. He felt like a kid with a pacifier, but it helped. He'd tap its stiff, comforting weight, and settle down, occasionally get out the sketchbook, flip through the cream pages, admire from some remote vista in his mind the emptiness, close it, put it away. For a while, looking at pages that weren't saturated with blood was enough. But he never forgot about the sketchbook he hadn't finished. It was now under the bed in the motor home. When he dragged Doug's torso out of the Humvee, leaving one of his arms and both of his legs behind, Doug's blood had soaked Seth's cammies, run into his boots, bled into the sketchbook's pages. The LT dragged him away from the Humvee, so Seth took it on faith that Manny's and Brian's blood was in the mix. God knew enough of it spilled into the dust and dirt.

That's when things went silent.

Right now he could hear Arden's heartbeat, her breath, the way it hitched up and up as pleasure coiled around them. Right now, he wanted to draw. He swung his leg over the bike and pedaled slowly up Ninety-second Street, used a break in traffic to cross Fifth Avenue to the Runner's Gate entrance to Central Park, then sat down on a bench, pulled out the brand-new Moleskine and a Micron pen, and sketched her face and torso, glass of wine in hand when she realized the rent-boy game, all cheekbones, jaw, lips, the arch of her brows above her eye sockets, capturing the haunted look. It was as automatic as breathing, getting the essence of that moment when she was both haunted and turned on, a few lines, vague swirls for her hair. He'd need paint, or a metallic pastel, to fill in her suit, but this was the pose. Pale gold hair, gold suit, haunted eyes, sex mouth. That was Arden.

He flipped the page, sketched in his hand against her sternum. Grease in his nail beds, the low curve of her bra cup, the ruffles of the suit. The notch between her collarbones. The scars on her shoulder and chest. She was wounded, and still in the fight.

The fine gravel was pretty dry from the late summer heat wave. As a runner sprinted past, he kicked up tiny pebbles in his wake, and a bit of dust. Seth's throat tightened, his heart rate spiked, and a sweat broke out down his back that had nothing to do with the late-summer humidity. His fingers spasmed, ruining the sketch with a jagged line, as if someone jostled his elbow. His eyes stung as he looked up, around, anywhere but at the drawing. A blood-bath of a sunset behind trees heavy with summer-dark leaves, the top of the stairs leading to the gravel path around the reservoir, joggers in all shapes and sizes crunching along, bikes speeding past him on the drive.

Fuck this. Phil wasn't canceling on him. He shoved the sketch-book in his bag, swung his leg over the bike and set off along the park's winding paths to emerge on the West Side, where Phil lived with his mother. The red-brick buildings, spanning half a block, air-conditioners whirring in windows, the treatments different from apartment to apartment, felt substantial, real, after Arden's narrow, otherworldly showpiece of an apartment. Still straddling the bike, Seth paused by the door and buzzed the Dorhaus apartment.

"Yes?"

"Ma'am, it's Seth Malone. I'm here for Phil."

"Come on up," she said.

The door buzzed. Seth hauled it open, then disdained the elevator and took the close, warm staircase to the ninth floor. The smell of Hamburger Helper hung heavy in the hallway, the sound of a baseball game behind 9A, baby crying behind 9B, NPR behind 9C. Nine D was open. Seth knocked anyway, then stepped in to come face-to-face with Doug's duffle bag, the contents strewn around the living room.

His diaphragm spasmed. He expected the shrine, the folded flag in the triangular case under the boot camp graduation photograph of an unsmiling Doug, his brown eyes serious. He'd been with Doug when the picture was taken, joking around in their dress uniforms, self-conscious, proud. Young. Fuck, but they were young, then. Doug still had some baby fat on his face.

Notched in the frame was a copy of the picture he tucked into the back pocket of every Moleskine he carried. He didn't need to move to look at it more closely. He had it memorized, the broad grin on Doug's face, Manny's head tipped back in laughter, Brian's hands on his hips, always the father figure despite being the youngest, and himself, head bent, his cheek creased with his smile. They wore filthy cammies, stood ready for patrol just outside Sangin.

But the day-to-day reality of the contents of Doug's seabag, dirty laundry, car magazines, toiletries, yanked the high right out from under him. This was the reality he had to stay in, a cramped apartment with a shrine, the loss hovering in the air, acrid and metallic all at once, like blood and the residue of explosives. Frozen in time. Arden's world and apartment felt very far away.

Phil leaned against the kitchen door frame, drying a plate with a dishtowel, his eyes giving away nothing. His mother came out from behind him, drying her hands on her apron. He'd last seen her at the funeral, and he should have been here before now. "Seth," she said.

He gave her an awkward hug. "How are you?" she asked, searching his face. She'd aged years, maybe a decade, in the past six months.

"I'm fine," he said. The standard bullshit. "Good. Keeping busy."

"Can I get you something?"

"No, ma'am," he said, and threw Phil a hard look. "I'm here for Phil. We're going to the movies." God. There was his iPod, dust and dirt ground into the case, the connections of tangled earbud cord. He'd drawn Doug with those earbuds in a hundred times.

"I don't quite know what to do with all this," Mrs. Dorhaus said, looking around the living room.

"You don't have to do anything with it, Ma," Phil said.

"I have to do something with it," she said.

"Do you want some help?" Seth asked gently, because the right thing to do was help her, steeling himself to do it.

"No. You boys go out and enjoy yourselves," she said. "I'll just . . . put this away."

Seth left his bike in the hallway and waited while Phil closed the door. "She does this," Phil said, his voice tight. "She unpacks the duffle, stares at all his stuff, then packs it up again. It's like she thinks one day he'll come home and unpack it."

He knew how she felt. Seth often found himself waiting for someone to check his body armor, or to even be breathing in the same space he was. "We could have stayed," Seth said.

"I can listen and remember all the good times we had together, and then I snap, can't take it anymore. Basically, I'm fine until I'm not fine," Phil said matter-of-factly. He looked at his watch. "I'm not fine now. We've got time to kill before the movie starts. Let's hit the bar."

He followed Phil down Columbus to a nondescript neighborhood bar, and into the dim lighting. The outside didn't look like much, but the interior was all right, booths along the back wall, stools at the bar, tables in between, and televisions in every corner. Two women sat in a booth at the back, not bothering to hide the way they were checking out Phil and Seth. Phil ordered a shot of whiskey and a beer. Seth stuck to beer.

"How's Britt?" Phil said in the tone of a man who knew the answer.

"What makes you think I've talked to her?" Seth said, trying to stall him.

"Because I talked to her a couple of days ago, and she mentioned she got a new car. 'How did you get a new car?' I asked, because last time I checked she was living paycheck to paycheck waitressing at Ruby Tuesday's and going to school while her mom watched Baby B. 'Seth sent me the money,' she said. 'Seth,' I said. 'Seth who rides a bike in Manhattan and lives in a motor home?'

'Seth,' she said." Phil swallowed the rest of his beer, and signaled for another round. "Where the fuck did you get twenty grand?"

Fuck. Busted. "I did a job for a guy," Seth said.

Phil's face was comically astonished, visions of hit men or drugs dancing in his head. "You did a *job*? For a *guy*?" he repeated incredulously. "Cash under the table? What the *fuck* have you gotten yourself into? Twenty fucking grand?"

Working as Ryan's personal delivery service was nothing compared to being Arden MacCarren's muse. "It's not like that," Seth said dismissively. "I delivered an orchid."

"Is *orchid* code for something? Weapons? Heroin?"

"It's code for a fucking pain-in-the-ass delivery. I rode as slow as I ever have, carrying that thing through Manhattan. Avoiding potholes is a bitch when you've got a three-hundred-dollar plant cradled in your arm. They're fragile."

"You're shitting me."

He'd put a few things together since he met Arden, paid a little more attention to the world she lived in, the world Ryan came from. Ryan was throwing money around for a reason, and it had something to do with being the whistleblower on the MacCarren Ponzi scheme. "I deliver a lot of flowers and food. Rainy nights, no one wants to go out and pick up two buck chuck and wontons at Trader Joe's. This guy had the kind of money where twenty grand was like five bucks to you or me. He wanted me on standby for the summer."

"That's not normal. Normal people don't make those kinds of offers, and people in their right fucking minds don't take them," Phil said. "That's movie shit. That's mob or gang shit."

"It wasn't the mob," Seth said. "It was Wall Street. Britt needed a new car. I sent her the money so she could buy one. All it would take to derail her was the transmission on that shitty Escort going out on her. Now she's got a fighting chance at finishing school. Which is what Brian wanted for her."

Phil opened his mouth but what came out was a girlish, flirty "Hi."

Seth turned to see the girls from the table, holding their cocktail glasses, smiles as bright as the shiny fabrics they wore. "Hi," he said. Phil shut his mouth.

"I've got that," she said to the bartender, thrust her credit card between them, then tapped the globe and anchor on Phil's forearm. "Thanks for your service."

"Thanks," Phil said easily, and tossed back the shot. Seth couldn't read Phil's reaction. As far as he knew, Phil wasn't seeing anyone. His last girlfriend didn't last the deployment.

"I'm Amber," the talkative one said, and held out her hand.

"Carlie," the other one said.

Handshakes all around, then the drinks arrived and they clinked glasses.

"How long have you been home?"

"A couple months," Phil said.

"Few months," Seth said, when she and her friend turned expectant eyes on him. There were rules for situations like this, and rule number one was Don't ruin your buddy's chances. He settled in to play wingman. A few minutes of conversation established that the girls both worked in retail. They displayed equal curiosity about Seth's bike messenger work and Phil's status as a college student.

"Where are you going?"

"I'm in the general studies program at Columbia," Phil said.

Eyes brightened, eyebrows lifted, a little laughter.

"It's pretty boring compared to bike messenger work," Phil said. "You should see him ride."

Seth flicked a look at Phil. He didn't need Phil deflecting attention from himself to Seth.

"Are you going to school, too?"

"Not right now," Seth said. He could see their thoughts spinning like a slot machine, trying to match up attraction and the lure of danger with future employment prospects. Being a bike messenger was great for one-night stands, not so great for anyone thinking about white picket fences or an apartment in Manhattan.

"He finished his degree while we were in the Corps," Phil said, once again turning the attention back to Seth. "And he's an artist."

No joy. Being an artist fell into the same category as bike messenger. Great for sex, no future prospects measurable in dollars and sense. "Were you in the same unit?"

"Nope," Phil said.

Seth opened his mouth to head this off, because he could see the train barreling down the tracks at top speed, but he had literally no idea what to say. Talking to Arden was so much easier than this.

"How do you know each other?"

"He served with my brother," Phil said, jerking his thumb at Seth.

"Is your brother still in the Marines?"

"He died."

And there it was, the crash, the smiles disappearing, the eyes widening. Shock was universal, and so easy to draw. "God. I'm sorry. Wow. That's awful. Um . . ." One of those girl-communication glances, and they both went to the restroom.

"What the hell?" Seth said.

Phil slugged back the rest of his beer. Based on the total lack of tact on Phil's part, Seth wondered how early he'd started drinking. "Doug's dead, so I'm *wounded*. There's a certain type that likes that. The good news for you is that those two prefer healthy former Marines. You should go for it."

"No way," Seth said. "We had plans."

"The movie will be showing tomorrow, or next week," Phil said. "Go ahead. I'm telling you I don't mind."

"I'm not ditching you," Seth said.

The conversation happened low and fast, finishing just as the girls emerged from the restroom, freshly tousled and lipsticked. All Seth could see was Arden's pale gold hair and violet eyes, the lush pink of her mouth after she kissed him until he forgot everything.

"We're going to a party in Tribeca," Amber said. "Want to come along?"

"I've got to get going," Phil started.

"No thanks," Seth said, cutting him off. "We've got plans. Nice to meet you. Thanks for the drinks."

"What the fuck?" Phil said when he and Seth were standing on the sidewalk. "You got a girlfriend I don't know about?"

"Do you?" Seth shot back.

"I didn't mind when the dress blues got me laid. I mind a hell of a lot when wounded does."

Seth got that, the penetrating stares, the soft, tender looks, invisible pets and strokes. Well intentioned. Useless.

"Jesus. Girls buying us drinks, inviting us to parties, and we walk away. Doug would be so pissed at us."

Seth huffed out a laugh. "Yeah."

Phil shoved his hands in his jeans pockets and hunched his shoulders. "There's this wall between me and the rest of the world. I know what I'm supposed to do. I just don't want to do any of it. If I do the things I'm supposed to do, like go out and drink with girls, I lose it."

"Lose what?" Seth said.

"Time, mostly. There's about seven hours from Tuesday night I don't remember. I remember being in a bar on the Lower East Side. Then I woke up in some strange girl's apartment, hungover, still high, and wearing fuck-all. I had no idea where the fuck I was. I had to use the GPS on my phone to find my location."

Jesus. Seth stared at him. He was supposed to be looking out for Doug's younger brother. Scenarios spun through his head, mostly about the kinds of diseases you could get from sharing needles or having unprotected sex. "Jesus," he said finally. "Phil. What kind of high?"

"Pot. I'm not stupid."

"You don't remember seven hours," Seth retorted.

"No one else brings him up," Phil said, bringing to the surface what had been lurking in the depths all along. "Mom says it's like she only had one son."

Seth could only imagine how Phil felt. He'd lost friends, brothers, but not like Phil, who'd idolized Doug, spent his whole life trying to live up to his older brother just as intensely as Doug praised him, guided him, mentored him. He shoved his hands in his pockets, said nothing, because there was nothing to say. Being here would have to do.

Phil looked at him out of the corner of his eye, then looked at his watch. "Can we just go to the fucking movies and not think about it?"

They looked at the electronic marquee over the ticket booth a little while later, considering a list of romcoms, family dramas, cartoons with talking squirrels, and by unspoken agreement avoiding the action movies packed with explosions. Hollywood used the worst day of his life as entertainment. They settled on a bromance comedy; Seth bought the tickets, Phil bought the popcorn and sodas. "You realize everyone's going to think we're dating," he said, as they settled into their seats.

Seth shrugged and claimed his soda. "Nothing wrong with that," he said.

"You seeing anybody?" Phil asked before cramming a handful of popcorn in his mouth.

Seth thought about Arden, drenched in gold, her tumbled,

witchy hair. He thought of the way she got more real when he drew her, the angle of her jaw he'd felt under his palms now a fine line in his sketchbook, and deep into his soul. He thought of the arrangement they'd made, what he'd unwittingly confessed, just so she wouldn't be alone in her need.

"No," he said, and put her out of his mind.

— TEN —

A few days after the humiliating baby shower, Arden swallowed the last of her coffee, rinsed the mug, and went back upstairs to dress for the first trip back to the MacCarren Foundation offices since the day the FBI raided her family's homes and offices. She chose her outfit carefully, a tailored pantsuit in black with a stark white blouse underneath, the collar high enough to hide the faint bite mark on her neck. Her hair she left loose, then tucked into a twist, then simply brushed back in a low ponytail. Lipstick to give her face some color. Big pearl earrings that were a Christmas present last year, the heirloom pearl necklace her grandmother gave her on her sixteenth birthday. More slowly, she slipped on her watch, then the ruby ring she customarily wore on the middle finger of her right hand.

She'd never really done this, totaled up the value of what she wore with an eye to its worth, but after the debacle at Melissa's party, she'd started to reassess her possessions. The ring was a signature piece, custom-made in the twenties by Cartier at her great-grandfather's request, for her great-grandmother. The provenance made it worth far more than the value of the stones, and she had a dozen pieces of similar quality and historical value in boxes in her dresser, more in a vault. Her mother had a hundred pieces like that, acquired over decades of familial wealth, handed down from her mother's side of the family. Would they also be seized by the government and sold?

She twisted the ring on her finger. There would be an FBI escort at the offices this morning, and she no longer pretended they weren't sizing her up on every level. She looked at the ring, tilting it so the faceted stone caught the light. There was no point in pretending she wasn't Arden MacCarren. The ring was legitimately hers, worn every day since her twenty-first birthday. Including today.

After texting Derek, she poured coffee into a travel mug, then waited by the front window until the SUV pulled up. The press must have gotten wind that something was up, because a wedge of photographers were all but lurking by the head-high wall protecting the steps to her front door. She slid on her sunglasses and hurried down the stairs.

"Morning," Derek said as he opened the low wrought-iron gate for her, then put his body between her and the photographers as she trotted to the idling vehicle's rear passenger door. Unflappable, her Derek. She could have kissed him.

"How did they know I was going out?" she asked.

"I don't think they did," Derek replied. "Daria Russell just moved in down the street. They were staking her out and saw me drive by. They've probably memorized the plate number."

"Two birds with one stone," Arden said with a sigh. "Poor Daria. First Ryan Hamilton, now me."

"What's the schedule?" Derek asked.

"We're meeting the FBI at the foundation offices," she said. "Home after that."

"You got it," he said and rolled down Ninety-second Street.

The shouts and flashes were muted by the big vehicle's sound-proofing and tinted windows. Steadfastly ignoring their shouts, Arden sipped the coffee, felt her heart rate trip and stutter, then start to race. She pulled out her phone and once again tried the New Zealand number she had for Garry. The phone rang seven times, then eight, then someone picked up.

"Hello?" It was a rough male voice, not unlike Garry's, but she couldn't be sure.

"Garry?"

"Arden?" he said.

Relief swept through her, leaving her dizzy. "Garry, where the hell have you been? I've been worried sick about you."

"Out with the sheep," he said, then cleared his throat. "I just got back last night. Sorry. I haven't talked to anyone in over a month."

"Did you read my emails? You know what happened, right? Dad and Charles were arrested for running a Ponzi scheme out of MacCarren."

"I skimmed them."

Silence. "Garry? Did I lose you?"

"I'm here."

New Zealand had changed her already quiet brother. "Garry, you have to come home. I need you here."

A pause. Arden was so used to the rapid-fire pace of her life that Garry's silences to process things seemed like they belonged to another geologic era. "It's got nothing to do with me," he said finally.

"Garry. You are a MacCarren. I need you here. Mom needs you here. She's a walking zombie. Neil says they're going to go after the foundation. Whatever Dad and Charles did, we can't lose the foundation, too."

Silence, but this time it was freighted in a way that sent a spear of sheer terror straight through Arden's bones. "Oh my God. Did you know? Is that why you left?"

"I didn't know," he said. "I knew something wasn't right. It was never right, the way they were. But I didn't know what they were doing."

Another dizzying wave of relief spiraled through her. "Look," she said. "The FBI has been asking me every five minutes if I've gotten in touch with you. They want to talk to you. I think you're too low priority for them to send someone to New Zealand to escort you back here, but I'm not going to lie to them. We've talked, you know the situation. Pack a bag and book a flight home."

"Mom won't send the jet for me?"

She blinked in astonishment. "Garry. *Read the emails.* We don't have a jet anymore. The government impounded it the day of the raid. If you have any friends left who will loan you a private jet, by all means, ask them to send it for you, but I wasn't allowed into Melissa Schumann's baby shower on Saturday. Remember Melissa? She lived with us after her mother found out her father had knocked up both the nannies?"

The silence this time was tinged with shock. "Okay," he said, and she finally heard the Garry she used to know. "Give me a few days. I need to handle some things here before I leave."

"Soon, Garry, sooner rather than later you need to be on a plane," she said. "I have to go. The government has some crazy idea that the foundation was somehow connected to the scheme. I'm trying to keep them from confiscating that, too. Call me when you've made arrangements. I'll send someone to the airport for you."

The paparazzi had abandoned the foundation offices, for now. Clustered outside the door but flagrantly not talking to one another were Neil, speaking into his phone; Special Agent Daniel Logan, clutching a cup of coffee and looking as bland as it was possible for a six-foot, whip-lean man to look; and her assistant, Emma, who was texting and sneaking covert glances at the two men.

Derek double-parked, turned on the flashers, and walked around the hood of the car to her door. Arden heard him give a sharp whistle to get Emma's attention. "Open the door."

Emma snapped to, unlocked the building's door, and when she opened it, Derek opened the car door. Arden was out, across the sidewalk, and into the building with a grace and speed that would have made her mother proud. She took the stairs to the second-floor offices and unlocked them herself.

The room was an open floor plan, modeled after the trading floor she was used to. Her desk was in the middle of the space, with Emma's to the right. Three glass-walled conference rooms lined the windows overlooking Hudson Street. The room smelled musty, and dust had gathered on the surfaces. She set her bag on her chair and turned to face the people who'd followed her up the stairs.

"Good morning, Agent Logan. How can we help you?" Arden said to Special Agent Logan, as if she hadn't run into him in his wife's shop, as if he hadn't walked through the front door of her family estate wearing a gun and a bulletproof vest. Reality tilted slightly, and she tightened her grip on the back of the chair.

"I need the foundation's financial records," he said, and handed what she assumed was a subpoena to Neil. He opened it and began reading.

"For which dates and accounts?" Arden said.

"All of them," Logan said.

Arden looked at Neil. They'd talked about this in the shattered days after the raid. He'd looked through them, Arden had reviewed them, but they weren't about to hand over anything until asked. Neil nodded.

"Emma," Arden said quietly. Her assistant sat down at her desk and started transferring files from the foundation's servers to a memory stick Logan handed her. Arden also sat down and started pulling grant applications. Turning over the records didn't affect the foundation's operating schedule. The process was all online, requiring documentation that had to be checked before a decision was made to fulfill the grant. She would ask Emma to do that from home and see if they could answer some of the immediate requests in the interim.

While Emma waited for the files to transfer, Arden looked around the office. The walls were lined with pictures of the lives changed through the foundation's work. While many nonprofits like theirs chose global initiatives, Arden's mother and Arden both chose to focus on problems closer to home. Inner-city education, health, hunger, homelessness were all topics near and dear to her mother's heart. The great-granddaughter of a settlement house founder, she'd learned to consider her work a continuation of her family's legacy.

The photos on the walls were of inner-city kids clutching schoolbooks and notebooks. Teens with college-acceptance letters and stars in their eyes. Families growing their own food in gardens started in neighborhoods where obesity rates soared due to lack of access to fresh vegetables and fruits. Asbestos and lead-paint-removal projects shouldered up against pictures of her mother, Arden in the background, with the politicians claiming responsibility for clean air and water legislation. MacCarren Foundation had done good in the world, decades of good.

She couldn't lose this. If she faced facts, MacCarren was gone. But the foundation could live on, could be the legacy that redeemed their name.

"All done," Emma said. She gave Arden a quick look, then offered the memory stick to Agent Logan.

"Thank you," he said gravely, gave them a small nod. "I'll let myself out."

"How's Aunt Lyd?" Neil asked after he left.

"Not well, but I finally reached Garry. He'll be home in a couple of days."

"That's good news," Neil said. "I'll call you later. I'm due at a deposition."

When he'd left, she turned to Emma. "I'll contact our outstanding requestors and update them on the situation. In the meantime, I'd like you to take some of the off-cycle grant requests home with you and do the due diligence on their supporting materials. The ones that pass muster, please send me for review."

"About that," Emma said. "I've found another job."

So that's what her assistant had been doing with her paid two-week vacation, as well as flying somewhere she could get a deep tan. A flush stood high on her cheeks. She wore vintage Chanel ballet flats and a Trademark shift dress, and the gold medallion with her initials on it. Arden had a similar necklace, with her own initials, back in her jewelry box. The daughter of one of her mother's friends, Emma was working for the foundation to gain experience and firm up her connections. Arden often hired the daughters or sisters (and in one very memorable, successful case, the son) of friends for that very reason. She'd been in a position to gift favors, and did so happily.

"I see," Arden said. "May I ask where?"

Emma glanced down at her outfit.

"Ah. Well, fashion really is your first love," she said. "It was time for you to move on, anyway. You're ready. You'll do well there."

She'd chosen a good time to leave, when Emma still had people's sympathy, but not staying so long people began to doubt her. She always asked the departing assistant for a recommendation for her replacement, a schoolmate, a friend at loose ends with a drive for philanthropy, a sister or cousin. This time she didn't ask.

Emma worked her keys off the ring, then handed over her

employee badge. Her computer was already sitting on the desk. She'd come prepared.

"Thanks," Emma said awkwardly. "I learned a lot from you."

"I'm glad," Arden said. "I wish you all the best."

She stayed in the empty office the rest of the afternoon, tidying things, gathering what she needed into boxes and onto her computer. She sat at her desk and drew the office as it was, empty, quiet, desolate, and wondered what would become of her if she lost this, too. The sun was setting when she texted Derek to meet her out front; she'd have some boxes to transport. He carried them down the steps and stacked them in the back of the SUV, then escorted her into the backseat.

"Just stack them in the foyer," she said when they arrived at the town house. "I'll carry them upstairs. Thank you."

He stacked the boxes neatly along the wall where Seth usually propped his bike. Arden made a mental note to move them.

"Why haven't you quit?" she said baldly. "Emma did today."

He looked at her. "I've worked for your family for a long time," he said finally. "I was in your dad's security detail when you had the panic attack at work."

"I remember," she said. She'd done without a driver before the panic attack, no security at all. Just a doorman and relative anonymity. But after that, after her heart started to race while she was driving, after crossing a street made her light-headed, using a driver made sense. Protected her. Derek was preternaturally quiet, big, and faded into the background. He protected her without seeming to protect her.

"I've seen a lot over the years. You can't work this close to people and not see things. Your dad usually forgot we were around. You don't."

Tears sprang to her eyes. The few friends she had left meant the world to her now. The ones who stayed by her through this.

"Thank you," she said, wondering at the helplessness of the words. They meant everything and were overused to the point of meaninglessness. "Thank you."

"You're welcome," he said. "Sure you don't want some help getting the boxes upstairs?"

"No," she said. "I can manage them. Enjoy your evening. I don't think I'll need you tomorrow."

"Just text me if you do. Arm the security system when I leave," he said, and closed the front door behind him.

She keyed in the code to set the system, then wondered when she'd next leave the town house. She traded her suit for faded jeans and a tunic. Fall was here, the highs barely reaching the sixties, darkness claiming the day earlier and earlier with each passing week.

The records were all in paper form; shifting the foundation's process to paperless technology was on her list of things to do in the upcoming off-cycle, so she spent an hour carrying the boxes into the dining room, poured herself a glass of wine, and opened the one labeled *off-cycle requests*. Emma was efficient; they were stacked in the order received and complete, with the incomplete requests at the back of the pile. Only after she was halfway through did she think to check the submissions in-box.

Request withdrawn.

There were several, no, a dozen, nearly twenty in the in-box. All polite, thanking the foundation for the consideration, but given the "uncertainty," they'd prefer to find funding elsewhere. *Uncertainty. Instability. Current situation.* Like the MacCarren Foundation was a third world country the State Department had issued a travel warning for.

New first order of business: sort through the applications to find the ones still willing to ask her for money. She did that and ended up with basically even stacks, one of withdrawn requests, the other still interested, or at least who hadn't actively withdrawn their request. She considered the files, and for the first time, wondered whether she should admit defeat.

No. Admitting defeat would mean giving up the last vestige of the life she had, the influence and good MacCarren money could do in the world. Right now it felt like all she had left.

The town house's solid walls and sound-deadening windows muffled most outside noise. She could hear her own breathing, the shallow inhales, the huffed exhales. The sturdy rope of her life's work she'd planned to cling to through the coming months now as tenuous as a cheap string.

Something about the angles of the files, stacked somewhat haphazardly, interested her. She got out her sketchbook and drew the files and her open laptop, practicing the vanishing point, letting her mind drift as twilight absorbed the light in the room. She was checking out, and she knew it, thinking about what she'd draw to put in the end-of-class show, rather than the shambles her life had become. But the computer and files, each nearly pristine, gave her only surfaces to draw, lacking a depth to draw her deeper into the subject, into herself.

Her phone vibrated beside her. She glanced at it, and saw a text from Seth on the home screen.

You home?

"Ask and ye shall receive," she said with a little laugh.

Yes. Why?

Look out your window.

She set her pencil in the sketchbook and closed it, then walked over to the wall of windows in the front formal reception room and peered through the edge of the drawn curtains to look down on the street below. The paparazzi were still there, although fewer in number. Manhattan was still there, something she didn't take for granted. Bewildered, she scanned the people on the street, and picked out Seth, almost out of her range of vision, leaning against his bike, messenger bag slung over his shoulder, his helmet in one hand, phone in the other.

I see you. She sent the text. He looked up, but didn't wave. She appreciated the discretion.

Dinner?

I'd like that.

Any recommendations? I don't know this neighborhood.

She didn't want healthy. She wanted junk food, pure and simple.

Marco Polo does a decent pizza.

He clapped the helmet on his head and buckled it one-handed, then disappeared down the street. The sun set while he was gone, and the photographers called it a night as a group, walking in the direction of the buses running down Fifth Avenue. In a couple of minutes, the street was empty. Seth was still her secret.

She tidied up the files, and had opened a bottle of wine when the doorbell rang. She opened it to find Seth leaning against the doorjamb, a pizza box balanced on one hand, the helmet dangling from the other. He looked at her through his eyelashes, a smile curling one corner of his mouth. It took a moment for the shoe to drop—the sexy smile, the pizza in his hand, his ability to adapt on the fly to whatever role-playing game suited the moment—but when it did, laughter riding a very fine line between amusement and hysteria pealed from her throat. She choked it back, because all she needed was a picture or video of her laughing going viral. *Arden MacCarren, enjoying life while thousands suffer.*

Seth's smile softened into a real one. "They're gone," he said. "Your pizza, ma'am."

She swallowed hard, dug her fingernails into her palms, and fought off the panic. It was so close, scratching at the underside of her skin, fighting to be free. "I'm not sure I have enough money to pay for it."

"We can work something out," he said, and rolled his bike through the open front door.

The pie was from a quintessential New York pizza place that sold slices and whole pies, garlic knots, bottled soda, and not much else. It smelled fantastic—basic mozzarella, tomato sauce, and a worthless carb white-flour crust. For the first time in recent memory, her stomach growled.

"Sounds urgent," Seth said, and spun the box around and onto the dining room table.

"What can I get you to drink?" she asked from the kitchen.

"I'm good," he said, following her into the kitchen, and pulled a six-pack of beer out of his messenger bag. They were still sweating, so he must have picked them up from one of the grocery stores on Lex or Second. She turned the oven on to warm while he put the beer in the fridge, keeping one back for now. She got two plates down from the rack hanging over the sink, and poured herself a glass of wine while he slid a piece onto her plate, two onto his. A quick rummage in the fridge brought out a container of Caesar salad and another of fruit. Napkin and glass in hand, she followed him back into the dining room.

He held up his bottle of beer. She tapped her glass to it, then bit off the tip of her piece. He folded his in half, New York–style, and did the same, decimating nearly a third of the slice.

"I didn't get a chance to grab lunch," he said when he swallowed.

"Me, either," she said. "I'm surprised to see you here."

He smiled at her. "I was riding by and saw your light on. It was a whim."

– ELEVEN –

Arden fiddled with the edge of her napkin and sipped her wine, her eyes dark and conflicted. For a moment Seth wondered if being a whim bothered her, then set it aside. If he had to guess, he'd say she was both surprised and touched that he'd stopped by out of the blue. No guess at all, she was definitely on edge.

"I like being your whim," she said lightly.

He glanced at the files and laptop at the other end of the table. "Bringing work home?"

"In a manner of speaking," she said.

"Want to talk about it?"

"I'd really rather eat this pizza and forget about it," she said.

And why would she assume he'd be able to help her? He was a bike messenger, a former Marine, a guy who modeled nude for money. She had no reason to assume he'd be anything more than a distraction. Anyway, it didn't matter. He had obligations. Responsibilities. No room in his life for another one.

"Tell me about your day," she said.

He mentally ran through the deliveries. All over Manhattan, one in Queens, a couple across the bridge into Brooklyn. "I spent the day playing in traffic," he said easily.

She smiled. "Is that what you call it?"

"Among other things," he said.

"Why work as a bike messenger?"

Unbidden, Phil's question came to his mind: *This is what you're doing with your life?* But Arden's words were tinged with curiosity, not judgment. "I like being outside. I like the rush of riding in Manhattan traffic. I like the challenge of pitting myself against the clock, the traffic, my own endurance."

It was the truth. He did like that, but it sounded shallow in this context. Chasing a rush when he was a Marine meant something. Chasing one alone, even with the motivation of the people left behind, sounded different. He'd never wanted to be alone, but this was the way his life turned out.

"Another slice?"

"I'll get it," he said, but she took his plate and got up. "You're not afraid of the traffic?" she said from the kitchen. He heard the box scrape against the oven rack, then her hissed breath just before pizza hit the plate.

She came around the corner with three slices steaming on the plate and a second beer in hand, pausing to transfer one piece from his plate to hers and hand him the beer. He blew on the melting cheese, then folded the slice double, taking the time he needed to chew to think about his answer. "I am, but I'm not. Fear is a warning, not a command. Respect the situation. Pay attention. Only fools don't feel fear. Courage isn't the absence of fear. It's feeling the fear and doing whatever impossible task is in front of you anyway."

She thought about this as she finished her first slice, then arranged the second neatly on her plate. "Give me examples."

He really didn't want to talk about it, but there was something else behind this. "Like walking point on a patrol into a wadi you know is riddled with insurgents. Like driving down a road you know was mined last week. Like going door-to-door in a village never knowing if a sniper's got a bead on you from a window across the street. Like getting into a Humvee knowing the road was mined last week, and driving on it regardless."

It was more than he'd talked to anyone besides Phil since he got out. He hadn't had to explain this to anyone. The people he knew and loved already knew all of this.

"And riding in Manhattan traffic compares to that?"

"No," he said frankly. "But it's the best I've got."

"Why are you here, not back in Wyoming? Don't you have family there?"

He couldn't tell her about dust, how little there was of it in Manhattan, how dusty country roads were. "My parents are there. I'm an only child. One of my friends who died left behind his kid brother, who was also a Marine. He's having trouble adjusting to civilian life."

"Phil," she said. "The guy you were going to the movies with."

He nodded, on the verge of telling her about Brittany and Baby B, but something stopped him. He didn't want to be that guy, the wounded one who got the big eyes and the soft, patting hands, and the whispers. He'd been a part of something special, a kind of bond that nothing, not even death, could break. Most people couldn't even begin to comprehend what he'd had, what he'd lost, what he was determined to honor.

"You have responsibilities," she said quietly. "I get that."

They finished the rest of the meal in silence. "Do you have anything going on tonight?" He shook his head. "Can I?" she asked, glancing at the ceiling where, above them, her easel was always set up in the living room now.

"Sure."

He started unbuttoning his shirt, but she stopped him. "I want something different this time," she said. "Can you do something Marine-ish?"

"Marine-ish?" he said, humor fizzing in his veins. It felt good. Light.

"I don't know what I want," she said. "Something you'd do, a pose you'd hold, a way you'd sit or stand or whatever."

"You really don't know anything about the military, do you?" he said.

"Not a thing," she said ruefully. "Show me."

A faint ping went off on his internal radar, not a siren blaring, just a ping he couldn't shake that faded into the silence. He watched her, but the radar swept around, giving back a clear screen. Then he got to his feet and took the stairs to the second floor, where Arden lived and slept. He could feel her behind him, like he used to feel Manny at his back as he guarded their backs. The hair on his nape lifted, but he kept on moving until he stood in the small space made by rearranged furniture, then he did something he hadn't done for months. He came to attention.

Heels together, toes apart, legs straight but not locked because locking his knees ensured he'd pass out in formation. Every recruit learned that in a week or so, either from personal experience or from watching the poor fuck who did pass out. Stomach in, shoulders back and down, but chest not puffed out, elbows slightly bent, fingers curled, thumb aligned with the side seam of his pants. Chin lifted, thousand yard stare, and just like that, he was back in his body, hearing.

His heart did a jittery little dance in his chest, cha-cha-cha-ing against his breastbone like automatic fire. He was aware of Arden in his peripheral vision, hand moving in the rough scribbles of gesture drawing, fluid movements contrasting with the bony angles she shouldn't have, cheekbones and collarbones and wristbones, her hair like gold in the setting sunlight.

"It's too formal. Too distant," she said distractedly. "Too still."

He tried to remember that she had no idea what this meant, what coming to attention meant to him, the thousands and thousands of times he'd done it, how deeply it was carved into his bones.

She looked up, tucked her hair behind her ear, leaving a smudge of charcoal on her ear. "You're not here," she said. "Where do you go?"

Except he was. "Back," he said. Why was he answering her questions?

She stepped out from behind the easel and circled him, pacing slowly, stopping to look at the arrangement of his shoulders and spine. The sword burned down his back, a leftover sense memory from getting the tattoo. He'd thought nothing would ever feel that alive again.

"Back where? Boot camp?"

"No." Stop answering these questions. "Morning roll call."

"What's that?"

"Every morning and evening we'd muster for roll call."

"So they'd know if you were there?"

Ignore the amusement in her voice. She doesn't know.

Because the whole mattered more than the individual parts. He'd surrendered himself to the mission, the brotherhood, and the pain of missing it bloomed sharp and metallic in his mouth. As if he'd bitten into metal. "It imposes order. Sets you to military time and military life. Doesn't matter if you came in off patrol two hours earlier. You get up and answer roll call."

His voice wasn't his voice. Did it always sound like that, or was his hearing still off?

"Where would you go? Oh. AWOL? Surely not in Afghanistan."

People did all kinds of crazy things in war zones. What kept you there, what kept him there, were the other members of his platoon. Letting down your buddies was a sin worse than death. "Nowhere to go," he said, then cleared the quiver from his voice.

Still behind him, she said, "May I?"

He gave a jerky nod, like his chin would meet the stiff upright collar of his dress uniform if he nodded too deeply. The next thing he felt was her palms on his shoulder blades. They rested there, tentative, pressed, thumbs and fingers seeking the edge of bone and muscle, the dip into his spine, then down and around to his ribs. She did it again, her breathing even and unaware. He swallowed, feeling an indescribable tension as his body and mind struggled to be in two places at once.

"Where are you?" she asked, her voice light even, fading into the background of waning light.

He was back at the roll call after the IED. It was tradition. Even though everyone knew Manny, Doug, and Brian were dead, and half the people in the room had picked up body parts and pieces of their kits, tradition held that their names were called at the next roll. That's when it felt real to him. Hearing their names, then their ranks, and his own voice saying, *Lance Corporal Dorhaus is no longer with us. Lance Corporal Gibson is no longer with us. Corporal Lopez is no longer with us.*

That was his right, his responsibility, his role as the person left behind. Not the gunny's. Not the LT's. His. His voice, saying what had to be said. That's what you could do with words, but how did you draw absence? How did you depict what wasn't there? Three human lives snuffed out, and no way to show it.

That's when the silence started, the silence that was flickering off and on like a poorly tuned radio, even in this room, the absence of even his voice now. Her fingers curled around his ribs, no more than heat and faint pressure, but he had no doubt they were the only thing keeping him on his feet. He had sixty pounds on her, probably more, and a few inches, but she was holding him up.

He inhaled. His body betrayed him into breathing, into taking what it needed to fill his blood with oxygen to deliver to the cells. She stepped back, and he found he could indeed stand. Even in failure, he still stood.

"Give me something else," she said. "Less rigid."

The next breath shuddered into the air. He made a big show of rolling his shoulders, cracking his spine side to side, then shut off his brain and found himself dropping to one knee. He used to wear kneepads to protect his knees from hard surfaces, rocks, shrapnel left in the dirt; Arden's carpet served the same purpose. His arms and shoulders curved into position around the imaginary weapon cradled in his arms.

"Interesting," she said.

He could feel the nearly eight pounds of rifle in his arms. He'd lived with it for so long, carried it everywhere, and when he wasn't carrying it, it was within arm's reach at all times. He could field-strip and reassemble it in less than twenty-five seconds, insert clips and clear obstructions with his eyes closed. Left elbow on left knee, left hand supporting the barrel, right hand curled around the grip, finger on the trigger. Head tilted, cheek pressed into warm metal, eye aligned with the sight and squinting under the visor of his helmet. Dirt and hills in front of him, not an upscale apartment, no leather purse on a table in the hallway, money and girl gear spilling out of the open top. His shoulder automatically adjusted for the kick. His bones and muscles settled into a new formation, one as utterly familiar as attention. All imaginary, all more real to him than the floor under his knee.

He'd drawn it again and again, trying to capture what couldn't be held.

"May I?" she said again.

He wondered what it was about him that was telegraphing *do not touch* signals, but at some level he recognized she was doing the right thing. He nodded, felt the stock push against his cheek. He held nothing. His arms curved around fucking air, but he could feel metal against his face.

This time she laid her hands on top of his shoulders, resting them there for a few seconds before squeezing gently. "They're different, and not just because the pose is different."

"You give it nowhere to kick," he said. "You absorb each recoil."

"That's not what I'm looking for, either," she said after a few seconds.

He wasn't sure how he felt about her shopping through his poses, his body, like she was trying on clothes.

"What are you looking for," he snapped as he straightened.

"I'll know it when I see it," she said mildly.

Hands on his hips, he glared at her. She wasn't flinching from him. Somewhere in there was a woman who routinely dealt with, or stood up to, men being men. Swearing, sweating, flailing, yelling, throwing things, losing their cool spectacularly, Arden had seen it all. That strength was there, under the pale skin and the shadowed eyes.

"Fuck," he muttered.

"Not yet," she said. "Give me something else."

"For someone who won't show me what she draws, you've turned into quite an *artiste*," he said, giving the final word the derisive drawl it deserved.

"Maybe I'm an *artiste*," she said, with a French pronunciation, "and the rest of it is all crap."

He stared at her, waiting for her, no, willing her to tell him what she was keeping hidden. She stared back, then looked away. "Something else," she said.

Impatient, tired, and still back in Afghanistan, he walked over to the wall that separated her bedroom from the living area, put his back to it, and slid down until his butt rested just above his heels. Forearms on knees, hands dangling in space in front of him, he let his head rest against the wall and closed his eyes.

"That's really interesting," she said, mostly to herself.

With his artist's mind he took himself out of his body and considered the pose. Lots of U-turns, knees to hips and up the spine. The folds of his cargo pants, the line of his throat emerging from the collar of his shirt. Hands dangling into space, deceptively innocent, up close a great exercise in drawing negative space.

"Why that pose? Why is it different?"

She was asking herself, and him. She'd form her own answers as she drew. He didn't need to answer her. He did. "After a patrol, we'd come back to the base and hunker down behind a wall of sandbags, smoke, decompress," he said, realizing even as he spoke that he felt not smooth drywall but the uneven, rounded protrusions of stacked sandbags.

"So this isn't pure Marine," she said.

She was already drawing, pencil moving swiftly and smoothly over the paper. The sound was unmistakable, somewhere between a gliding scratch and a rasping glide. He kept not looking at her, and as long as he didn't look at her, he could see the ghosts in the room. Manny to his left, Doug and Brian to his right. Always the same order. Doug and Brian both chewed dip, shared their cans with each other. The day before they died, Brian offered Doug his last lipful. Doug refused it. *Fuck you, I'm not taking your last dip.* They'd split it, Manny offering a steady stream of chick-flick commentary about grand gestures and true love, Seth just happy to be there, just happy to be alive. He'd pull out his sketchbook and start drawing.

The sense memory was so vivid he almost reached into his right cargo pocket.

This was pure Marine for him. This was what it meant to be a Marine. Manny's shoulder pressed to his—the only way he'd take comfort—Brian's compulsive *'Scuse me* every time he farted, Doug's detailed retelling of Phil's latest act of bravery. The way they watched over his shoulder as he drew. The way they pointed out things, learned to see the way he saw, bringing him interesting bits of debris.

Arden had gone silent, lost in the drawing. As the minutes passed, he realized he'd inadvertently given her the pose he found easiest to sink into and hardest to bear. He tried to sort through the conflicting, confusing emotions. He was lonely, but so what? Aside from a few years in the Corps, he'd been lonely all his fucking life, the only child of parents caught up in their own lives. It wasn't that. There was a ringing wrongness to holding this pose, so loud he was surprised she couldn't hear it. Feel it. He shouldn't be here. In this apartment. With this woman, sure, but he wasn't supposed to be here at all. He was supposed to be with them, and he wasn't, and it was impossible to take.

She peered out from behind the easel, startling him, then came to stand in front of him. He looked up at her.

"May I?" she asked softly.

Another quick, jerky nod, although he had no fucking clue what she was going to do. Or why she would do it. She went to her knees in front of him and sat back on her heels, then reached out and put her hands on his thighs, behind the spot where his forearms rested on his knees. Slowly, she slid her palms down his thighs to the join with his hips, her thumbs coming to rest on his cock. She wasn't trying to turn him on or feel him up; after a pause, her hands glided up his torso to his shoulders. Another pause, then they continued to cup his jaw. She was staring at him, studying him, her gaze restively curious.

She turned his head slightly to one side, then the other. "You have different tan lines," she said.

"The bike helmet straps are different from the combat helmet straps," he said, curtly, trying to close a barn door when the horse was out and in the next county. Arden was in. Whether she knew it or not—and he prayed she didn't—she was in.

"*Hmm,*" she said, and went back to drawing. She drew for what felt like hours, but based on the incremental changes in the sun was probably less than the forty-minute sits at a drawing class. "That's all," she said finally, distantly.

He straightened, slotting his spine and hips back into place. She stretched, too, fingers woven together above her head, up on tiptoes, side to side. Her back cracked and popped. She was looking at him, but he couldn't read the look in her eyes. Desire? Maybe. Curiosity? Definitely. Sympathy? Unbearable.

He couldn't do it. Memories crowded close, and suddenly he couldn't bring himself to touch her, to be touched, so he started moving toward the door. "See you tomorrow?" he said to cover the fact that he was all but fleeing her house.

"Unfortunately, no," she said. "I'm going to spend the day with my mother. I won't be back in time for class."

"Oh," he said. "Okay."

"Good night, Seth," she said. She didn't say anything more, just followed him down the stairs, opened her wallet, counted out the twenties, and handed them to him. His fingers brushed hers when he took them, the brief contact electric, tingling.

He gave her a wordless nod, trundled his bike out the front door and down the steps to street level, then fled.

Only when he was biking across the bridge did he wonder why she'd been so quiet. This should be no big deal, using stances drilled bone-deep in his body as fodder. He was her muse, helping her learn. But somehow this had become about him, not just

Arden. Not the sex—he swerved around a truck emerging from an alley, ignored the honk and yell—okay, maybe the sex started it. Maybe it was the combination of sex and drawing, the sex the bold foundational lines, the framework to contain the more subtle elements, the shading, the texture, the negative space inside every human soul.

What seemed like a simple thing to do for others had started to work away inside him. Without his knowledge, let alone his consent, whatever this thing with Arden was it wasn't just about her anymore. It was about him.

He rode to Brooklyn, let himself into the motor home, and paced the short, narrow hallway for a minute. The sketchbook in his closet all but glowed in the fucking dark, like he should toss the one in his pocket and pick up the one he'd set aside while it was still damp with blood. Draw what he could to fill the gap in his life.

That was a hopeless task. Nothing could fill this emptiness, no drawing, not even if he had a hundred years and the skill of a draftsman. He was just a grunt who liked to draw knights and dragons, who knew that dreams of quests were nothing more than entertainment. To shake it off, he reached instead for his phone, sent another text to Ryan Hamilton, and to his shock, got three dots and an immediate response. I'm fine. Thx for checking in. Just off the grid for a while.

Relieved, he pulled up his recent calls, tapped Phil's name, then sat down on the bench seat, and cradled his head in his hands. When Phil answered, he said, "Do you miss it?"

"Fuck, no," Phil said, amused, knowing exactly what he meant. The background noise, music, laughter, conversation, sounded like a party. Then the noise quieted. Seth heard the flick of a lighter and a quick draw. "All the time. Every fucking second of every fucking day."

"Yeah," Seth said. "It was miserable. The suck. Some days I'd do anything to go back."

"So go back."

He thought of the people who weren't there anymore, and the people here he owed. "I can't."

Another inhale. Seth heard a door open, then close. "How are you?" Phil asked.

No way was Doug's brother supposed to be checking up on him. That was his job, not Phil's. "Fine," Seth said. "Working. I sleep fine; I'm eating. Working."

"Let's try that again, without the bullshit. How are you?"

"It wasn't bullshit," Seth said, thinking back less than an hour to his session with Arden, the way he bolted afterward. The press of his nearly empty sketchbook against his thigh as he hunkered down in her living room. "I'm fine," he said, heard his voice grow stronger before the silence rushed in again, nearly drowning his final words. "There's nothing wrong with me."

—TWELVE —

A rden woke early on Sunday morning. The plan was to be in East Hampton for brunch around eleven, but the advantage to insomnia and bad dreams was being up early enough to beat traffic. She texted Derek, asking him if he'd mind leaving earlier, not expecting a response at this hour. She pulled on a robe and padded into the kitchen, too tired to yawn. She started the water for the French press coffee, and her phone vibrated in her hand.

Sure. What time?

Pick me up at 8.

She stepped into the shower more to wake up than to get clean, towel-dried her hair, then pulled on a pair of khaki pants and a sleeveless linen top. The pants were loose on her hips, so she added a belt and a pair of worn brown leather sandals, her go-to favorites. The coffee she poured into two travel mugs just as Derek texted he was turning the corner.

She should have looked outside before she opened the town house door, but she didn't. One second she was standing on the landing outside her front door, the next the world splintered into shards of images and sounds, photographers crowding forward, shouting her name, blocking her path to the street at the same time tires screeched and a horn blared on Fifth Avenue, then the sound of a thud she knew in her bones, metal hitting the human body, a hoarse cry. Her hand flew up to protect her head, her heart rate soared, her vision tunneled, and her knees buckled. The energy emanating from the paparazzi took on a fierce glee; they crowded closer, *what's happening why are you fainting Arden are you sick Arden does your family make you sick now.*

Then a hand closed around her upper arm and hauled her both upright and through the crowd, knocking people to the side. Both travel mugs tumbled to the sidewalk. Arden barely held on to her purse as Derek, using his body as a shield, shoved her into the backseat. The slamming car door missed her foot by an inch. An intrepid soul hauled open the other passenger door and shoved a camera into the space. She recoiled, the body and camera were hauled back, and that door slammed. Derek all but hurled himself into the driver's seat, slammed the door, and hit the locks.

"Jesus fucking Christ," he said, then hit the horn loud and long.

"It was a pedestrian. Someone hit a pedestrian," she whispered. "I heard it. I heard the cab hit her."

Flashes went off, visible even through the tinted windows. Bodies blocked the windshield, cameras hoisted, their shouts muffled into a dull roar. The engine revved up. She could see the needle spiking hard to the right. Photographers scattered like birds, their fists hitting the sides of the vehicle in frustration, or anger. Derek roared down the street, away from the horde. The last thing Arden saw was the Ciao Bella Gelato sign before Ninety-second Street tunneled to black.

Someone was saying her name. MacCarren. *Ms. MacCarren.*

"Arden!"

Derek. She was shaking, sweating, and her stomach, which had nothing in it except two swallows of coffee, lurched sickeningly. "I'm okay," she whispered. "I'm okay. I'm okay."

It was a litany, a prayer, one she recognized from the moments after the cab struck her, when the world was a dizzying spray of streetlights and lit windows and shouts. The doormen from the building she'd been hit in front of, crouching over her, yelling at the cabdriver, hovering in the background. *I'm okay. I'm okay. I'm okay.*

Except she wasn't okay. Broken shoulder and collarbone. Torn ligaments, a shattered knee, a moderate concussion. Blood trickling down the side of her face. She felt no pain, was crawling like a wounded animal in the middle of the street, trying to get away. *I'm okay. I'm okay.*

She looked down at her hands. A bit of coffee had splashed from the open spout onto her chinos. Her purse, which had been dangling from her elbow, lay on the seat beside her, phone and red leather journal disturbingly close to spilling out. "Where's my coffee?" she said stupidly.

"You dropped the mugs," Derek said. "I thought, under the circumstances, I'd leave 'em."

"I'm okay," she said. She would not burst into tears. "Did they see?"

"I got you into the car before you . . . I don't think they saw." Derek's eyes flashed to hers in the rearview mirror. "You really should think about hiring more security. A bodyguard."

She would not, under any circumstances, erect another barrier between her and life. "I'm sorry. Dealing with this isn't part of your job description."

He shrugged. "No skin off my nose," he said.

"Thank you," she said again. "Have you had breakfast?"

"No," he said.

He was changing his answer. She could tell. Maybe he'd eaten. Maybe he had plans to eat lunch in East Hampton after he left her at the house. Derek was a local and knew all the best greasy spoon diners. But he'd said no, and she'd asked, and she was grateful to him.

"Let me buy you breakfast," she said. "For getting you out of bed so early."

He pulled over and double-parked in front of a deli, then turned on the flashers. "I'll get it," he said. "What do you want?"

She handed him yet another twenty. "A bagel with lox and cream cheese," she said. She wasn't sure if her stomach could handle anything else. "Another coffee, too, please."

He came back with a full white paper sack, handing her sandwich back to her without ceremony. Her heart was jittering six different directions in her chest. Hands shaking, she shoved her phone back in her purse, but set the journal on her lap and dug around for her pencil bag. After Seth left the night before, she'd started to rough out her drawing for the show at the end of class. The Marine-ish poses had been the breakthrough, the insights into Seth's character he'd never shown her before. She had a better understanding of the impulse behind everything he did, enough to feel she could perhaps draw something worth showing.

Except that wasn't the right way to approach it. Her fingers doodled Seth's hands, dangling in space. She got the impression they weren't often empty, held a gun or a pen or a piece of equipment, and the emptiness seemed wrong. Was he holding on to something that wasn't there anymore, refusing to let go of what he needed to leave?

When she looked up from the sketchbook, they were in the heart of East Hampton, driveways curving back to shingled houses set back from the road on green-velvet lawns and protected by thick privet hedges, then into the dead-end roads lined with trees leading to "beach houses" backing to the ocean. Derek pulled through another, smaller cluster of paparazzi, neatly contained at the gates by two suited men.

With the fainting episode outside her town house, she'd just handed the paparazzi another excuse to dig into her life, extend the MacCarren news cycle another day, or longer. The panic attack on the trading floor wasn't news, but someone would remember, when prompted. They'd use this as an excuse to dig deeper into her family's history, expose what little they had left to the world, dig out the cabdriver who hit her, the doormen who protected her on the street, the EMTs, doctors, and they'd all talk . . .

Derek braked to a halt beside the house. Tufts of beach grass sprouted from the sand piled against the weathered fence. Beyond that, the beach was empty, secured in all likelihood by more of the suited men at the gates. The ocean was a sullen gray, matching the sky. Arden got out of the SUV and hitched her bag higher onto her elbow.

"When should I come back and get you?"

"I'm not sure," she said. She needed to stay strong for her mother, but she already felt a quart low, and it wasn't even ten in the morning. "I thought I'd stay through dinner."

"But you plan to go back to the city tonight?"

"Yes. I'm not sure. Perhaps. I'm sorry," she added. She used to send Derek an hour-by-hour timetable for the week, with adjustments made on the fly, but very few of them.

"Not a problem. Fifteen minutes' notice and I'm here."

"Thank you," she said, then stopped Derek when he turned to circle the car. "Derek. Thank you. Your loyalty . . . right now . . . means so much to me."

He waved her off. "I'll wait until you're inside."

She crossed the parking area, skirting the six-car garage and taking the flagstone path to the multilayered deck at the back of the house. Through the kitchen window she could see Marla, the housekeeper, slicing fruit at the big island. Her mother was nowhere in sight. She looked around the compound, remembering the FBI vehicles parked in the driveway, the grass, blocking the garage doors, men and women in windbreakers tromping through the house, including Daniel Logan, handing her a search warrant, asking her and her mother to take the children upstairs while they ransacked her father's study, taking computers and God alone knew what else.

Her mother couldn't continue to live here much longer. Arden rapped on the sliding glass door hard enough to make her knuckles sting.

Marla wiped her hands on her uniform apron, removed the security stick from the track, and unlocked the door. "Miss Arden," she said.

"Hello, Marla," Arden replied, and set her purse on the opposite end of the rectangular granite-topped island. She inhaled a shaky breath and sat rather heavily on one of the barstools.

Other than Marla's local radio station, the house was eerily quiet. Normally her mother entertained here year-round, inviting relatives from out of state for sailing and beachcombing for weeks at a stretch, friends for days, business associates for weekend trips. The compound had eleven bedrooms, a guest house on the property, and another smaller beach house around the point. On a typical Sunday, for brunch Marla would supervise three kitchen helpers and servers, serving buffet-style. Today the house was completely empty.

"Who's here?"

"Your mother," Marla said.

"No one else?"

"Miss Serena hasn't been back since the day of the raid," Marla said.

No one else. A month ago the house had been full of people, including Ryan Hamilton and some model he'd brought with him. Ryan Hamilton, who'd played them all so very well, sitting at their table, eating their food, sailing on the *Indomitable* with Grandpa and Arden, and all the while gathering information to bring them down. Expose them. "Did she go back to Greenwich?"

Charles's wife, Serena, was a Connecticut socialite who'd pursued Charles with exactly the right combination of interest and independence. She was a carbon copy of their mother, beautiful, elegant, interested in art and decorating, in charity causes and international travel. She'd spent two years gutting their apartment in the city and redecorating it, and four months choosing their private jet. When she did a thing, she did it well, which meant the divorce would be quick, severing Charles from her life, and the girls'.

"West Palm," Marla said, taking a cantaloupe from the fridge. "Her parents' place down there. Farther away from the press."

"Mom must be devastated." She lived and breathed her granddaughters' lives.

"I don't think she feels much at all right now," Marla said with the bluntness of a longtime family employee.

"Valium?"

"Among other things."

"Arden?"

Arden turned to find her mother standing at the foot of the stairs curving around to the second floor. The main floor of the house, broken only by the fireplace, was open on all four sides, the chimney rising through the second floor. Floor-to-ceiling windows on the south and west sides opened to the beach and the ocean beyond. Beyond the kitchen was an east-facing breakfast room, and a formal dining room that could seat thirty. The space was broken into different seating areas, one around a grand piano, another a cluster of overstuffed chairs around the fireplace.

Her mother shuffled slowly forward into the gray light, and Arden sucked in her breath. Her mother looked every single second of her fifty-seven years. More. Lines normally animated by laughter and the sheer delight of being alive now looked clawed into the skin around her eyes and mouth. Antianxiety medication reduced the energetic spring in her walk to an old woman's tentative step. She wore chic Chanel ballet flats, not slippers, but the moves were as tentative as her grandfather's shuffling down the nursing home hallway.

Raw emotion propelled her across the floor to sweep her mother into a hug. *"Shh,"* she said. "I'm here, Mom."

"Arden," she said again as she looked at her only daughter, then at Marla, then at the food. "Is it time for brunch?" she asked, her voice somewhere between its customary cheerfulness and a bewildered child's.

At that, Arden leaned back to better study her mother's face. Her pupils were the size of dinner plates, shock submerged under a tide of pharmaceuticals. She'd made the right decision, telling her mother to stay in East Hampton rather than returning to their Fifth Avenue apartment. There weren't enough drugs available legally to make her mother fit to cope with the city, the press, the publicity.

"Not yet, Mrs. MacCarren," Marla said gently. "I'm cutting the fruit. I'll start the eggs Benedict in a few minutes. Coffee?"

"Tea, I think. Let's go sit by the windows, Mom," Arden said.

Her mother looped her arm through Arden's and let her move

them to a cluster of wingback chairs overlooking the beach. Marla brought the tea tray, and left them.

"How are you?" Arden asked as she poured her mother a cup. Steam rose into the air, carrying a hint of chamomile.

"I'm awful," her mother said in a bewildered tone. "Really awful. They don't have words for this."

Arden huffed out a laugh. "I know."

"Serena left, with the girls."

"Marla told me."

"I miss them, but I can't leave your father right now. Serena wants me to. She wants me to cut off all contact with him, and with Charles, but I can't abandon my husband and son. She can. She can leave her husband, my son," she said, her voice tremulous, "take the girls, run away, but I'm not leaving my family, my home."

Arden made a noncommittal noise, and added cream and sugar to her mother's tea.

"Have you been to see your father?"

Her father and Charles had effectively shunted everyone else to the side: her mother, Serena, Arden herself. Garry was the only one who went voluntarily, fleeing the tight father-son duo for ranches on the other side of the continent, then the other side of the world.

Fury swarmed up her throat and down her spine. How like them, how fucking *like them*, to keep these secrets, then leave the second-class citizens of the family MacCarren to pick up the pieces. She swallowed hard, chased it with hot tea. "No, Mom," she said as gently as she could. "I'm not going to go see him. Or Charles. Neil's coming over for brunch. We'll talk to him about it then."

"He is?"

"Remember, Mom? I texted you."

"Oh."

Arden pulled out her phone to show her mother the string of

texts. Her mother nodded vacantly, then looked at the red leather notebook. "That's new?"

"Yes," Arden said, latching onto the familiarity of beautiful design and shopping. "I bought it earlier in the weekend," she said, leaving out the disastrous baby shower experience. "I'm taking a drawing class with Betsy."

"She's still speaking to you?"

"Of course she is. She's my best friend."

"Best friends don't steal their friends' fiancés."

The theft, such as it was, had happened five years earlier. Her mother wasn't quite with it at the moment. "She stole *a* fiancé, Mom," Arden said, trying to make light of it. "Just one. And I think he went willingly."

"Yours. Her best friend's."

Arden didn't say anything, just smoothed the cover of the journal with her hand. "He loves her in a way he didn't love me. Anyone who looks at them can see that. I want them to be happy."

"You never did fight for what was yours," her mother said. The drugs had loosened her tongue. Arden knew she'd thought these things but not said them. The teacup drooped, threatening to spill over the lip, onto her linen slacks. Arden took the cup and set it on the table between them.

"It was a fight I didn't want to win."

Her mother didn't say anything else, just held out her hand for the journal. Arden gave it to her, knowing her mother wouldn't actually see the drawings. "Very nice," she said.

"Thanks, Mom," Arden replied, recognizing her mother's standard response when something was subpar but social niceties prevented her from saying that. Her mother majored in art history and painting, a connection she shared with Serena. Arden's scribbles wouldn't attract her interest.

The front gate buzzed into the kitchen. Marla answered, then called, "Mr. Neil MacCarren's here."

Her mother's head turned vacantly toward Marla. "Thank you," Arden said.

By the time Neil appeared on the deck, dressed in khakis, an oxford, and a blazer, his canvas briefcase in hand, Arden had the door unlocked and open. He stepped through, smoothed his hair, and gave Arden a quick kiss on the cheek. He took her mother's hand. "Nice to see you, Aunt Lyd," he said.

"Any trouble at the gate?" Arden asked under her breath.

"I'm used to ignoring press hordes," Neil said, making light of it. "How are you?"

"Fine."

"Liar."

Arden looked at her mother, who'd wandered into the dining room. "I don't know. Still in shock, maybe? I keep waiting for anger to come, but so far it's just this weird combination of shock and disbelief," she said, editing out her final emotion. Desire, low-level and ever-present, simmering in her temples, her stomach, her sex. She thought of Seth, of the possibility of seeing him tonight, of what might happen after class. Heat flared in her cheeks. Discomfited, she looked away, adding, "My past isn't helping. It keeps ambushing me. Someone got hit by a car on Fifth just as I was leaving the town house today. I was in the car before the panic attack happened," she said when Neil's gaze sharpened.

He ran himself a glass of water from the fridge. "Feeling numb is fairly normal," he said. "It will pass."

"How do you know?"

"In my job, your worst day is my average day. I've seen this before. Not this close to home, not on this scale, but I've seen it."

"Great. How do I deal with it?"

He smiled at her, his wry, quirky grin as sharp as the rest of his angular face. "Get physical. Run. Box. Swim. After her mother died, a friend of mine used to buy plates at IKEA and break them."

She lifted an eyebrow at him.

"Seriously. Hit the gym."

"I can't hit the gym," she said. "Everyone with a cell phone will take a video of me falling on my ass in kickboxing and sell it."

"Get a personal trainer and someone to hang a bag in your house," he said. "Do something physical. It'll help."

"Brunch is ready, Miss Arden," Marla said.

The eggs Benedict with salmon was delicious, the fruit cut into identical pieces and served in cut-glass dishes. Neil cleaned his plate. Arden ate enough to make Marla nod with satisfaction. Her mother, already a proponent of Wallis Simpson's advice that you can never be too rich or too thin, picked at her food and stared out the window. When the meal was over, Marla cleared the dishes, served coffee and tea, and retreated to the kitchen.

Neil pulled out his laptop and a sheaf of papers. "I have good news and bad news. The good news is that I've looked through the details of the trust," he said. "Arden, I'll start with you. Your assets are distinct from your father's. The town house you live in is owned by the trust your grandfather set up. Your trust fund came from your grandfather and as such is separate from the current generation's . . . situation. As long as the investigation doesn't turn up proof that you knew about the fraud, you'll be fine."

She nodded. This was no better or worse than she'd expected. She had something, an education, a work history. She could and would work.

"Aunt Lyd," Neil said, then gently repeated her name, "your situation is different. Under the law, anything you owned jointly with Uncle Don is fair game to be confiscated and sold at auction to reimburse the victims. That means you're going to lose this house, the Fifth Avenue apartment, the house in Vail, the one in Palm Beach, and most of your assets."

Silence. "What can she keep?" Arden said, desperately searching for something positive in all of this.

"The truth is, not much. The trust that came from her parents is separate and fairly well-protected. Hollow Hill Farm is also separately deeded and managed. They can't seize it—"

"I'll lose everything. Cars. Jewelry. Art."

Her mother picked a fine time to get coherent. Neil nodded to each word. Arden reached across the table and gripped her mother's hand.

"The clothes off my back?"

"Possibly," Neil said.

Her mother went back to staring out the window of the house she'd loved more than any other she'd lived in.

"That leads me to the MacCarren Foundation."

"What about it?"

"The government is going to go after the endowment."

Her mother's eyes turned to Arden. "No," she whispered.

"Can they do that?" Arden demanded.

Neil fiddled with the papers. "They can. If nothing else, it makes them look like they're doing everything they can to get the money back for investors. They're already talking about filing lawsuits against everyone who knew your father well and withdrew their earnings, rather than reinvesting with your father."

"Arden, no," her mother whispered.

The foundation was her mother's pride and joy. Discovering that her life was a fraud had devastated her mother. Losing the foundation might destroy her.

"What can we do?" Arden asked. There had to be a way to fight this, not for her father's sake, but for her mother's.

"I don't know," Neil admitted. "All I know is that with hundreds of millions of dollars in the foundation's accounts, it's going to be a feeding frenzy."

Her mother was visibly agitated, tears trailing from her eyes. "The foundation?"

"Mom, why don't you go lie down for a little while? Neil and I will handle this."

She got her mother settled in the bedroom, tucking her in as she would tuck in one of her nieces during a sleepover treat with Aunt Arden. When she took off her mother's glasses, her mother peered farsightedly up at her and said, "Are you the best person to represent us? Arden, you were never the strongest child, and now . . ."

"Garry is on his way back from New Zealand," Arden said, knowing this would reassure her mother. She patted her shoulder, felt the fragile joint under the layer of cashmere blanket. "Don't worry, Mom."

She returned to the main floor. Neil had a second cup of coffee and was standing at the windows overlooking the windswept beach.

"How bad is it?"

"The foundation has been run with impeccable integrity since your mother started it decades ago, but the money your family donated was essentially taken from MacCarren investors. The precedents for this are few and far between. Legally, we can fight, but from a publicity standpoint . . ."

"We're going to look terrible."

"I'm thinking ahead. The case isn't at that stage yet. Everyone's still caught up in the criminal charges—who did what, who knew what and when. It's my job to think about you and Garry and Aunt Lyd. You have some decisions to make, and I want you to be prepared for them before it actually becomes a point of contention."

"Or a news story. Thanks, Neil."

"Now for the worst news," Neil said. Arden braced herself. "The special agent in charge notified us yesterday that if your mother doesn't move out voluntarily by the end of the month, they'll begin eviction proceedings."

"What happens then?"

"It could take a while, but if she refuses to leave, she'll be forcibly removed by the sheriff's department. She has no ground to stand on to keep this house, Arden. If she doesn't leave gracefully, under her own terms, it's going to be brutal, and ugly."

Visions of that publicity nightmare spun up in Arden's head. "I'll try to get her together," Arden said.

Neil nodded. "I'll let myself out."

She picked up her journal and crammed it back into her purse. Out on the water, the *Indomitable* drifted with the current. She was a beauty, a Herreshoff yacht bought eighty years ago and restored a couple of years ago. She would be sold, too, at auction.

Outside the door, Arden rubbed her forehead. She should be a good daughter and stay. But her mother was in no condition to talk, and if Arden stayed at Breakers Point, it would only solidify her mother's resistance to moving. And her skin felt too tight, her chest too small for her heart and lungs. Betsy had her sketchpad, an easel, pencils. Neil said to get physical.

And Seth would be there.

- THIRTEEN -

Sunday afternoon found Seth stretched out on the bed in the motor home, scrolling through the text messages on his phone, at war with himself. Habits were hard to break, and right now two different habits jostled for his attention. The newer habit was to saddle up and surrender himself to the city's ambient noise so he didn't have to listen to the silence in his head. But the delivery-service apps were all but dead, making it not worth his time to bike into Manhattan and wait for a job to appear. Normally he'd do it anyway, but today another, older habit knocked insistently at the door of his psyche.

He felt like drawing. His thumb chafed against the underside of his index and middle finger, the movement automatic for adjusting a pencil or pen. Details inside the motor home sharpened and faded. He recognized the signs, a pressure in his chest, a tension demanding release, and new signs as well. His skin felt too tight, like he was filling up with sketches demanding to get out. Right now his soul didn't seem to care if his mind said drawing was something he used to do.

Restlessly, he rolled over and plucked the new Moleskine from his cargo pants pocket, opened it to a clean page, then uncapped a Micron pen. Okay. So far so good. A quick dragon that came out a little like a chicken marching off in a huff, the lone knight fighting off the dragon he'd seen in the shop window in the West Village. Standard stuff for him. Easy.

Not right.

He dropped the pen into the crease in the notebook and scrubbed his hand over his face, reached for his phone again, intending to see if there was anything new in the world since he last skimmed the news websites three minutes earlier. The background screen on his phone caught his attention, the picture of the four of them; he picked out the details that made them a unit. Doug was easy, almost a caricature of a serviceman, but Seth never could quite get the set of Brian's jaw, the way he folded in on himself, all long legs and arms and angles out of geometry class, or the way Manny's personality flashed out of his eyes, even behind the shades and under the helmet. Despite seeing the picture dozens of times each day, despite drawing them hundreds of times over the years, he was losing their faces.

Determined to recommit them to memory, he tapped through to the actual picture in his camera roll and picked up the pen again. But his lines were off, failing to capture impulse behind the pose, all the little nuances that drew them together. The way Manny was looking away but every other sense totally attuned to them, Brian's Gumby-like limbs, Doug's easy grin, the one he so rarely saw on Phil's mouth.

"Fuck," he said, and tossed the pen at the sketchbook, talking to his muse as much as to himself. "What do you want from me?"

More.

Little zings through his arms and fingers accompanied this single word, audible through the static in his mind, drawing his eyes back to the sketch of the lone knight. It fit with his past work, except it didn't, and deep down he knew giving in to this impulse would set him on an unfamiliar road. Only when the tension became unbearable, immense and filled with static, did he roll over and pull a larger sketchpad and his box of pastels and pencils from one of the storage drawers under the bed. When he jostled the contents of the box, the corner of the unfinished Moleskine appeared, the edges of the pages saturated with dried blood.

Not now.

He pushed it to the back of the box and closed the drawer. With the pillows tucked at his back, he started to draw the details of the knight, bigger, the shoulders, the lifted chin, big eyes, a full mouth with messy pink lipstick, blond hair tumbling out from underneath the Spartan helmet. The big sketchpad braced against his knees, he lost track of time as he drew, minimal lines then filling in the color with metallic pastels. They didn't make the right shade of wheat gold for her hair, so he layered the colors, smudged and smeared until he had the sheen just right.

Arden. He'd drawn Arden, not a faceless knight. He could hear his own breathing, deep and even in the silence, and felt ashamed that he couldn't get his buddies right.

"You'll get it back," he said. His voice sounded strange in the motor home's dim, close air. "You just haven't done that for a while. She's what you see now. You'll get it back."

The muse made no comment on that. Time to head into Manhattan to model for Micah's class. Knowing Arden wouldn't be there left him with a layer of relief over a visceral disappointment. He was forgetting them, and he couldn't forget them.

Not even for her?

Not even for her.

He rode over the bridge into Manhattan, going a little out of his way to ride uptown along East Park Drive. The city was putting on a pretty fall show, the air cool for September. He arrived at Betsy's apartment on time today, rolling down the path along the big Egyptian temple in the Met. When he swooped around the corner, he was surprised to see Arden claiming her bags from the back of a big black SUV. A driver in a suit and shades held the door for her.

"Thank you, Derek," she was saying.

He rolled up next to the door and swung off the bike, two movements he made automatically. The driver, big enough to double for an NFL linebacker, swung around and stopped just short of shoulder-checking him into the potted evergreen in a cement pot. Hand to her throat, Arden flinched back against the rear wheel well and dropped her bag of drawing supplies.

"Hey, easy," Seth said, one hand raised, the other neatly twitching the bike upright and out of a dogwalker's path. "It's me. It's just me."

Derek the linebacker looked at Arden for confirmation, but she was staring at Seth like she'd never seen him before. He wasn't sure he'd seen this woman before. Right hair, right stubborn line of her jaw, khakis, a loose linen top in a pale blue, and sandals, but the expression on her face was scarily blank.

Then it smoothed out. "Seth. You scared me half to death."

"Sorry," he said, as much to the driver as to Arden. The big guy relaxed, or pretended to relax. He knew how to handle himself. "You said you weren't coming."

"I changed my mind," she said, her voice either shaky or obscured as she crouched to pick up the scattered art supplies. He leaned the bike against the polished brass pole holding up the building's door-to-curb awning and helped her. "Okay? Got everything?" he asked, stopping himself just short of patting her down like he'd pat down Manny to make sure he had everything, straps tight, locked and loaded.

"Yes," she said. "I'll walk home, Derek. Put the car away and head home yourself."

She looked around quickly, lifted her chin, and strode up the awning. Seth followed in her wake, wheeling the bike next to her, a little bewildered. She seemed to relax once they walked through the heavy brass doors. "I'll take that, sir," the doorman said, and reached out one white-gloved hand for the bike. He was good with faces, clearly remembering Seth from a couple of weeks ago. "Ms. Cottlin said to go right up."

He pushed the elevator button for them. The doors closed, leaving Seth and Arden in a square space of gleaming brass. She stared straight ahead, breathing shallowly. In the twenty-four hours since he'd seen her last, something had happened to her face. The skin clung more tightly to the bones, and her eyes, never vibrant, were full of ghosts.

"You okay?" he said quietly.

"Fine," she said. "I just . . . didn't sleep well."

He recognized that for what it was, a lie told in the hopes that if it were repeated often enough it would be true. He stayed silent when the door opened and Betsy swooped down on Arden. She gave Seth a quick glance and clearly modified what she was about to say.

"I'm so glad you could make it," she said, giving Arden a quick hug, then pulling back to peer into her face. "How's Lydia?"

"As well as can be expected," Arden said, obviously falling back on platitudes.

Betsy's gaze sharpened, then she took Arden's hand. "Come help me with the wine," she said, and drew her down the hall into the kitchen.

Seth dropped his messenger bag to the floor in the hall, and walked into the living room that looked over the park. Micah was there, as were Sally and Libby, wine in hand, discussing a trip to the High Line for a nature drawing class. Seth gave them a quiet nod, poured himself a glass of ice water, and stepped to the side, waiting for the class to begin.

Waiting for Arden to come out of the kitchen. When she did, she had a wineglass in hand, Betsy's arm around her shoulder, and a little bit of color in her face. All that did was take her from deathly pallor to ICU resident. Something was going on there, something she wasn't letting him see.

Betsy nodded at Micah. "Seth, if you please," Micah said, and waved into the circled easels.

He shucked his cargo pants and button-down shirt, draped them over the back of a red leather chair, and resolutely did not look at Arden when he walked into the pool of sunlight on the parquet floor. Micah ran the class through the warm-up poses, then broke to arrange the platform for a long sitting. Seth ended up sitting twisted with the bulk of his upper body weight on his right arm and shoulder. It was a complicated, spiraling pose, and based on the absolute silence in the room, engaged everyone quite nicely.

He could see Arden in his peripheral vision. Without having seen a single thing she'd drawn, he could tell she was surrendering to the process, dropping into the act and art of drawing. Micah wandered among the easels, making quiet suggestions, adding a quick line now and then to demonstrate something. When he reached Arden's easel, Seth saw his eyes widen.

"You've been practicing," he said in a tone Seth had heard rarely in other classes. Impressed surprise. Enthusiasm even. "You're moving from surface, from contour lines to character, personality, essence, to unity. You're present to that possibility, open to it, without trying to make it happen."

"No pressure there," Betsy said from the other side of the circle. Laughter. Even Arden smiled, but her face was still pale. She looked at him without seeing him, a pattern that continued through the break—when Betsy's housekeeper brought out trays of chocolate-dipped strawberries, cheese and crackers, fruit, and little slivers of cake—through the second session, right up until Micah called time.

"Draw every day. Whatever you see. Try to focus on nature, things made and well used. It's okay to copy other artists. Go to the Met or the Museum of Modern Art and copy drawings. It will help you find your voice, give you something to incorporate or push against," he added over the clamor of sketchpads closing, pencils and erasers sliding into pencil bags.

Seth made his circuit of the easels, saving Arden for last. "Can I look?" he asked, keeping his eyes on her face.

"No," she said, rapid-fire. "Not yet."

On one hand, he understood. He didn't want anyone peering into his sketchbooks from the war, either. But on the other hand, he wanted to know what Arden's weary, battle-tested eyes saw in him. The desire sat oddly in his chest, perched like a bird at the very end of a swaying branch, kept out by the other birds, huddled together, taking up all the strongest spaces.

She stuffed the pencil case into her bag. "Come over tonight?"

Again with the undertone. He kept his back to the other people in the room, protecting her from prying eyes.

"Sure," he said.

"I'll meet you downstairs."

Seth took the elevator to the ground floor, reclaimed his bike from the doorman, walked outside and turned north, then leaned the bike against the building's corner. Spent the five minutes he waited for her trying to identify how he felt. Anticipation. Uncertainty. Disloyal. Alive. Not sure how to go on. Confident that something else was bothering Arden.

When she walked out of the building, sliding her sunglasses onto her face, she hit him like a ton of bricks. Same white-gold hair, same pale skin, same big hollowed-out eyes. The khaki pants and linen shirt looked rumpled. She should look like a lost child, fragile, in her too-loose pants and her scarred skin. Instead, all he could see was strength, like something stripped away everything and left only the core of her. Steel. A little nicked, like swords actually used in battle. Scuffed. But still steel, still deadly.

"Don't be anyone else today," she said when she reached him.

He fell into step beside her, wheeling the bike between them. "Fine by me," he said. Right now he wasn't sure who he was at all.

She hung back for a moment, then came up on his other side, like she wanted to get closer, no obstacles between them. He stamped down on the sweet sensation spreading through him. "Does Betsy lay out a spread like that every time she has someone over?"

Arden nodded. Smiled, if you could count a bit of a quirk of lips a smile. "We met at boarding school. Her parents worked abroad so she shuttled between school and camps. Sometimes she'd stay with us over a holiday. She loves having a place of her own, welcoming people, feeding them."

If Betsy could get Arden to eat, he'd stand naked in her living room every day of the week. "You didn't eat much."

"I haven't had much of an appetite lately."

They reached her town house. He hoisted the bike onto his shoulder and waited while she unlocked the door and keyed off the alarm system. "Can I get you anything?"

"I will if you will," he said with a little smile.

"Of course." In the kitchen she opened the fridge and pulled out plastic deli containers containing various cold salads. A loaf of French bread was tucked into a bread box on the counter. She loaded up a battered tray, black lacquer with a dragon inset, which had to be an antique, handed him the tray, then picked up her drawing bag and led him up the stairs, but didn't stop in the living room.

He raised an eyebrow.

"May I draw you?"

He loved the polite way she asked, like this wasn't what they did, him stripping off his clothes for her, then fucking her. "Sure."

"I want to do this in bed," she said.

He loved that about her, polite request, then *bam*, the sharp left into the unexpected. "Whatever you want," he said.

"You can eat and loll at the same time, right?"

"A decade in the Marine Corps and I can eat and do just about anything," he said, and followed her down the hall.

The bedroom windows overlooked the backyard, which was saying something in Manhattan. From this vantage point, Seth could see Arden's garden, enclosed by a high brick wall, and the brick path running the length of the narrow space, the flower beds cut back and neatly mulched for the winter. A weathered table and chairs for two sat on the tiny brick patio, a closed umbrella standing guard between two raised planters filled with chrysanthemums.

"Nice," he commented. Central Park was half a block away, and she had a yard, too.

"I prefer the rooftop deck," she said as she pulled back the white duvet and top sheet. "More sunlight."

"There's a rooftop deck?"

"I'll show you sometime," she said distractedly, then set the tray to one side of the mattress and gave him a little nod.

"Where do you want me?"

She sat on one corner, crossed her legs like a little kid, and tucked her hair behind her ears. With her back to the windows, he had a hard time seeing her expression. "Get comfortable," she said.

The room shimmered with the things they weren't saying. He stretched out on his side, crossed his legs at the ankle, and braced his weight on his arm. It wasn't the most comfortable position to eat, but he'd make do. He took one of the little plates and set it on the sheets in front of him, then added some of the sliced bread, cheese, a few carrots, and a couple of cookies. It was no wonder she and Betsy were so thin. They set out mouthfuls of food then picked at them like birds.

She set her sketchpad on her knees and bent her head. He ate slowly, trying not to get crumbs in the sheets, watching her, not caring if she noticed, trying to figure out what she saw. Based on the pattern of her glances, she was working on the line from his shoulder to his hip like her life depended on getting it right.

"What?" she said.

"Nothing," he said, pinching together bread and cheese. "Come here."

"You're distracting me," she said, but obediently scooted forward a little, then bent even farther forward and opened her mouth for some bread smeared with a spicy lobster dip.

She didn't back up, but stayed within arm's reach. Concentrating. Blocking something out. He'd seen it before. Done it before. Reached for lines and hash marks and shading because as complex as they were, they were less complex than reality.

He popped the cookie in his mouth, then reached out and ran the tip of his index finger around the knobby bone of her ankle. One slow circle. Pause on the pulse tripping beside the bone. Another circle, bigger, just as slow, not stopping this time, nudging up the leg of her chinos.

"Am I distracting you now?"

"A little."

Her voice was fainter, her gaze fixed on the sketchpad, and

pink bloomed on her cheeks and throat, as if the color in her skin drew its strength from her voice.

The room was cool, the air-conditioning a faint hum, the sunset colors leaching to city-style perpetual, artificial twilight. He'd never seen night so black until Afghanistan. Daylight was the same, but night, night was different here. It caught Arden's hair, lay over it like a sheet of dirty silk, threw her face into relief. He found himself memorizing her cheekbone, the plane underneath it, the curve of her ear, the way the muscles tensed and slackened as she concentrated, then lost it under his finger.

Hand up the leg of her pants, he rolled forward, getting his knees under him.

"Stop," she said, and flipped to a new page.

He stopped, hand still curved around her calf. What felt smooth three seconds earlier now felt awkward as hell, but she was sketching madly, face alive, drawing, of all things, the line of his back and the curve of his ass. She made him aware of his body in ways he'd never been before. With a shock, he realized that's how he could make this okay. He'd just sublimate the ache in his chest into physical desire. That was fine. Getting obsessed with her strength, needing her for that, was not fine. She could need him, use him as her muse, but that's where it ended. He pushed aside the vision of her as honed steel or a knight and angled his head just enough to get his point across.

"Okay," she said, and he completed the move, leaning in to kiss her.

Her mouth opened under his, lips soft and warm, swollen from her biting them as she worked. He licked first the lower, then the top, the edges of her teeth.

"I can't work like this," she said, the words of a complaining diva, but the tone one of laughter.

He bit her lip, then spoke against her mouth. "You want to draw?"

"Yes," she said, like she was explaining the blindingly obvious. What he heard was Maybe. No.

"I'll get out of your way," he said, and shifted sideways to put his mouth to her bare shoulder. The shirt was loose enough that he could shift it with his mouth, first to her neck so he could kiss the round curve of her shoulder, the bump of bone under the skin, then to the edge of her shoulder so he could kiss the collarbone. His lips crisscrossed over the scars there, then nuzzled into the hair falling against her throat.

"What happened?" he said.

"Car accident." Her pencil scratched against the paper, more slowly than before, but still assured.

"What are you drawing?"

"Your feet. Your . . . um . . . instep. No, arch. Not instep."

He smiled. Slipping concentration. Good. He remembered his feet in Afghanistan, the way the skin would rot and peel after weeks of patrol, how they'd stumble back behind the wire and take turns bullying each other into taking care of their feet. The doc always came around for a check, but there were twenty-two of them and one of him, and he'd walked patrol with them, too. So they did it for each other, because it took some of the weight off the doc's back. Because they loved one another.

"You have adorable toes," she said.

He blinked against the sting in his eyes. She reached out and stroked a single finger down his arch. "Not ticklish?"

"Not really," he said, and held himself still while she learned his foot, the flat of his heel, the curve around his arch, the pad of each toe, then picked up the pencil again. He shifted his weight.

"Are you looking down my top?"

"I am now," he said, and peeked. "Take it off."

"That's not how this works," she said, then made an inarticulate noise of protest when he gripped the hem and pulled it up. The pencil went one way, the sketchpad another. Her bra, a pale coffee brown silk, looked familiar.

"Where did you get that?"

"Irresistible," she said, distracted.

He'd seen it on a mannequin there on a delivery earlier in the summer. Sitting back on his heels, he reached out and brushed his thumb over her nipple. While he wasn't looking at the sketchpad, the line quivered when her nipple peaked. He did it again, and watched her eyelids droop. He sat back on his heels, but she held out her hand.

"You, too," she said, and nodded at his shirt.

Never in his life had he regretted buttons more. He made swift work of the first two before she muttered, "You're too fast, or I'm too slow. Slow down."

Class was easy, because boot camp erased any inhibitions he had after years in locker rooms. Shuck everything, sit or stand or stretch. Hold the pose, because any physical challenge shut down his brain.

This was hard, on her bed, in her bedroom. She was watching him, not quite the dispassionate artist, not quite a lover, but close enough. Close enough, when the last thing he wanted was to get close. He slipped the third button from the placket, feeling more self-conscious than he did when he undressed for a big class at CUNY. It was hard to sit under her gaze when she not only saw him, she saw into him. Maybe not through, not yet. It wouldn't take long.

He shrugged out of the shirt and tossed it to the floor.

"Tell me about it," she said abstractly. "The tattoo."

He controlled the flinch. "It was Manny's idea," he started. He pulled out his phone and showed her the picture of the four of them, laughing—that was his background, his screen saver, his reason for living. She studied it carefully as he named them, tracing her fingers over the image. "When our first tour finished, we decided to get tattoos."

"Why that one?" she asked, handing back his phone, returning to her sketchbook.

"We all got the same one," he said.

She filled in some section, middle of the page. He kept his eyes resolutely forward. She didn't want him to look. He wouldn't look. "Why that one? When I first saw it, I thought it was a cross."

"I was a kid when I enlisted. Seventeen. I graduated early so I could join. I used to draw fantasy stuff. Dragons. Trolls. Elves. The epic quest, *Lord of the Rings* stuff."

Her gaze flicked up to him. He'd startled her out of her trance, and he wasn't going any deeper, how he used to daydream about quests, missions, companions, a band of brothers he'd never had. "What?" he said defensively. "I was a kid."

"It's very cool," she said.

"The guys used to mock me, until I started drawing them."

"I have brothers," she said. "Mocking seems to be part of the Y chromosome."

He laughed. "Eventually they wanted me to draw them. If I did a quick sketch and handed it out, it turned into a thing, a badge. New guys knew they were in when I drew them. It was just a thing I did, you know? Always with the fantasy elements, never meant for it to be anything else. But when the tour was over and the four of us were back home, we got drunk. I was drawing stuff, Manny decided the sword was *sick*, and we got tats of it. It made sense at the time."

She was looking at him, eyes wide, lips parted. He'd been in plenty of strange situations, but this one, kneeling on Arden's bed, both of them shirtless, the world held at bay by brick walls and silence, the sheer shroud of secrecy they created together, this one was the strangest.

"How many tours together?"

"Four," he said. By the end they thought they were invincible. Why wouldn't they? They were young, infallible, and the quest didn't end with a mortality rate of seventy-five percent. It didn't end with the heroes dead and the mute scribe sent back to tell a tale.

"Which ones are from the other tours?"

He pointed at the dragon, then at his version of the devil dog, a stubborn-looking bulldog braced on squat legs, eyes narrowed as it peered into the distance. *Semper Fi Do or Die* ringed the image.

"And the last one?" she asked, scanning his chest.

He looked at her, his voice throttled.

"I'm sorry," she said, his misery reflected in her eyes. "God, I'm sorry. I should have thought."

"It's okay," he said. "You didn't know them."

For a minute he thought she was going to reach for him, pat him softly on the shoulder and tell him he'd get over it, that in time he'd heal. He braced himself for the pity he didn't want, the empathy he couldn't bear, but then Arden handed him a gift.

"Would you turn around? I'd like to see the sword and dragon from the back again."

Relief swamped him. He swiveled around, presenting his back to her, and used the time to get himself under control. The dragon's muscled back and lashing tail extended nearly to his hip; the sword down his back was the reverse of the one on his chest. To a casual observer they looked the same.

"The runes are different," Arden said with a questioning lift at the end.

"Yeah," he said. He'd done them himself, using a book of

Elvish he'd bought off the Internet. God, what a geek he'd been, believing in heroic quests. So fucking young. Only the extremely poor joined the Corps for the money. It was about the mission, the platoon, his friends. He was stupid enough to believe in honor and duty and service.

She gave a pleased little noise, and for a few minutes the only sound in the room was pencil against paper and his heart, beating in slow, agonized thuds, reminding him of all the times he'd prayed it would just fucking stop. His heart. The universe. Something to end this.

"Take off your pants, please," she said behind him.

He laughed, swung himself off the bed, and shucked the rest of his clothes. "Same position?"

"Please."

It really shouldn't be hot, the way she said *please* with that distant, dismissive air of expectation, like someone raised her with both manners and the unshakable confidence that she'd get what she wanted. He settled on his heels with his back to her, and waited while she sketched, his cock thickening and lifting with his heartbeat. He thought about her in that coffee silk bra and her too-loose pants. He thought about the tight, hot clasp of her sheath, the way her eyes closed as he pushed into her.

"Okay." Distracted. Like she was somewhere else.

He turned around. The sight of her was like a fist to his chest, and had nothing to do with his erection. She'd seen something in his back, in the sword.

Before he could investigate, her gaze flicked down and she smiled a rare, broad smile. "How come that never happens in class?"

"Two reasons. I'm not an exhibitionist. Micah made it abundantly clear that if I got off on women looking at me naked, I'd be thrown out of the class and blacklisted from every art school in the city. Modeling for art students is the easiest money I've ever made."

"Have you made most of your money in the Marine Corps?"

He laughed. "Yeah." The mood shifted, with his not-quite-a-lover, not-quite-a-friend. He used to laugh all the time, with Manny, Doug, Brian. Life was tedium punctuated by moments of sheer terror, but Christ, they laughed.

"What's the second reason?"

"It's usually fucking cold in the rooms," he said, and reached across the pad for the button at the top of her pants. He could curl his fingers into the waistband with room to spare.

She laughed again, while beckoning him forward. All four fingers, like a motherfucking boss, not like a flirty girl. Good. Get this back on her territory, not his. He left his hand in her waistband and knee-walked forward until he could fit one thigh between hers and tugged gently. Sketchbook in one hand, pencil in the other, she got to her knees and let him unfasten her pants and push them down. Pencils clinked against each other as they worked off her pants, leaving her in the bra and panties, and him utterly naked. When he tossed the khakis to the floor, she lifted the sketchpad and held it in front of her like a shield.

"Just a little more," she said, and this time it was softened with a smile.

He wanted her, but he could wait, let the desire that pushed away the memories simmer under his skin until she felt it, too. "How do you want me?"

"Lie back," she said.

He stretched out, head and shoulders on one of her big pillows, one hand tucked behind his head, the other resting on his hipbone. Close enough to his cock to make him calculate the distance in inches between fingertips and erection. "No, look at me," she said when he turned his head away from her.

He'd never felt this vulnerable.

She scooted closer, and he watched her lose herself in drawing. Her shoulders relaxed as she worked; he'd only noticed how much she had hunched over after she straightened. He tried to shift into soft focus, make her a blur of pale skin and gray silk, but all he could look at was her bra strap, slipping in slow motion from her shoulder to lie against her biceps. The cup gaped a little, giving him a shadow glimpse of nipple each time she exhaled. He didn't want to want this.

He couldn't look away.

His fingers twitched. He stilled them, breathed in for four, out for four, in, out, then found himself reaching for his cock to squeeze it, take the edge off.

"No."

"What?"

"Your face changes when you want something."

Another direct hit to the solar plexus, stilling all the motion in his body. Blood, breath, everything dragged, stopped flowing. The response of prey to a hunter, or a Marine laying a trap. He wasn't sure which role he played right now. He dragged his gaze from her breasts to her face and found her looking at him. Not his body, not his erection, but his face. His fingers curled, but he forced himself to move his hand back to his hip. His cock throbbed, and a bead of precome formed at the tip. His hips shifted restlessly, another involuntary movement, and his hand tightened in the hair at the back of his head.

She exhaled slowly, and because he was looking at her face, he saw the blood stain the skin of her cheeks, her lips soften and part. His movement had drawn her gaze down; she flipped to a clean page and went for the torso and hips now. He'd never had a woman look at him naked like she did, seeing, seeing, putting together pieces he hadn't realized were broken. Some thinking part of his brain knew this problem wouldn't be fixed by gripping his cock, but fuck, he wanted nothing else.

"Go ahead," she said. Like she'd heard him thinking. Like she knew all his secrets.

He wrapped his fingers around the shaft and squeezed. Relief rushed through him, followed hard by a surge of sensation, sweet and hot and sticky in his veins.

She was watching, her pencil halted, midline, gaze fixed on his hand. He drew his fist up the shaft, slicked the precome around the head, stroked back down. Her gaze trailed up his torso, watched the muscles clench in his abdomen, then continued to his face. Knowing that his face had changed, he wondered what she saw, tried to discern it from the tiny shifts of muscles and the pattern of her breaths.

"That's good, too," she said, and resumed drawing, her arm moving in the big sweeping gestures of capturing the essence of a man with his cock in his hand.

It was need, he realized. She showed it in a completely different way, leaking out behind the tight restraints of blank expressions and not reacting. The deeper they sank into drawing and sex, the more she cracked. But he was the one in real danger. She drew him back into his body, made him want, made him feel; both those things would keep him from taking care of the people left behind.

The room had darkened while she drew and he casually stroked himself, until her face was deeply shadowed and the city's ambient light was the only thing illuminating his body. With a frustrated sound, she set the sketchpad to the side and rolled off the bed. His eyes were adjusted to the low light, so he saw her hips sway as she walked, the lower curve of her buttock revealed by the silk tucked into the cleft. She closed the blinds, then turned on the lamp beside the bed.

A disquieting blend of lust and emotion simmered inside of him, tipping to one side, then the other, swirling together. He wanted the scale firmly weighted to the side of lust, not emotion. It was time to put things back in balance.

Holding her gaze, he lifted his hand and beckoned her forward.

FOURTEEN

His spine. God. His *spine*, as straight and strong as the sword alongside it. She'd die with that image burned into her brain, muscles and bone forming a deep groove, the sword steel-straight alongside it, the hilt stretching across his shoulder blade. How did the Marine Corps make men like that? What kind of man chose that sort of tattoo? In the sword, the dragon, the dog, she'd been given the key to him, if she could just find the lock it opened.

The ordinary white lamplight, filtered by the shade, gave him an unexpected, unreal cast. It dispelled the shadows, but at the same time transformed him into an alien creature, and unlike turning on the lights to make nightmares flee, it did nothing to lessen the dangerous edge to his face.

She'd never had a man like this in her bed. She wasn't sure she'd ever had a man like this in her *life*. She knew of a few boys who'd attended one of the military academies or joined the officer training corps after their junior years in college, but they were few and far between. Their path just didn't include the military, the possibility of dying in battle.

The surface shifted like his tattoos when he moved, hinting at textures and depths and dimensions she'd barely glimpsed. Then he let go of his cock and gave her the same beckoning move she'd used on him. *Come here. Now.*

She padded to the bed, knee-walked across it to his side, stopping to lift the abandoned tray off the bed, then straddled him. Hands by his shoulders, knees by his hips, her lips pressed to his. His mouth was soft skin that firmed as she kissed him, the pressure making his lips swell, heat. His tongue flickered against hers, the touch lightening as she held herself away from his body—mouth, breasts, hips barely caressing him. He arched up into her body, his hands firm on her hips. Strength restrained. He could pull her down, roll her, fuck her, and they both knew it. The control implicit in his grip sent heat streaming from her back brain down her spine, trickling over her ribs and hipbones to pool in her nipples and sex.

"You want that?" she murmured against his mouth.

"You know it," he said, and closed his teeth on her lower lip.

She lowered herself to her elbows. A hard beat of pleasure coursed through her at the full body contact, although silk still covered her breasts, pressing against his chest, and her mound against his cock. Sweat slicked the skin where they touched, and the incomplete, out-of-rhythm contact of their breathing drew attention to the bare-skin contact at their abdomens. It felt like a tantalizing promise of the synchronicity that could come.

His hand closed around her buttocks as his hips circled under hers. A faint rasping sound, the friction of hair against silk, rose into the air. She smiled, then bent and kissed him, still not giving him anything more than light pressure, a brush of lips, a hint of tongue. She wanted to tease him, but this was also for herself. These islands of time in a sea of turmoil only grew more important to her each time she found one. She washed up on the beach of him, clung to him like a life preserver with no thought of how she'd swim to shore, content just to be with him and breathe until the wreckage washed up on whatever solitary island she'd live on for the rest of her life. Seth wasn't in her future. The last thing she needed right now was a man.

But this wasn't just any man . . .

"Hey," he said softly. "Come back."

She snapped back into the moment to find herself sprawled on top of Seth. He was looking up at her, brow wrinkled.

"Sorry," she said, hastily. No man wanted proof positive of a woman's mind wandering during sex.

"No big deal," he said, gently smoothing his hand from the top of her thigh, over her butt cheek to her hip, then back down.

"How did you know?"

He smiled. "You get distant. Nervous, tense, kind of twitchy. You stop breathing."

Oh, God.

"It's all good," he added. "Still into this?"

The question was amused. He knew how into this she was, just not why, exactly. And she was into it. But this possible shift, this tenderness, made her skin itch. To combat it, she shifted her weight to her left elbow, hitched her hips away from his just a bit. His hands tightened, then relaxed, letting her do what she wanted to do. She slid her fingers into the elastic waistband of her panties. They were damp, clinging to her skin. His eyes followed her hand, watched intently as she spread her folds and drew her fingers through the slick heat between her legs. She made a soft noise at the contact against sensitized skin, and carefully circled her clit, then withdrew her fingers.

He watched her hand the whole way up to his lips. She drew the moisture across the skin, starting to swell from her kisses, then exhaled a shuddering breath as she bent to kiss him. This time she didn't tease, just licked the taste of her arousal from his mouth, and when he gripped her wrist and turned her hand to his mouth, she helped him lick it from her fingers. Then his hand guided hers down again, back into the hot silk between her legs, his fingers twined with hers, gathering moisture. She relaxed the muscles in her arm and shoulder, let him guide her fingers this time to the tip of his cock. He circled the tip, smearing their fluids together. His cock flexed, the muscles in his abdomen jumped, and heat speared sharp and electric between her legs.

She forgot everything but the skin-on-skin contact, their breathing, shallow but falling into rhythm. Transfixed by the image of his bigger hand enclosing and guiding hers, the pulse of blood under the thin skin, she watched a moment longer, then glanced up at his face.

Hot blood in his cheeks, his lips, his eyes. Their eyes locked, he let go of her hand to slide his fingers through her hair and cup her head, then wrapped his arm around her waist to hitch her closer. She draped her leg over his thigh and braced her head on her elbow, looking down at his face as she set a slow rhythm.

Murmured words taught her what he liked, harder, slow. Precome slicked her hand as she stroked. He pulled her closer and drew her mouth down to his, giving her the rough, quick breaths, the tense and release of his muscles. He pulled her hand to his mouth and licked the palm, and when she started stroking again, the sensation was strong enough to make him dig one heel into the mattress and arch into her hand.

She kissed him, the faint taste of sweat and precome dissipating in his mouth, deep then light. In the lamplight she saw sweat form at his temples, on his chest and abdomen, his athlete's body shedding heat any way it could. The scent of sex and lust was in her mouth, her nose, her blood. He groaned, lifted his head to look down at her hand.

"Say when," she whispered.

"Not yet," he growled.

She slowed her touch, drank his groan from his mouth. Her bra and panties clung to her skin. She'd never been so hot, so turned on, in her life, couldn't resist rubbing her body like a cat against his. The movement sent her bra strap down her arm, making the cups gape away from her breasts. He looked, groaned, closed his eyes, looked again, hips thrusting up into her fist.

"So fucking hot."

"Tell me why," she whispered. She'd always felt ridiculous trying to be sexy, but with Seth, right now, it felt totally natural. She leaned forward, let her partially exposed breast graze his chest. "Tell me why."

"You look messy," he said indistinctly. "Like you're about to get fucked, like you really, really want it."

Emboldened, she let his cock slap against his belly and hooked her thumb in the elastic of her panties, then wriggled the clinging silk down to expose her hip, the top of her rear end, then pressed her hot, damp sex to his hip. His hand clamped down on her hip when she licked her own palm and set her hand to his cock.

It was hot and sweaty, tantalizing and far too good to stop. Her hair trailed over his face until he tucked it behind her ear and drew her forehead down to his. Her arm was aching from holding her head up, so she stretched it above her and lay her head on her biceps. He turned to face her. "Gonna come," he said in a near soundless voice. His gaze was locked with hers, eyelids quivering, his mouth brushing hers.

"Yes," she said, timing her downstrokes to the lift of his hips. It felt far too rough to her, harder than she'd expected, a full-body lift that only intensified when she rolled more of her weight onto his torso and leg. His cock swelled in her hand, then he groaned as his orgasm pulsed over her circled fingers.

His heart was pounding, the beats too fast to separate into a pulse. His chest heaved as he drew in a full breath, his muscles quivering as the tension eased.

"Be right back," she said, and patted his abdomen.

In the bathroom she washed her hands, the water cooling the hot pulse in her wrists, then wet down a facecloth for him. The woman in the mirror was nearly unrecognizable, suddenly possessing the mouth and eyes and tangled hair of a model. Her bra strap still drooped, and her panties barely reached her hips. She thought about tidying herself up, then didn't. This wasn't over.

Back in the bedroom Seth was sprawled on the bed, eyes closed. She set one knee on the bed and wiped the semen from his stomach. He startled under her, opened his eyes, then took the cloth from her hand to finish the job. She held out her hand for the used cloth. He jackknifed upright, tossed the cloth onto the tiled floor of the bathroom, then wrapped both arms around her waist and tumbled her onto the bed. She yelped when a pencil lost in the sheets pricked her skin. He reached under her and swiped it away.

"Your turn."

"Yes, please," she said. Desire had turned into something else, something that thickened her voice into a throaty demand. Her sex was so slick, the silk clinging and sliding against her clit. She'd never felt like this, like her blood had turned to honey in her veins.

He reached under her back and unfastened her bra. She sighed with relief when he lifted it away, the cessation of friction at first a relief, then not enough. He cupped both breasts in his hands and squeezed, then used tongue and teeth on one nipple while he pinched the other. The hard tips swelled even more; she lifted, undulated under him, soft, breathy gasps sharp and distant in the room. He worked her panties down her thighs until she could kick them off and spread her legs.

His hand drifted down, petting gently until he learned her body, then parting her swollen folds and circling her clit. She tossed her head and whimpered. He leaned over her, studying her intently. "Not enough?"

"No," she said before she could stop herself and say something polite. "More," she added,

His middle finger slid down, gently circled her opening, then dipped inside. Again, relief, but not enough, and now her clit throbbed, abandoned. He bent over her, protective, possessive, powerful male.

"You want something inside you?"

"Yes," she demanded.

He added a second finger, working them teasingly in and out, brushing the top wall of her vagina in such a way that the flesh quivered.

"More," she demanded again.

"I'm being careful here," he said.

In response she set her fingernails to his shoulder and the small of his back, and dug in.

"Yes, ma'am," he said, his voice dark, amused, full of promise.

The third finger, thick, blunt, stretched her enough to make her head drop back. He still wasn't going deep, but the thing he was doing, his fingers slightly curled and stroking patiently, made her quiver with anticipation.

Then he deepened the stroke slightly, applying pressure as he pulled out, and a shock wave of pleasure pulsed through her. She let out a shocked, disbelieving cry. He made a very male, very satisfied noise, pressed the base of his thumb to her clit, and set about taking her apart. She let him. Every ounce of focus was on his hand between her legs, the pressure firm and relentless and steady, three fingers stretching her, teasing a previously unknown spot inside her. She could feel her muscles quivering as the long-denied tension coiled deep. His lips hovered over hers, the erratic pressure and flicks of his tongue a delicious contrast to the fabulously, predictable movements between her legs. He understood, she thought with the few remaining functioning brain cells, how critical constancy was when it came to a woman's orgasm.

The pleasure swelled until her skin strained to contain it. Gasping, she turned her face into his throat, inhaled sweat and sex, felt his teeth close gently on the exposed tendon in her neck. She came, sharp cries tearing from her throat in time to the heated beats dissolving all her edges. He didn't move. If anything, he curled even more tightly over her, around her, until he was the only thing anchoring her to the earth.

She went lax, breath heaving, cheeks stinging as the blood began to ebb back into her veins. Her sex fluttered as he gently withdrew his hand, resting it on her hip. She let her eyes close, trying to hold on to the blankness that would fade all too soon, real life rushing back in as her breathing and heart rate slowed.

"You okay?"

"No," she said, telling him the truth for once.

He laughed, a soft huff of air she felt on her ear, saw lift his chest and contract his abdominal muscles.

"I don't know what to do with this," she said.

That did not get a laugh. She wasn't sure what she meant. She didn't know what to do with this kind of intensity, with this kind of pleasure, this kind of contentment, if she were honest. Like the build to her orgasm, she'd spent so much of her life in a constant state of tension that the absence of it left her reeling. It felt wrong to have this now, but right now was all she had. If the panic attacks and the raid had taught her anything at all, it was that the past was gone, the future was uncertain, and now was the only thing she could count on.

See it. Apply the contour drawing skills and really see the now. It can't be taken from you.

"I don't either," he said.

At least she wasn't alone. They lay in silence a little while longer. Then he patted her hip. "Mind if I take a shower?"

"Only if you mind if I join you," she said, eyes still closed.

"I'll go heat up the water."

The bed dipped as he got up, then she heard the shower turn on. She slowly sat up, rubbed at her eyes with the heels of her hands, then looked in the mirror. Mistake. Her skin was blotchy, the flush of arousal still vivid on her upper chest and cheeks. She was past bed-head and into sex hair. She smelled like sex; the whole room smelled of sex. Blood pounded in her ears, a steady fast rhythm underscored by her still erratic breathing. The taste of both of them lingered in her mouth. Semen, her juices, his sweat, her own, licked from her lips. Every sense engaged, almost no mental processes online.

Is this what it meant to feel alive?

Seeing herself like this was unbearably intimate. Her eyes slid away just as she heard the shower door swing open, then closed. Gaze resolutely fixed in front of her, she scooted to the end of the bed, stood, and hitch-walked into the bathroom. Seth stood under the spray, arms folded across his abdomen, looking at the drain. When he saw her, he opened the door.

She stepped in and let the water course over her, soaking her hair. The scent of them streamed down her body and away, stinging between her legs. She turned her head up and opened her mouth to rinse away the taste, and felt the muscles knit themselves back into their customary tight pattern.

"Is this for me?" he asked, pointing at an unused bar of plain, unscented soap resting in the tiled niche.

The soap was a concession to reality. She was sleeping with the artist's model from her drawing class. It was only polite to let him shower afterward, and to have on hand a soap that wouldn't embarrass the hell out of him. "You mean, do I have a supply under the cabinet for the men in my bed?" she asked lightly.

"Well, yeah," he said, not joking at all.

"Yes, I bought it for you. I have a toothbrush, too."

"Thanks," he said, and lathered up.

She reached for the almond-scented body wash. The shower was custom-built, tiled in a swirling pale granite, had jets at various his-and-hers heights and plenty of room for both of them. He finished before she did, but stayed under the spray.

"My shower's about two inches wider than my shoulders," he said in explanation.

"Enjoy it," she said and rinsed her hair.

He toweled off more quickly than she did. When she came back into the bedroom, he wore his underwear and shorts, and had his arms through his shirt.

"It's pretty late to ride home," she said with a glance at the clock. "You can stay. If you want."

Once again he stopped in the act of dressing. "Are you sure?"

"You're working in Manhattan tomorrow, right?" She scrabbled under the pillows until she found her nightgown, shoved between the mattress and headboard by all the activity. "There's no point in biking to Brooklyn for a few hours of sleep, then biking back," she said through the soft cotton. "Unless you'll sleep better in your own bed."

He let his elbows drop, then tossed the shirt on the chair next to her dresser. "I get up early," he warned. "Breakfast delivery rush."

"That's fine," she said, eager to let the promise of untroubled sleep settle over her. She retrieved the duvet from the floor, twitched the bedding into place, climbed into bed, then realized he was still standing there, a hesitant expression on his face. "What's wrong?"

"I draw myself to sleep."

There was a hint of defensiveness to the statement, like he'd revealed something secret. She yawned hugely. "Whatever you need," she said, and burrowed into the covers. He left to rummage through his messenger bag and returned with a black hardback sketchbook, and a black leather zippered pouch worn white at the corners, dust embedded in the creases. He dropped his shorts, arranged the pillows against the headboard, and thumped into the bed in his underwear.

She tapped the sketchbook's rigid black cover. "Are these the kind you carried in Afghanistan?"

"Yeah," he said. "Reporters tend to use them, too. The covers take a hell of a beating and protect the pages inside. Mine were always the color of the dirt by the time I finished with them because the dust worked its way into everything," he said, stroking the cover with his fingertips.

"Can I watch?" she asked, curious.

"Sure," he said easily.

He drew the circle of easels in Betsy's living room. Her hand dropped automatically to his chest when he lifted the sketchbook to open it, splaying across the bare patch of skin just under the sword's hilt. Sleep was creeping up on her, but she couldn't resist stroking the spot. Something about it seemed bereft, oddly empty on a torso otherwise covered in ink.

"This tour's tat was going to go there," he said.

He wasn't looking at her when he said it, his words as even as his gaze, focused on the blank page in front of him. Like drawing let him open up inside, reveal himself.

"Oh," she said.

"We had the tat picked out," he said. "The date our first tour began, and the date we went home for good."

But they didn't come home. Her throat tightened. She traced the sword's hilt, then its blade, over his abdominals to his thigh and back. "I'm sorry," she said finally.

He didn't even shrug.

He drew the view of Central Park from Betsy's windows, a view he must have memorized during the sitting. His recollection was picture-perfect, not detailed, but somehow capturing the feel of the park in such a way that the drawing could only be that particular stretch of Fifth Avenue. He drew the strawberries, nestled together, condensation gleaming on the chocolate as it warmed from the fridge. He was fast, unerringly capturing the essence of what he drew in a few quick strokes.

When she fell asleep, he was still drawing.

He'd said that wrong. He *used to* draw himself to sleep. Back before. He hadn't since his sketchbook absorbed his friend's blood.

The habit itched at him again. Why not? He had his sketchbook, and pencils were scattered all over the floor.

He drew her, asleep by his elbow, capturing the way her mouth relaxed but her brow furrowed, as if easing into sleep worried her. He shaded in the sex flush on her cheeks, so unlike her normally pale face, and his hand added the suggestion of chain mail, transforming her into a shield maiden. His shield maiden. He drew, from memory, the fierce look on her face while she leaned over him and took his cock in her hand. He drew her huddled back against the SUV, the split second of sheer terror on her face burned into his brain. He drew the room, memorizing the details, the big bed, the linens and upholstery and shades all white.

He drew himself in the mirror, not quite looking, just the hint of shape he could discern in his peripheral vision, her arm draped over his torso, her leg entangled with his. She anchored him in time and space, drawing him back to earth, the sound of his breathing low and resonant in his ears, his heart ticking in his chest.

He drew until his eyelids drooped, and he drifted into sleep.

Arden awoke to Seth's hand on her shoulder. Blinking, she looked at him. He wore the cargo pants, the right leg cuffed to avoid snagging the greasy chain, and a tight-fitting long-sleeved jersey. His eyes were solemn, mouth soft.

"I'm leaving, but I didn't want you to wake up alone."

"I usually wake up alone," she said, groggy. "What time is it?"

"Just before six."

He was hunkered down on his heels by the side of the bed, studying her. She sat up, pushed her hair out of her face, and wondered how bad she looked having fallen asleep with wet hair. "What?"

"Do you always dream like that?"

That woke her up in a hurry. "Like what?" she asked cautiously.

"You were having one hell of a nightmare around four."

"I don't remember," she said. But then images surfaced. She was handcuffed to a chair under a fierce bright spotlight, like the ones used to interrogate prisoners, blinding them, hiding the identity of the interrogators. Creatures snarled and snapped at her from just outside the ring of white light, teeth made of razor blades glinting as they lunged, blood dripping from their huge, misshapen jaws. Her stomach dropped, remembering the fragments, which propelled her out of bed. He was the one who should have bad dreams, or PTSD, or something.

"You need the code for the security system," she said as she hurried past him, down the staircase to the entryway, where the sight of her purse drew her up short. Did she pay him for last night? He'd modeled for her, but it had quickly turned into something else, something difficult to describe even after she had lived through it. Better to err on the side of caution; she remembered what he'd said about making all his money in the Marine Corps. If she asked him if that counted as a modeling session, he would say no.

She dug out her wallet and thumbed through the twenties, counting out the modeling fee and the tip.

He'd followed her down the hall more slowly, and paused beside her to shift the messenger bag's strap over his head. "Do you know how to ride a bike?"

"Of course I know how to ride a bike," she said absently, and handed him the cash.

He tucked it into one of the zippered pockets in the bag without bothering to count it. "Come for a ride with me."

New York City traffic, even inside an enormous SUV, often badly startled her. There was no way she could handle traffic on the unprotected seat of a bike. She let out a short trill of laughter that sounded brittle rather than confident. "No way. I've seen bike messengers ride, and there is no way I'm doing that."

His brows drew down slightly. "Not work. A pleasure ride."

"Riding through New York City traffic isn't my idea of fun."

"So we'll ride through the park, or along the water."

She stared at him. "I'm not . . . athletic. I can't ride a bike."

"You just said you could. Unless your shoulder and knee can't take the stress after the accident."

He said it so calmly, giving her an easy way out. Claim weakness, get a free pass out of the situations that scared her. Her chin lifted. "My shoulder and knee are fine. I *can* ride a bike," she said, remembering pedaling around the big driveway of the Hamptons house as a kid, riding around the Great Lawn in Central Park with her nanny in tow. "I just *don't*."

"Why not? It's not about being athletic. It's about getting out, getting some exercise, getting some sun. It's a way of being in touch with the world, adding dimension to your drawing."

"Seth, it's a sweet invitation, but no, thank you," she said, using the firm voice that sometimes kept her heart rate from skyrocketing, like she was reassuring her mind that yes, she understood, she would not do anything daring or risky or public. "I have work today. I've put off foundation work for the last few weeks to deal with things, but I really need to get back to normal life."

With the emphasis on *normal*, so much for sounding cool and collected.

"Okay. That's cool."

He just looked at her, not judging, not hurt. She almost said they could do something else, like go to the movies, or dinner, or a walk, but then she remembered the unpredictable horde of reporters and photographers quite possibly watching her door right now. All he'd said was that he needed this, too. Nothing else. So she kept her mouth shut.

"Thanks for coming over. Stay safe today," she said, and opened the door. The street was empty except for a suit-clad neighbor who walked a shih tzu to Starbucks every day to bring his wife a latte. In a matter of seconds, Seth was down the stairs and through the gate. He gave her a nod, fastened his helmet, and swung his leg over the bike. He turned the corner on Fifth Avenue just as Arden closed the door.

— FIFTEEN —

The phone, vibrating and ringing on her nightstand, dragged Arden from a restless sleep. She pawed her hair back from her face and focused on the screen.

Mom.

" 'Lo?" she said.

Muffled weeping on the line. Phone clasped to her ear, Arden rolled to her back and tried to remember what day it was. Wednesday. Yesterday she'd had a meeting with Neil and made phone calls to the dwindling number of requestors in the foundation's giving cycle. A quick glance at the screen showed just after three in the morning.

"Mom," she said. She sat up, turned her back to the wall, and arranged the pillows behind her. The one closest to her head still retained a hint of Seth's unique scent, skin, sweat, and the bike grease. "What's wrong?"

Sobs finally resolved into, "Where am I going to go?"

It sounded like her mother was coming to terms with leaving

Breakers Point. "Mom, you've got options," she said. "You know you can move in with me."

A hiccupping laugh, then, "Darling, you don't really have the space for me."

"There's plenty of room, Mom. I'm only using the main and second floor. We can fix up a bedroom for you off the kitchen, overlooking the garden."

"There are too many stairs. I told your father to put in an elevator, but he wouldn't listen."

"We can put in a lift. Or, Garry bought that apartment on East Fourth years ago—"

"It hasn't been renovated since the seventies, and Garry's coming home. He'll want to stay there."

Arden took a deep breath and counted to ten. Her town house was nearly three thousand square feet. Garry probably wouldn't stay longer than it took for things to settle down. Her mother didn't want her problem solved. She wanted to roll back time to the end of the summer, when she was the queen of their rarefied social circle, with homes all over the world. She wanted Arden to listen.

"Garry's not going to stay, Mom. He's got the ranch in New Zealand. That's his home now. And Joni's offered you their guest house in West Palm. You love Florida in the winter."

"I can't go to Florida," her mother said in a tone of disbelief.

"Why not? You'd be close to the girls—"

"I can't leave your father. He told me yesterday he hired a new lawyer, one of the Delmonicos, I forget which one, but Charles went to Yale with his daughter, and that everything would be cleared up. It's all just a big misunderstanding."

Suddenly wide awake, Arden sat bolt upright in bed. "He's fired Neil?"

"He said Neil wasn't being aggressive enough."

"Mom, it's not a misunderstanding. I've seen the accounts, the fake trades, and statements. The IT people who automated the process gave depositions earlier in the week. It's over."

"Your father says it's a very complicated mathematical model, too complicated for anyone but him and Charles to understand, certainly more complicated than the government could understand."

Or Arden. Arden, the mathematics major with an econ minor, certainly couldn't understand it, or have the nerves to run any part of the business. The sheer megalomania in that statement, even when presented with evidence, took Arden's breath away. "It's actually really simple, Mom. He took in money from new investors to pay out old investors, and himself. What was complicated was constructing elaborate lies to make the returns make sense. Dad's been lying to you for decades, and he's still lying to you."

"Don't you dare talk about your father that way! He is your *father*, and my *husband*. He's a good man, a good provider, and if you were a good daughter, you'd go defend him."

Arden bent her head. "A good daughter. I don't even know what that means anymore. I've tried so hard to be a good daughter I've lost sight of the goal. Those words are meaningless."

"They are not meaningless," her mother said, outraged. "You know perfectly well what they mean. They mean standing by your family, fighting to retain what belongs to us."

"Mom, when you support your family with money stolen from people, nothing belongs to you."

"He didn't steal it. He just didn't have enough to pay everyone back at that single moment in time. It was a cash flow problem. He says this new lawyer will clear everything up, and there's no need for me to leave the house."

"Mom," she repeated, "I need you to listen carefully. If you don't willingly leave the house, the government will forcibly remove you, in front of television cameras from all over the world. The images of you being evicted by the sheriff will play on every major television station in every country and make the front page of every major newspaper and Internet news site. That will only make things worse."

"Rick Dunlop would never do that to me. I contributed to his reelection campaign every year."

"A fact he's now having to explain to voters," Arden shot back, searching desperately for something, anything, that would convince her mother to leave Breakers Point of her own accord. "Think of the girls. Think of Serena having to explain that to the girls."

"I'm sure she's not letting them watch the news right now."

Her mother wasn't living in reality if she thought the girls' friends at school weren't taunting them with this. She waited in silence, out of arguments.

"They're punishing *me*," her mother said in a small voice. "I didn't do anything except love your father and use a significant percentage of what he made to do good in the world. Doesn't the foundation count for something? Surely they can't take that away, too. You're going to make sure they won't take it away. It's our work. Yours and mine. What will you do if you don't have the foundation?"

In her mother's mind, it was simple. She'd keep her house, Arden would keep the foundation, and her father would make everything all right again. "I don't know, Mom. I'll find something."

"I'm going to do what your father tells me."

"And I'm telling you to call Joni and take her up on her offer of the beach house in West Palm. Go to Florida for the winter, see your granddaughters, and let me deal with this."

"I'm glad Garry will be here to help you."

Arden bristled. "Garry has spent the last eight years herding sheep in what can literally be described as the far side of the world. Sheep, Mom. The stupidest animal alive."

"His IQ was higher than yours or Charles's. So much potential."

He was the one smart enough to get out of this. The words trembled on the tip of her tongue, but she bit them back. "I'll be glad to see him," she said. And wring his neck.

"When does he arrive? Did we send the jet for him?"

"Mom. The FBI took the keys to the jet the day of the raid. You've been allowed to stay in the house only because Neil called in favors. His reprieve won't last much longer. You need to decide. Me, Fourth Street, or Joni's house in Florida."

Her mother hung up on her. Arden slid down in the sheets and rubbed the heels of her hands against her eye sockets. The tension was ratcheting up, tightening all the muscles in her neck and back. Maybe Neil was right. Maybe an exercise program was the way to go.

She checked the day's weather: calm, clear, and cool. Then she texted Seth. Still interested in going for a bike ride?

Going back to sleep was a lost cause. She got up, made coffee, and took a cup upstairs to the living room where her easel stood. She sipped the coffee and flipped through her sketchpad. She'd toyed with working up poses of Seth from Betsy's class, but she couldn't get the sketch of Seth sitting on his heels with his back to the wall out of her mind.

She clipped her sketchbook to the frame, then put a sheet of heavyweight paper on the easel. She closed her eyes and called his face to mind, the narrowed, wary eyes, the stubble that was heaviest around his mouth, the dip at the center of his upper lip, the slight curve of his lower lip. She would ask him to sit like this for her again, because this was the essence of Seth. She drank coffee and drew until her trembling fingers prompted her to eat something. A container of Greek yogurt in hand, she stood back and looked at the drawing. It was a good start. Something was happening she found difficult to describe. Her vision was clearing, not her eyesight but rather the filter through which she viewed the world, the one she was only vaguely aware of.

Her phone buzzed at seven, startling her out of her zone. The text was from Seth.

Absolutely. Runner's Gate at nine ok? Weather looks good this AM but not afternoon.

Aren't you working?

I'm giving myself a day off.

She tried not to read too much into that, and failed. Sounds good. See you then.

Then she went downstairs into the basement storage room and looked at her bike. During a year at Oxford, a year away from being a MacCarren, she learned the basics of bike maintenance, so even though both tires were flat, the chain dry, she could get it ready to ride. She pumped up the tires, greased the chain, and then hoisted the bike onto her shoulder and carried it up the stairs, the brick walls snagging on the seat and handlebars as she did. She peered through the gap in the curtains. No photographers today. Maybe it was too early, or a celebrity's life had imploded. She wasn't about to turn on the news and find out.

Dressed and ready, she pushed the bike up the sidewalk and across Fifth Avenue to Runner's Gate, where she stopped. She adjusted the strap of her bike helmet and tucked her shades more firmly at the bridge of her nose. Hair in a ponytail, head and face mostly hidden by the helmet and straps, she wore jogging leggings, a cropped zippered jacket in Manhattan's ubiquitous black, and a pair of running shoes notable only for being boring white with equally boring white laces. No neon, no trendy blue or pink or green. She was as anonymous as she could possibly be. This was a brilliant idea. She smiled, actually anticipating being outside in the chilly fall air, riding through the park's glorious show of color, using the pretty morning to talk down the anxiety.

I'm fine. It's not like what happened. I'm not on foot. I'm on a bike. Central Park has bike lanes and only a couple of stoplights. The north end isn't heavily traveled, either. It's not the same. I'll be fine.

"Hi," Seth said.

"Hi yourself," she replied.

Seth wore black tights like her own, a jersey, and his helmet. He leaned his bike against a park bench and turned to hers, squeezing the tires, testing the brakes, checking the handlebar alignment.

"What are you doing?" she said, amused.

He looked at her. "Checking everything over. It's a habit."

"An interesting one," she said. Never before had she gone on a ride with someone who did a safety check before they set out.

He unzipped a small bag on the back of his bike and riffled through the contents. "I've got a spare inner tube that will fit your tires," he said.

"Do you normally carry spares?" she asked.

"For my bike, yes. For yours, no. I took a guess at the size of your bike and picked them up today on my way here."

"Thanks," she said, touched.

"You should get a kit, just the basics to repair punctures, air up your tires, that kind of thing."

"Seth, I rode a bike for a year during my exchange year." She remembered daily rides through Oxford's cobbled streets and narrow lanes, thinking she was finally cured. When the panic attacks returned, she resolved to find another way to deal with them. Unlike Garry, leaving for another continent wasn't an option. "I can fix a puncture and a loose chain. If I can't fix it, I'll call Derek to come get it, deliver it to a bike shop, and pick it up later," she said with far more bravado than she felt.

He laughed, the sound rich. "Let's go," he said, and swung his leg over.

She followed him into the park. At midmorning on a weekday there wasn't much traffic on the drives that circled the park, mostly nannies or moms with swaddled kids in strollers or on trikes with handles. They rode north along the east drive toward 110th Street. The north end of the park was less busy, hilly, wilder than the south end, large chunks of rock erupting from the earth, and trees loomed over the path, their leaves thick and rich in color made brilliant by the sunshine. Seth rode on the outside, next to her, but without talking as he looked around. Always alert.

She downshifted to compensate for the slow climb to the northwest corner of the park. Seth just eased back on the pedals, keeping pace with her. It was a gorgeous day for a laid-back ride through the park, and it went so smoothly it tricked her. She was fine as they rode down the West Park Drive, past the American Museum of Natural History. She was fine as they negotiated joggers and nannies, passing the Delacorte Theater, then swinging wide to pass Strawberry Fields.

She was fine until she turned onto Central Park South and merged into traffic. Cabs and cars were bumper to bumper, merging into one lane to avoid a power district crew at work. She could hear Manhattan on the other side of the wall enclosing the park, the cars and the jackhammers. Her heart rate accelerated, at first imperceptibly, then faster and faster as she couldn't draw a deep breath. One car honked, startling her, then a second, then there was an all-out honkfest as drivers vented their impatience into the park's serene air. Braced as she was, when a truck's horn went off right next to her, her heart swelled to the point where she thought it might explode, her throat closed off, restricting her breathing, and her vision tunneled to a pinprick of light.

The bike's handlebars wobbled in her sweaty hands, nearly tipping her into the truck, or under its wheels. Arden's stomach lurched up to her throat; the only thing that prevented her from vomiting was the fact that she could neither breathe nor swallow. She was going to lose control of the bike, swerve into a vehicle, and die. She tipped sideways, put out a foot to stop herself, felt her knee buckle. The bike's frame dug into her calf and thigh. Sound dopplered around her, amplifying over, then disappearing under her racing heart.

Then the clatter of a bike hitting the pavement. Not hers, which was still tangled around her leg. From a distance she could hear Seth's voice. A big hand closed around her handlebars, guiding her back upright, Seth's strong arm caught her and supported her to the curb. Somehow he got her and the bike to the side of the road and up onto the paved path. She sat down hard, right in the middle of the path, hands curled into talons and trembling near her face.

"Arden," Seth said. "Arden."

All she could think was how uncommon her name was, and he kept repeating it, and everyone was watching. Staring. At her. At Arden MacCarren, falling apart once again. "Stop saying my name," she managed to gasp out.

His mouth shut with a click. In her blurred vision, she saw him snag his abandoned bike out of the road, onto the patchy grass. Then sat down next to her and wrapped both arms around her. He murmured nonsense noises, soothing noises, put his big hand by her face and tucked her into his shoulder. It should have felt confining, the last thing she needed when she was flying apart, but somehow, she could breathe. Maybe it was like breathing into a paper bag, maybe it was the unique scent of Seth, his skin and clean sweat and the total lack of pressure in his embrace. He was so strong, so solid, he would hold her and hold off the world while she fell off the edge into the abyss.

When it was over, she inhaled one long shuddering lungful of air, the first she'd taken since the panic attack started; she exhaled the same way, reminding her brain that her body knew how to breathe, and if it would just get the fuck out of the way, things would be fine.

She felt his head turn, his nose nuzzle into her hair.

"Where's your phone?"

"Zipped into the back of my jacket," she whispered.

His hands, strong, steady, gentle, circled her, unzipping the pocket, withdrawing her phone. "Passcode?"

"Zero-two-seven-six."

His arm still around her, he tapped in the code. "I'm going to text Derek to come get you."

"That's probably for the best," she said. The attacks left her weak. Weaker. She could probably walk the bike, but there was no way she could ride it any distance. The only thing she could do was sleep off the aftermath, and hope the headache wasn't too killer.

More tapping. She sat up, inhaled crisp, cool air, then rubbed her face and eyes. A quick look showed no one was watching her. Just an average day in New York, crazy woman having a hand-flapping, breath-heaving, legs-shaking meltdown in the park. Nothing to see here. Her rational brain knew that, of course, but the crazy fear knew nothing but its own frenzy.

Seth wasn't looking at her. Giving her space, or creating distance between them. "He's on his way," he said.

She didn't know what to say. She should say something, explain this, but she'd told him nothing. Just then, an SUV pulled into the park drive and stopped at the yellow barricades. Derek got out, stuck two fingers in his mouth, and whistled. "Stay here," Seth said. He walked her bike to the SUV, where Derek had the back open. Seth handed off the bike, then came back to get her. He put his arms under her elbow and half hauled her to her feet. "One step at a time," he murmured when she tripped over her own feet. "Eyes ahead."

She made it to the SUV, where Derek waited with the door open, and got herself into the seat with no more than the suggestion of Seth's hand at her waist. "Go," he said to Derek. Then Derek shifted into gear. She caught a glimpse of Seth holding back a line of taxis while Derek backed up into Fifth Avenue traffic.

"That was a terrible idea," she said to Derek, and closed her eyes.

She opened her eyes when the SUV braked in front of her town house, then fought back the urge to vomit. A couple of the most persistent photographers leaned against the wrought-iron fence enclosing her small front patio. Derek cursed under his breath. "Stay here."

He opened the hatch and pulled her bike out of the back of the SUV, carried it down the steps to the basement door, and trundled it inside. Then he came back and opened her door. "Now."

One last burst of energy carried her through the cameras shoved in her face, to the front door, and inside. Derek had to move the car, which was double-parked, and anyway, she didn't want to see anyone right now. Instead, she sank to the foyer floor and closed her eyes.

A minute later, the doorbell chimed. She ignored it, as Derek had a key and knew the security code.

Knock knock knock. "It's me."

Seth. She got to her feet, flipped the lock, and opened the door.

He slid through the gap and shut it again in the photographers' faces.

"I still have your phone," he said.

God, he was handsome. Really handsome. Shoulders like the hilt of a sword, with his body the blade. "Thank you," she said, hand braced against the wall for support. "Just . . ." Her knees weren't up to much at this point, so she just waved her hand at the hall table, where her purse sat.

He set it down and looked at her. His body was as relaxed as she'd ever seen it, his gaze as focused and clear as the brilliant fall sky. "I'm sorry," she said shakily, fighting back stupid, useless tears. "I never cry. Just . . . that was the second one in a week . . ."

He put his arm around her waist and looped hers over his shoulders. "Let's get you upstairs. You'll sleep better in your bed," he said.

His arm was warm, and strong, and her arm around his neck made her feel as if she were doing some of the work. In her bedroom she crawled into bed and fell asleep.

She awoke to a steady rain coursing down her bedroom windows. She'd slept through the sunny morning and into the afternoon rain, and knew she'd sleep through the night, once she fed herself. The panic attacks reduced her body to its most basic needs: food, water, sleep, which was good. It took a day or two for the humiliation of the panic attacks to subside, and if she spent the first day eating and sleeping, the second day wasn't quite as bad.

She took a shower, toweled her hair damp, then dressed in warm fleece leggings and a loose sweatshirt. When she walked down the hall to her living space, she stopped abruptly. Seth sprawled in the armchair, one leg draped over the arm, drawing in his Moleskine.

"Hi," she said.

He finished the shading, then closed the sketchbook. "I hope it's okay that I stayed. I didn't want you to wake up alone," he said.

"I really do wake up alone most days," she said, trying for humor.

"You shouldn't. Not after something like that," he said.

She felt raw, vulnerable, and utterly ashamed that he'd seen her that way. She turned away, then turned back and squared up her shoulders. "Yes. Well." She cleared her throat and forced herself to look at him. "I have panic attacks," she said.

"Uh-huh," he said. "You hungry?"

"Yes," she said.

He stayed close while they walked down the stairs, and somehow steered her to one of the stools under her breakfast bar. She sat there while he ran her a glass of water, then rummaged through her fridge and came up with eggs, onions, red peppers, mushrooms, and feta cheese. She watched him whisk eggs, then pour them into a pan to set while he diced the rest of the ingredients.

"I should be cooking for you," she said.

He lifted one eyebrow, all but daring her to give it a shot.

"But this is nice. You're good at this," she said, watching him work.

"It doesn't look all that different from coming off a combat high," he said. "I've dealt with lots of those."

Startled, she laughed, then put her head in her hands. "That's real. Real fear, a real situation. Mine is all in my head."

"How long have you had them?"

"Fifteen years." For a while she'd been able to count days, months, years between attacks, marking time as normal, like a sober alcoholic or someone who's experienced a traumatic event that completely reordered her world. After a while she gave up. "They started when I was thirteen. I was hit by a cab crossing Park

Avenue. I broke my collarbone, fractured my shoulder, broke my left leg, and tore a bunch of ligaments in my knees. I hit my head pretty hard on the way down, too. Something about the noise, the horn, the tires, embedded itself in my brain. I'm hyperalert, I guess. It's hard to live in Manhattan if horns trigger unreasonable fear-based responses. But then they disassociated from horns and started happening when I was stressed out."

He made an "I'm listening" noise as he swept the vegetables into the eggs and folded it in half. She watched him cook in her kitchen, carefully stowing the utensils in the dishwasher, wiping down the counter before he got down two plates. It was all bizarrely normal, so she kept talking.

"The first one was at an eighth grade speech competition. I had a bad one when a wave swept my feet out from under me on the beach in Ibiza," she said, remembering the sting of saltwater in her nose, her father and Charles laughing, Garry running out to rescue her. "That's when the various treatments and interventions started. But the attacks only got worse, more frequent. Finals weeks. I had my most public one on the trading floor. There was a documentary crew on site, filming something about MacCarren, and I totally lost it. That attack confirmed what they'd always thought, that I didn't have the inner strength, the will of steel to work at MacCarren. They were so eager to shunt me off to the side. I tried everything I could to stop the attacks. They didn't stop. The Ponzi scheme is only part of the reason Betsy scheduled the class. She's been working on a way to cure me almost as long as I have."

"She's a good friend," Seth said. "That explains the scars."

"Four surgeries," she said. "My mother despairs of the scars. So disfiguring."

"But you don't hide them."

"No," she said. "The last thing I need is another complex."

"You're not a woman with complexes," he said.

She didn't know what to say to that. "Why did you stay?" she asked.

"Because you have eggs, and I don't. I really felt like an omelet."

His eyes were smiling, even if his mouth wasn't. She smiled back, but didn't let him off the hook. "Seriously."

"Seriously?" He draped the dish towel over his shoulder. "Mostly it's because you're the only thing I've wanted to draw since I got home from Afghanistan."

"Really? Why?"

He shrugged. "Sometimes you draw things to learn how. Sometimes your muse gives you the subject. Lately I don't seem to be picking."

"Can I see?"

"You show me yours and I'll show you mine."

"Fair enough," she laughed, and was still laughing when he flipped the omelet onto a plate and set it in front of her. She cut it, gave him half. He ate while the second one cooked, then they split the warm second one.

"What's it like?" he said.

Describing them was easy. Preventing them proved to be the difficult part. "The world gets narrow. Like a tunnel. The doctors say my brain is dumping adrenaline into my body faster than I can process it."

"I know how that feels," he said. When she raised her eyebrows, he added, "You just described the average combat experience."

"Really?"

"And your hearing disappears, or barely audible sounds become really distinct, like the tink of shell casings hitting your leg or the dirt."

"Yes," she said. "I could hear the bike wheel ticking earlier today, but nothing else. My heart goes crazy, and I can barely sip air." She laid her fork and knife across her plate. "Everyone tells me to breathe through it, but breathing is part of it. I was intubated and I had a bad reaction to the sedative—these horrible nightmares about not being able to breathe. It drives me insane to not be able to get a breath, because an elephant is sitting on my chest, and then have someone say 'Just breathe, honey. Just settle down and breathe.' If I could breathe, I would!"

He snorted. "Sounds like a medic telling someone to clot."

"Usually I get so light-headed I pass out. At that point my brain's shut down and my body takes over, and I breathe again. I've tried everything. Every kind of therapy imaginable. Yoga. Meditation. I've given up everything from gluten to dairy to caffeine. I thought if I got back into drawing, I'd learn to focus on something outside the chaos in my body. They get worse when I'm under prolonged stress. Right now . . ."

"You're under prolonged stress," he finished.

"There's no one but me. My father and brother are in prison. My mother is falling apart. My other brother is on his way back from New Zealand. But for right now, it's me and my cousin Neil handling all of this. I am the public face of the MacCarren implosion, and I'm a train wreck waiting to happen."

He ate the last bite of his omelet and aligned his sketchbook with the edge of the table. "Let me get this straight. You were hit by a moving vehicle and hospitalized, then had multiple surgeries. You've finished college and grad school, you tried working in one of the most stressful segments of the business world, and instead ended up working for a globally recognized foundation. And you think you're a train wreck?"

She blinked. Seth had done his research into her life, and never said a word. "I think the panic attacks were originally about the horns, the accident, but they've changed since then. They're about not measuring up. They're about failing my family, about being exposed as a fraud. A fake MacCarren. They're about the threat of shame, exposure."

"It's human instinct to want to belong," he said quietly. "Families, friends, tribes. That's why shame and ostracizing are effective deterrents."

"Right now some people would be filing a petition to change their name," she said. "I want to redeem the MacCarren name. Not change it."

He collected the plates, rinsed them, and loaded the dishwasher. "Tell me about your family," she said.

"Not much to tell," he replied. "I grew up in Cheyenne. My parents are professors at the university. My dad teaches Shakespeare and my mom teaches medieval history."

Her jaw literally dropped. "Your parents are college professors."

He smiled. "Yup."

"Why didn't you go home after you were discharged?"

"I'm the extroverted only child of two introverts who are happiest working in separate rooms. I love my parents, but my life is here, on the East Coast."

His face had closed off, so she didn't push. He wiped the counters down, then turned to her. "Does drawing help?"

She thought about the last few weeks. Something was helping . . . The drawing, or Seth? She couldn't identify which of the two was helping, but now wasn't the time to tell him he was crucial to her mental stability. "Yes," she said. "The single-minded attention on one thing that's right in front of me definitely helps."

"Okay, we keep doing that, but we switch it up a little."

"You want me to model for you?" she asked, trying to follow his train of thought.

"Another time," he said. "I meant we record us together."

"Doing what? Drawing?"

He looked at her, and the other shoe dropped. "You want to record us having sex."

Even as she said it, she recognized the tension in her body, profound arousal fighting with profound fear. "Why do you think this will work?"

"It sounds like the trigger—the horn and the exposure—are connected to a sense of shame, a sense of not measuring up. That's why you panicked on the exchange floor, why it gets worse when you're being judged. Everyone looks ridiculous when they're having sex. So do that, and watch yourself at your most ridiculous. What could be worse?" he said, and carried the plates into the kitchen.

She thought about this for a moment, trying to discern what her body wanted, what her mind feared, Seth's intentions. Efficacy was so much a part of her life. She judged, valued, weighed, considered everything from grant applications to investment returns.

"It's supposed to be fun," she said, part question, part thought.

"It's a way for you to lose yourself in your body and see you're okay," he said easily. The tink of silverware and dishes as he loaded the dishwasher, then straightened. "It's about seeing yourself, about letting go, being in the moment, totally in your body. And it's about seeing you the way I see you."

Her breath caught at the thought of seeing herself through Seth's nonjudgmental eyes. "How do you see me?"

He smiled. "Watch for yourself."

"What if I don't want to do it?"

"Then I'll tell you how I see you, or draw you. But think about it. You have a camera that records video, right? We use that. You don't even have to let me see it if you don't want to. Think of it as a series of gesture drawings."

"What if we start and I change my mind?"

"Then we shut off the camera and go back to what we were doing," he said with a laugh.

"Oh," she said. Her whole life seemed like an all-or-nothing proposition at the moment. "All right. I'll think about it."

"Get some sleep. Text me when you're ready."

"What if I'm never ready?"

"Then text me when you want to draw. It's not an ultimatum. It's an offer. That's all."

He bent down for a kiss, the contact fleeting, warm, tingling, then deepening, heating. "Do you want . . . ?" he murmured against her mouth.

"I want," she said. She knew that. In the total chaos of her life, she knew she wanted Seth. "My body, however, wants sleep."

He chuckled, drew back. "Okay. Go sleep," he said, and started toward the foyer, obviously intending to clear out and give her some space.

"You can stay," she said. The words were out before she could stop them. "If you want. Or not. It's raining," she finished.

He probably got his best work in the rain, making deliveries so other people could stay warm and dry. He had a life, friends, a mysterious inner world she felt she'd barely glimpsed.

"I'd like that," he said, and picked up his messenger bag, then followed her upstairs.

It was a quiet evening, cool enough for her to start the gas fire. She read for a little while, then closed her book and fell asleep wondering how much more she would reveal to the man who was rapidly becoming the only thing she needed.

— SIXTEEN —

When Seth woke up the next morning, Arden was in the living room, bundled into a thick robe and working away at the drawing on the easel. She was working with an 8B pencil, shading something, based on the rapid back-and-forth of her hand. "I made coffee," she said absently.

Telling himself that until he had caffeine he didn't have to think about how much better he slept with another person in the room, he went downstairs and poured himself a cup, then came back up the stairs. "How many floors are there?" he asked after he'd had his first sip.

"Four, not including the basement. There's one more above us, bedrooms I don't use and a bathroom, and access to the rooftop deck."

"You mentioned that," he said.

She smiled. "Come on," she said, and exchanged her pencil for a coffee cup.

Hand on the mahogany rail for balance, she led him up the stairs to the top floor, then opened a six-paneled door that could have been a bedroom or bathroom but was actually a flight of stairs. "Close the door," she instructed, "or the cold air rushes all the way to the basement."

At the top of the stairs she threw the bolt and opened the door. They stepped out into a hidden garden. The unobstructed westward view showcased an expanse of the reservoir and the trees of Central Park. Tall evergreen bushes tucked against the wall overlooking the street provided some measure of privacy. Sturdy patio furniture clustered around a small table, with a gas grill and a portable heater tucked in a corner. The plants looked chilled, their leaves quivering in the slight morning breeze.

"Poor things. It's time to take these inside for the winter," she said, examining the leaves.

"The city looks totally different from up here," he said, turning his attention eastward, catching a glimpse of rooftops and water towers stretching toward the river.

"Perspective," she agreed, and came to stand beside him. Steam rose from her coffee, the rich aroma lingering in the chilly air. "Height and distance make everything look different."

They stood there companionably for a few moments. Seth's brain lurched oddly from the past, quiet moments in the freezing Afghanistan or Iraq mornings, coffee brewed over open campfires and shared all around, to the present. Arden eased into a chair and tucked her bare feet into her thick robe, and studied him. Seth returned her gaze, afraid to show too much, unwilling to let even that fear show.

"Let's do it," she said.

A heat strong enough to dissipate the chill in the air flooded his veins. He was surprised he wasn't steaming. "Okay. When?"

She shrugged. "I should go see my mom today," she said. "Could you take tomorrow off?"

"The whole day?" he asked, puzzled.

"I want to do something else before we . . ."

"Okay," he said. "What do you want to do?"

"I want to go on a date."

He choked on his coffee but managed to get it down. "A date?"

"Maybe not a date," she said. "I want to do something with you, something casual, something different from what we usually do. I want to go out. Just . . . go out and do something."

"Are you sure?"

"Hiding from everything," she said with an encompassing flip of her hand that took in her house, the city, and most of the world, "is the first step down a slippery slope. I'm not losing ground."

How could she not see what a fighter she was? She was attacking so fiercely, refusing to concede anything to anyone, negotiating terms. By the time this was over, she'd believe that with every cell in her body. "Okay."

"I thought we might—"

"Stop right there," he said. He was all about gender parity in every aspect of life, but when it came to relationships, there were some things gentlemen still did. Planning a first date was one of them. "You want to go on a date. I'm going to take you on a date."

She frowned, smiled, and wrinkled her nose at him, all at the same time. "Great," she said. "Where are we going?"

"Out," he said, and finished off his coffee. "I'll pick you up at ten tomorrow."

"Ten in the morning?"

"Ten in the morning." There wasn't much point in having a flexible work schedule and dating a woman who didn't need to work at all if he didn't take advantage of it. He bent down for a quick kiss. "See you tomorrow."

His hearing cut in and out during the day, like a television with a faulty cable link. *No signal* reigned for the most part, but every so often he got a full blast of Manhattan's sounds to go with the high-def picture. Horns, a subway thundering by under his feet, an idling semi right next to him as he waited for the light at Fourteenth Street. It was odd, annoying, but for the most part easy to ignore because the city was always louder than his beating heart.

The next morning he took the subway to Ninety-sixth Street and followed the flow of traffic lights down to Arden's street, where he paused on the corner and assessed the situation. A few photographers loitered on the sidewalk equidistant between Arden's town house and Daria Russell's. They were drinking coffee, smoking, chatting in a desultory fashion. Seth pulled his phone from his pocket and texted Arden.

Ready?

The reply came immediately.

Yes.

He slipped his blade shades in his pocket, squared up, and set off at a brisk walk down the opposite side of the street.

They didn't even look at him twice. He wore khakis, a button-down, a thin cotton sweater over the shirt, and his running shoes, his best effort to blend into the Upper East Side, and it worked. He felt naked without the combat helmet or bike helmet or the shades. Halfway down the street, he texted Arden.

Now.

He crossed the street, coming up her side just as she opened the door and hurried down the steps, falling in behind her and obscuring her from the photographers' view. "Turn left at the corner," he said quietly, refusing to look behind them but listening for running footsteps. He heard an uptick in the chatter but without being able to see Arden for sure, they were reluctant to chase her and maybe miss a Daria shot.

Only when she was around the corner and out of immediate range did she turn to face him. He gathered her close then turned uptown and held up his arm for a taxi. One pulled to the curb almost immediately. He opened the door for Arden, and followed her inside. "Fifty-third and Fifth," he said through the open window. The cab pulled into traffic, and anonymity.

Arden shut off the television screen explaining how to ride in a cab, and turned to face him. "Hi," she said.

It took him a moment to recover speech, because she looked like something out of a fashion magazine. She wore a black leather jacket that looked like alligator or crocodile, nipped in at her waist with wide fur lapels and buckles at the wrists and hips. Her black swirling skirt pooled at midthigh. Black tights for warmth, black motorcycle boots with low Vibram soles. Her red leather sketchbook peeked out of a black bag not much smaller than his seabag. But the killer was a black beret tugged down low over her forehead and ears, black-rimmed glasses, and barely there color on her lips. She looked fragile, delicate, all bones and angles, but underneath she was steel. Only a strong person could take the kinds of hits she'd taken in her lifetime and still be in the ring. He was drawn to that character trait. Where everyone else saw weakness, he saw pure, ringing steel.

He should just walk away, but he couldn't, not from her.

"I didn't know you wore glasses," he said finally. Stupidly.

"Contacts, usually," she said. "I have an astigmatism. That was cool. Very stealth, covert ops, James Bond, Jason Bourne."

"Good job wearing shoes that don't make any noise," he said in return, playing along.

"Fifty-third and Fifth," she mused as the cab drove south. They were already in the high Seventies, traffic moving along quickly now that the morning rush was over. "MoMA?"

"Sound okay?"

"Sounds great. I haven't been in ages."

When they got to Midtown, the cabbie pulled to the side of the avenue and punched the meter button. Seth handed a twenty through the window and followed Arden out of the cab. They set off down the sidewalk, moving briskly until Seth caught her elbow.

"Slow down," he said quietly. "We're not in a rush. Whatever happens, we'll handle it together."

She exhaled, paused, then continued the exhale, reminding herself to breathe, he thought. A slow inhale, then she straightened her shoulders, tucked her arm through his, and let him set the pace.

The museum had just opened for the day, the line of people waiting to get in moving quickly through the grand lobby and into the galleries. "I have a membership," Arden said under her breath.

No one was looking at her, the New Yorkers' unconscious gift to one another, privacy, a seeming ignorance of another person's presence. "Do you want to use your name here?" he asked.

She hesitated. "No," she said finally.

He paid for both of them and picked up a floor plan before guiding her to the elevator bank. "Let's wander," he said.

The next ninety minutes were spent in near silence as they browsed the galleries, following the art through doors and around corners until they ended up on the uppermost walkway connecting the building's gallery spaces. Arden's face, pinched with worry when she walked down her town house stairs, had relaxed and taken on a bit of color. She rested her forearms on the metal railing overlooking the atrium, and turned to look at him. "Now what?"

He turned his back to the railing and leaned against it. "What spoke to you? Made you wonder?"

She tilted her head, considering the question with a seriousness that was both characteristic and far too much work. "The orange Rothko," she said. "It's—"

"*Shh,*" he said. "Not yet."

He led her back to the gallery where the vibrant painting was on display. While there was a horde of selfie-taking tourists in front of Van Gogh's *Starry Night*, this gallery was quiet, people walking through, but not stopping. They sat down on the padded bench facing the painting. "What are we doing?" she asked.

"We're going to look at it."

She looked at the painting. Her attention wasn't obedient. She didn't do it because he'd told her to look at the painting, but because that was the task, the mission, the job, the purpose and point. And if he'd learned anything about Arden MacCarren, it was that she'd master the task, or die trying. But this wasn't a task she could throw herself at and beat into submission. So he sat there, not moving, and observed her. Over the course of several minutes she crossed her legs, shifted her weight, leaned forward, then back, cocked her head, tucked a loose strand of hair behind her ear. Each movement released a hint of perfume, the smell of animal skin she wore—the beret smelled like it had just come out of the back of her closet, dusty, a bit like sheep. Her breathing varied widely from rapid and shallow, then slowed, and the fabric of her tights whispered against her skirt as she crossed her legs again.

Slowly, slowly, she settled, focused on the picture, the gradations of orange and red. He should have been doing the same thing, but all he wanted was to immerse himself in her, try to get to the core of her, the fundamental impulse that drove Arden MacCarren to never, ever quit. Even now it streamed from her like heat from the hood of an idling car, self-contained, fast moving, revving up when the time came.

He reached for her hand, wove his fingers through hers, and lifted the back of her hand to his mouth and kissed it. Her attention was now fully focused on the painting, but she gave him a distracted smile without looking at him. Unobtrusively, he touched his tongue to his lower lip and tasted the lotion she used, her skin.

Other visitors came and went, glancing casually at the painting, taking selfies, smiling apologetically at Seth and Arden but never really looking at them, then moving on. Arden's body relaxed almost imperceptibly, until she was breathing deeply, her shoulder pressed into his, her fingers loosely linked with his.

When a tourist tripped over her foot backing up to get a bigger shot, Arden seemed to surface. She blinked, smiled at him, her eyes curious, but she didn't speak.

"Come on," he said, and led her to the cafe.

When they were settled in a corner table with a cup of soup for her, a sandwich and chips for him, and cake for dessert, he said, "That's all you're eating?"

"I put a pot roast in the slow cooker before I left," she said. "I thought . . . you might like to stay for dinner."

"Sounds great," he said casually, like the date turning into an all-day thing was no problem. And it wasn't. It was easy, too easy for him to forget who he was, where he belonged. "Why that painting?"

She let her soup cool on the spoon while she considered her answer. "The color, I guess. At first it was just vivid, but then it became intense, like a challenge. I didn't want to look at it, so I looked at it for a really long time."

He chuckled. "You are something else."

"But then I just let it go," she said. "I let my eyes go into soft focus, so the color field wasn't the object of my attention, but just part of my awareness, part of the space in the room, then in the museum, then the city. It became permeable, like I could walk into it, through it, see it from the other side of the wall."

He felt his eyebrows lift ever so slightly. "Go on."

"If art is a representation of the artist's view of reality, I wondered what Rothko's view was when he chose those colors, how he could stand to work with those colors day after day. I looked at the painting for what? Fifteen minutes?"

"Forty."

"Really?"

He nodded. "Forty minutes. You'd still be there if that woman hadn't tripped over your boot trying to see the world through her phone."

She blinked, obviously pleased and bewildered. "Okay, forty minutes. But as I wondered, imagined coping mechanisms, what he was thinking, the way the color changed as the light shifted, I felt the color saturate my . . ."

She had paused. "Your soul?"

"Well, yes. Which is ridiculous."

"Why is it ridiculous? You don't have one?"

"I don't talk about having one." She ate another bite of cake, sipped her coffee. "The painting doesn't have an obvious subject. It's not of dancers or war or a café under a night sky. But the subject is light. The painting had a life of its own, and for a little while, I was a part of it."

They finished lunch and left the museum to a warmer autumn afternoon. "Where to now?"

"A walk in the park?" he suggested.

"I'd like that," she said.

It was a slow ramble back up to Ninety-second Street, winding through the fall color, leaves in yellow and orange and red gathered against curbs and park bench legs and fences. People stared at Arden, tall and slim and obviously wearing clothes that cost as much as a small car, but with the big sunglasses she'd swapped for her other glasses, no one seemed to recognize her. "Which painting would you have chosen?" she asked as they walked along Poet's Walk.

They passed a woman in a trim gray business suit juggling six balls while someone filmed her; they stopped to watch the show. "You've obviously studied art," she said.

"My degree is in art history," he said. "Lots of theory, lots of drawing. But I was in the Corps while I got the degree, and overseas for a big part of it. Most of my work was out of books. I visited museums when I was stateside, but even that didn't seem like homework."

"Have you thought about becoming an artist? There are so many venues now, digital and traditional."

He shook his head. "It's just for me," he said, then stopped, frustrated.

"There's nothing wrong with that," she said when they came to the fountain at Seventy-second Street. The boat pond stretched away from them, ducks gliding across the surface, avoiding the casual boaters.

"It's not enough," he said, then stopped again. He'd had enough, once. He didn't need much. Food was fuel for his body; he'd slept wet, freezing, half-awake and listening for gunfire, mortars, RPGs. A thirty-year-old motor home was enough. What satisfied him was the camaraderie, the purpose, the friendships. Belonging. "I want to do more than make art. It's too easy."

"Says the man who's made most of his money in the Marine Corps," she said with a smile. "Your definition of difficult is most people's definition of impossible. Easy for you isn't necessarily easy for anyone else."

The problem was that civilian life wasn't cut out to provide the things he wanted, had become accustomed to, not in the intense way he'd had them before, not when lives were on the line every single second of every single day. Combat stripped away pretenses, illusions. You knew who you were, who your friends were, what mattered. The rest of the world felt like a movie set, something he would watch in the rec room before heading out on patrol.

He longed, with every fiber of his being, to give more, to be worth more. Doug, Manny, and Brian had given everything, their lives, leaving no road map for What Happened Next. None of the books dealt with that, what happens when the mission's accomplished, the quest ends, they all live happily ever after.

The sun was setting when they emerged from the park at Ninety-first Street, walking the long half-block to her town house. Tantalizing smells came from the kitchen. Arden pulled off her boots while she opened the Crock-Pot lid, turned to wash her hands, and make a salad.

"It's a Crock-Pot," he said.

"What?" she said. "Think I'm too fancy for a Crock-Pot?"

"Well, yes," he said. "My mom uses a Crock-Pot."

"If it makes you feel better, I had the ingredients delivered from Dean and DeLuca." She bit off a carrot and smiled at him.

"Whew," he said. "Are you working on your piece for the show?"

"Yes," she said, and opened a drawer for a meat thermometer. "But you still can't see it."

"That smells good," he said, his mouth watering.

"Good," she said. She tugged the digital meat thermometer from the roast and inserted it again at the front. "Done. It's best if we let it sit for a few minutes while I make gravy."

"Gravy?"

"You eat pot roast without gravy?"

"No, but—"

"Just hush and let me cook," she said, then handed him the bottle of wine and a corkscrew. "It's strange. I've seen you nude a dozen times, no formalities, just shuck your clothes and get on the pedestal, but for this I thought we needed wine and food."

He laughed as he seated the corkscrew, pushed down the levers, and wriggled the cork free. "It smells really good."

She set two glasses on the counter. He poured out a red wine, first for her, then for himself, and clinked glasses with her. He swallowed. "Very nice."

"Thanks," she said, pleased. "I don't do this often, but it's really satisfying."

The tenor in the room had changed, throwing him off balance again. The scent of a home-cooked meal, something he didn't do often, given how easily the motor home heated up. The contrasting textures of her clothes, from the silky tights to the rough leather of her jacket, made his fingertips itch to touch her. In his mind he kept seeing flashes of the shield maiden he'd drawn last night. Vikings and Arden clashing together in his mind.

"Why did you decide to do the video?" he asked.

She shrugged, then sipped her wine again. "It seems like the most fearless thing I can do. It's the craziest thing anyone's ever suggested to deal with the panic attacks. And I really want to see how we are together." She pulled a serrated knife from the butcher block and handed it to him. "Will you carve, please?"

He carved, she added dumplings and vegetables in a pretty arrangement. They carried their plates to the table, and sat down at two places set with mats and napkins in antique silver rings. She took her place at the head of the table, glancing at him only when he held her chair for her, then snagged the wine bottle from the granite breakfast bar and topped off both their glasses.

Suddenly awkward, he waited until she picked up her fork and knife before following suit. The meat all but melted on his tongue. "That's good."

"I'm glad," she said, adding a bit of carrot to her fork.

They ate in silence, something he appreciated. She finished before he did, sipped her wine, watched him with a lazy smile on her face. "How did you become a bike messenger?"

"Filled out the applications on the apps, went through a background check, bought a bike."

She snorted. "You just threw yourself into Manhattan traffic?"

"I studied the map, memorized the streets below Houston, but yeah. I hit accept for a job, did the job, did it again."

"Unbelievable."

He shrugged.

"Ever think of doing anything else?" She made a little noise, studying him in a way that made him really nervous. Not judging. Seeing. She saw him like no one had seen him since the day the IED went off.

"Not really," he said. Which was partially true. The IED blew up more than his friends. It blew up plans for the future, too.

"What didn't you have in mind?"

Like that. He huffed out a little laugh. "What do you mean?"

"We don't make choices in a vacuum. I, for example, am very aware when I do something that my mother might like it, but my father might hate it, or I'm doing it to prove something to Dad and Charles."

His friends used to be his framework. "I have two unrelated skill sets that don't translate well into the civilian world. I'm a grunt with an art history degree. Do I need to do something else? Use my degree? Make something of myself?"

"Only the something you feel called to be," she said. "I think you're already quite something."

Her cheeks were flushed, her eyes a little glassy. His tense, anxious art student was a little tipsy, and a little flirtatious. He smiled at her, leaned forward in his chair, and kissed her. "I think you're something special, too."

"Frightened by my own shadow," she said.

"Fighting the fear that's as close as your shadow," he said. That's what was missing from the drawing, her shadow, a demon she's facing off against. He made a mental note, and kissed her again.

"Not here," she whispered against his mouth. She got to her

feet, took his hand, and drew him down the hall to her bedroom. Her sketchpad and pencils were strewn on the unmade bed.

"Got the camera?"

She opened a closet in the foyer and pulled out a digital camera, then trotted up the stairs, shucking her jacket as she went. He popped open the memory card slot. Sixty-four gigs. Plenty for what would likely be maybe an hour of recording. He set the camera on the bureau that was only a bit higher than the bed itself. He hunkered down and positioned it so the bed filled the frame. He wasn't thinking about angles or close-ups, just getting the action, such as it was.

"I want to draw first," she said. "Ease into it."

"Okay," he said. "Where do you want me?"

"Get your sketchpad," she said with a quick smile. She was settling herself against the pillows mounded at the headboard, her knees tucked demurely to one side, tugging her skirt down to her knees. The black skirt and fitted turtleneck and her flushed cheeks stood out against the sheets the same color of cream as her skin.

"You want to draw me drawing you?"

"I want to draw you drawing. Whatever you draw is up to you." She flipped to a clean page in the sketchpad, gathered the pencils, then glanced up at him. "If that's all right with you."

He modeled for her all the time. They were about to make a sex tape. Suddenly refusing to let her draw him seemed ridiculous. He noted instead his body's response to the suggestion. Sex tape: business as usual. Her drawing him while he drew: rapid heart rate, sweat breaking out at his hairline and under his arms, tightening in his gut. It was, he realized, more intimate to him than sex.

That awareness hit him harder than a sucker punch, and left him just as breathless. Which was good. His hearing was definitely coming back, breath and heartbeat elevated, audible.

"It's fine," he said, his voice coming from a distance. She'd come at him sideways, slipping under his defenses, and suddenly here he was, eating dinner, drinking wine, looking at art, and having sex. If that wasn't a real relationship, he didn't know what was.

"Great," she said, with another one of those quick smiles.

His sketchbook was downstairs, in his messenger bag, along with his pens. He paused to look at the kitchen and dining room, their plates abandoned on the table, the roast pan on the counter. It looked like a home, the kind of home people made together, where one cooked and the other cleaned up, a task that could wait if something more important came along. Like sex. Or art.

The bedroom was eerily quiet, a fact he noticed only because he couldn't shake the feeling of déjà vu. On his way to the bed, he tapped the button to start the camera recording. When he sprawled on his side of the bed, flattened the sketchbook, and picked up a pen, placed the déjà vu. He was drawing with a friend. The close physical proximity, the steady silence that didn't need to be filled, the sense that they were in something together.

Oh, shit.

Her brow creased into a frown; she made an impatient noise and erased a line, then brushed the eraser debris into the bed. Without thinking about it, he reached out and tucked her hair behind her ear, so the light from the bedside lamp felt soft and warm on her cheekbone and the shining fall of her hair. She was deft with the pencils now, her hand confident, turning the sketchpad to give her better access to a section without smearing the drawing. He idly captured the curve of her ear, the strands of hair flowing behind it, feeling the sinuous line in his fingers as well as seeing it on the page, not really in the drawing, not really in the room, waiting for her to make the move.

Without thinking much, he flipped through the pages. His sketchbook was a record of his life, what he saw, what was on his mind, but the gap between the drawings he made before the IED went off and his recent sketches of Arden felt wrong, like a drawing missing a crucial element.

Enough of this. Drawn to the textured tights, he set his hand on her knee and stroked it up to the hem of her dress. The fabrics were smooth and warm, retaining her body heat in the cool weather, and contrasted with the fitted cashmere turtleneck she wore tucked into the skirt. No easy access here, tights and sweater and skirt combining to cover her in multiple layers from her chin to her toes. He moved his hand back down to her thigh and brushed the back of his thumb against her mound. Her hand movements slowed, and a soft heat rose into her cheeks. He kept at it, not rushing, until she set the pencil and sketchpad to the side and turned to brush her thumb across his lips.

He looked up at her, closing his eyes only when she bent to kiss him. Red wine, warm mouth, already plush from her nibbling on it as she worked. She pulled back, looked at him, her eyes studying him with intensity, and it took everything he had not to react, to be the blank page on which she drew this version of herself. She could be as bold or as shy as she wished.

When she urged him to his back and straddled his hips, he knew not even this would dent her essential boldness. Her willingness to face her fears, to stare them in the face even when they sabotaged her again and again, blew him away. Her hair slid loose from its mooring behind her ear, curtaining their faces as she dropped tempting kisses on his cheek and jaw before licking into his mouth. Some level of his mind remembered the camera, pointed at their heads in the pose they held, but he wasn't about to remind her of it.

She lifted her head and peered down at him. "Come back," she whispered. "Come back to me."

Desperate to cloud her vision, he slid his hands under her flirty skirt to her hips, clasping them tightly as he rolled her to her back.

He settled between her legs and matched her kiss for kiss. Her hands scudded up his back to grip his shoulders, then his upper arm, then set to tugging his shirt free from his khakis. Bracing his weight on one elbow, he reached under her skirt and started working her tights down. It took some maneuvering from both of them to get them down and off, but when he did, it was so worth it, he glided his cupped palm from her calf to her bottom, feeling the tights' texture pressed into her skin.

When he reached the curve of her bottom, warm, loose silk covered his hand. The smile that curved her lips, pleased and shy and challenging all at once, told him she was wearing something different underneath. Rather than investigating immediately, he closed his eyes and explored by touch. Firm curve under his fingers, the contrast of the jut of her hipbone and the soft curls covering her mound under his thumb, soft fabric gathering at his wrist.

When he couldn't wait a moment longer, he nudged her skirt to her waist. It caught under her opposite hip but lifted enough to reveal midnight blue silk in a form he couldn't name. They were cut like shorts, elastic waist, and stopped just at the tops of her thighs.

"Tap pants," she said. "They're very retro Fifties pinup girl."

He heard one word out of three. "Pretty," he said. They made her pale skin glow like stars in the night sky.

"Thanks. Another Irresistible purchase," she said as her fingers went to the buttons of his shirt and unfastened them. She spread the fabric to either side, baring his chest for her fingers, now trailing over the bare spot in the tattoos covering his shoulders and torso. Solemnly she pressed the tips to his mouth. He kissed them, then she drew teasing, skimming fire down the blade of the sword on the left side of his torso, slid her hand into his pants to flatten it against his cock.

He groaned and thrust into her hand. His skin was heating,

the blood simmering just under the surface as he slipped backward in time to caveman. His body got a bit heavier, the better to feel her under him, and his hands gripped her hip and her hair, to hold her for demanding kisses broken only by her frantic efforts to get his shirt off. When that wasn't enough, he pulled her turtleneck off over her head. Her hair crackled with static electricity and stayed in a wild halo around her head until he smoothed it down with his palms. Now that he could see the set, the bra matched the tap pants, the kind of styling he'd seen in old movie and pinup posters or Katy Perry performing for troops. He stroked both hands down to her shoulders and over her breasts to her waist.

Right now he was the one who couldn't breathe. Unable to resolve the emotions, he kissed his way down her body, then shouldered her thighs apart.

He slid his arms under her thighs and stroked her abdomen through the silk, drew the inseam to the side, and delved into her folds with his tongue. She gave a shuddering, gasping breath, and twisted in his arms. He slid his hand up to cup her breast and stroke his thumb across the nipple, peaked under the silk. Her hand gripped his hair as he licked her, slow, steady strokes timed to the rhythm of her hips. But even with the cues, a tighter grip on his hair, her thighs trembling on his shoulders, the quickening lift of her hips, he wasn't ready for the shocked, disbelieving cry as she went rigid. He licked her through it, gentle touches, until she went slack in his arms.

He slid his arms free, rose to his knees, and put his hands to his zipper, his awareness narrowed to her face, her hands, the searing heat between them. She scrambled upright, forgetting grace in their haste to get naked; she hurried out of her bra while he shoved his pants and underwear down. She got a condom from her nightstand, and he pulled her close as she smoothed it down his length.

The sweat drying on her skin might be chilling her. "Cold?" he murmured.

"A little," she whispered back. Her eyes were dreamy yet full of a comprehension, like she'd seen through the veil to the other side. "You'll warm me up."

With his arm firmly around her waist, he tipped them onto the bed, then reached back for the sheet and pulled it up to his shoulders. "Better?" he asked.

"Yes," she said. With a soft, slow touch she stroked his face, and again he couldn't shake the sense that she saw something in him he didn't want shown to anyone. He wanted to blur her awareness, get her head back where it needed to be, in her body. He aligned the tip of his cock with her hot, wet opening, braced his hands on either side of her head, and canted his hips forward, slowly gliding deep.

Her eyelids fluttered closed, and her breath stuttered, halted, eased from her lungs. Better. Not thinking about him. Not feeling anything for him, definitely not with him. Make it about the body, the source of all their troubles. He pulled out, slid back in, again, again, then adding a bit of force to the strokes, watching her drop deeper and deeper into sensation. Great. Perfect.

So why was he the one kissing her? Why was he the one stopping to check in with her when he could read the signs, hear the sirens of her sighs and gasps, the unmistakable way her legs tightened and drew up, the way her hands flattened at the base of his spine. The deep rose blush forming on her collarbone told him everything he needed to know about where she was in her body.

So why did he stop and whisper, "Arden"?

The look in her eyes when she opened them, dazed, vulnerable, so far gone in the pleasure they created, hit him in the empty spot in his chest. Without really thinking about it, he rolled her. The sheet got caught underneath them, barely covering her hips, but she seemed far less concerned with the cold room. She looked down at him and laughed with sheer delight, then started to move. Okay, this was better. She had her hands on his chest, grounding him as she rocked back and forth, her hair and breasts swaying with each move. He slid his palms up her damp spine, gripped her shoulders, urging her into each gliding stroke.

But then her soft cries grew sharp and helpless. When she dropped to her elbows to capture his mouth, he was gone again, drawn into what he didn't even know he needed. Her mouth on his, her body against his, her hands in his hair, her tight heat clenching around his cock as she came, and when had the edge of orgasm become the edge of falling apart? He fell, pushing up into the soft depths of her body, and the hoarse cry torn from his throat reminded him of the last time he'd felt this vulnerable, the last time he'd been this present in his body, to this kind of total silence. Then the silence was punctuated by his breath and heartbeat, only his, an unmistakable sign that the world was utterly changed.

But now Arden's heart raced with his, her breath mingling with his as they shuddered through the aftershocks. The sense of wrongness he'd been trying to draw for days clarified into crystal. He'd never felt more alive than that moment in Arden's bed, her breath teasing his lips, her hand curled around his nape.

He wasn't alone anymore.

– SEVENTEEN –

Arden felt she really should get off Seth. Unable to hold herself up, much less walk, she'd collapsed onto him like someone had removed all her bones. Seth's hand gave random, subtle twitches on her hip as his grip loosened. She smiled at the evidence that a man strong enough to bike around Manhattan all day was reduced to trembling by sex with her.

Sex they'd just filmed.

Suddenly motivated, she clambered off him, and the bed, leaving him the sheet as she scurried to the camera, picked it up, and tapped the button to stop the recording.

"Did we just do that?" she asked, staring at the back of the camera. The controls were like partially understood hieroglyphics. A blue light was flashing, but stopped when she found the menu. The play symbol appeared on the screen, the video ready to be viewed. "I guess we did."

He kicked free of the sheet and headed for the bathroom,

leaving her staring at her camera like it was a bomb. No fade to black like in the movies, just Seth in the bathroom, dealing with a condom, and her, naked, her sensitized nerve endings heated like they'd been rubbed with sandpaper. A little shiver ran through her. The air held a definite chill now that the sun had set.

She'd actually forgotten about the camera. When had the awareness of being recorded disappeared? Before the sex heated up, which meant during the drawing. At least she'd accomplished that goal. Drawing was now second nature, something she could do to ground herself in the moment.

Seth emerged from the bathroom. In the dim light the tattoos seemed alive on his skin as he stooped to pick up his underwear and pants. She left the camera on the bureau to snatch her robe from the hook on the back of the bathroom door and pulled it on. As she did she caught a glimpse of herself in the mirror, and stopped half-in, half-out of the robe. Her hair wasn't so wild she couldn't run around the corner and pick up takeout from the Italian place. Her lips weren't so swollen that it was obvious what she'd been doing. The flush on her skin could have come from a healthy workout. She looked like herself, but better.

Happier. That's how she looked. Vibrant and alive and happy, but a sustainable happy. The kind of happy that came along routinely, say two or three times a week after amazing sex. She'd paid hundreds of dollars for facials that didn't leave her with this inside-out glow.

But there was a chill in the room. She belted the robe at her waist, then went back into the bedroom.

"Do you want to watch it?" she asked. "I can get the rest of the wine."

He didn't. She knew that expression, even if it only lasted a millisecond on his face, of coming face-to-face with something terrifying. Seth Malone, who confronted armed jihadists, roadside bombs, death and its aftermath, Manhattan traffic, was afraid to watch this video.

Then it was gone, smoothed back into his habitually blank expression. "Sure," he said.

"We don't have to," she started.

"Afraid to be on the other side of things?"

Ninety percent teasing, ten percent edge. "No," she said truthfully. "I thought you might be."

He pulled up his pants and zipped them, but left the button undone. "No big deal," he said with a smile, and the edge was gone. "I model for art students and I spent twelve years in the Marine Corps. I've got nothing left to hide. Let's do this."

Seth had arranged the pillows against the headboard. He hadn't bothered to put on his shirt, perhaps because he was always dressing and undressing for her, enough wardrobe changes for a model or an actor. *Always naked, never seen* popped into her head. Arden sat cross-legged beside him, held the camera in both hands, and tapped the play button with her thumb.

The opening was a bit self-conscious as they got comfortable on the bed without engaging each other immediately. Her nerves were obvious to her, although Seth didn't seem to track her glances at the camera that stopped when she realized he wasn't going to pull some caveman stunt and immediately go after her. The way he'd stretched out on his side with his head toward the camera and his legs crossed at the ankle was totally natural. Watching people draw was really boring, only slightly more interesting than watching paint dry. If she hadn't known what was coming, she would have shut off the video. Her heart gave a funny little skip as she watched herself draw, the fierce concentration, the furrow in her brow, so worried. A wave of tenderness for herself rippled through her, eddying along her nerves, into her awareness.

But then something happened, like it happened while she looked at the Rothko. Without either of them moving, the boundaries between them blurred, shimmered, disappeared. Seth didn't move, but the line of his body changed, relaxed, and became something that made her fingers itch to draw, because that . . . that was the thing that was missing from her main piece for the show. And she changed, self-consciousness dropping away, every line in her body subtly different. She'd forgotten the camera, and everything was different. She no longer looked like a woman carrying the weight of the world on her shoulders.

Is that what she could look like? Be?

Her awareness shifted to Seth. Did he see it, too? In her peripheral vision, his expression hadn't really changed, and more to the point, his body was no more or less tense than before. Maybe he didn't see it. Why would he see it?

"Is it difficult to draw in that position?" she asked. With his head braced on one hand, he used the edge of the other to keep the sketchbook immobilized and drew with it at the same time.

He shrugged, a movement she felt against her back rather than saw. "I can draw anywhere," he said.

On the screen he reached out to tuck her hair behind her ear, and she realized why he'd seen it. Seth saw everything, taking in the world the way she was trying to learn to do. She looked at the sketchbook, the cover black and pristine, no dust, no dirt, and something clicked into place for her, tiny disparate pieces of information suddenly coalescing into understanding. The cover was so clean because he wasn't drawing. Seth could eat anywhere, sleep anywhere, draw anywhere, but right now, he was at home nowhere. Because for Seth, home was people, not places, and his friends were gone.

She felt as if she'd taken an arrow to the chest, spearing deep. It had been right in front of her all this time, and she hadn't seen it, because he was so bloody naked all the time, so accommodating, needing nothing, asking for nothing, always at someone else's side, playing the role of brother, husband, father, model, art teacher, the man in her bed.

It was almost a relief when her on-screen self bent to kiss him, because surely, *surely* the sex would be less revealing than this. She noticed, in the graceless scramble to get their clothes off, that her scars were barely visible in the light.

"We should have turned on a lamp," she said. "It gets dark so fast now, and we're kind of shadowy."

He didn't respond.

"It's rather art house," she added.

Shut up, Arden.

She glanced at the time, and saw that they were about halfway through the video before they started having sex. Twenty minutes. It would have been perfunctory, even laughably boring—oral, missionary, a bit of oh-so-super-exciting woman on top for the big finish—except the lines of their bodies, the essence of them together, was of total trust and abandon. They were lost in each other. Found in each other.

The sound she made when she came sent a shock wave of pleasure straight through her sex, and a sudden blush to her face. "Oh, God," she said. "Am I always that loud?"

He chuckled. "You are."

"I don't really hear it when it's happening," she said, thinking her way through what she meant. "It's not as loud." Because her heart was pounding in her ears and she was somewhere else, far away, so deep in pleasure, sound reached her from across a vast chasm.

On the screen she'd slumped forward over Seth. His legs were stretching out under the sheet, but she could see her toes uncurling, the muscles in her legs going slack, then she clambered off the bed, picked up the camera. The replay button appeared in the middle of the screen. She powered off the camera.

"Well," she said into the awkward silence. She had to be careful here, rather than shoving the view screen under his nose and saying *Look! Do you see what you're doing to yourself?* He hadn't done that to her. She would return the favor. "That was interesting. I don't think it will cure my panic attacks, but it was . . . informative."

"Yeah," he said, and shifted down to the end of the bed. He shouldered into his shirt and started buttoning it.

"Plans?"

"I might hang out with a friend," he said without looking at her.

It was an excuse. Seth never made excuses. Not for what he'd done, what he did now. He didn't have to. He'd paid for his life with blood, sweat, and tears. But he was making an excuse now. He plucked her underwear from the floor and tossed it at her feet. "Are you mad at Ryan?"

It took her a second to make the connection between her tap pants and Ryan Hamilton. When she did, via Simone Demarchelier's Irresistible, she thought about it for a long moment, trying to separate Ryan from her family's total destruction. "No. He did the right thing. I can't blame him for choices and decisions my father and brother made over and over again. I don't know that I want to talk to him anytime soon, but I'm not angry with him."

"He's with the woman who owns Irresistible."

"I know," she said. "That was the affair of the summer. The gossip was scorching hot."

A distraction to go with the excuse. She wondered if he understood what she meant when she said he might be afraid to be on the other side of things, rather than the one who sees things, goes deep into another person's soul, looks around. As either the artist or the model, Seth deftly managed attention and scrutiny, using his pen or his bared body to prevent anyone from seeing inside him. Even his job as a bike messenger kept him moving at top speed, focusing attention on the people whose lives were blown apart by the IED. Look at all these people left behind, brothers, wives, children, and pay no attention to the man in the middle of it all. The silent one, the one with no claim of blood or marriage but used words like *love* and *brother* without hesitation. The one who'd left his family of origin and lost his family of choice.

He picked up his messenger bag and lifted the strap across his body, then turned to leave.

"I had a nice time today," she said. "Thanks for taking me to MoMA. I'll never see a museum the same way again."

"You're welcome," he said. "I'll . . . I'll text you later."

"Be safe," she said.

She of all people couldn't help him find his way through that wilderness. Instead, she let him go. For the first time in their relationship, she didn't pay him.

If he'd known how the day was going to turn out, he would have ridden his bike to Arden's town house. Instead, he was on foot, all but jogging toward the Lex line at Ninety-sixth Street. He needed movement. It was cool, crisp, a perfect night for a ride. Night rides were the best, the speed and rush of wind in his face, and the adrenaline rush of substandard vision would set his skin humming like it was electrified. With his bike he could play chicken with taxis, SUVs, semis making deliveries, scream after that near-sexual rush that only intensified as he pushed himself to stay even with a taxi, the cab's metal frame and whirring wheels an inch from his leg.

Instead, he was on foot, unable to stop thinking about the sex he'd just had. That wasn't "I didn't die in Afghanistan" sex. It wasn't "I didn't die at all" sex. That wasn't "I'm getting on with my life" sex.

That was "you reorder my world" sex. That was "life will never be the same" sex. That was "I'm falling for you" sex.

That was exactly the kind of sex he didn't want to have.

He took the stairs down to the subway two at a time, swung through the turnstile, and walked from the station to the end of the platform all the way down to the other end. Keep moving. The train's single headlamp appeared in the depths of the tunnel, but he didn't stop moving, not even when the wind and noise hit him. The speed of the local train was barely enough to soothe his need for movement, as was his short jog from the Grand Army Plaza station to the motor home. But when he unlocked the door, dropped into his bed, the truth caught up with him.

The video laid him bare. It wasn't the expression on her face. It was the expression on his, before, during, and after. He'd never seen himself like that, desperate, yearning. He was the one with the pencils and pens, the one who saw and recorded, who found the essence in others and gave that back to them. But in that video, he was the one being seen, the one looking at a future like it was something he wanted. It made him hot and cold, ashamed and afraid and hopeful, all at once.

It made him feel things he had no business feeling.

"Okay. Fine," he said, not sure who he was talking to. His muse, probably. He reached under the bed and pulled out his big sketchpad—the one that held an in-progress drawing of Arden, the one of her with her hair loose, studying him as he modeled for her—and his pencils and pastels. As he worked, the pencil in her hand became a dagger, the tunic a shirt of chain mail, the easel a shield. Her boots became greaves. He added the gold he'd come to associate with her in his mind, and the drawing took on the mystical-quest feel he too often fell back on.

When was he going to learn that the quest was over? It had failed, a spectacular train wreck, engine in the ravine, steaming, flames coming from the linked cars. And yet he reached for this again, and again, falling back on what he knew, except what he knew no longer existed.

An eerie stillness settled in his mind. It was the blank calm of the convoy before the IED went off, a single moment of stillness where you knew everything and nothing, all at the same time. It wasn't stillness in terms of noise or motion, but rather as if the universe had come to a halt before white light, concussive sound waves gave way to shrieking metal, then hoarse screams.

He reached back under the bed and drew out the sketchbook he'd been carrying when the IED went off. Dust was embedded in the textured black cover, while blood had dried on the pages, adhering the edges together. He trailed his fingers over the cover, smelled old blood and dust, then pressed the pad of his middle finger against the top edge, intending to open it.

"I can't," he said.

You'll have to eventually echoed in his mind.

"No."

But when he woke up the next morning and dressed for a day on the bike, he slid that journal, not the new one, into his cargo shorts pocket.

Arden shoved her sketchbook into her purse, slid her sunglasses from the top of her head to her nose, and hurried out the door to the SUV. She was reworking her rough drawing of the photo on Seth's phone, but rather than adding details, she was paring them back, seeking to evoke their deep bond with as few lines as possible. While she drew, Derek drove her to Kennedy, where Garry's flight was due to land in less than an hour. Derek dropped her off and went to wait in the short-term parking lot. She wore big sunglasses, no makeup, a bare-bones outfit of jeans, flats, tunic sweater with a denim jacket over it for warmth, and reveled in a moment of anonymity as she waited in the baggage claim area.

Would she recognize Garry? He'd been gone for years, hadn't come home for holidays, hadn't called, sent few emails and fewer pictures, mostly of mountains and sheep. To the best of her knowledge, he didn't even have a cell phone. She understood his desire to run as far away as possible; if he could have gotten accommodations on the international space station, he would have. Remote New Zealand was about as far he could go, with a decent climate and no ongoing civil wars, and still be on the planet.

She recognized him immediately, standing tall and straight as he loped down the stairs to the baggage claim area. Deeply tanned and dressed in jeans, boots, and a sheepskin jacket, he scanned the crowded, echoing space with his electrifying blue eyes, and caught Arden's gaze on the first go-round.

She wanted to run to him, to hug him close, to fall apart on his shoulder as she had so often when he was still at home, but that would mean making a scene, and that was the last thing she wanted to do. So she let him cross the floor to her, and held back the tears.

"Arden," he said quietly and hugged her tightly.

"Garry. I'm so glad you're home." She laid her hands flat on the thick stubble on his jaw and searched his eyes. "How are you? How was the flight?"

"Long," he said. "Crowded. I haven't been around this many people in years."

"Do you have luggage?" she asked, glancing down at the

overnight bag in his hand. A tablet was tucked into the outside pocket, but otherwise, it didn't appear to be half full.

"No," he said.

"Garry."

"I left clothes in my apartment," he said. "And at Hollow Hill Farm. We still own that, I see."

He'd caught up on the situation. "Yes, the trust owns Hollow Hill. But the clothes are years old."

"They'll be fine."

"Men have it so easy," Arden muttered and texted Derek to come get them. "Derek's on his way."

"Derek is . . . ?"

"My driver."

"I thought he might be a boyfriend."

"No. My driver."

"Anyone in your life right now?"

Well, that was a complicated question. She thought long and hard about it before saying, "Maybe. Which is not important, because we have plenty of other things to think about. I assume you're caught up."

"I spent the flight reading the news coverage, your emails, Neil's emails, and the indictment," he said.

That explained the tablet. Trust Garry to attack "the situation" as ruthlessly as he'd avoided it. She lowered her voice, trusting the ambient noise of planes, cars, rolling suitcases, people greeting and parting ways to cover their conversation. "The short version is that Mom's going to lose everything she and Dad owned together. Dad fired Neil, but I kept him on to represent me and the foundation. He's putting up a fight, but it's a lost cause, and we all know it. She'll be able to keep what was hers before the marriage, so it's not like she'll be destitute. But forty years of her physical world is about to disappear. We're not sure how much

Charles will keep of the money Granddad gave him. Again, Neil's fighting to keep that and somehow transfer it to the girls. You and I have our money, obviously. That money is completely removed from the business. Mom's refusing to leave Breakers Point."

"And the FBI is threatening to evict her."

"We're not quite there yet, but Neil says yes." She took a deep breath. "The real problem is that they're also going after the foundation's assets," she said, and heard her voice quiver as she did.

Why was this still the problem for her? Why was this the thing she couldn't face? Because it was the only MacCarren work she'd been allowed to do? The investment side was gone. But the foundation, which had been hers, wasn't.

Garry wrapped his arm around her and tucked her into his shoulder. She fought back the tears, the impending sense of doom swelling in her chest. She could not fall apart at Kennedy. When she lifted her head, she recognized a photographer snapping pictures ten feet away as one who'd been staking out her building since the story broke.

"Oh," she gasped. She straightened out of Garry's embrace, turned the opposite direction.

"Welcome home, Garry," the photographer said, continuing to snap pictures. "How long are you staying?"

Garry turned the other direction and started walking away, subtly giving Arden some privacy and neatly cutting off the photographer at the revolving doors. Derek was pulling up to the curb when a horn honked, setting off a cascade as the waiting cabs all released their frustration at once. She startled, felt her heart rate shoot straight to the moon, and the impending sense of doom swell until her vision began to blacken around the edges. Then she heard her name through the hammering pulse in her ears. She looked up and saw Derek, standing on the driver's side running board. Garry grabbed her elbow and hustled her through the cars to the SUV. The locks thunked open, Garry hauled the door open and shoved her inside, all but sitting on her as he clambered in after her. Another thunk, and the cocoon closed around them. The photographer stood in front of the vehicle, taking pictures through the windshield until an NYPD officer got in his face. Hands raised innocently, he backed up to the sidewalk, and they drove away.

It didn't work. Drawing didn't work, sex with Seth didn't work, seeing that beautiful video of them together didn't work. Nothing was going to work, nothing. She would succumb to this over and over for the rest of her life. Shudder after shudder rolled through her body, from her teeth to her toes, and not even Garry's solid body at her side, the familiar scent of lanolin and denim and the cream he rubbed into his boots, could stop them.

"Where to?" Derek asked.

"Breakers Point," Garry said, his hand curled into Arden's shoulder. "I'll see if I can talk some sense into Mom. When do we meet with Neil?"

"Tomorrow morning," she said, hearing the quaver in her voice. Hating it.

"*Shhh,*" he said. "It's okay."

She gave a wild little laugh. "It's not okay, Garry," she said, then straightened and grabbed her journal to pull herself together. It fell open to the latest sketch of Seth and his friends, caught forever in laughter and sunshine. "It's not the panic attacks anymore. It's the hope. After every single one, I hope that's the last, that I'll find a way to fight them off. It ends, I realize how ridiculous my fears are, I feel ashamed of myself for giving in to them, I try again. I'll be rational. I'll be in control. But once the dominoes start falling, I can't stop them. I don't want to stop them anymore. I just want to hit bottom so I can stop hoping."

— EIGHTEEN —

"I'm not saying it's the only right thing to do," Garry said. "I'm saying it's one right thing to do, and we have to consider that."

Arden took a deep inhale, then let it out slowly, trying to send Garry a subtle hint to settle down. It wasn't even nine in the morning, but his voice was already impatient. He'd not been able to talk sense into their mother, but given the amount of mood-altering medication she was on, that wasn't really his fault. Everyone involved needed to be in his or her right mind today, so they'd put her to bed without a Xanax. She was alert, sitting across from both of them in Neil's conference room, and determined to go down fighting.

"But there's legally no way they can take the money," she said.

"I'm not sure of that, Aunt Lyd," Neil said. "Regardless of the outcome, they're an effective method of calling attention to a situation. The longer you fight this, the worse you look to the media, and the longer it takes to move on with your lives."

"But if we give up the foundation, we lose the reason for moving on!" her mother said.

"Mom," Garry started.

"You hush," she said, pointing her index finger at him. Arden nudged him under the table. Garry scribbled something on his legal pad and edged it to Arden. *We should have let her take the Xanax.*

This is best if we're all clear and calm, Arden wrote back.

". . . And a significant portion of the money in the foundation's accounts was legitimately raised. Yes, Don made donations, we all did, but—"

"You're splitting hairs, Aunt Lyd."

Arden rose to her mother's defense. "She's doing what we always did at the foundation. We weighed one good against another. This is no different. Which is the greater good: giving money to people swindled in the Ponzi scheme, or distributing it via the methods and organizations we've always supported?"

"That's not how the government or the public perceives the situation," Neil said.

"It's not a situation. It's our legacy! Don't we owe something to the future, to the people who donated to the foundation, who supported our goals?" her mother said.

"What's the ratio of outside funding to MacCarren money?" Garry asked.

Her mother's mouth shut with a snap. "About twelve percent," Arden said.

"So we could give most of it back."

"It'll be a hell of a tax nightmare," Neil pointed out, "but yes."

"You can't *return gifts,*" her mother said, outraged.

"Aunt Lyd, think of Arden and Garry," Neil pointed out. "People are demanding some kind of public restitution, some kind of atonement. They're going to have to live with the fallout from this, as are their children."

"I am thinking of them, or at least of Arden. This is her life's work."

I'm twenty-eight, Arden thought. Twenty-eight years old. I never wanted this to be my life's work. Is my life over at twenty-eight?

"The fact is," Arden said, "there is no way we can make this right. Even if we turn over the foundation's assets, we can't even return investors' initial investments, let alone twenty years of promised returns."

Neil sat back, troubled.

"I want to make this right, Neil," she said, hearing the words for the first time, knowing them to be true. But she had to think of her mother, too, also still standing in the wreckage left by her husband and son. "If I could, I would make everyone whole, give them what they invested, plus a reasonable return. But I don't know how to do that, and what's more, how do we restore trust? Four generations of MacCarren work, ruined by greed and arrogance and narcissism. No grand gesture is going to make that right."

Garry sat beside her, his expression remote. Arden couldn't tell if he was back with the sheep in New Zealand or plotting something. His gaze reminded her of the look on his face when he constructed an elaborate Rube Goldberg machine that would take up the entire main floor of Breakers Point, or the look he had before he disappeared out west.

"Exactly," her mother said with satisfaction. "Now that we've settled that, I want to talk about what we need to do to save Breakers Point."

A junior lawyer came in, tapped Neil on the shoulder, murmured in his ear. "Excuse me for a moment," Neil said, and went into the hallway. Arden got to her feet and stretched until her spine popped, then pulled her sketchbook from her bag, hitched one hip onto the window ledge, and looked at the last of several increasingly spare sketches she'd made of the picture on Seth's phone. It was pared down to the barest of bare bones. To remove one more line would make the drawing's framework collapse, destroy the unity. It was completely different from her drawing for the show, and yet just as good.

Garry wandered to examine the pictures on the wall. In her peripheral vision, Arden could see Neil and the junior associate, heads together over a cell phone. Then Neil looked up, straight at her, and for once he wasn't wearing his impassive face. He looked astonished.

He said something to the associate, who set off at a run down the hall.

"What?" she said when Neil opened the door and sat down at his laptop. "What happened? Is it Dad? Charles?"

Neil cleared his throat, the gesture so uncharacteristically nervous her heart nearly stopped. "Arden, are you seeing anyone?"

"No, not really," she stammered. "Not dating anyone, not exactly."

"Have you recently been intimate with anyone?"

"What? *Why?*"

"I don't know how to say this, so I'm just going to say it." He cleared his throat, and Arden's stomach heaved its way into her throat. Neil was never at a loss for words. "An individual recorded you having sex with him and sold it to one of the gossip websites."

"That's not true," Arden protested hotly. "It was on my camera. I recorded it." She was so intent on defending Seth that the full implications didn't hit her until after the words were out of her mouth, in the air. "Wait . . . what?"

"I'm sorry," Neil said. "Say that again?"

"We made the video together," she repeated, although less vehemently. "How do you know about it?"

The blood drained from her face. She felt it happen, knew the sensation intimately, because the sudden drop in blood pressure was a frequent precursor to fainting. Neil didn't answer for a moment, then said, "Arden, do you remember the first meeting with the FBI, and I said you needed to treat your devices like they could be confiscated at any point in time?"

"Yes," she said, bewildered. "I used my camera, not my cell phone or my tablet, and I deleted the video right after we made it. It was . . . We were trying . . . What happened?"

Neil's eyes closed briefly. "It was uploaded to your cloud account, and your cloud account must have been hacked. We emptied it out immediately after the raid because you kept foundation records there, and we changed the password, but . . ." His voice trailed off. "The video is on Gawker right now. Social media's gone berserk. The news outlets are starting to pick it up."

"I didn't know," she said. Her lips were numb, her entire body ringing like a fire alarm. "It was on the camera less than an hour."

"I don't understand," her mother said. "What's happened? What video?"

"Would it be possible for the individual in question—"

"Seth."

"Seth," Neil continued smoothly, "to join us?"

"I don't know. Maybe. I'll call him."

Arden found Seth's contact information in her phone and tapped the call button, then watched the seconds tick by on her screen as she tried to identify what she felt. She should feel something. Ever since her first panic attack she'd always felt something, low-level anxiety escalating to fear and from there, eventually, to the overwhelming sense of impending doom.

Right now, at this very moment, she felt nothing at all.

" 'Lo," he said.

"Seth, I need you to come to my lawyer's office. Sixty-eighth and Third."

"I'm in the middle of a run. Can it wait?"

"No. The video is out."

"Out? What do you mean, out?"

"I don't want to talk about it over the phone. Please. Come to Neil's office."

"I'll be there in fifteen minutes."

The call disconnected. Arden stared at her phone. "Fifteen minutes," she said.

"Someone tell me right now what's going on," her mother said.

"I made a sex tape, Mom. Someone stole it from my account and sold it to the media."

Her mother's mouth opened, closed.

"I'll get you some water," Neil said.

Talking about the lawsuit against the foundation seemed pointless. Neil excused himself again. Garry said he was going to step out. Arden, connected to the law firm's secure Wi-Fi, ran a search and got back results of the video on news sites and social media, all posted within the last hour. It had gone viral and apparently crashed Twitter. The news-media pages showed only what they called relevant portions, tastefully obscuring body parts, but the whole thing was on YouTube, Reddit, streaming live on news sites.

She tapped play, and a news announcer's voice piped into the conference room. A still of her and Seth in what she could only describe as a clinch was frozen on an enormous screen in the background.

"What's the explanation for the scars? They're quite severe," a woman wearing makeup applied with an airbrush machine asked another woman, who nodded sagely.

"Arden MacCarren was hit by a cab when she was a teenager," the woman said, somehow managing to sound sorrowful despite sheer glee over what would likely be massive news ratings. "According to my sources, she needed several surgeries to recover,

but the accident left lasting psychological scars, too. Arden's suf-
fered panic attacks ever since, including one just prior to her leaving MacCarren for the family foundation . . ."

It had taken less than an hour for someone to connect her scars
with the accident, and from there to her panic attacks.

Everything she'd wanted to hide was now all over the Internet.
Forever.

She couldn't figure out what she felt about this. She shut down
her browser and closed the computer, as if putting her Internet
head in the ether-sand would make it all go away.

The conference room door opened again to admit Garry, Neil,
and Seth. He wore his usual messenger uniform of a jersey and
cargo shorts, with running tights for warmth underneath, but his
face was a total blank, hard and angular, his eyes simmering with
barely leashed fury.

"Neil, we need a minute," she said.

"It's fine," Seth said, cutting her off.

Neil ushered Seth to the table, offered him a water. The junior
associate sat down at his laptop while Neil flipped to a new page
in his legal pad, got Seth's full name, date of birth, address. "You
work as a bike messenger," he said, his gaze fixed on Seth. Never
took anything for granted, did Neil.

"Yes."

"How long have you been a bike messenger?"

"About six months."

"And before that?"

"I was in the Marine Corps."

She forgot that his tattoos weren't common knowledge, that
his devotion and loss were written on his skin but not for everyone
to see. "Were you deployed?"

"Four times."

Another note on the legal pad. She could see Neil's brain

branching through options, like a decision tree under construction. Sane or crazy? Manipulative or damaged? Gold digger or independent type? Clock tower shooter or suicidal? "How did you meet Arden? Deliveries?"

"I was taking a drawing class," Arden said. "He was the model."

She didn't think it was possible for lawyers as experienced as her cousin to show shock, but Neil's jaw literally dropped open. "You were the life model for an art class."

Seth didn't even blink. "Yes."

Arden stepped in. "I asked him to model for me. I was in the class because I thought it might help with the panic attacks. Manage them."

"Was there a financial arrangement?" Neil asked delicately.

"Of course, there was a financial arrangement," Arden snapped. "Life modeling is a skill you pay for."

"And then you became . . . intimate."

What had they become? Intimate, yes. Entangled? Absolutely. He was as wrapped up in her, like gold threads in cloth, as she was in him. She thought about those fall days, the sunlight fading in strength as her own strength grew, Seth's eyes, his mouth, the sheer weight and substance of his presence. "Obviously, Neil," she said.

Silence had never felt so absolute. Her mother, who had an appropriate response to any situation, gaped at her. Neil had found his poker face again, while the junior lawyer appeared to be running through some mental Rolodex of God only knew what. Garry, the bastard, covered his mouth with his hand, but his eyes were deeply amused.

"Okay, so we spin this," the junior associate said. "We downplay the paid-model thing. He's a specialist in trauma, we play up the panic attacks, their history, longevity, the trauma that caused them."

Arden and Seth spoke at exactly the same time. "No."

"Absolutely not."

A pause. No one moved. "Not one word of that will be spoken," Seth added. Thousand-yard stare. He was gone, somewhere she couldn't follow him.

"It's a strategy we should consider," Neil said tentatively.

"It's a pack of lies," Seth said. He held the room entirely in his hand. "She's not a victim who needed someone to swoop in and save her. I'm no one's savior." He looked across the table at Arden. "Excuse me, please."

"Seth, wait!" Arden shoved her chair back and hurried around the end of the table. She caught him in the hallway and drew him into an empty office. He slid his sunglasses on while she closed the door. "I'm sorry. I didn't even know the camera had wireless capabilities, let alone that it uploaded to my cloud account. I vaguely remember the clerk at J&R setting it up for me, I don't know . . . something must have—"

"This isn't your fault," he said. "One of two things happened: either some scumbag journalist or hacker got into your account, or someone leaked the password. Either way, someone invaded your privacy. Not your fault."

"Our privacy," she said quietly. "Someone invaded our privacy. That's the problem here, isn't it?"

The privacy invasion, or the fact that it was theirs. Their privacy. Their lovemaking. The heated intimacy bent and twisted before it could harden into steel. This should have wrecked her. Instead, her entire body rang like a clarion call, the horn raised and blown, summoning her. To what?

To the rest of her life.

He shrugged. "Tell your team to do whatever they think is best. Make me a trauma specialist, a rent boy, your art class fling, whatever. It doesn't matter."

"Because it's somehow better if you're just some rent boy I picked up for a fling? How does that make it better? It makes me the worst kind of woman I know, and makes you nothing. It's also a *lie*!"

He looked away, then back at her. She reached up and took off the blade shades, so much a part of his Marine persona that the tan lines were stark on his skin, even as fall deepened toward winter. He looked at her, and the stark pain took her breath away. He shifted his weight, looked away first. "Look, the timing's not bad. The class is over in a couple of weeks. It's probably best if . . ."

"If we end this now rather than then? Sure." Her laugh was brittle, the kind of laugh a woman made when she was past the point of caring. "An art class fling. Everyone has them. It's *de rigueur*. Someone has to sleep with the model."

She said the words because she wanted to see him react to the way she diminished what they had. He flinched. Imperceptibly, but it was there, a flash of shock in his eyes. *Yes*, she thought. *You don't like this, and yet you're doing it. Stop.*

"Why won't you let me in?" she asked quietly. "Why won't you let me help you like you've helped me?"

His hand went to his cargo pants pocket, the one where he kept his sketchbook. "Arden, you don't understand, and you don't need to understand."

"No, you don't want me to understand. You won't let me inside so I can understand. I've touched every inch of your skin, drawn you in dozens of different poses, but you've never let me touch you, really touch you. I know they died, but you won't tell me how you feel about them dying. That's because you won't tell yourself how you feel about them dying."

The silence, brittle before, now vibrated with a tension that made her gut clench. He went totally still. She'd hurt him, and she knew how. *Duty* and *honor* were just empty words without the emotion of love behind them. He knew that better than anyone she'd ever met. She'd brought her sketchbook with her, red as blood, red as life. Now she opened it, flipped hastily through the pages until she found one, then tore it free and handed it to him. "Seth, I want you like I've never wanted another man. I wanted you for you, for me, for what we could be together. You have to go on living because you're alive. They aren't. To deny that, to live only for them, is to deny yourself. One of these days, you'll have to stop running. When you do, you'll find you're not as alone as you think you are."

He took the drawing. Without looking at it, he folded it and put it in his pocket. Then he left.

Arden walked back into the conference room to a group of people studiously not looking at a device with playback potential. They were probably the only five people in New York City not staring at a screen right now.

"We don't spin this," she said. "There will be no spin, no comment at all. My public life is fair game, but my private life is off-limits. The only official statement we make is the following: *No comment*. Nothing else. Not one word."

Even as she spoke the words, she knew something was changing inside her, growing, stretching wings, filling her from the inside out with a fierce power. Her private life, her interior world, had been on display for far too long. Everyone knew about the panic attacks, her attempts to treat them. No more.

No more.

"We're done for the day," she said. "Mom, Derek will take us to Breakers Point. I'll help you pack. Where are you staying, Garry?"

"I'll come with you to Breakers, then I'll head out to Hollow Hill. I'm fine. Don't worry about me."

"What about the foundation?" Neil said.

"Give me one more day, Neil," she said. "Twenty-four hours, and I'll have an answer for you."

Derek pulled up in front of the mauve granite building just as they exited the doors. Arden and her mother climbed into the backseat, where Arden automatically opened her sketchbook. It opened to the page she'd torn out, the page she gave Seth when he walked away.

She couldn't feel that right now. She flipped to a clean page and used the first pen she found to draw her mother's hand, the tracery of blue veins, the slender fingers and perfectly shaped nails. She still wore her wedding ring.

"I can't even imagine what this will do to your father," her mother said.

Surely Dad knows I have sex sat heavy on her tongue. She swallowed it, and said instead, "It happens, Mom. I'm not the first woman to be targeted, and I won't be the last."

"At least we still have the foundation," her mother said. "Your father can be so proud of that. And Garry's back."

"Garry doesn't want anything to do with the foundation," Arden pointed out, biting back, *and Dad doesn't give a shit about it, either.* "You heard him."

"He's a MacCarren. It doesn't matter what he wants," her mother said.

"It does, Mom. He left once and did quite well without the foundation, or any MacCarren money. He'll leave again. If you want him to stay, you can't shove the foundation at him."

"Why doesn't anyone want it?" her mother all but wailed.

Because Dad treated the foundation like a halfway house for failed MacCarren investment bankers. Again, she counted to ten, swallowed bitter words. "Because we're not you, Mom. The foundation is what you wanted. Not Garry. Not me."

Her mother's eyes widened. The car trundled along, a silent pod moving with other silent pods, taking people to and from the places and spaces of their lives. She added texture to the cuff at her mother's wrist, the band of her Cartier watch.

"What are you going to do?"

"I'm going to pack you a suitcase and have Marla box up the rest of your things and put them in storage. Then I'm going to put you on a plane to West Palm."

"Arden, you have to—"

"—do what I think is right," Arden finished. "You turned the foundation over to me two years ago. It's mine. You're going to Florida. I'm going to think about our future as a family, and make a decision."

At Breakers Point she texted Betsy, who set things in motion on her end, then she packed her mother's suitcase, and booked her on the last flight to West Palm. She called Neil and updated him, making arrangements to send over a list of her mother's property to be collected later. She and Derek dropped her mother at Kennedy at the private plane hangar. In moments her mother was airborne.

Derek drove her home, then went off to whatever private life he lived. Inside the town house, closing in on midnight, Arden sat down in her living room and looked at the incomplete drawing of Seth she was finishing for the end-of-class show. Ever since the accident—half her life ago—she'd been spinning like a top jerked around by a toddler. Lately the hits had come faster and faster, from unexpected places. Seth. The baby shower. The panic attack in the park. The video. The video getting out. She felt like the universe was sending her a message, using bigger and bigger circumstances to make a point, shouting, coloring in bigger, broader swaths in an effort to tell her something.

The picture drew her eye. It was of a man in an extreme situation, living with the threat of death and failure every day, but all the while radiating paradoxical strength and woundedness, determination and fear, surviving under the most crushing circumstances, because Semper Fi never ended. She would never get tired of looking at Seth, could spend hours watching him like she'd study a painting by a master. He was complex, shrouded, shaded, finding strength not in individual success but in brotherhood and belonging, in fighting the fight that had to be fought.

Safety was an illusion. So was peace. But she could find calm in the chaos, a harbor in the storm, and be that for someone else.

She was at the end of her rope. The only solution she could understand, the only one that made any sense, was to reach out and cut the rope.

"I'm turning the foundation money over to the authorities."

The words were quiet, calm in the darkness. She waited for the aftershocks to shudder through her, the doubts and questions and automatic assumptions that questioned her decisions, her worth as a person.

They didn't come. The calm space she'd found with Seth was now her center.

"I'm closing the MacCarren Foundation. The money will be transferred to the advocate charged with distributing assets to the victims of the MacCarren Ponzi scheme."

Nothing. Just calm. Like she'd been hanging a millimeter off the floor, so close to solid ground there wasn't even a jolt when she landed.

She looked at the easel, the picture on it, of Seth, but not any of the poses from their class with Micah. He'd shown her that strength, the steel inside her that would vibrate from blows, but not break, not bend, not shatter. He'd walked beside her through the worst weeks of her life, never doubting her but always challenging her, never questioning but always opening space for her to find herself.

It was the best gift anyone had ever given her. He'd given her the tools she needed to find herself.

At four A.M. she still hadn't slept, so she pulled on a pair of jeans, a fisherman's sweater, and her boots, went downstairs, and walked down Fifth Avenue to Betsy's building. The streets didn't seem so threatening at night, empty and beautiful in that emptiness, light pooling on the corners, familiar landmarks shrouded and sleeping. The night doorman had the door to Betsy's building open before she got to the door.

"Ms. MacCarren," he said, poker-faced. "Is Ms. Cottlin expecting you?"

"No."

He buzzed, and Betsy's sleepy voice filled the intercom even as Arden's phone lit up. Are you downstairs?

Yes.

"Go on up," the doorman said.

Betsy opened the door dressed in a chenille bathrobe, her bare feet curling away from the cold tile, and looked at Arden, her face filled with love and horror and amusement. Arden said the first thing that came to mind.

"I finally found a way to convince my mother to move to Florida."

Betsy's laugh trilled down the scale, bouncing around the empty hallway, as she enveloped Arden in a big hug. "Oh, honey."

Arden hugged her long and hard, then unwound the scarf from around her neck and shed her coat onto the coat rack by the door. "You watched it."

"Of course not," Betsy protested. Arden raised an eyebrow.

"Okay, I watched it. Everyone has watched it. What did your mother say?"

"She said Dad would be so disappointed. Among other things." This time Betsy's laugh resonated off the windows. "I told her I was disappointed in him, so we were even."

"What did Garry say?"

"I don't think he watched it, because most brothers don't want to see their sisters having sex, but he said, 'Good for you.'"

Nick wandered in, shoeless, his tie around his neck but not tied, a cup of coffee in his hand. "Hi, Arden," he said, and bent his head to kiss her cheek. At least he'd seen her having sex before.

"Hi," she said.

"Make another pot of coffee, would you?" Betsy said, pressing a fond kiss to his recently shaved cheek. "I want *pain au chocolat*. Will Le Pain deliver this early?"

"Give them another hour," Nick said. "I'll stop by on my way to the train and send someone over."

"What does Seth have to say about all of this?"

Arden shrugged as they followed Nick into the kitchen. "I'm not sure. He left."

"Left where? Your apartment? The city? You?"

"All of the above."

"Over a sex tape?"

Arden flicked a quick look at Nick, saw his I-know-what's-going-on-here-but-I'm-not-saying-anything face as he poured coffee into two cups. "It wasn't just a sex tape," she said.

"Ah," Betsy said, and took the coffee her husband offered her. "So he saw that, too."

"Betsy, everyone on the planet with an Internet connection saw everything."

"Not really. The sheet actually hid quite a bit. It looks more like soft-core porn than one of those celebrity tapes. It's dark, and you're badly positioned. You can tell it was a spur-of-the-moment thing, not something you were doing for the attention."

"Thank you, Mike Nichols."

"You know what I mean. It was about the two of you, together, not about tits and ass. Even if I didn't know you, it's almost too intimate to watch."

"I think that was worse," she said. She sipped the coffee, trying to keep her emotions under control. "It was special."

"Anyone with eyes can see that," Betsy said.

"Between us," Arden continued. "Now everyone's seen it. I can't decide if he thinks he's failed me—he takes honor very seriously—or if he's furious that he's been exposed, too."

"The guy takes off his clothes to model for art students," Nick pointed out as he sat down in the breakfast nook and tied the laces on his oxblood wing tips.

Was that just a hint of jealousy from her former fiancé? He could see exactly how different she was in bed with Seth than she'd been with him, the two of them wrapped in a cocoon they spun of touch and look and taste. There was something about them, something special. She knew it. Seth knew it. But she wasn't afraid of it, while Seth was. He'd had it, and lost it.

"Does he need a job?" Nick added, snugging the laces on his second shoe.

"He's got a job," she said.

Nick lifted an eyebrow. "A career, then. We've got an executive development program," he said. "If he's got a degree and any aptitude at all, he might be a good hire for us. The government is making a real push to hire veterans."

The last thing Seth would want is to be part of some quota. "I'll tell him," Arden said, but even as she spoke, she knew Seth wouldn't want that job. He was wired to take care of people, not compete against them.

"He's not going to want that job," Betsy said after Nick left.

"I know," Arden said. "But it was nice of Nick to offer."

"How did you react to the video?"

"Did I have a panic attack? No. Shockingly, no. I did not."

"Why not?"

"Because I'm angry. I'm really fucking angry."

"Finally!" Betsy said, slumping back against the chair.

Clarity washed over her. All along she'd been trying to convince herself that the jumbled mess of love and loyalty knotted inside her was clean, hard, clarifying anger. It wasn't. She'd been shocked, horrified, hurt, scared, in denial, then scrambling to stay on top of the wreckage left in her father's wake. *Finally*, as Betsy said, she was nearly rigid with fury.

"It was a vulnerable, intimate moment that's now on display for the world. He was mine. He was the first thing I had for me, not for MacCarren." And now he was gone. She swallowed the lump in her throat, and clung to the anger. "It's like I'm standing on the other side of a raging river, and I don't know how I got there. I can't see the stones, or the bridge, or the boat. All I know is that I'm different. Not cured. I've had too many long stretches without a panic attack to think I'll ever be cured. But I'm different."

"You are," Betsy said quietly. "I can see the change even from the first drawing class."

She was going to cry, because the relief was so profound, so transformative, to find herself on the inside of something, on the inside of herself. She'd found herself, but the man who guided her through the turmoil had disappeared under the rapids.

She took a shaky breath. "I've decided to turn the foundation's endowment over to the law firm working to reimburse investors. It won't make everyone whole, but it will help. I'm letting it all go. I've told Neil to keep anything Mom and Dad bought before he started the scheme, but otherwise, to let it all go. It's the only way we can move on."

And she'd already moved on. These were the details, the pesky loose ends to tidy up and tuck away, no longer the only thing on her mind. Short of death, she'd survived not one but two arguably worst-case scenarios, and come through stronger. She would no longer let fear rule her life, and she would stop asking for permission to do what she knew was right. She thought of the swords tattooed down Seth's chest and back, and wanted one for herself. A wild, warrior woman with tattoos on her breast. Why not?

"I might get a tattoo," she said absently.

"Why not?" Betsy said rhetorically.

The doorman buzzed again then sent up a delivery man carrying croissants, *pains au chocolat* fresh from the oven, and two enormous hot chocolates from Le Pain for them.

"I'm not going back to sleep," Betsy said.

"Me, either," Arden said, and bit into the pastry.

– NINETEEN –

The morning after Arden told him he wasn't as alone as he thought he was, Seth set out to prove it by biking into Manhattan to meet Phil for breakfast at a twenty-four-hour diner in the East Village. His friend, dressed in what were obviously last night's club clothes, was hunched over a textbook, spinning a pen around his thumb joint as he read.

Seth tossed his helmet on the booth bench and slid in after it. Phil raised red-rimmed eyes to his. Definitely out late, maybe even up all night, maybe even still drunk, but not that drunk, and definitely not high.

"So. What's new?" Phil's eyes were dancing, bright with the kind of vivid glee, a sheer, joyful delight, Seth hadn't seen on his face in a very long time. "Seen any good movies lately?"

"Very funny," Seth said.

Phil signaled for the waitress and tapped his coffee cup for a refill, then said, "I have to say, of all of Doug's friends, you're the last one I would have expected to do something like that. Doug might have, if he was drunk off his ass. Brian would have, but only with Brittany, with candles and roses and music and all that shit. Manny . . . who knows? In the right mood, Manny would have done it with two girls but he would have been just as likely to not do it at all. He was one unpredictable motherfucker. But you?"

Seth gave him a level look.

"Come on," Phil said. "It's not that bad. The lighting sucked, for one thing. You took too long to get to the action, too."

Seth felt a muscle pop in his jaw. "Leave it," he said.

Phil's eyebrows drew down. "What's the big deal? Give it one news cycle, maybe two, and it's gone. Based on what I read, she's got bigger problems than making a sex tape with you."

She did have bigger problems, and the video would never be gone. Not for Arden, and not for Seth. He'd seen, and once he saw, he couldn't unsee, erase his memory, rewind with a zip, and forget it ever happened.

The waitress refilled Phil's cup and poured fresh for Seth. "Get you anything?"

"I'm not hungry."

"We'll both have the Make My Day," Phil said as he slid the laminated menus to the edge of the table. "Over easy for me, scrambled for him. White toast for both. Why do we call them tapes, anyway? No one's used videotape in, like, years," he added when the waitress left.

"No idea," Seth said, studying Phil, who was adjusting the scalloped edge of his paper place mat. "Are you high? Is this a pot-munchie binge?"

"I'm not fucking high. I've been up all night and I've got three hours of class today. I need fuel," he said, his voice rising as he spoke. "Jesus Christ, Seth. What does it take with you?"

"Me? What are you talking about? You're the one who's drinking too much, you disappear for days—"

"I'm reacting normally to combat stress and losing my brother. My behavior is within the normal boundaries for a grieving veteran, something I know because I fucking go to the fucking support groups and see my fucking therapist like a fucking grown-up. You, on the other hand, are riding right off the fucking rails!"

Phil's voice rose with each *fuck*, his index finger thumping on the stained laminate table surface. Seth stared at him, along with the customers in their immediate vicinity.

"You act like it didn't happen, like if you step into their boots, they won't be gone. Manny." *Thump.* "Brian." *Thump.* "Doug." *Whump.* Edge of his fist this time, making the coffee jump in Seth's untouched cup. "It happened. They're *dead*. You have to accept that and move on."

Seth's temper slipped, Phil's voice and fist tapping open a fine crack in the thick pane of glass between him and the world. This was Doug's baby brother, a stern voice in the back of his mind reminded him. What would Doug do? He thought of their interactions, the fights Doug described, in-your-face explosions that disappeared just as quickly. "I have accepted it," he snapped, low and sharp. "I was there. I pulled your brother's body out of the fucking *Humvee*. I smelled his blood, Manny's, fucking Brian's, boiling on the burning fucking undercarriage. You think I haven't accepted it?"

—*Whump* smoke and fire billowing out of the vehicle's distorted frame time frozen shattered glass meat cooking—

"That's exactly what I think, you dumb grunt." Phil held up a fist, and jabbed out his thumb. "You won't call any of the veterans organizations. You're living in permanent limbo, a job that's about being in motion, a house you can drive away, or ditch." He added his middle finger to the index and thumb. "You've got no real relationships going besides me and Britt and Baby B. Even those aren't real, Seth. You're my brother, but you're not Doug. You're taking care of Britt, but you're not Brian. You could

probably be Manny, whose exploits on leave in Thailand are fucking legendary, but who the fuck wants, really *wants*, to be Manny?
What you had on the video, that was real!"

His breath caught in his throat.

Phil raged on, ignoring the looks from other customers. "Unless
she's some kind of rich girl getting off with the Marine, in which
case you're still the luckiest fuck ever. That's who you are now.
You're alive, living in the greatest fucking city in the world. Fucking act like it!"

"I can't!" He didn't know it was true until he said it. He wanted
to rage the building down. He wanted Arden, wanted to be wanted
by her, and he couldn't . . . he couldn't.

"Why not?"

The anger welled up inside him. "Because I owe people! I owe
my brothers! I thought you'd understand that!"

Phil sat back and blew out his breath. "Now we're getting
somewhere. Do you want to owe them?"

"No! God *damn* it!" He'd rage the fucking city down if he
could. "I don't want to owe them a goddamn thing. I want your
brother, my best goddamn friend, alive, here, at this goddamn
table. I want them all to meet her, and her to meet them. I want
them to be the honor guard at our wedding, godfathers to our
children, telling her stupid stories about me so I can tell her stupid
stories about them, because she'll fit right in with them. With us.
But there is no us anymore, and I don't know who to be without
that. Don't you get it? There's no rule book for this life. Nobody
writes about it, makes movies about it, tells stories about what
happens after." He could hear his voice tightening, thickening.
All movement around them came to a halt, although whether that
was real or just a part of his imagination, he didn't know. "I'm so
fucking angry with them—"

He stopped. Fists clenched, vibrating on the edge of violent destruction, and nowhere for it to go. "I should have died with them."

"You didn't. You got in the second vehicle like you'd done a hundred times, but this time, you lived. Life's random. Get angry, Seth," Phil said quietly.

He swallowed hard, the lump of everything he was fighting to keep inside straining his throat. "The city will burn if I let it out."

Phil threw him a disbelieving look that was almost a slap. "This ain't the 'burbs, cupcake. New York City is pretty fucking impervious. You'll burn if you don't. You hate the anger because if you feel it, you have to admit you're still alive, that you didn't die in that IED explosion. You're faking it, biking like a crazy man, artist's model, flaunting it to everyone, but inside, you haven't admitted that you're angry. You lived and they died, and now you have to go on living."

The whole diner was silent, even the short order cook staring out from the window to the kitchen. The waitress was frozen between tables, a plate of hash browns and eggs in one hand, the coffeepot in another. Seth had two options: hit Phil until the blood ran from his knuckles and Phil's face, or run.

He ran.

Outside the diner he unlocked his bike and set off, pedaling erratically, chest heaving, no idea where he was going, swerving in and out of traffic, cutting off semis making late-evening deliveries, until he found himself at the GWB, heading out of the city into a tangle of highways, heading upstate on 9W, riding like he was racing the sun to the western horizon, pushing himself until his muscles were screaming. He could do this. He'd outrun this before, outridden it. Drawing wouldn't do it. Arden was too deep in his soul, and if he put pen to paper, it was all over.

She wasn't playing to script. She didn't call, or plead, or push. Every time he was with Arden, his soul rung with the clang of struck steel. She was the honed steel sword, a warrior he could trust at his back, the last thing he ever expected to find in this new world he shouldn't be living in.

With words, sure. He'd made no promises with words, never said I love you, or even I really like you, much less what he really felt, which was *I think you're fucking amazing, stronger than the steel in a dress sword, stronger than the guys I fought with. I'd take you at my back in a fight anywhere, anytime, against any odds, because you, Arden MacCarren, are better than a hero. You pick up the pieces left when life detonates. You make do. You just do.*

No. He'd made her promises the only way he knew to make them. He'd made them with his body, with his heart. He'd ridden beside her while she conquered her fears, lain still so she could find a way to see the world, tucked her into the curve of his hip while the sweat dried on their bodies after they burned each other to cinders. The Marine Corps oath was a spoken vow, a ritual, but the bonds were forged in blood, sweat, tears, in torn ligaments and wrenched joints, in exhaustion. That's the bond he'd forged with Arden.

Sweat trickled down his temple, jaw. He rubbed his shoulder against his jaw, swerved across traffic and onto a two-lane black-top road curving into the countryside, slowing when his muscles turned to jelly. He came around a curve and saw the road transition from blacktop to dirt. He sat up straight, braking as he back-pedaled, and ran right over a piece of metal partially hidden in the groove where the pavement ended. It sliced through his tire, sent him weaving crazily into the weed-strewn shoulder.

"Fuck." He stumbled off the bike, jerked the handlebars around to keep the frame upright. *Keepoutofthedirtkeepout-ofthedirt*, and he was scrambling backward like the time he'd come face-to-face with a scorpion.

It didn't take a genius to see the damage. The tire and inner tube were cut as cleanly as if a surgeon had taken a scalpel to the tire. He took a cursory look at the shard of metal, identified it by the shade of green as a blade from a piece of farm equipment, then picked it up and flung it into the ditch.

He reached for the quick-release strap of his messenger bag and realized that in his haste to get away from Phil and his spook-ily Arden-like insights, he'd left it in the booth. He was alone in the middle of bum-fuck nowhere upstate, with a limp, flapping tire and inner tube, and no repair kit.

The realization hit him like a body blow, the memory of the camaraderie, getting checked over before he went out on patrol, the physical nature of that. Someone always had his back. But he was alone, really alone, because he'd run away from everyone who mattered to him, and now he was stranded.

He shoved his hands over his head, squatted on his heels, then got to his feet and blew out his breath hard as he looked around. It was pretty country, thick trees lining the south side of the road, fields fenced in stone to the north. Goldenrod nodded in the ditch between the road and the field. Not a house in sight, and even if he walked back to one of the big houses, and even if someone was home, and even if they had a car big enough for his bike, and even if they were willing to give him a ride to a bike shop, even if there was a bike shop within twenty miles, he still had to ride back into the city.

Right now that felt like climbing a mountain with a fully loaded field pack on his back.

Hands still linked behind his head, he looked at the bike. Sweat cooled on his chest, under his arms. In a little while he'd be cold. None of the bike messengers had cars. Phil didn't either. He could probably scrounge one up, rent one, worst-case scenario, but Phil was probably in class, his mother at work.

The only person he knew in the city with a car was Arden, and he didn't know if she drove the car. He'd only seen Derek behind the wheel, never Arden.

He could smell the dirt, the particles lifting into the air, catching in his nostrils. He wheeled the bike a few yards away, putting pavement between them, and tried to think. The only thing he could think was, *Call Arden.*

He didn't want to do it. He knew if he did he was putting himself in real danger, but he didn't have a choice.

She picked up on the third ring. "Hello, Seth," she said.

"Hi," he replied, then cleared his throat and tried again. "Hi."

"Are you okay?"

Apparently the throat-clearing thing hadn't worked. "I'm fine. I need a favor," he continued. "Can you come get me? I blew a tire."

"Sure, but don't you have a repair kit?"

"It's the tire, not the tube, and anyway, I forgot the kit."

"You forgot the kit."

"I forgot the kit. Look, if it's a problem, I'll—"

"It's not a problem. Where are you?" He heard a subtle note in her voice, familiar but hard to identify. Caution, maybe.

He looked around. The middle of nowhere, aka a field along a dirt road branching from a blacktop road that connected to the 9W. "I don't know." It was a pretty big admission for a Marine. "Upstate New York."

"Upstate New York?"

"I went for a ride." He used the location services, read her his GPS coordinates, then waited while she put them into her maps app.

"Seth, you're nearly forty miles outside the city," she said. "I'm on my way. Don't go anywhere. I'm on my way. Get somewhere safe."

He wheeled the bike to a curve in the road where he could see oncoming traffic but not the dirt road, and leaned against the stone wall to wait for her. The silence was too familiar, reminding him of the rural villages in Afghanistan, the quiet particular to places where people grew things: animals, crops. The farmer who owned the field behind him was growing squash and pumpkins. Their vines lifted and swirled in the dirt like green, tendriling waves anchored to the dirt waves by fat, orange buoy gourds.

Dirt. He hadn't smelled the earth, inhaled it deeply, since he left the Marine Corps. A total absence of dirt roads was one of the advantages Manhattan had over Wyoming. He hadn't heard silence like this since then, either. Military bases were never quiet; the outposts often were, but something rang under this silence, lurked under it, threatened to explode from his ears. He was breathing hard, hearing his breath in his mind, just like he did after—

He got up, paced around the curve, then back again. Checked his phone. Battery life low from searching for a signal but okay. Leaned against the wall again and felt the dirt rising at his back, threatening to crash over him, pumpkins, vines, and all. Checked his pockets out of habit, felt the folded sheet of paper Arden had given him in one cargo pocket, his notebook in the other.

Looked at neither. Focused on breathing in the smell of tar from the blacktop. Watched the road for Arden.

When she came she was barreling along like a team on a rescue mission for one of their own, hunched over the wheel, phone in one hand. Her hair caught the sun even through the windshield, her enormous sunglasses obscuring her eyes, but the determined set of her jaw came through loud and clear. She was so intent on getting to him that she drove right past him, around the curve, onto the dirt road. Dust rose into the air, dislodging something inside him, some piece of information he got at gut level before his brain put the awareness into something as superficial as words. Intuition. A gift from the other side, landing with no more impact than a gently lobbed packet of sauce from an MRE, Doug's voice echoing in his subconscious, *Here you go, man*, Brian's laughter, faint and familiar.

He shook his head once, intending nothing more than to pull himself together. Walk around the curve onto the dirt. Make casual conversation. Hoist his bike into the back of her SUV. Get the fuck out of here.

He walked around the curve to see taillights flashing red through the dust she left in her wake. Particles clotted in the hairs in his nostrils, and the smell, so familiar, so horrible, the flashing red lights, *red dust eerie silence aftermath*.

A figure appeared in the dust, slender and strong. Its mouth moved, but he didn't hear a word because he'd stopped dead.

"I'm sorry," Arden said as she walked through the settling dust to the macadam road where Seth stood with his bike. "I was so focused on the phone I missed you by the side of the road. That's a metaphor for modern life if there ever . . . was . . . one . . ."

Her voice trailed off. Seth stood in front of her, staring at her, his body present but nobody home behind his eyes. She'd seen that look before in her own eyes, just when a panic attack hit, terror, loss, loneliness. Desolation. It was a look of utter desolation, the kind of wreck and ruin left behind when a city was sacked, taken from within.

Or a soul.

She watched Seth disappear before her eyes, his mind going to a place she knew well but yet couldn't follow him into. His hand spasmed on the bike's handlebars. Automatically she looked at them, then at the front tire, which was slit from side to side. So that's what happened. Irrelevant. The kind of daily obstacle he would normally overcome automatically. Except today he was thirty-seven-point-three miles away from her Upper East Side town house, and he was falling apart in front of her eyes.

She said nothing. After fifteen years of people trying to help her through panic attacks, she was an expert on what to do or not do when someone fell apart.

The first sign that he wouldn't stand there until doomsday was a choked inhale, quickly swallowed. He still wasn't seeing her but rather some mirage she couldn't imagine in any real detail, but again, knew.

Another sound. A sob. Again, swallowed, and oh, how she ached for him. She stepped across the line demarcating dirt and blacktop, and put her hand on his shoulder.

He shook her off. Turned away, and in the same move, shoved the bike away like it had betrayed him. It skidded across the blacktop to balance precariously on the gravel shoulder, teetering on the ditch. He went to his heels, thudded his fists against his head, breathing hard, words she couldn't quite understand under the ragged breaths.

Another sob, almost a retching heave. She stayed where she was, waiting for him to lose the fight he'd fought for so long but couldn't even hope to win.

What broke free was a hoarse growl that became a bellow of pain and anger and sorrow and rage, aimed first at the road, then at the sky as the sobs tore free. He stumbled in a circle, then tripped to his knees on the dirt road, pounding the ground with the sides of his fists. *Why? Why?* tore from his throat until even that word was gone, leaving only wordless howls the heartless blue sky absorbed without a ripple. He staggered upright again, then, shoulders hunched, fists clenched, he stalked in a wide, uneven circle around her, obviously searching for an outlet, not really seeing her. His shoulder bumped hers, but she gave no ground, just lifted her chin and watched him blow to pieces in front of her very eyes. When his swerving path took him into the bike's range, he picked it up by the frame, staggered through the withering weeds in the ditch to the stone wall, and hurled it into the field. Then he drew back his fist, aiming at the wall.

"No!" Arden shouted, leaping across the road, down into the ditch. Desiccated stems and leaves crunched under her feet. Her ankle twisted, sending her stumbling into Seth's arm. "Not—"

"—your hand. Seth! Not your hand!"

She was there, slender fingers wrapped around his biceps, physically holding him back from punching the stone-and-mortar wall. Sunlight glinted off her hair, turned her eyes to gold coins fringed with black lashes. The eyes of the dead, covered with coins to pay the ferryman's fee across the river.

She shifted her weight from one foot to the other, and she was there, in her eyes, alive, fearless, fighting, always fighting. Arden, gold and gleaming.

"Not your hand," she said again, gently.

For a long moment he stared at her. He wanted the pain that would come from driving his fist into rock until the skin bruised and swelled, until his knuckles cracked, until his blood mixed with the dirt, as their blood had. He wanted to hurt and be hurt, to exact the price from some goddamn thing that would give him restitution for what had been taken from him in a single second of light and sound, what he could never make right with his life.

It would never be enough, and yet it had to be enough. The impossibility of it all was tearing him apart.

The sob that tore from his throat was different this time. He crumpled to his knees. She jammed her shoulder under his arm and turned with him until he was hunkered down with his back to the stone wall. The curves of stones and gaps between them felt like a wall of sandbags, and that made the sobs worse. He rested his forehead on the heels of his hands, and cried until his throat was raw. He breathed in sunshine, and the scent of her hair, and her perfume, and the oddly mixed smells of fall, things shriveling while the pumpkins bloomed on the vines, the dirt that buried as easily as it gave life. Face buried in her neck, her arms tight around his shoulders, he cried out the loss, and breathed in life.

When he was done, at long last, he realized the gift he'd been given when her SUV drove past him, throwing the dust of his past in his face. It was the gift of having Arden by his side for the inevitable breakdown, the noise and violence of it. He'd faced his loss and grief and anger with her. With the strongest fighter he knew.

After a long, long while, he could hear again, not just his own wrenching sobs but the full range of country road sounds, his breathing and hers, his heartbeat, birds and the leaves and dust settling back to earth. Every muscle in his body ached. He sat back and wiped his face inelegantly on his shoulder and sleeve. Arden inched away and looked at the tree line with interest, giving him some space to pull himself together. He drew up his knees and let his hands dangle from them. After a moment, she patted his thigh, and paper crackled in his pocket. He reached into the pocket, felt the sketchbook from Afghanistan, and the page Arden had torn from her notebook.

He remembered what she'd said at her lawyer's office. *You have to stop running, Seth. When you do, you'll find out you're not as alone as you think you are.*

She was here. He had to look at it.

"Not if you're not ready," she said, as if she could read his mind. She probably could. Right now he felt as bare and exposed as a patch of road rash.

He slid the folded paper back and forth with his thumb, caught a glimpse of blue ink, not her usual choice of medium, a curving line that made his heart stop, because he knew that line. He knew it. He'd lived it.

He opened the fold, and stopped breathing.

Using what appeared to be a calligraphy pen and midnight ink, she'd drawn the picture that was the home screen on his phone, not an exact duplication of the photograph, but the essence of the pose. Doug's ridiculous frame captured in a line of broad shoulders tapering to a narrow waist. Manny's forehead, nose, lips, enigmatic, utterly unique. Brian's arms spread wide, seemingly trying to encompass all of them, and Seth in the middle, hands shoved in his pockets, head tipped back as he laughed. In her lines was the truth of them, that they wove a fabric of a love he could never hope to duplicate, never thought he'd feel again. The spare lines captured both who they were and the loss he felt without them, the empty places on the page mirroring the emptiness of his soul. In just a few lines she'd captured both what they were, and what they were not now.

"It's good," he said. The words came out garbled. He cleared his throat, felt his eyes fill with tears again. "It's really good."

"Thanks," she said easily. Cross-legged in the dirt, she gave a quick, sidelong glance at the sketchbook page he still held. "I'm proud of it."

"It's really good," he repeated. Like a *fool*. "Just a few lines and you nailed us."

"Everything about the four of you shone through in that picture. I just . . ." She shrugged.

She just . . . did what was incredibly difficult to do. Drawing was a skill you could learn, seeing was a gift, getting inside their tight circle almost impossible, but she'd done it.

He tipped the paper back down, so he couldn't see the drawing. She plucked a few tiny weeds from between pebbles and dirt, tore them apart, rolled the stems between her thumb and finger. Arden MacCarren, sitting in the dirt in upstate New York, like she had all the time in the world, nowhere else to go, no one else to be. He looked at her, and in that moment knew he was done having the sex he could have after surviving Afghanistan.

He looked around the bucolic countryside, the dirt road. Fucking dirt roads. His bike wasn't made for that kind of riding, but a Humvee was, and it still didn't matter. Safety was an illusion, the world was a merciless place, all we have is each other, and even that can be taken away. He'd tried making himself a moving target, minimizing the collateral damage, shoring up the ruins of people's lives, denying he had one of his own.

Until Arden, wearing a suit of gold, picked up a pen that was mightier than any sword or gun, and fought at his side.

He was ready, instead, to have the life he could have, after Afghanistan.

"Now what?" he said, as much to himself as to Arden. Nature certainly didn't bother to answer him, too busy getting on with things, powering down for the winter, geese flying south overhead, the breeze rustling the dry leaves, a snake side-winding through the gravel at the side of the road, heading somewhere on serious snake business.

"Thirsty?" Arden said, keeping one wary eye on the snake.

"Yeah," he said.

She got to her feet, then held out her hand to help him to his. A sword, gilded gold, straight and strong and true. He took it, did most of the work himself. He had to outweigh her by eighty pounds, but it was the thought that counted. Then he followed her back to the SUV.

She handed him the water. "What set that off? Anger over getting lost?"

He nodded at the dirt road. "Dust." When her brow furrowed,

he added, "The roads were all dirt. When the IED went off, it took a while for the dust to settle. I haven't smelled dirt like that since I got out. I guess dirt is my horn." Admitting something. Still not looking at her. His face still felt hot from the ride, the fury, the crying. "I was really angry. I am angry. It's exhausting to be this angry and not admit it." He swiped at his face. The grit in his skin, his eyes, felt familiar. Tears welled up, partly due to irritation, partly because he couldn't seem to stop crying. Months of not-crying finally coming due.

"I didn't know you could drive," he said.

"Of course I can drive," she said with a smile. "I just don't very much. You really didn't know where you were?"

Maybe she meant right now, maybe she meant metaphorically. It didn't matter, because he was smiling back at her. A real smile. "I could live off the land indefinitely. I wasn't paying attention." His smiled faded. "I really wasn't paying attention. To being alive, to you, to anything."

He was now. Images and emotion surged through the newly channeled, raw grooves in his heart. He wanted to see how she turned out, how laugh lines once again suppressed the grooves of grief bracketing her mouth, the wrinkles that would form under her eyes. He wanted to see her exhausted with joy after delivering their child. He wanted to see her in Central Park, pushing a toddler on the swings while a baby slept in the carrier on his chest. He wanted to see her walking a child to school along the city streets before she went into the office. He wanted to bring her a coffee, then sit by her on a park bench while the kids played soccer. He wanted to lay down with her at night knowing that whatever hell the day brought, she was next to him, wrinkles and stretch marks and crow's feet and age spots.

The images flared in his mind as bright as the bomb blast that burned away his vision, one after the other, as fast as an ignition switch. And just like that bomb blast, all that remained when he got his vision back was the future he could have, if he'd only accept that it was his for the taking. He would honor the dead with his life. It was the only thing worth offering to them. His life, his whole life, well lived, in unity with himself, the world around him. He'd found the essence of the pose, of his changing, shifting life. It was Arden.

"Thanks," he said.

"My pleasure," she replied. "Are you hungry? Derek keeps energy bars in the console, and I brought chocolate croissants from Le Pain," she said.

He lifted an eyebrow at the chocolate croissants.

"I was with Betsy," she said.

That's all it took for the odd combination to make sense. "Yeah, I'm hungry."

She opened the back of the SUV and hitched herself up onto the black carpet, then offered him the array of food she'd brought. He drank a bottle of water in three long swallows and ate two protein bars before he slowed down to sip another bottle of water.

"This isn't what my future was going to look like," he said, out of nowhere. With Arden, conversations started and stopped, picked up and took left turns, nothing to finish because it was a lifelong thing.

"I know that feeling," she said.

"I don't have any idea what I'm going to do."

"Me, either," she said, looking around the countryside with interest. "We have a farm about forty miles that way," she said, pointing behind her shoulder. "Organic farming, maybe?"

He tried to imagine his city girl in boots and a barn jacket, and failed until he added a horse, probably a thoroughbred. After savoring that image for a moment, he dug through the bag of pastries in search of the promised chocolate croissant. "I do know that I want to figure that out with you."

"You sure about that? I'm a disgraced socialite. I know the panic attacks. They come and go in cycles. I'll probably never be entirely rid of them, and the fallout of the last few weeks will follow me all the days of my life."

"We all walk with ghosts, Arden." He took a bite of the croissant. "I thought I could keep them alive by being what their families needed. A brother to Phil. A provider to Baby B. Doing all the things Manny would never get to do." Just saying the words brought the tears flooding back. He swallowed the croissant and the lump in his throat.

"You were trying," she said. "No one can fault your dedication to the people you love."

"I can't stop taking care of them. But I will stop trying to be the men they lost. They're gone. I have to let them go, so I can stay."

"That sounds like a good plan," she said.

"You saved me," he said. "They saved my life so many times, but you saved me, too."

"I'm in good company, then," she said. When he looked back at her, one eyebrow raised, she added, "You taught me how."

– TWENTY –

A couple of weeks after Arden stood in front of a crowd of reporters and announced she was closing the MacCarren Foundation and turning over the endowment to the arbitrator responsible for distributing reparations to the victims of the Ponzi scheme, she rang the street-level bell for Irresistible.

"You're sure about this," Seth said as they waited for a reply.

"I'm sure," she said. "It's actually a little exciting. I don't know how this is going to go. I'm kind of enjoying being Arden, not a MacCarren."

"Welcome," a voice called through the intercom as the door buzzed open. Arden made her way up the stairs, Seth close on her heels. The showroom was empty but for a sales associate arranging an array of colorful lace bodysuits on a display rack by the windows.

"How may I help you?" she asked.

Arden had to give her credit. Her face showed not the slightest sign of recognition, just a relaxed, pleasant, helpful attitude. "Is Simone available?" she said.

"Do you have an appointment?"

"No."

"Let me ask," the associate said.

Arden looked around the showroom with interest. "Great examples for drawing drapery," she said under her breath.

"I'm happy to draw you in anything you like from here," Seth replied.

Simone appeared in the workroom doorway, her red hair caught up in a messy twist secured with one black lacquer stick and two yellow pencils. "Hello, Arden," she said, and crossed the room to give her a kiss on both cheeks.

"Ma'am," Seth said.

"Lovely to see you again," she said to Seth.

"I'm looking for Ryan," Arden said. "He's all but disappeared since the summer, and I thought you might know how I can get in touch with him."

Simone's blue eyes grew wary. "May I ask why?"

Arden gave her a wry smile. "I have a business proposition for him."

Simone studied Arden's face, then apparently came to a decision. "He's here," Simone said, and tilted her head toward the workroom.

Arden followed her through the door. Ryan was indeed in the workroom, lying on his back with his feet against the wall, a Bluetooth earpiece in one ear, eyes closed as he murmured to himself in French.

"He's practicing language tapes," Simone said in explanation.

"In French," Ryan said without opening his eyes. "*En français. Je m'entraîne à apprende le français avec un logiciel de lange. A qui parles-tu, ma chérie?*"

His eyes widened when he saw Arden. In a smooth motion he swiveled to the side and got to his feet, tugging the Bluetooth earpiece free as he did. Arden stared at him. She'd barely known he existed until that horrible day at the East Hampton house. Her father and brother rarely admitted anyone to their closed circle, and she'd found Ryan's presence bewildering, until the FBI explained how he discovered the scheme, then pretended to want a seat at the table in order to gain their confidence and get a full confession. He'd used a wild summer of expensive girlfriends and parties to provide his cover, and apparently fallen rather hard for Simone Demarchelier in the process.

Finding him on his back, wearing corduroy trousers and a sweater with a turtleneck collar and elbow patches, earnestly repeating French phrases, disarmed her. "Hello, Ryan," she said quietly.

"Hello, Arden," Ryan said. He crossed the floor to shake Seth's hand, but looked like he was thinking better of offering his hand to Arden. She held hers out first.

He took it, studying her face as he did. "What can I do for you?" he asked, then winced. "Sorry. That's not where I want this to start. I want you to know that I *am* sorry. It was clear from the beginning that you and the rest of your family were innocent bystanders. I swear I had no idea the FBI would raid the house while women and children were there."

Women and children. The chivalrous language surprised her again. "You're not to blame," she said. "The FBI is not to blame. Dad and Charles are at fault. No one else, and especially not you."

"Still. I didn't want it to go down that way."

She shrugged. "It did. We go on."

A silence fell, broken only by the cheerful French female voice piping transitive verb forms from Ryan's earpiece. He swiped at his phone and shut her off.

"Can I get anyone a drink? Tea? Water? Wine?" Simone asked.

"I'd love some tea," Arden said.

The ritual of making tea and setting out a selection of cookies eased everyone through the most awkward moments. They sat on the sectional positioned in front of the three-way mirror. Simone poured for herself and Arden. Ryan and Seth stuck to water.

"Where are you working now?" Arden asked when she'd taken her first sip.

Elbows braced on his knees, Ryan rolled his water bottle between his hands. "I'm exploring options," he said dryly.

She lifted an eyebrow.

"Recruiters aren't exactly beating down my door. I've had a couple of offers from friends to 'help me find something,' but they're being loyal, not serious. I'm not sure I want to go back," he added. "I'm also not sure what else I would do."

"Sounds familiar," Arden said. Beside her, Seth smiled.

"I'm sorry about the foundation," Ryan said, as if remembering yet another thing he should apologize for. "I didn't think the government would go after that, much less get it."

"I gave it to them. I could have fought them, but in the end, I wanted a clean break. It's best for my mother, my nieces, and for me."

Ryan made a noncommittal noise.

"So," she said, far more casually than she felt, "I'm going to start over. Build a new investment bank based on the ideals my great-grandfather started with a hundred years ago, honesty, integrity, hard work, fair profits. Garry's back from New Zealand, at least for the time being, acting in an advisory role. Would you consider coming on board?"

His brow furrowed. "As your employee?"

"As a founding partner. Hamilton MacCarren has a nice ring," she said.

At that his eyebrows shot toward his hairline. "You're going to use your name," he said.

"The name MacCarren used to mean something positive. It will again. Until it does, I refuse to be ashamed of it, hide it, deceive people." She drew breath. She'd told no one but Seth, Neil, and Garry about her plan, asked no one else for input or advice. No more living in fear. No more asking for permission. "My share of the profits will be donated to the victims' fund, until the last investor is repaid."

His eyes were alight as he stared at her. "You're going to open an investment house using your name, and repay the people your father and brother stole from."

"Yes."

"Even though you have no responsibility for their theft."

"Yes. I've seen the worst unchecked greed can do. That experience is worth something, and integrity means more to me than it ever has. The way I see it, what happened is an asset, not a liability. We'll also put money and time behind efforts to strengthen regulatory oversight," she added. In for a penny, in for a pound.

Simone sat back, her eyes alight as she studied Arden. Ryan huffed out a laugh. "Hell, yes, I want in on this."

Arden smiled. "I hoped you would."

Early December

Arden trotted up the stairs to the town house's front door and whirled through, into the foyer. "Hello?" she called as she toed out of her boots and tossed the mail on the hall table.

No answer. She and Seth were due in the West Village for the end-of-class gallery show Betsy and Micah organized. While she'd spent the day in meetings with Garry, Neil, and Ryan, focused on getting Hamilton MacCarren up and running, Seth had taken the day off for an appointment with an adviser to register for courses in NYU's masters in counseling program, with a specialization in art therapy. He'd given his future a lot of thought and decided to dedicate his career to helping returning veterans cope with their experiences in the military. It colored everything they did—marriage, work, family life—and seeking help from another veteran eased the stigma and removed the "civilians don't understand" roadblock.

He wasn't exactly living in the town house, but he wasn't exactly spending much time in Brooklyn, either. They'd had a quiet, separate Thanksgiving—Seth in Wyoming with his parents, Arden at Hollow Hills Farm with her mother, Garry, and Serena and the girls, who had flown up from Florida for a week. The girls' ponies were stabled at Hollow Hills and would stay there until Serena decided if she was going to make a permanent home in West Palm, or return to the city. She'd been worried that filing for divorce would end her relationship with Arden and her mother, but in fact, they'd all become much closer. They were survivors, Seth commented, when she mentioned this. Drawing strength from one another would only make the road easier for all of them, especially the girls.

She stripped out of her office clothes and considered what to wear to the show. Her grandmother's vintage Chanel little black dress would suit perfectly, with a deep V-neck, wide shoulder straps, and a full skirt. She'd paired it with a short, swingy coat, also vintage Chanel, then tugged on a pair of ordinary black cotton leggings and her flat-heeled Frye boots, picked up a suitable pair of heels, and headed downstairs.

Seth let himself and his bike in just as she reached the main level. She went up on tiptoe to give him a quick kiss. "How was NYU?"

"All set," he said, then held her at arm's length to look her over. "The leggings don't seem to go with the dress," he observed.

"I thought we'd bike down to the gallery," she said. She'd

acquired an assortment of chic biker girl gear, including a retro white Electra Townie that suited her far better than her sporty hybrid bike, with matching saddlebags, a rear rack, a helmet in a fabulous shade of cranberry, and a wool-lined black trench that sported reflective tape that billowed out as she rode, making her highly visible to motorists. She held up her heels. "Panniers or your messenger bag? I don't have anything else to bring. Betsy arranged all the food with Edith."

"Messenger bag," he said with a smile, and tucked the shoes inside.

"What's so funny?" she asked.

"The day after I met you, I took a couple of pairs of shoes to an I-banker's assistant in Midtown."

"Did she tip you?"

"I don't remember."

"*Hmmm* . . . Room for improvement, then," she said, and gave him another lingering kiss. "You look very handsome," she said as she patted his chest.

He wore a pair of dark wool slacks, a button-down shirt, and a shawl-neck sweater with leather patches at the elbows, and even with the reflective strap around his calf to keep his pants leg free of his chain, he looked very hot, and very content. The expression sat more easily on his face than it ever had, but today there was an aura she'd never seen before. A hint of the shell shock had crept back in.

He winced at her touch. "Easy there."

"What's wrong?" she asked, wondering if she'd misread the look in his eyes.

"Nothing. If we're going to ride down, we should get moving. I'll show you later."

The ride from the Upper East Side to the West Village was sheer joy, the street lights bright enough to ride comfortably, the shops starting to bring out Christmas decorations, and the weather clear and crisp. They rode through the park to Fifty-ninth Street, exited onto Eighth Avenue, and took that all the way to Bleecker Street, where decorations turned charming and a Christmas tree lot was set up near Abingdon Square. Seth rode behind her when they biked together. Worried she would hold him up and reluctant to be watched over, she'd bridled at leading them until he explained that a) he didn't care how slowly she rode, b) it would kill him to look back after eight blocks and find he'd left her having a panic attack in city traffic, and c) it was an act of considerable trust to let him "watch her six," and would she please do him the honor?

Phrased that way, she couldn't say no.

Outside the gallery, a velvet rope manned by Derek and one of his friends provided security to cordon off the few paparazzi who'd gathered in the hopes of a picture worth selling. But to Arden's immense relief, the world had moved on from MacCarren, and from her and Seth. Guilty pleas entered by both her father and brother and turning over the foundation's assets had worked to bring the whole sordid chapter to a quick, if ignominious, end. She was old news now, and happy to stay that way.

They chained their bikes to one of the racks springing up around the city to facilitate alternative transportation. Once inside the gallery, Arden ducked into Edith's office and exchanged the tights and boots for her heels. Suitably attired, she rejoined Seth upstairs.

The room held a few familiar faces, Betsy and Nick, Sally and Libby and Micah, people connected with them. Ryan was there, talking quietly with Daniel Logan; Simone Demarchelier was avidly discussing couture invitations with Tilda Davies and the assistant Arden recognized from her ill-fated baby-shower shopping trip, while the gallery owner, Edith, chatted up Sheba Clark. Phil was there, and his mother, and a couple of men and women

Seth had met through Phil's former military support group. It was a friendly crowd, no critics or dealers, just a small celebration. Edith's assistants circulated with glasses of champagne and tiny appetizers. The drawings were arranged by student, a final piece surrounded by their earliest attempts and other drawings made outside of class. Libby's were precise, Sally's earnest, Betsy's full of exuberant energy. To fill out the spaces on the wall, Micah exhibited a couple of the drawings he had made while his students worked. They were far more adept and interesting than any of the students'. Arden made a note to ask him whether or not she could purchase one or two that captured flashes of Seth's strength and vulnerability.

"Is it strange to see yourself on the walls like this?" she asked Seth as they walked past renditions of him in various nude poses.

"Not really. It's what happens if you model for students or artists. At some point in time, you're going to see a drawing of your naked body on a wall."

They came to Arden's selections, displayed at the back of the room. "Do you want me to look?" Seth asked in a low voice. He stood solid and unmoving in the middle of the gallery, his hands wrapped around hers, his gaze fixed on hers. "I don't have to."

"Yes," she said. "I want you to look."

He wove his fingers through hers and walked to the back of the space. Choosing from all of her sketches wasn't easy. She'd chosen some that, to her mind, revealed their relationship more completely than the video: him in bed, sheet low on his lap; him sitting in the chair with one elbow on the armrest, one finger stretched to his temple, the others under his jaw, eyes dark with desire. These pictures and more spiraled around her final exhibition work, and that was the one that halted Seth's breathing.

She'd drawn him hunkered down on his heels, face turned to the viewer, but his eyes focused on a detail she'd added: a picture, held in his right hand. She knew what was on that picture, four men, three of them gone, leaving the fourth to forge a future in the fire of loss and pain and suffering. She wished, as she did every time she looked at the picture, that the figure would look up at her.

The real man standing beside her did just that. "You see me," he said, almost inaudibly. "How did you see me?"

"Seth," she said quietly. "Who you are radiates from you and touches everyone around you. I would have been blind not to see it."

"They're very good," Micah said. They turned to find him behind them, arms folded, enigmatic smile on his face. "You're wasted on Wall Street."

"But necessary. Thank you," she added, confident in her choices.

"Have you seen Seth's contributions?"

She looked up at Seth, eyebrows lifted. He smiled back, a flash of relief that he'd kept this surprise from her. "No," she said to Micah, who tipped his head to lead her to the back corner.

Then it was her turn to stop breathing.

Seth's drawings were far more complex and nuanced than any-thing drawn by the students; both the art teacher and the model had skills she couldn't hope to attain in a decade of practice. There were pictures of Brian, Doug, and Manny; pictures of Afghanis; rough, quick sketches of pilots; a Marine sitting in the doorway of a helicopter; a flag bearer holding the regimental colors during a ramp ceremony. There were pictures of her, one in her gold suit, her hair witchy and tumbled; another with the gold transformed into a warrior princess breastplate and greaves, complete with a shield and a sword and a Fuck-with-me-at-your-own-risk look in her eyes that made her laugh. "I want that one," she said. "I'm going to frame it and hang it in my office."

"Not for sale," Seth said immediately. "But I'm happy to make it a permanent loan."

"I like the sound of that," she said.

When the party petered out, they biked home in silence. Seth gently, absently rubbed his chest through the sweater as they stored the bikes in the utility room below street level, then walked upstairs. "What's wrong?" Arden asked.

"Nothing that won't heal," he said. "Come upstairs and I'll show you."

In their bedroom he eased the sweater over his head, then stood while she unbuttoned his shirt. She spread the fronts to reveal a white bandage taped to his chest, covering the empty space over his heart. One corner of her mouth lifted as she flicked a quick look up at him.

"Go ahead," he said, "but easy with the tape. This is one time when ripping it off quickly will hurt worse."

She gently pulled back the tape, starting with the upper right-hand corner and peeling down and away. The skin underneath was reddened, angry, lessening the contrast of the dark blue ink. She blinked, not believing her eyes. He'd gotten his final-tour tattoo, in the space he'd saved for it, over his heart.

It was the study she'd done of him, Doug, Manny, Brian, the picture she'd given him in Neil's office, the one he'd finally looked at on the dirt road. He'd inked her art on his skin. She swallowed hard, and blinked back stinging tears.

"While I live, they live," he said. "And you drew it, so it's like you're a part of us, too."

At that, the tears fell. "Seth," she whispered in a choked voice.

With his thumb, he swiped the tears away, then kissed her. "They would have liked you," he said. "Respected you. You're a fighter."

He'd seen her when so few others had. "It looks like it hurts," she said.

He shrugged, but carefully. "It goes away in a few days. Skin's resilient."

Mindful of the bandage, she reached up and wrapped her arms around his neck, looking up into his eyes.

"Arden," he said seriously, "I love you. I know it's fast, but I know the same way I knew with my friends. It's a bond you can't explain to anyone else, but—"

"I know," she said. "You don't have to explain that to me, because I know. I love you, too."

Wrapped securely in his arms, she let the silence settle over her. She breathed in, breathed out, and knew she was alive. She breathed in, breathed out, and knew peace.